shameless expectations

ADRIAN J. SMITH

EREKA PRESS

shameless expectations

Hope has holes
    in its pockets.
    It leaves little
    crumb trails
    so that we,
    when anxious,
    can follow it.
    Hope's secret:
    it doesn't know
    the destination—
    it only knows
    that all roads
    begin with one
    foot in front
    of the other.

—Rosemerry Wahtola Trommer
    *How to Love the World: Poems of Gratitude and Hope – Edited
by James Crews*

one

"Athena's running late."

Monti wrinkled her nose, though she pushed the perturbed feeling down. She shouldn't allow that to come up. She was here as a favor to her sister, and to get a little extra cash for her bills, but that was it. And if she was delayed five or even fifteen minutes, then she would live.

Hell, everyone would live.

"That's okay." Monti folded her hands behind her as she followed her big sister through the halls of the house. She hadn't been in a clinical setting for therapy or massage in over a year, but Fallon had begged her to come and help out her boss.

Apparently the woman was desperate for sleep.

From Fallon's descriptions, Monti hadn't realized how much of a prison this house was. It was gorgeous, for sure, but the energy was what threw Monti. It wasn't warm or friendly. The curtains were all drawn in, the lights were dimmed, and all of the doors were shut. People moved from one place to another as they worked, which she remembered Fallon mentioning once.

Athena had an office in the city for her legal clients, but because those were rare and a lot of her other work was done from home, she worked from home most days. She remembered this if she dug down for the information Fallon had fed her through the years. Monti rolled her shoulders as she followed half a step behind her sister. She still couldn't figure out why she'd agreed to this job. She really didn't need it, and she didn't want to mess anything up between Fallon and her boss.

"I really appreciate you giving this a shot. I know I strong-armed you into it, but Athena's tried everything." Fallon seemed tense in a way Monti hadn't seen her in a long time. Not since—well, she didn't want to think about that.

"What do you mean everything?" The more information Monti had going in, the better she might be able to help. She hadn't stopped being a therapist because of her lack of confidence. No, it was something else entirely.

Fallon stopped short in the hall, locking her brown eyes on Monti's. "I mean everything. She's been to all the doctors, all the naturopaths. She's tried CBD—that was a disaster. Not doing that again."

Monti's face pinched. It was the newest fad, that was for sure, but depending on the person, it wasn't a good fit. Still, Monti didn't have the reason that Athena wasn't sleeping. Starting with the problem was usually the easiest way to find the solution. Although getting sleep was a good place to start.

"Like I said on the phone, I thought with all your training…"

"Yeah. Makes sense." Monti shoved her hands in her pockets. "But I haven't done this in years. You're lucky my licenses are even up-to-date."

Fallon dropped her gaze to Monti's hands, pointed, and shook her head. "You can't do that when you're with her."

A line formed in the center of her brow, but Monti pulled her hands from her pockets and stretched her fingers out like someone had slapped the tops with a ruler. "All right."

"I'll tell her you're here, and hopefully she won't be long." Fallon led the way into a small library.

The walls were lined with shelves full of books floor to ceiling. It was honestly Monti's dream. She could lose herself in here for hours if she had the time and permission to do so. With the door shut, she walked the line of shelves and glanced over them. The selection was a wide variety, from classics like Tolstoy, to law texts, to religious ones, and even modern self-help. But there were shelves lined with fiction books, ranging in all genres.

It looked like Monti's eReader had vomited all the books into this one room. Smiling, Monti picked one of her favorites and ran her finger along the spine. She didn't dare pull it off the shelf without permission, so she left it sitting right where she found it —just caressing it a little.

"I'm sorry for the delay." The woman's voice was a shock through the room. Loud and firm. Precise.

Monti jumped before she turned around to face the door. She looked so small. Not because she was a tiny woman but because she just didn't take up much space. Monti could only assume this was Athena, the great lawyer, and Fallon's boss. Who else would be in the room? But she hadn't exactly introduced herself either.

"I'm Monti Schroeder."

Athena nodded at her but didn't move forward to take Monti's outstretched hand. Nerves swirled in Monti's stomach. She briefly leaned into them, acknowledging their presence, and then moved away to release them. When she looked back into Athena's blue eyes, they were still just as cold. Her hair was pulled back into a ponytail at the nape of her neck, bangs cut at an angle down each side of her face. Her makeup was pristine.

"Your sister said you're good."

"I am." Monti wasn't sure how to respond to the non-question. She could talk about her credentials all day if needed, all the studying she'd done over the years, but that wasn't what would give Athena permission to trust her. "Ms. Pruitt, forgive me, but if you don't want me here, I can leave."

Athena pressed her lips together tightly, to the point they almost disappeared. "You're not my first choice."

"So I heard." Monti gave her a small smile, hoping the humor in her tone would break the ice a bit. Instead, she was greeted with a blank stare. "Why don't we start with why you think I'm here."

Athena winced, her fingers at her sides clenching tightly before loosening. Did she even know she was doing that? Athena was pale, as if she hadn't stepped into the sun in months. "I haven't slept in weeks."

"Well, I doubt that." Monti bit her tongue. She needed to excuse the judgment and remove it from the conversation. But she wasn't wrong. It was impossible for Athena to go weeks without sleep and still be alive.

"I can't sleep well. It's affecting my work." Athena cut her a sharp look.

"Fallon says you've tried alternatives."

"Medications, studies, herbs." Athena still stood by the door, poised as if she was going to need to escape at any moment.

Monti relaxed her stance and glanced at the two leather wing-back chairs next to each other with a small table in between. "Mind if we sit?"

"I don't do therapy."

"Didn't say that's what this was, but noted." Perhaps Fallon had told Athena of her training already. That would explain why Athena didn't need to ask. "I was asking because I thought it might be more comfortable."

Though something told her that Athena was never comfortable.

Athena said nothing as she walked stiffly to the closest wing-back and slid into it. She crossed her legs, her slacks riding up on her ankle, revealing her black flat shoes. Monti took her time, observing Athena as she walked closer. It seemed with each step she took that Athena tightened even more. Her shoulders tensed, the muscle in her jaw bulged, her breathing quickened.

Trying not to disrupt Athena's calm any more than she already had, Monti sat in the chair and relaxed as best as she could. She wanted to present the most non-confrontational front as possible. Athena clearly needed a safe space, and the onus was on

Monti to create that. Although without the proper time to do that, Monti was going to be shit out of luck.

"I'm a clinically trained therapist, Ms. Pruitt, but if you don't want therapy, we don't have to do that. I'm also a trained massage therapist–think more clinical than a spa."

"I'm aware of your qualifications, *Monti*." Athena's glance of disdain and annoyance was pure. The use of Monti's first name was a pitiful attempt to put Monti in her place, and they were both well aware of that fact.

"Then you know why I'm here. And you can either accept my services or I can leave. The choice is yours." Why was she being so obstinate? Monti was here as a favor to Fallon, yes, but also because she needed the cash. But she didn't have to get it from Athena. There were always other ways. And she was supposed to be creating a safe space for Athena. This wasn't going to plan. This was why she'd left the practice entirely.

"I have no other choice." Athena raised her hand and pinched the bridge of her nose, a giant diamond of a ring winking in the light on it. "I haven't slept in weeks. I need to sleep in order to function."

"Something we can agree on, then." Monti placed her palms together and leaned down. "I can attempt to help you, if you'll let me."

"I don't like to be touched."

Monti looked up at Athena, finding the truth in her words. The vulnerability in Athena's voice was filled to the brim with shame, and even from the next seat over, Monti could see the tears build and then vanish.

Oh, she's good at this.

Monti was going to need to be on her A-game for this one. Fallon hadn't prepared her for the depth of mess Athena was stuck in. The question remained, however, would Monti be able to crack Athena?

"I have to ask, Ms. Pruitt, why am I here? You don't want therapy and you don't like to be touched. There are alterna—"

"There aren't." Athena jerked, her movements tense and sharp.

"I'm not understanding what you expect from me. And I want to make sure before this conversation goes any further that we're on the same page. I'm here because Fallon said you need help to sleep. There are some things we can try, but unless you're willing, they won't work."

Athena pressed her lips together, lines forming. She paled. Was this shame again?

"Do you mind if we start again?" Monti offered. "Because I must have done something to set off your alarm bells."

Athena's blue eyes locked on Monti's, and there was a slight shake to her head. Though the move was almost imperceptible. With a deep breath, Athena turned to face Monti better. The first sign that Monti might be making progress of some sort. Was the way in to be blunt?

"You didn't do anything." Athena pinched her nose again before rubbing her temple and closing her eyes. Instead of her shoulders relaxing they tightened. "It's hard to think."

"Because you're exhausted." Monti watched Athena carefully. Her clothes covered her from ankle to wrist to neck. The only skin showing was that of her face, a bit of her neck, and her hands. What was the purpose of that? Her clothes looked uncomfortable, warm, and as if they consumed her to hide her. "Can we try something?"

Athena glanced at her warily.

"We'll stop whenever you want. I'm not here to push your boundaries or make you feel unsafe. I'm here simply to help you sleep."

"What's your suggestion?" Athena leaned forward before catching herself and straightening her back.

She was sleep-deprived—to the point that she could barely hold herself upright. Monti breathed deeply, softening her tone. She needed to be calm and open, allow Athena to trust her even if just a little to help her today.

"I'll touch your hands and your scalp only. And again, if it makes you uncomfortable, you can tell me to stop any time and I will. I'll start with your hands—that way you can see me." Monti put her hands out to the sides. "The choice is yours. If it doesn't work, you can chalk this up to one more alternative that failed."

Athena stared down at Monti's hands, her eyes closing slowly before she popped them open again. "Just do it."

"Ms. Pruitt, I'm not sure you fully understand, but I want you to accept this, not simply acquiesce that it's your only choice. You do have a choice." Monti watched Athena carefully, the way she contemplated and processed what Monti had said.

"I'm willing to try."

"But a part of you isn't."

"There's always a part of me that refuses to be touched. I just have to shut her up." Athena looked Monti dead in the eye and raised her eyebrow. "Doesn't everyone?"

Monti chuckled a little with a slight smile. "Everyone has different parts for different reasons, Ms. Pruitt."

Holding out her hand, Monti waited to see what Athena would do next. This wouldn't be the end of the discussion by any means, but it seemed to be a good start. Athena was more open to what Monti had to offer at least. Monti slowed her breathing and pulled a calmness toward the center of her chest. Once she found it, she grasped onto it and held it there.

Athena hesitated, which Monti expected, but after a few seconds, she reached forward with her left hand and slid it into Monti's. She said nothing as she waited to gain just a few more ounces of trust.

"I'm going to start with your palm and work my way through each of your fingers. When we're done with this hand, we can start on the other one. Satisfactory?"

"Yes," Athena answered, her tone much softer this time than before.

The difference startled Monti. She looked into Athena's eyes, the slackness in her jaw, the ashen color just under her skin that her makeup wasn't quite covering up. Monti took another breath and started slowly. "When I started school for massage therapy, it's because I was fascinated by the body and how every part of ourselves is interconnected."

"I don't need the lecture, Ms. Schroeder."

"Would you prefer silence?" Monti asked as she slid her thumb along the center of Athena's palm and up to her fingers.

"Talk about anything other than what you're doing." Athena's voice was breathier than it had been before.

"How many of these books have you read?" Monti watched Athena carefully.

Athena sighed heavily. "Not all of them."

"But a lot of them?"

"Yes," Athena agreed. Her body seemed to be getting heavier by the moment.

"Which ones do you prefer?"

What would pull Athena's attention when she wanted to relax? Monti was pretty sure it wouldn't be the law books, though maybe if they started reading those Athena would fall asleep.

"Depends on my mood."

"And what you're going through at the time, I assume." Monti moved to Athena's fingers, skillfully avoiding Athena's giant wedding ring. She started with her thumb and smoothed the muscles and tension in them. She wished she had grabbed some of the oil in her pocket, but she hadn't wanted to disrupt Athena even more, and if the touching thing had to do with certain sensations, then oil could make it worse. "I'm also a mood reader."

"Is that what we're called?" Athena turned to lock her eyes on Monti's, and she honestly looked sleepy, as if the tendrils of slumber were pulling at her.

"Yes, ma'am. But my library is electronic. I'd love to have a library like this. It's gorgeous."

"Years of collecting."

"I don't know where I'd put it. I don't stay in one place for very long, and I'd hate to move the books so frequently." Monti finished with Athena's pinky. "Was that all right?"

"Was what…" Athena trailed off, staring down at her hand in Monti's. "Oh…yes."

Had she forgotten Monti was touching her?

"May I have your other hand?"

Wordlessly, Athena lifted her right hand and placed it in Monti's. The angle was awkward, but Monti didn't want to scare Athena away. They melted into a soft silence, and it was comfortable. Monti worked while Athena just breathed. She spent a bit of extra time on Athena's right hand, knowing that the move to her scalp would be a huge ask.

"Ms. Pruitt?" Monti finally asked, her voice calm and quiet. She didn't want to startle Athena. "Are you ready for the craniosacral massage?"

"The what?"

"Your scalp." Monti held herself still. "I'll need to stand behind you."

"Yes."

Monti stood up slowly. She moved with care, wanting to make sure that Athena was aware of where she was at all times. Monti brushed the pads of her fingers over the clip holding her hair in the ponytail at the nape of her neck. "Can I take this out? I won't tangle your hair as much."

Athena said nothing as she reached up and slipped the clip out. Monti touched her shoulder briefly. "Let me know if you want to stop. Please."

"I will."

Monti started at the front of her head. She took everything slowly and step by step. She worked methodically. Athena rested back into the chair, her shoulders tightening and then relaxing. Her hands on the arms were lax, fingers loose. Her breathing became deeper, slower.

Almost scared to look, Monti was certain she had fallen asleep. She finished the massage and slowly moved around the chair. Athena rested with her eyes closed, her lips slightly parted, completely asleep. Smiling, Monti moved to the wall of books and snagged one she'd never read before.

The Tao of Pooh.

Monti sat in the chair she'd left before, sent Fallon a quick text to let her know she was successful and to bar anyone from entering the library, and then she started reading. She could get lost in a book while Athena slept. It was all the payment she needed.

two

Gasping with a start, Athena jerked awake.

She curled her fingers around the arms of her favorite wing-back chair in the library, one of the few places she ever felt comfortable. The room was dim, only the lamp in the corner and the one on the table turned on. Her eyes were so damn blurry that it was hard to see, but she wasn't willing to release the chair yet. She might need her hands free.

Athena blinked to try and clear the sleep from her gaze. She slowed her breathing and her heartbeat, then turned to find Monti, sitting in the chair opposite hers with a mug almost to her lips, a book resting on her thigh, and one ankle crossed over her knee.

"Before you ask, it's been three hours," Monti said, her voice that same calm it had been when she'd started the massage. "No one has been in here except me and Fallon."

Athena released a breath, the tension that had been riding in the top of her chest falling almost immediately. Well, as much as it ever did, because if she paid attention, it never completely vanished. She rolled her shoulders and released her grip on the arms of the chair.

Three hours.

Straight.

Without interruptions.

That was honestly the most sleep she'd had in one go in weeks. Athena looked around her library, blinking. Her brain wasn't catching up fast enough with what was actually happening. "What time is it?"

"A little after six."

Athena held in the curse. She had so much work to do, work that couldn't be missed. She was lucky that she hadn't missed any scheduled meetings. Brushing her hand through her hair, Athena stopped. Her hair was still down around her shoulders, loose. Monti had pulled the clip out and set it on the table.

One quick glance told her it was still there.

She'd never been comfortable sleeping with strangers in the vicinity before. Why was this so different? It was probably because she was so exhausted that her body had just given in. Athena pursed her lips and glanced at the book on Monti's thigh.

She'd read that one multiple times. Monti must have caught the direction of her gaze, because she closed the book and set it on the small table between the chairs.

"I didn't think you'd mind if I read while you slept."

"It's a library." Athena stopped there, the rest of the sentence obvious. Books were meant to be read, and she wouldn't have them there just for aesthetics. But Monti wouldn't know that. They'd never met before, and despite Fallon's several mentions of her elusive sister, Athena hadn't cared to pay too much attention.

"How are you feeling?" Monti's tone was back to that smooth quality, which immediately reminded Athena of a therapist's office.

She'd been in those enough over the years and none of them had helped. She watched with rapt curiosity as Monti brushed a hand through her short hair, the soft brown strands popping back into place. Monti Schroeder was a curiosity if Athena had ever met one. Monti was unlike her sister—casual, relaxed, clearly smart—to the point they were almost complete opposites.

"Where did you go to school?" Athena didn't drop her gaze. She always wanted to see what everyone wasn't saying, and that usually was written all across their bodies.

"Is that really your question?" Monti drew her eyebrows together, canting her head to the side slightly.

"Yes."

Monti sighed and waved a hand out in front of her. Then she took a sip from her mug and rested her free hand on her knee, curling her long fingers on her knee. "I received my undergraduate degree in sociology from the University of Puget Sound, and my master's in psychology from Colorado State."

"You move often."

"Yes." Monti stared at her, quite directly. It was unnerving, but Athena didn't move. This was likely how it felt when she stared at people. "And you?"

"Harvard Law." She hadn't expected the pushback at her own degree. She'd gone to school to get a break from her parents, and as an attempt to find something to do with her life, something out from under their thumb.

"*Impressive* is what I'm supposed to say to that, but when you come from money, it's easy to get a degree wherever you want."

Cold rushed through Athena. "Excuse me?"

"I'm not saying you didn't earn your degree. But economically speaking, you had an advantage that others didn't." Monti seemed to pale slightly.

"An advantage I used."

"Well, why wouldn't you?"

Athena ran a single finger over the wood in the arm of the chair, the feel of the smooth material calming her. She did it again as she worked through her upset over Monti's implication. She knew she'd grown up in a privileged household. Coming from money was something she'd always known would be a burden, but she'd dealt with it the best way she knew how. From what she'd gathered about Fallon, that wasn't the case for their family.

"Are you feeling more rested?"

Jerking with a start, Athena realized that she had missed something in the in between, when she was lost in her thoughts. She had been doing that more and more often lately. Perhaps with a few hours of sleep, she would be able to find her brain again. "Yes."

"Good. Most people forget about the skull when they do massages. But I've found them to be quite useful in easing migraines and relaxing the rest of the body. Everything is interconnected." Monti took another sip from her drink before setting it down, the tassel from the tea bag swinging in the movement.

What kind of tea would Monti Schroeder drink?

"Yes, well, it's an odd feeling," Athena mumbled, not sure what to do. Which was a rare occurrence for her.

"It can be." Monti slid forward, elbows on her knees, fingers steepled together. "Do you want to talk about it?"

"Talk about what?" Athena's tone was sharp, but that phrase was one that would always set her off. And she had work to do. Why was she still sitting here entertaining a conversation? Yet Athena couldn't make herself leave.

"Why you're not sleeping." It was a statement, not a question.

"Stress. Why does anyone not sleep?" Her defenses kicked into her high gear. All that nervous energy piled together and swam a violent whirlpool in her chest, pulling everything toward the pit of her stomach.

"There are as many reasons as there are people in this world."

Athena paused. Perhaps she wasn't giving Monti enough credit. She was educated, even if she hadn't managed to live in one place very long and she wasn't currently working, according to Fallon. Athena clenched her jaw. "Thank you for your services, Monti."

Monti's lips parted, as if she was going to say something, but she stopped.

Athena pushed to her feet, her toes curling slightly as tension rippled along her calves, up into her thighs, her stomach, and her shoulders. Three hours of sleep would have to be enough. She had a case she needed to work on, and she was running out of time because the trial was coming up.

"Ms. Pruitt, I need to check in with you about the care you received today."

"You did. It was satisfactory." Athena snagged the book and started toward the shelf where Monti had pulled it from.

"No, we didn't."

When Athena spun around, she found Monti still studying, fingers steepled, but she was leaning back in the chair like she owned it. Like she belonged there. The feeling disturbed her. Athena froze on the landing, the shelves at her back. "I found it useful."

"Was the touch too much?" Monti's tone softened as she asked, as if she already knew that the question itself was going to cause upheaval. How was Monti so insightful?

And perhaps Monti did know exactly what this had done to her. Maybe Monti Schroeder had been paying attention. It was rare that Athena had found someone who was able to do that after only one session. It released even more of that tension. But Athena resisted that feeling. It was uncomfortable and against her nature. Still, the thought occurred to her that Monti might as well just unravel her.

"It was fine." It wasn't a lie. Athena had almost forgotten that Monti was a stranger, touching her. If Athena closed her eyes—which she wouldn't do—she could still feel the sliding of Monti's finger against her. Stopping that train of thought, Athena stiffened her shoulders and set herself back on track.

But each time she thought about going back to before, even though it was only a few hours ago, it was another stab to her heart. She hadn't done the job of protecting herself from someone else—she'd let Monti get too close. Athena reached up and brushed her fingers through her tangled hair. She'd almost forgotten about that, and the sharp tug was a good reminder of how she'd already let her guard down too much.

Self-conscious, Athena pulled her hand down to her side and

gave Monti a hard stare. She wanted her clip back, and she wanted her hair back in place. Everything in here was disordered, and it shouldn't be. This should be the simplest and purest place for her to be in the house. It was always that. Yet with Monti here, it was something else entirely. Monti was nothing more than a disruption, and Athena couldn't have that. It would throw her into chaos that she'd never recover from.

"Ms. Pruitt, I'd like to help you, but unless you actually answer my questions, nothing is going to improve."

"Help me? You're here as a favor to your sister." Those defenses Athena had were still up. But again, normally she would have walked out of the room already, disappeared from the conflict. And she found herself unable to leave, still staring at Monti and her dark brown eyes, her calm countenance.

"True." Monti dropped her hands. "And I can leave anytime I want. Do you want me to?"

Yes. The answer was on the tip of Athena's tongue, but she couldn't make herself say the word. Because she wasn't sure that was what she wanted to say. Three hours of uninterrupted sleep had been blissful, and if Monti could give that to her again?

Athena might just let her stay.

"I have work to get done." It was Athena's go-to defense, and it always worked.

"Far be it from me to get between you and work." Monti put her hands on her knees and pushed up to stand. She had long legs, just like Fallon. But beyond a few commonalities in their looks—their eye color, their body shape—they were complete opposites. Monti stepped away from the chair, her hands automatically sliding into her pockets.

Athena tensed sharply and took a step backward. Something moved into her throat, clogging it. She couldn't scream. She couldn't breathe properly. Her heart thundered, making it impossible to focus. Sound raged through her ears.

"Ms. Pruitt." Monti's voice cut through everything.

Athena grasped onto it and clung. Monti was the better alternative to the flash she'd seen. And all she had to do was focus on the other woman in the room to stay present in the here and now.

Athena blinked. She took a steadying breath and looked directly at Monti.

"I forgot. I'm sorry." Her hands were out next to her sides, palms toward Athena in the most non-threatening way possible.

Damn. I thought I was better with that already.

Swallowing the lump that clogged her throat, Athena straightened her spine. "Fallon will see you out."

Without another word, she stalked toward the door and walked out. She couldn't go back in there. She couldn't face Monti and her embarrassment from *that* episode. It had been years since she'd been this bad, and the fact that it was coming back up now? She hated herself even more for it. The hallways were quiet, which meant most of her staff was already gone for the day. Soon enough, Fallon would leave her, and she would be all alone in her house.

In the quiet.

Athena pushed that thought to the side. She could manage one more night. She had every night for the last twenty-two years. Though it would help if Kevin was home. Even if they didn't sleep in the same bed, it eased her discomfort knowing that someone else was in the house with her. Someone she could actually trust. Athena walked into her office suite.

"Ms. Pruitt." Fallon stood up immediately.

"You can send your sister home, Fallon."

"Um... Is everything okay?" Fallon paled, that nervous energy she always seemed to carry with her fully present now.

Athena inwardly winced. She should take better care, though most days she struggled just to keep up with her own needs and had nothing left for anyone else. She nodded sharply. "Fantastic. Send her home, and when you're done, feel free to leave yourself."

"All right." Fallon sounded nervous.

Athena didn't have the time for it. She walked into her office and shut the door. Everything was just like she left it. Papers and books on her desk, her computer on but asleep. She relaxed and closed her eyes briefly before she stepped toward her desk.

She'd been working on this case for months now, and they were finally gearing up for the trial. Athena ran her fingers through her hair, belatedly realizing that her hand shook. This case was affecting her more than it should, but something about it bothered her.

Her client had been stalked for twelve years and no one had done a damn thing about it. Not only was it unconscionable, it was ridiculous. The amount of turmoil and resistance her client had faced throughout the last decade because she was a woman and because no one had listened to her was without reason.

It wasn't the first case Athena had taken on like this. It wasn't the first time she'd dealt with issues this terrible if not worse. But this one case affected her more. And for the last three months that she'd been working on it, Athena hadn't been able to put her finger on why.

Except twelve years was a long time.

Almost as long as twenty-two.

And if in twelve years nothing had been done, no one had listened, it gave Athena very little hope that twenty-two years would make any difference. Which left her exactly where she was.

Alone.

Working.

And trying to find justice for someone who stood a chance at getting it.

Because hell knew Athena didn't stand a chance.

Athena pulled the heavy law book in front of her and opened it to where she'd left off. She always did prefer to work with books over electronics, so long as she could manage it. Sliding her finger along the rough paper, Athena lost herself in the words.

She wouldn't lose.

Not this time.

three

The sun shone against Monti's skin, warming her cheeks even though the air was chilly this time of year. The park she'd found was beautiful, and with the people bustling around it she could almost take her mind off the fact that she'd broken her fast of massaging.

And for what?

A few dollars and a curt dismissal.

She frowned, trying to push back the entitlement that she felt bubbling up in her. Athena had no idea who she was and clearly had her own demons to face. Monti couldn't judge her quick reactions because every person was their own person.

At least that's what she kept trying to tell herself.

It wasn't really working.

Sighing heavily, Monti closed her eyes. She crossed her legs, the cold water from the morning dew seeping into her loose pants. They'd no doubt be damp for hours afterward, but she could live with that. It would be a good reminder of what she'd discovered on this journey.

Monti centered her breathing. She focused on it, the in and out of air from her lungs. Starting with the top of her head, she ran through the meditation quickly and then paused, letting her body work its magic to find the peace that she so desperately longed for. The one thing that was elusive in her life that she'd left everything behind to find.

And yet she still couldn't grasp onto it.

Pain. Frustration. Annoyance.

It all slipped through her faster than a gunshot, though the wounding it left had the same rippling effect. Sometimes she wondered if she was ever going to find peace.

Or if it even existed.

Giving up, Monti stood up and brushed her pants off. She smiled at a young woman who jogged in her direction, sweat dripping down her face as she moved at a steady pace. It had been a while since Monti had taken any kind of lover. She'd been so focused on trying to find herself that she'd lost track of even paying attention to someone else. She didn't need love, definitely not the physical sort.

What she needed was peace.

Her phone buzzed in her pocket, and she smiled at the gentle reminder from Fallon about lunch. She'd lost track of time. With the constant gray skies, it was harder to keep track of it all. But then again, she'd never been particularly good at that. Brushing her short hair behind her ear, Monti stretched her legs as she took the long walk back the way she had come.

Peace.

What did that even mean?

She hadn't had peace her entire life. She'd been born into chaos, and while she'd distanced herself from it, that myth of peace still hung over her. Fallon was the only good thing to come out of that house. Then again, Tia choosing to raise them had been the second-best thing. If only they'd been ripped from their home sooner. Running her fingers through her hair, Monti kept her pace a meandering stroll.

She needed to right her mind before she went into a conversation with her sister. Their relationship had enough stressors in it that they didn't need to add Monti's worries to it. And Fallon would understand if she was late. She always did.

Monti walked and walked and walked. By the time she reached the coffee shop where Fallon had said to meet her, she was forty minutes late. She'd definitely get a reaming for this one, but she'd needed the time to think. Even if she didn't come up with any solutions.

There are no solutions. Only journeys.

The words echoed in her mind, but she couldn't recall where they came from. It could be from any number of teachings, and did it honestly matter which one? She wasn't looking for an answer. Just peace. And she'd been careful not to make peace the answer, hadn't she?

"There you are!" Fallon's smile faltered slightly, as if she could immediately sense Monti's overcast mood that morning. "What's wrong?"

Monti cringed. Yup, her sister was always sensitive to the emotions of those around her. And Monti was no exception to that rule. How was Fallon handling her boss not sleeping? Monti's guess was not well.

"Nothing." Monti slid into the seat across from her sister and plastered on a smile. She really shouldn't do that, but she also didn't want Fallon to worry any more than she already did. And if Fallon was good at one thing, it was worrying. "I was meditating at the small park along the river. Have you been there?"

"No." Fallon squinted into her cup. "I haven't found the time."

"Which means you haven't made it," Monti challenged. She used to think the same way as Fallon. But it was really because she wasn't making the time to do anything that was life-giving for her. Monti had stopped that as soon as she found out how detrimental it was to her.

"Fair." Fallon raised an eyebrow, her gaze sharp. "And what have you made time for?"

"Meditation." Monti smiled, settling into that feeling of calm she found whenever she did a practiced meditation. Well, most of the time she did one. Lately, it had become harder to find her center, harder to be encompassed by that calm. "And I've been exploring this city again, with new eyes."

"What does that even mean?" Fallon rolled her eyes as she sipped her coffee.

Monti laughed lightly. "It doesn't really matter." She ordered a tea when a waitress came over. They settled into silence. Monti knew where the conversation was going to go, just the same way that it always did.

"When are you going to settle down?" Fallon asked.

And there it was. The question Fallon always asked and the one Monti always avoided.

"Never." Monti pressed her palms flat against the wooden table, the unfinished surface smooth against her skin with how worn it was. "I like being a nomad."

"I don't like not knowing where you're at."

"You always know where I'm at." Monti thanked the waitress and sipped her tea. "You always know how to get hold of me."

"If you answer your phone."

"I'll always answer for you," Monti charged back, hoping it would be enough but also knowing that it wouldn't be.

"You don't."

"I'll try to do better." That age-old frustration burned in the top of her chest, but she really didn't want to deal with it, not today. The check that was being deposited into her account would keep her going for another month easily. That and the connection to Athena Pruitt for one massage were things that Monti was grateful for.

"You always say that."

"I do," Monti agreed. She couldn't fault Fallon. There were times when she would go silent for days and weeks at a time, just to try and find herself in the midst of everything going on in the world. There was no way she could do that with her sister nagging in her ear. So she dropped it and took a sip of her burning hot and not quite steeped tea.

Fallon sighed heavily. "I've missed you."

"Same." They could at least agree on that. It had been far too long since they'd sat together in the same room. "You could always come with me, you know. I was planning a trip to Belize in a few months."

"I don't know, Monti. I don't think I can get the time off."

"You deserve the time off. Take it." Monti had never understood what pull Athena had on her sister. They were stuck together, and if Athena said jump, Fallon asked how high. "Come on, it could be a fun sisters-only trip."

Fallon canted her head to the side as if she was really contemplating it. "But I'm going to want to be spoiled if we go. I don't want to be sleeping in caves or going on long ass hikes. I want to sit at the beach with a margarita and a good book—or five."

Chuckling, Monti grinned. "I think that could be arranged. I can go on all the hikes, you stay at the resort."

Pursing her lips, Fallon slowly shook her head. "I don't believe you'll come back to drink with me at night. Or that you'll even book us into a resort."

"Definitely will." It was a lie, and they both knew it, but they didn't have to say it out loud. Monti didn't drink quite like Fallon did, always one to watch what she put into her body with great care. "Ask Athena for time off. We can go together."

Fallon pulled her lower lip between her teeth. Was she really contemplating this? It would be amazing if she was, and Monti would stay at any resort just to have some one-on-one sister time.

"With this trial coming up, I don't think I can." Fallon's face fell. "It's... this is a tough one, and I've never seen her like this before."

"Sleepless in Seattle?" Monti snorted at her own joke.

Fallon gave her a flat look. "So funny. Har, har, har."

"Hey, it was funny!" It was helpful that Fallon knew Athena so they could actually have this conversation. Not that Monti would reveal anything personal beyond what was already in the open. She was fastidious about confidentiality. Athena's story wasn't her story to tell. "Anyway, she can't keep you working forever."

"I know." Fallon nervously twirled her hair around one of her fingers. "But she's worrying me, Monti. I'm serious. I've never seen her like this."

Monti shrugged. Sure, she was curious what was setting Athena off so much, and at the same time, it wasn't really her job to figure it out either. But she wanted to. That urge to help Athena hadn't gone away. In fact, in some ways, it had only gotten worse. She hated that part of herself sometimes. Monti couldn't help Athena unless she wanted it, and just pushing her way in to satiate her own curiosity wasn't going to do anyone good.

"You worry too much," Monti answered, turning her thoughts back to her sister. "And she's your boss. Put up some better boundaries."

"Athena is more than my boss."

Monti frowned. They weren't in a relationship, were they? Fallon had never said anything about being interested in women. Then again, she barely ever talked about being interested in anyone. Shaking the thought from her brain because it wasn't her business, Monti sipped her tea again, this time getting the full burst of flavor on her tongue. It was amazing.

"I take care of her," Fallon added finally.

"So you have a codependent relationship," Monti said simply, the words blunter than she wanted them to be, but she couldn't take them back now.

Fallon glared. "We do not."

"Sure, you don't."

"Don't use your big fancy degrees on me, missy."

Monti threw her hands up in mock indignation. "I would never dare."

"Sure, you wouldn't." Fallon smirked, but they fell into a comfortable silence. "When would we go? Winter?"

"If you wanted. We can go whenever. It's not like my schedule is booked up."

Fallon hummed, as if she was imagining the beach already. Monti wished she was a visual person like that, but she'd tamped down her visual acuity so much in the past years that it was a struggle to visualize just for meditations.

"I'm going to visit Mom soon. It's her birthday."

Monti knew the question was coming as soon as Fallon brought it up. But she didn't want Fallon to ask it. Seeing the disappointment on her face would be too much. Though Monti had only ever given in to the request once.

And once was enough.

"Do you want to go with me?"

"Fallon…" Monti trailed off, hoping that Fallon would come to the conclusion already. "You know I don't."

"But will you?"

Now that was a different question than normal. "I'll have to think about that one."

Monti could probably force herself to go for her sister's sake, but that would be it. She still didn't want to go. There was nothing there for her. Monti was about to speak when Fallon's phone rang in her purse.

"Sorry." Fallon fished around and snagged her phone, answering it immediately.

Monti tuned out the conversation, wanting to give her sister privacy. The answers were rapid fire and quick. Monti stared at the counter in the back of the shop, and the very beautiful woman standing behind it. She was bubbly and excited to see new customers come in.

But was that her personality or something she simply *wore* for the job?

Those types of questions always plagued Monti, no matter where she went. She was unable to escape her constant need to dig deeper and discover who every single person was underneath the surface.

"I'm sorry," Fallon interrupted her thoughts, bringing Monti right back to the table. "Athena needs me back."

"It's not a problem. I'll catch up with you soon."

"For sure." Fallon bent down and gave Monti a half hug. "Please don't be a stranger."

"I promise," Monti whispered. And this time, she meant it.

After Fallon left, Monti finished her tea and wandered around downtown a bit more. She couldn't stop thinking about Fallon at work, however. More importantly, she couldn't stop wondering about Athena. Just what was it that caused her to become the person Monti had met?

Everyone had a past. Everyone had things in their lives that formed them. Monti's was tragic. Then again, whose wasn't? Monti shoved her hands into her pockets as she walked, then smiled to herself. She could do that today. At least for now. Perhaps a run in the park or another round of yoga would do her some good.

She needed to meditate on what it was about Athena that had captured her attention. What was it she wanted to figure out and why? Because Monti had learned early on that those yearnings usually said more about her than anyone else.

Soon enough Monti would be gone, off in her van to her next destination—once she figured out where that would be. And in her wake, she would leave no one worse off without her. And *that* was the only thing she knew had to happen. The less impact she made, the better off everyone would be when she left.

Then they would all be able to find peace.

four

"Fallon, I need you to set up a meeting with Gwen Fudala for the upcoming week." Athena said the words quickly as she walked through Fallon's office to get to hers.

"Uh… sure." Fallon quickly sat down and started typing, but something in the way she tensed caused Athena to stop.

She knew she was an exacting boss, that she demanded high quality from her employees, but was she being a bit too harsh? With her inability to get proper rest lately, she was left trying to figure out how to control each urge to snap in anger. And Fallon, unfortunately, had borne the brunt of the moments when Athena hadn't managed to keep herself in check.

When Fallon finally looked up at her again, a small piece of Athena chipped off. She had been too cruel lately. Rubbing her thumb into the center of her palm to try and bring herself back to reality, Athena glanced at Fallon and debated what to say. An apology wouldn't be enough, that was for sure.

"How was lunch?" There. That was a satisfactory apology without it being an apology. Right?

"Oh. It was all right."

Fallon rarely asked to leave for a longer lunch, but Athena couldn't remember off the top of her head why she'd made the request today. She went back through every memory of the conversations leading up to the lunch and couldn't piece it together. If she'd been sleeping regularly, she would be able to do that. The fact that she couldn't remember things like she used to was killing her slowly from the inside out. And it made her wonder just exactly how she was going to get through another case and another trial.

"My sister was late," Fallon added, the frown evident on her lips. "Really late."

That's right. She was meeting with Monti. Monti who had touched her. Monti who had come in and given her a few hours of blissful, restful sleep, which had allowed her the mental capacity to finish the injunction she wanted to file. Athena dragged in a deep breath, an easing of the tension in her chest as she blew out the warm air. Why was it that just thinking about Monti and what she'd accomplished did that?

She parted her lips to answer Fallon, but wasn't quick enough.

Fallon looked Athena over and said, "She's always late, to be fair, but this time it was worse than normal."

Athena was glad that Fallon hadn't inherited that trait. She wouldn't still be working there if she had.

"She didn't used to be, but ever since she quit her job and started living on the road, she doesn't really have to conform to normal society in quite that way like the rest of us." Fallon twisted a pen between her fingers, a nervous habit that Athena had noticed on more than one occasion.

"She's a free spirit," Athena finally added to Fallon's one-sided conversation. She felt compelled to say something, especially now that she'd met the infamous Monti, but nothing quite came to mind that would soothe Fallon's obvious distress.

"She'd call herself that." Fallon winced as if she'd revealed something that she hadn't meant to.

But what could it possibly be? Athena didn't understand sibling dynamics at all, since as an only child she grew up in a vacuum. She was raised to be the heir to her family's fortune and essentially to figure out what to do with all the riches when her parents died. Which they had. And she'd upheld her end of the bargain so far.

"Or at least I think she'd say that's what she's aiming for," Fallon mumbled the last part.

Athena had almost missed it. She stayed standing in the entryway to her office, not sure if Fallon wanted her to come closer or not or if she could even manage to be in such close proximity to another person. But the question rolled through her mind, and Athena couldn't stop herself from asking, "She's not free?"

"Is anyone ever really free from their past?" Fallon's brown eyes locked on Athena's, the truth in her statement hard-hitting.

Athena was shackled by her past. She was so tightly confined that she couldn't remember the last time she'd felt a bit of that freedom Fallon was talking about. Or joy. Or even just settled peace. But for right now, she needed to escape this conversation before it got much deeper than it was already. Turning on her toes, Athena walked into her office and closed the door behind her, leaving Fallon to deal with whatever scheduling needed to happen.

As she sat at her desk, with books and everything laid out before her, Athena couldn't focus. Those few hours of blissful sleep had done wonders in the short term, but for the last several hours, she'd been back to the state she was in before.

Unable to get anything done.

Exhausted.

Distracted.

Which meant she really might not want to meet with Gwen so soon. Pulling out her hair clip, Athena ran her fingers along her skull and her neck, attempting to mimic what Monti had done and failing miserably. Body work was never something she under-stood. But Monti obviously did, because the way her fingers had worked along Athena's muscles had been nothing less than a miracle.

Logically, Athena knew that her body was connected to everything, each part of her connected to the other, but how? How did she fix one part in order to force her body to rest and sleep? Because that was what eluded her right now. She couldn't focus.

Standing, Athena walked to the large window. She crossed her arms and stared out at the rainy field outside. The forest was beautiful with the trees surrounding her, the greens dark this time of year because the sky kept feeding them no matter what. And the gray of the skies almost always suited her mood. She never understood sunshine, or basking in it, or allowing the rays to kiss her skin.

Sure, she'd read about that in books, she'd even attempted to experience it a few times at her beach house in the Florida Keys. But it had all been a waste and she'd given up. She'd come stumbling inside and holed herself up in her library with a good book where her mind could be teased into learning. This house was her home now, the place where she would live until she died.

What a morbid thought was that?

Athena wrinkled her nose and shifted her stance. If she were braver, she'd go on a walk outside. Throw on a jacket and some hiking shoes and disappear into the forest for hours, losing all track of time. She was willing to bet that Monti wouldn't think twice about doing that.

The knock on the door was sharp.

Athena jumped, spun around, and put her hands in fists at her sides. Her heart raced wildly, and she couldn't calm it down. That had been worse than normal lately. And she couldn't make it stop.

"I was able to get ahold of Ms. Fudala, but she can't meet with you until next week."

"Perfect." Athena knew the word came out sharp when she hadn't intended it to, but it really was optimal. It would give her extra time to sort herself out before they had to talk through details of the trial.

It was the trial.

The thought settled into Athena's very being. Ultimately, Athena knew, she should never have agreed to take it. There was a reason she'd limited herself on cases in the last five years, and this was it exactly. When she'd looked over the initial request, she couldn't ignore the fact that Gwen Fudala had seen no justice. And she deserved to find some peace, even if Athena thought that was a crock of bullshit.

"Also, Francine with Shiloh's Home called with dates for the next gala and to personally request you attend." Fallon looked so nervous. Had Athena scared her that much?

"Oh?" Athena crossed her arms, her hands grabbing hold of her elbows as if she was hugging herself.

"Would you like me to respond that you'll attend?"

"If it fits with the schedule, yes." She loved that particular foundation. It worked with sexual assault victims, sharing their story, helping them find closure along with single parents and young women. If only that was available to everyone. "Let Kevin know. He'll want to come with me."

"Yes, ma'am." Fallon ducked her chin. "Would you like the usual donation?"

Athena thought a moment before responding with a shake of her head. "Double it."

She might regret that decision later, at least her haste in making it. But on a very basic level, she knew she never would. They were doing good work, and they needed the funds to be able to continue.

"Is that everything?"

"Um..." Fallon seemed shy all of a sudden, in a way Athena rarely saw her.

She held the silence, waiting for Fallon to continue. It wasn't like she could concentrate on work anyway right now, despite trying. Her energy waned in a way it hadn't in decades. She needed Kevin home, but he was on a three-week trip to Indonesia with his long-time lover. What were husbands for if they were constantly gone and with someone else?

"What do you think?"

Athena blinked, having no idea what Fallon had just said. She really had to get better control of herself, figure out what she was missing and why she couldn't just relax. Athena wracked her brain for any memory of what they had been talking about, but she couldn't even bring up the start of the conversation.

What the hell was wrong with her?

"You have no idea what I just said, do you?" Fallon's face fell. She drew in a deep breath and let out a long sigh. "I asked how it went with Monti. You've been suspiciously quiet about it."

"Suspicious?" Athena raised her eyebrows in surprise. "It's hardly suspicious. She came to do a job, she did it, and she left."

"And *you* slept." Fallon crossed her arms, giving Athena a pointed look.

Curse her for bringing that up. Because as much as Athena wasn't avoiding it, she wanted to. Monti's fingers had been magic on her skin, and the sleep was heavenly. And Athena didn't exaggerate. Ever. She would love to bring Monti back into the house and try again. Even three more hours of uninterrupted sleep would give her what she needed to focus.

"I did," Athena admitted. Why was that so damn hard?

"So call her to come back."

Athena stretched her neck muscles, her entire jaw and chest tense from just that one comment. She'd thought about it. She really had. But to pick up the phone and make the request? Impossible. And yet to have Fallon do it was too much to ask. She was once again letting her own demons get in her way of living. Not that that wasn't a theme for her entire life. Live into the expectations of others and the ones she set for herself and she wouldn't have to look at what was falling apart around her. Right?

"I'm not sure that's a good idea," Athena finally answered, though she didn't sound too convinced herself.

Silence filtered through the room, and Athena wondered why Fallon hadn't left yet. Why wasn't she alone? Athena dragged in a ragged breath and faced her desk again. What had she been working on?

"Let me call her." Fallon's request was simple and quiet.

"Fallon..." Athena started, but she couldn't form the words. That had been why she'd hired Fallon, and why she'd kept her around for so long. The woman was obnoxiously good at anticipating Athena's every need and then pushing for it even when she rejected the help. Still, she wanted to say no. She wanted to deny that there was a problem.

"She's still in town. She will be for another week or two at least—I think, anyway. So let me call her. She could use the cash, I'm sure, and you could really use a few more hours of sleep."

"I don't think it's a good idea," Athena finally answered. The pull of the muscles in her shoulder was so intense she was pretty sure something was about to break. "I really just need to get some work done."

"You can't work if you can't focus."

Why did she have to be blunt sometimes? That was a trait both Fallon and Monti shared, and it irked Athena. She'd always been taught not to do that except when in the courtroom, and even then she felt as though she was working against herself every time she did it.

"It's not that bad," Athena said, flicking a glance to Fallon because they both knew she was lying through her teeth. Fallon's look said it all. Sighing heavily, Athena waved her off. "Fine. Call her."

"Perfect. I'll schedule her in."

Athena didn't answer as she sat back down at her desk. Work. That's what she needed to get done. This injunction wasn't going to file itself, and she'd been debating whether or not to expand their list of people to sue when it came to the individuals on the police force.

Who would she have sued in her own case? Hell if she knew. It was so long ago, and such a different time. She was a different person then. Biting her lip, Athena stared at the email that had just come in. A notification of a scheduled event. Monti would be there in an hour.

Good.

That gave her time to get things sorted before she had to distract herself with someone else for a while. When Athena looked up at her door again, Fallon was standing in it. But this time she had a nervous look on her face.

Athena couldn't keep up with everything going on.

Her brain was fried, and just trying to focus on the basics was hard enough. Managing Fallon's emotions was beyond her capacity right now. She wasn't even sure she wanted to ask what the problem was, afraid the answer would be too big for her to handle.

"Simon called."

"Oh?" What could her son possibly want now? And how had she missed the call? Or rather, why would he call Fallon instead of her? Athena tried to work through the possibilities but gave up when Fallon's voice reached her ears again.

"I told him you were in a meeting when he couldn't get ahold of you."

Leave it to Fallon to try and protect everyone. "What did he want?"

"He wanted to know if you were planning anything for his birthday or if he should schedule a time to come home for it."

Athena pursed her lips, the pressure building behind her eyes almost instantly. It wasn't that she'd forgotten that it was his birthday. It was that she didn't want to think about it. Some milestones were harder than others.

"What did you tell him?"

"To come home. I'll figure something out." Fallon turned her back and closed the door.

Left in the blissful quiet of her office, Athena collapsed into her chair. What was going on with her? She couldn't keep going on like this, could she? Something had to give.

It just couldn't be her.

She was too destroyed to break again.

Wasn't she?

five

"I need you to come back and see Athena."

Monti leaned back in her van, her feet up on the small bed she slept on, pillows piled behind her. She wasn't sure she wanted to go back, and she honestly hadn't expected this call. With the way Athena had left the room, Monti was pretty certain they would never see each other again.

"I don't think that's a good idea."

Fallon sighed, and Monti could imagine the stress lines on her face, the pinch in her cheeks, the thinness of her lips. "I don't think you understand. I *need* you to come back."

"I don't practice anymore."

"I know. I get that. But she hasn't slept since you were here."

"That was four days ago." Monti sat up, one leg curled under the other. Had it really been four days? On one hand it felt longer, and on the other, she could still remember Athena's steady breathing as Monti sat vigil over her while she slept.

"I know!" Fallon repeated, her voice nearly screeching. "I need you to come back."

"You need me or she needs me?" Because those were two different questions, and Fallon hadn't said anything about Athena asking for her. Not yet.

Fallon whimpered. Which answered Monti's question.

"It's not a good idea unless it's her idea."

"It'll never be her idea," Fallon muttered. "Come tonight at five. I'll make sure she knows you'll be here."

"No."

"Yes."

"Fallon..." Monti ground out her sister's name in a warning. "I don't practice anymore."

"But you're still licensed."

"That doesn't matter. I've given it up. I'm not doing this." Monti's back was up. Fallon had never understood why she'd left her careers, why she jumped from one job to the next, why she'd chosen to live in her van and do life exactly as she wanted. Without expectations. Without leaving a trail of people behind her who would miss her when she was gone.

"You're my sister, and that'll never change."

As much as Monti hated that Fallon was right, she also couldn't deny it. Cringing, she took a deep breath and pushed down that defensive line of pain that lashed through her. Fallon would be better off if she wasn't so attached, but Monti understood why Fallon was. Anyone would be, coming from their circumstances, especially because Fallon had been old enough to know what was what at the time.

"I get that," Monti said, finally, her tone softening. Why was this always such a war within her? Why couldn't she just find that elusive inner peace everyone demanded existed? "But if she doesn't want me there, nothing I do is going to work."

"Oh, she wants you here. She needs to sleep or all of us peons are going to rebel and tie her up in a closet for the rest of next week." Fallon laughed lightly. "Not that we'd actually do that, but she has a big client meeting coming up tomorrow, and she needs to be on point for it."

Intrigued, Monti wrinkled her nose. She hated that her sister knew how to get her each and every time. Helping people. It was her biggest weakness. "Fine. I'll be there at five."

"Thank you!"

Monti hung up and blew out a breath as she fell flat on her back and stared at the ceiling in her van again. What was she doing? Going back into that house, that prison of a house, to help someone who was so resistant to help wasn't going to accomplish anything. But she would do anything for Fallon, especially when she used that tone.

Her phone buzzed in her hand, and when she picked it up, there was a text from Fallon.

Fallon: It's 4:45.

"Shit."

Fallon had done that one on purpose. Monti scrambled out of the bed, slipped her sandals on, and got behind the wheel. It was going to take her twenty minutes just to get out of the city, and another ten to get to Athena's mansion on the hill. She clenched her jaw, not doubting that Fallon had already planned for that when she'd called, knowing that Monti wouldn't make it before five.

Damn her sister for having this figured out.

Monti arrived at fifteen after. The gates automatically closed behind her as she drove toward the front of the house and parked exactly where she had the time before. She had no supplies for this. Fallon knew that. She had oils, yes, but nothing else.

Rubbing her clammy hands over her thighs, Monti prepared herself. Athena was a closed book, yet there had been brief windows to see inside, though it was clearly out of necessity and not because Athena had willingly revealed those things. Monti centered herself with a quick meditation. She had to go into this with her mind open and ready for whatever Athena was going to share with her.

When Monti opened her eyes, Fallon was at the front door,

arms crossed, and giving her a serious look. She was out of time. Climbing from the van, Monti started for the door and rubbed her hands along her thighs. She was wearing yoga pants today, having come from doing some exercise at a park. It was probably for the better since she didn't have pockets to accidentally flip Athena out.

Perhaps if she came back again, she would make sure to dress in yoga pants.

"She's waiting for you." Fallon didn't seem all that happy.

"Has the boss been taking her lack of sleep out on her employees?"

Fallon's sharp look confirmed her suspicion. Monti swallowed hard. She hadn't meant to poke the bear, but she certainly had. She had to get better at this living-in-peace thing. One year on the road and she hadn't managed it, despite the fact that she truly did love living without responsibilities. It had taken a whole year for her to realize that those weren't the issue at hand.

"A few hours is all I'm asking for."

"I'll do my best, but if she's not ready for it, then it'll never work."

"Ready for what?" Fallon rubbed her lips together as they stopped outside the library door.

"To work on the problem."

"What's the problem?"

Monti shrugged. She didn't honestly know, but even if she did, she wasn't going to tell Fallon. That was for Athena only to disclose, whenever she was ready.

"Fine. Don't tell me."

"You know I can't."

"I know. I just wish..." Fallon sighed heavily, looking directly at the door, her face falling. "I just wish I knew how to help her better."

"It's not your job."

"Maybe not." Fallon put her hand on the knob. "You ready?"

"As ready as I'll ever be...I think."

Walking in, Monti was greeted with Athena standing at the farthest bookshelf. She pulled one book and then another, stacking them before rolling her neck and her shoulders. She was exhausted to the point she was barely upright. Her body listed from side to side as she attempted to grab the next book.

"I'd feel better if you sat down so you didn't fall over."

"I won't fall," Athena muttered.

"Could have fooled me." Monti moved to the chair she'd sat in before, wanting to give Athena the advantage of sitting where she preferred.

"I suppose Fallon told you why you're here."

"You're not sleeping." Monti rubbed her palms along the chair. "I honestly didn't think our last session went well enough for you to call me again."

Athena cut her a look so sharp that it could cut diamonds. If Monti were someone else, she would have laughed at it, but she knew intuitively that Athena would recoil if she did. Monti bit her tongue and eyed Athena over. She looked almost perfectly put together, still covered head to toe.

Yet there were dark bags under her eyes that were puffy and red. The makeup she wore barely covered it up. Her skin was paler than it had been days ago, and her fingers trembled as she grabbed another book.

"Athena, sit down."

Athena's chin jerked up, her gaze locked on Monti's face. How many people were permitted to call her that? Still if Monti wanted to make some sort of progress toward deepening their relationship, then they were going to need to break down some of these walls between them. Monti raised an eyebrow pointedly and waited to see if Athena would give in. She must be using all of her strength to stay upright.

"I don't want to pry if you don't want me to, but I get the sense that you're scared to sleep."

"I've never heard anything so asinine."

Monti grunted and rested in the chair. "I would never underestimate fear if I were you."

"I never underestimate anything, Monti." Athena walked toward her, stumbling down the one step that would lead her to the chairs.

Monti almost jumped up to catch her, but she held her ground, if only to prove her point just how tired Athena was. But she had to know. There was no other reason why Monti would be there if she didn't. Athena slipped into the chair next to Monti, nearly melting into it.

"Did you ask Fallon to call me or did she suggest it?"

"What does it matter?"

"It helps me assess the situation more fully."

Athena's lips thinned, and her eyes closed. It took her a long time to open them again, and Monti could tell she wasn't seeing clearly. "I asked her to call you."

Interesting. Monti had to approach Athena with gentleness, and she had to make sure that Athena saw her coming. She was jumpy, and Monti was fairly certain that if she startled Athena that would be the end of their working relationship.

"In the last session, you slept."

"I did." Athena's shoulders tightened. "And I need to sleep again."

"But the real question, or rather the real problem to solve, is why you aren't sleeping. Not just getting the sandman to take you."

Athena chuckled low. "I haven't heard that reference in a while."

"It seemed apt considering the circumstances."

"Agreed." Athena clenched her fingers into a tight ball before relaxing them. "I don't want to talk. I want to sleep."

"I'm not entirely convinced one can happen without the other." Monti saw the recognition flash across Athena's eyes before she closed them again. It was getting harder and harder for

Athena to avoid, and eventually, she would either talk to Monti or she would find someone else who could help her.

"It'll have to."

"Oh, denial. You are a mighty beast, aren't you?" Monti shifted in the chair, leaning forward. "If you don't want my help, Ms. Pruitt, then why am I here?"

"I can't think."

"Because you're not sleeping."

"I believe we've established that fact," Athena ground out. "Are you sure you have a master's in psychology?"

Monti chuckled. "Yes. Many years of my life dedicated to schooling that I may never use again."

"And why is that?" Athena reached for a small glass on the table that Monti had missed before. It was filled with an amber liquid, probably alcohol of some sort, though Monti had no idea which kind. Athena lifted the glass to her lips but didn't drink.

"I don't work in a clinical setting anymore, and I don't plan on returning." Monti rubbed her palms together. She had anticipated this line of questioning the last time they'd met. When it hadn't happened, she'd assumed she'd gotten away without it. "Two years ago, I realized I needed to do a deeper search. I needed to find peace."

"And have you found it?" Athena eyed her over the glass as she sipped. Her eyes were so blue, the red rims and puffiness such a stark contrast. It brought out the color in a way Monti hadn't expected. Her face was heart shaped. In another life, Monti could imagine Athena being the talk of the town, living up to her given name. "Monti?"

"No," Monti finally answered, brought back to reality by Athena's voice. "But I believe finding inner peace is an ongoing process. I'm not sure it's ever complete. Though I know many religions and religious leaders would say otherwise."

"So would many therapists."

"I'm not like many therapists." Monti's palms were clammy. Why did she feel like she was under fire?

"Of course not. Everyone is unique and different." The comment was flippant, and it stung.

Monti wasn't about to let Athena in on that fact, however. She didn't need more ammunition to toss Monti out. And what Monti really needed to do was figure out if the attitude was because Athena was exhausted or if she really was that cruelhearted.

Clenching her teeth, Monti settled her heart and calmed the defensiveness that rose up in her chest. That would only be a hindrance in this conversation. "The idea in any therapeutic situation, whether it's psychological, medical, or massage, is to create a safe space. I need to make sure you feel that, otherwise our session today won't go forward."

Athena stared directly at Monti, her eyes wide. Though Monti couldn't read the emotion running through her.

"Do you trust me?" Monti asked.

"You've done nothing to earn my trust," Athena barked back.

"I've shown up twice, and the first time, you did sleep. I'd say that's a small amount of trustworthiness."

Athena canted her head to the side, the lines of her neck long and tense. She swallowed, her throat tightening before it relaxed. The muscles in her cheeks followed suit, dropping as Athena slowly closed her eyes and opened them again. "Yes, you're right."

Monti hadn't expected that. But she would take the win. "The last time I was here, I massaged your hands and your scalp. How was that for you?"

"It was good." Athena rested her head against the chair. She seemed so aloof, but Monti was pretty sure this was entirely because of the lack of sleep.

"Good. I'm glad. I'd like today to work on a little more than your hands and scalp, considering that didn't seem to resolve the problem."

Athena hummed. "What do you want to touch?"

"Your shoulders and neck. Upper arms if you'll allow it. You don't need to take your clothes off, since I doubt that would make you more comfortable. But if you could remove your jacket..." Monti trailed off, already noting the tension rising in the room and seeing Athena's pulse skyrocket in the line of her neck.

"I don't like to be touched."

"I know," Monti responded, softening her voice immediately. This was delicate territory she was walking through. "And I'll respect whatever you tell me. I do believe that you hold a lot of tension in your neck and shoulders. I imagine you're in more pain than you realize."

Athena shifted, turning her upper body in order to look Monti directly in the eye. A thrill of hope ran through Monti's chest and settled into her stomach. This must be it, the moment she had been waiting for when they would take another step forward. Monti stayed still, scared she would frighten Athena back into her hidey-hole.

Athena raised a hand to her ear, brushing an invisible strand of hair, but she didn't tear her gaze from Monti's. Her words were precise and without ire as she spoke.

"You have no earthly idea."

Six

Every noise was loud in Athena's ears. Her breath. Her heart. Her brain that just wouldn't shut the fuck up already. That part of her that clogged her throat anytime she tried to do something outside of her comfort zone. She clenched her jaw, her molars grinding against each other and the sound reverberating through her head.

Even Monti was loud. The shifting of the fabric of her pants against the chair, the weight of her body as the springs groaned under her movement. The clicking of her nails against each other as she rubbed the backs of her fingers and waited for a response.

That panic.

It clawed at her.

Athena struggled to push it back down in her chest. She was safe here. She was always safe in this house. And Monti had done nothing that should set her on edge. So why was she? Was it only because Monti needed to touch her? Because of the scars and hidden secrets that might be revealed?

"You need to breathe," Monti's voice was gentle, and it floated to Athena's ears like a sweet balm.

Sucking cold air into her lungs, Athena breathed relief. When had she started holding her breath? Her brain was awash with everything lately. She just needed to get back to work. She needed to get back to normal.

"Athena." Again, Monti's voice in that calm, sweet tone. "Count to six."

Furrowing her brow, Athena did as she was told. This was something tangible that she could grasp onto, something to focus on that could center this racing mind of hers. When she got to six, she started again. Athena lost count how many times she had gone from one to six, but when she opened her eyes and looked at Monti, she could tell it had been too long. There was worry etched into her sweet young face, into the lines just starting to form around her eyes and her lips.

"Now count backward."

"This is horse—"

"Athena," Monti said firmly, her look stern. "Count backward."

Biting her tongue, Athena did as she was told. Though she only did it three times before a sense of calm took root in the center of her chest. She'd been missing that before. She clasped onto it and refused to let it go. The longer she focused on it, the bigger it grew. Eventually, Athena looked into Monti's curious brown eyes and nodded.

"Thank you," Athena murmured, making sure her voice wasn't too loud.

"I think that might be enough for today."

"No." Athena gripped the arms of the chair tightly, using them as her lifeline. When the same panic didn't swell in her chest again, she knew she'd made the right decision.

"I don't want to push you."

"*You're* not pushing me." Athena leaned forward in the chair and reached to her belly, undoing the three buttons on her jacket. She needed this. She needed to stop hiding and allowing everything to control her. And if one more person came into that inner circle, how awful could it be? A massage, especially clothed, was nothing. And she did trust Monti to listen to her no matter what. At least in these circumstances. She was paid to be there.

Monti watched with rapt attention as Athena shifted to pull her jacket off, the sleeves leaving her skin bare to the chill in the room. She resisted the urge to shiver as goosebumps slid up her arms. She couldn't remember the last time anyone had seen her like this other than a doctor. And if she mentally put Monti into that same category, maybe she could make it through this.

But Monti was anything but a cold, aloof, clinical doctor.

Even just being in her presence twice, Athena was certain of that.

Monti was young, lithe, full of energy and excitement. And she was damn cute.

Athena folded her jacket and rested it over the arm of the chair. Her back was ramrod straight, tight with tension, as she faced Monti and waited to see what would happen next. Where would Monti touch her? Where would the tension go when she did? Because last time...last time it had vanished into the ether.

"Why push yourself?" Monti asked.

Athena's lower lip quivered. She hadn't thought that Monti had understood that subtlety. But she didn't know why. She couldn't answer. Tears sprang to her eyes again, stinging, but she blinked and pulled them back in.

What was wrong with her?

"Something needs to change," Athena gave the best non-answer she could come up with on the fly.

"I agree." Monti leaned forward, elbows on her knees, but she didn't break Athena's gaze. "But my question was why?"

"Because...this isn't working."

"What's not working?"

Why did Monti have to be so infuriating with her questions? All Athena wanted to do was sleep, and in order to do that, something had to give. If that was allowing Monti to touch her again, then that's what it would be.

"I'm not working," Athena whispered out loud. Though

she'd thought the words at first were only bumbling around in her brain. "In this current state, I'm too exhausted to think."

"Something else we can agree on." Monti reached forward and held out her hand, as if expecting Athena to touch her willingly, to slide her fingers against Monti's.

But she couldn't do it. She couldn't force her body to move. "Athena."

Again that balm, that constant reminder that there were years of anguish etched into Athena's life and Monti had been spared that trauma.

"I need your hand if I'm going to massage you."

"Oh." Athena swallowed hard, and when she placed her fingers into Monti's, she trembled.

Monti's hand was warm, her skin soft against Athena's. The touch was instantly comforting. Athena sighed, the weight of the last hour lifting. Monti started with her palm, sliding her thumb along the muscles and bones.

"Don't you use oils?" Athena asked after a few seconds of quiet.

Monti moved up Athena's palm to her wrist, digging her thumbs in and releasing the tension. "I typically do, yes."

"Why aren't you now?" Athena tried to hold in the moan when Monti hit a particularly tender spot on the top of her forearm. She worked the muscle, popping the knot several times and applying firm pressure before it disappeared.

"Was that okay?"

"Yes," Athena dragged out, almost a hiss. She'd never been touched like this in her life. Never with such reverence. Never had it felt so good.

"Good." Monti worked higher into her biceps. "I haven't used any oils because we haven't discussed oils—preferred scents, allergies, but also if the feel of them would be something you'd like or hate."

"I..." Athena paused and looked over Monti's contrasting face. Did she realize that she stuck her tongue out the corner of her mouth when she was concentrating? "I don't know if I'd like the feel of it or not."

"We can always try, Ms. Pruitt."

"I don't like the scent of lavender." Athena bit back another moan, the tension in her shoulder instantly easing. It dropped like a heavy weight as Monti slid her hands back down.

"I have some oils in my van if you'd like me to get them. Or Fallon can." Monti stood up slowly and shifted to Athena's other side. She started the same process on her right hand.

Athena was entranced by the way Monti moved, so confident in her touches. Athena's chest rose sharply with each breath as she concentrated on every glide of Monti's fingers. "Next time."

"Will there be a next time?"

"I don't think one massage is going to solve all my problems, do you?"

Monti's lips quirked upward slightly, a beautiful tenuous pull of her mouth. It was the first time Athena had seen it, and it made Monti that much more stunning. She had to be younger than Fallon by at least five years, but this smile made her look so youthful and alive.

"No, I don't think one massage is going to solve anything," Monti whispered back. "Except maybe you won't be in as much physical pain as before."

"I can only hope."

"Will you allow me to massage your neck?" Monti touched her full palm against Athena's upper arm, resting it there until they made eye contact.

Athena halted, her entire being hanging on Monti's words. Her gaze dropped to Monti's mouth, her lips and how they were slightly parted, her tongue peeking out from behind them. The heat from her palm soaked through Athena and filled the cold she'd become so accustomed to. She almost couldn't bear it. She had to blink hard to break her chain of thoughts.

Moving away from the touch, Athena leaned forward and nodded. "Yes."

Anything to stop whatever was happening in that moment. Not between them—that was the one thing Athena *could* deal with. But what was happening inside her. That tingling and pulling, the desire to lean in and see what Monti would do next, to maybe chase after the tip of Monti's tongue. But that couldn't be right. She was too broken for anything to feel good.

Monti stood next to her. "You'll need to turn to the side. The chair is too high for me to reach over it."

"Oh right." Athena slowly turned, putting her back to Monti. Which was probably the biggest sign of trust she'd given yet.

Monti moved slowly, deliberately, as she pulled the clip from Athena's hair and set it on the table, not touching Athena in any way that they hadn't agreed to. Athena waited for what was next, knowing it would instantly set off all her alarms.

"I'm going to start at the base of your skull."

"Okay." Athena jumped when Monti brushed her fingers through her hair, pulling it over the side of her shoulder so it was out of the way.

"Athena?"

"I'm fine. Just ignore it."

"I don't want to move forward if you're uncomfortable."

How was Athena supposed to convey that she was always uncomfortable, not just in a room with a stranger, but with herself. And this case she was working was making all of that front and center. She hated that she'd agreed to take it on, but she couldn't deny Gwen all the justice she could possibly obtain.

"Athena," Monti said again. "What are you thinking?"

"It's not relevant," Athena answered. She felt as though she was swimming through molasses, barely able to keep up. "Go ahead."

"Are you sure?"

"Absolutely."

Monti touched her again, and this time Athena didn't jump. *Perfect.* She was getting better control of herself already. Monti started at the base of her skull, using the sides of her thumbs to add pressure to the muscles with precision. Athena rolled her head forward slightly, enjoying the feeling of the pain from the knots working themselves out. This had been exactly what she'd needed.

"You've been in a lot of pain from this." It wasn't a question, and Athena appreciated that.

She'd spent too much of her time answering questions in her life, and to have Monti come to the conclusion without her was a blessing in disguise. Monti moved down to her shoulders, and Athena couldn't hold back the groan this time when she hit a particularly troublesome spot. Often at night, Athena would rub that part of her shoulder in hopes of easing the tension.

"Don't hold back if you don't want to. I'm not going to tell anyone what's discussed or what happens in this room when we're together. And noises are natural." Monti said it without shame, as if she really meant the words. "You wouldn't believe the number of people who fart their way through a massage."

Athena snorted. "You're joking."

"Nope." Monti pushed a little harder in the cord of muscle down Athena's shoulder.

Again she groaned, then whimpered when Monti found a particularly nasty spot. She jerked when the library door opened, and Monti immediately moved to stand between her and the door, covering her from it. Athena appreciated it, and she snagged her jacket, ready to throw it on when she heard Kevin's loud accusing voice.

"Who are you?"

"Monti Schroeder. Who are you?" Monti put her hands on her hips, and she didn't budge an inch.

"Kevin Brock."

Athena snagged Monti's hand and pulled her to the side, dropping her jacket back to the chair. "Kevin is my husband."

"Y-your husband." Monti spun around and gave Athena a hard look that was an odd mix of curiosity and pain. What was that all about?

"Twenty-two years almost," Athena answered and raised her eyebrows at Kevin. She hadn't expected him home this early. He was supposed to be gone for another two days with his boyfriend. Athena stayed seated, wanting Monti to continue whatever magic she'd been working, but she knew Monti wouldn't without being expressly told. "You're home early."

"My trip was cut short." Kevin cut a look to Monti, no doubt trying to judge who she was, especially since it was clear Monti had been touching her. "Fallon said you were in a meeting."

"I am." Her answer was clipped, she knew. But she was annoyed he'd interrupted something that seemed to be going well. It was the first time she'd been able to focus on anything that day.

Kevin looked from Monti to Athena, clearly confused.

"I haven't been sleeping. Monti is a massage therapist."

"Ah." Kevin nodded his understanding, though he still wasn't budging or buggering off.

Athena dragged in a sharp breath, wanting to dismiss him already. "Was there something you needed?"

"No. I'll see you at dinner."

"Yes." Athena nodded her agreement. They had some catching up to do.

He turned and made it to the door before stopping and turning to her again. "Oh! There's a gala coming up on the twentieth. I RSVP'd for us. You should wear that gold dress you have. It'll match the theme."

The gold dress he was talking about was probably one of the most revealing gowns she owned. She'd never actually worn it to an event, though she'd bought it for one. Once she'd put it on, she couldn't stand to wear it out and have that much skin showing for the world to see. Athena swallowed hard, unable to form the words she wanted to say right then.

"You look lovely in it, too. Shows off your ass." Kevin giggled as he left the library, shutting the door behind him.

Monti took her time turning back, keeping her hands at her

side and in plain view where Athena could see them. "Twenty-two years, you say?"

Athena hummed. "We've known each other since he was born."

"You're older?" Monti raised an eyebrow at her. "I didn't peg you for being a cougar."

"Hardly." Athena lifted her chin to meet Monti's gaze, a direct and firm stare.

"I think that's exactly what marrying a younger man is called."

Pinching her face, Athena shook her head in disbelief. "Kevin is one year younger than me. When you grow up with money, the circles are small, and they keep them small on purpose."

"Are you saying you two were destined to be together?" Monti touched Athena's upper arm lightly, as if they were old friends having a conversation. Athena stared at it before dragging her gaze up Monti's arm to her lips and then her eyes.

"Anything but." Athena pulled away from Monti and out of her reach, a silent signal that the touch was too much. Monti retreated, brushing her hands over her hips. "Are we done for the evening?"

"If you'd like that," Monti answered.

Athena didn't want to be. She wanted Monti's magic hands back on her neck and shoulders. She wanted to relax even more than she already had. More importantly, she wanted to sleep. But none of those words left her lips. She couldn't make any of them move past the clog in her throat—the part of herself that prevented anything close to intimacy from developing.

She had no doubt Monti was judging Kevin, and their relationship. What kind of husband would come home from a trip and not kiss his wife? The kind who married for all the reasons except love. Standing, Athena left her jacket on the chair. She could do this. She could stand before Monti with her jacket off and not be embarrassed by her body.

"Never get married, Monti," Athena warned.

Athena clenched her fists by her sides, already feeling the

strain from before returning to her body. She snagged her jacket and slipped it on, buttoning it tight in the front of her body. She was three strides toward the door when she stopped and faced Monti full on.

"It only destroys what's sacred in a person."

SEVEN

"I'm sorry to call you here so late."

Athena stepped into the library. Monti hadn't been expecting the phone call, and she'd been on a long walk by the river, the chill air a sharp contrast to her warm muscles. But now the chill was starting to seep back into her bones.

"I almost told you no." Monti stood by the wingback chair, her fingers rubbing over the fabric on the top of it. She wasn't quite sure why she was there. Athena had called her, personally, since Fallon wasn't at work, but that still didn't explain why Monti had felt so compelled to be here.

Athena was a wounded soul, that much was clear. But Monti wasn't a therapist anymore. She'd given that up. She'd given everything up in her attempt to find inner peace. And yet, it still seemed to slip through her fingers at every step.

"I need your help."

Monti sighed heavily. "The thing is, Ms. Pruitt, that I don't think it's my help you need."

"I slept, you know, after the other day."

"Did you?" Monti brushed her hands along the top of the chair, not making eye contact with Athena. Why was she here again?

"Only a few hours, but it was more—"

"Than the four nights before," Monti chimed in.

Athena lifted her chin up, almost looking down her nose at Monti. "Yes. More than before. But I haven't slept since then."

"You do realize, I hope, that your issue with sleep isn't because of the muscles in your neck." Monti squeezed the chair, as if it was her lifeline. She really should just walk out of here. She should go back to her van, leave town, and find somewhere else to explore.

"I didn't ask you here for that."

"I know," Monti answered, finally looking into Athena's eyes. "But anything I do is only going to be temporary."

"I'm not asking for you to fix my problems."

Oh, but you are.

Monti resisted the words. She stared Athena down. The woman looked small again, as if she was being brought down by the world around her. Monti was once again reminded of how deep Athena's problems ran. This was a therapist's dream, someone who would be in sessions for years if not the rest of her life.

"Then what are you asking?"

"I have this case." Athena ran her fingers through her hair, mussing it. "I meet with the client tomorrow, and I need—*I need*—to be able to function for that meeting."

"So this is for the short term," Monti said, trying to make sure they were on the same page.

"Yes."

Pressing her lips together hard, Monti shook her head slowly. "This isn't a good idea."

Monti turned to walk away. She couldn't be there. She couldn't let them do something that wouldn't help either one of them. Athena needed more help than Monti could provide, especially in a simple massage. And until she got that help, she wasn't going to be able to sleep.

"Monti, wait." Athena raced toward her, her voice wavering.

Was that desperation?

"Please."

Monti faced her again, those pleading eyes, the sharp lines in her cheeks and jaw. It was desperation. There was no mistaking it now. Monti straightened her shoulders and debated her options. She could make it a requirement to continue working with Athena that she see a professional therapist.

"If we do this..." Monti started, not quite sure when she'd decided to agree to this farce "...then you need to give me a bit more than you have. And I strongly suggest finding a professional to work with."

Athena looked like she was going to object, but she stopped herself. The emotions that slid across her face went quickly, one right after the other, and Monti didn't have time to decipher them all. She could barely manage to keep up with what was going on. "I'll think about it."

"Well, that's better than nothing, I suppose." Monti crossed her arms. She looked around the library as if judging it now instead of before when she'd simply admired. "I don't have a table."

"A table?" A deep line formed in the center of Athena's forehead in her confusion.

"For a massage. I haven't been giving massages for almost a year, and I don't have a table."

"Do we need one?" Athena glanced toward the chair, no doubt thinking they could keep going in much the same manner as before.

"Your neck and shoulders are very tense, Ms. Pruitt. It would really help if I could have you lie down fully in order to best give you a massage."

"Oh." Athena's cheeks reddened, no doubt thinking about the fact that not only was Monti going to have to touch her again, but she was going to have to lie down for it.

"Is that all right?"

"I suppose." Athena ran her hand through her hair again, far more agitated than the last time Monti had been there. No doubt the lack of sleep was really affecting her by now.

"Would you like to try some oils?"

Athena nodded sharply, not really paying attention to what Monti had asked. "I can lie in a bed."

"That would work." Monti stood still, waiting for Athena's next move. "I have the oils in my bag if you want to show me where I'll be massaging you."

"Right." Again, Athena's hand was in her hair, as if the nervous habit was something she couldn't control. "This way."

Athena walked right past Monti, expecting her to follow. Bending her knees slightly, Monti turned on her toes and trailed after her. The halls were long, and they had to take several of them plus two flights of stairs before they stopped in front of a door.

This house really was a mansion.

How lonely must it be here? Alone most of the time except for employees? Then again, Athena did have a husband. Monti had to remind herself of that, even though the two of them seemed anything but close.

Before Monti could ask, Athena was pulling her jacket off and throwing it onto the chair at the desk. She probably worked from there often, most likely when she should be sleeping. It took Monti a moment to realize that Athena was standing awkwardly in the middle of the large room, as if waiting for instructions.

Was this Athena's room? Or a spare room?

The small touches here and there, the phone charger on the nightstand, the mug of cold tea, it all meant Athena slept here. Suddenly Monti felt like an intruder. Even when she'd been in a clinical setting, she'd never felt like this. She stayed put, her heart racing.

What was the right step?

What was she supposed to do next?

Athena folded her hands together. "I suppose I need to get on the bed."

Monti cleared her throat. "Uh. Yes. Um... put your head at the foot of the bed, on top of the covers."

Monti moved to the door to shut it, the resounding click of the knob mechanism sealing her fate in. She wasn't sure she should be doing this. It was inappropriate, outside normal boundaries. But Athena seemed more relaxed in this room already, and if her ability to take her jacket off that swiftly was any sign, this was truly the only safe place that Athena had in this house.

They needed to honor that.

Monti needed not to screw it up.

Athena was different here. Somehow confident. Not that she wasn't confident before, but this was a self-assurance that she lacked elsewhere. Monti shook her head. No—that wasn't right either. This was Athena comfortable with herself. Sliding her suddenly clammy hands along her thighs, Monti looked Athena over.

"Do you mind if I lock the door? I don't want to make you uncomfortable, but I really don't want interruptions like last time either."

Athena pressed her lips together tightly, flicking her gaze from Monti's face to the doorknob three times before she nodded sharply. "Yes, that's all right."

Monti turned the lock and walked away. The satchel she wore had three oils in it, one she was pretty sure Athena would choose, but she'd brought backups just in case. It seemed as though she'd actually made her mind up about this before she'd gotten out of the van. Hell, if she really thought about it, Monti had decided to help Athena as soon as she'd started driving in the direction of the house.

Setting the satchel on the desk, Monti pulled out the vials of oil. "I think you'll like this one."

Athena stepped in closer, standing almost side-by-side now. The light in the room was low, lamps on the walls instead of an overhead. It was the perfect mood setting for a massage. At least

Monti wouldn't be fighting that as well. Athena took the vial, twisting the cap off to bring it to her nose.

She hummed in pleasure. "Yes, I like this one."

"Want to try some on your hands to see if the feel is okay?"

Athena hesitated for a moment before she nodded. Monti leaned against the desk, squeezing the contents of the plastic vial into her fingers before rubbing her hands together to wet them. She held her hands out for Athena, and then she waited.

She already knew by now that this woman had a very complicated mental process she had to go through before she made any physical connection. And sure enough, as if on cue, Athena settled her hand into Monti's waiting fingers.

Monti started the same way she had the last two times. Often with people who clearly carried trauma, especially when it came to physical touch, the routine was the best way to keep things on an even level. So Monti worked Athena's palm and then each of her fingers, moving around the giant diamond ring that she now took a much closer look at. She massaged one finger after the other.

"How does it feel?" she asked finally.

"Good," Athena answered.

"Perfect." Monti dropped one hand and snagged the other. She stayed seated at the edge of the desk, her back to the window and allowing Athena to have complete control of the room. She could walk away any time she wanted. "I don't want to make you uncomfortable, but it would help immensely if you could take your bra off. Keep your shirt on, please, but the bra can make it more difficult to relieve your muscles."

She could feel the instant Athena tightened. The way her muscles moved in repulsion against Monti's suggestion. She'd specifically waited to have her hands on Athena's before she suggested it, so she could see exactly where Athena held that tension.

"But if you're uncomfortable at all, please leave it on."

Athena's pulse raced under Monti's deft fingers. Monti waited, giving Athena the time to work through everything internally before she said anything out loud. Athena pulled her hand away from Monti, the oil still slick on her skin.

"It'll be fine."

"I'll wait outside until you're ready." Monti started toward the door.

"Don't worry about it. Stay here." Athena stepped toward an en suite, shutting the door quietly.

It wasn't long before she emerged. Monti was grateful for that because if it had taken Athena any longer, she really would have started to worry. Athena had her arms crossed over her chest as she stood by the corner of her large bed. It was too large for one person, but Monti wasn't going to say anything. There was no way that bed would fit in her van.

Athena toed off her shoes and sat on the edge of the mattress, pulling herself backward until she was close to the middle. She looked at Monti, once again needing some kind of direction. She begged for it, truly. Monti stayed where she was, leaning against the desk.

"Lie on your back. That way you can still see me."

With a deep breath, Athena moved slowly. Monti waited until she was settled and ready before walking quietly toward her. She touched Athena's shoulder lightly and waited to have her full attention. "Are you ready?"

"I suppose."

"Athena." Monti had learned that using her first name eased that professional barrier down a little in a way that worked to her advantage.

"Yes. Yes, I'm ready," Athena corrected.

"I'm going to start with your neck and shoulders, okay? Any time anything is uncomfortable or hurts, I want you to tell me." Monti still didn't move until Athena looked up at her and nodded. Then, and only then, did she slide her fingers through Athena's hair, pulling it out from under her body and laying it out.

Monti poured more oil into her fingers and rubbed them

together to warm them before she started. "Have you seen a professional counselor before?"

Athena's jaw hardened, no doubt trying to find a way to avoid the direct question. Monti followed the line of muscle and pushed Athena's head to the side to stretch it and move it. She breathed slowly, focusing her attention on Athena's body and on what she wasn't saying.

"Athena," Monti tried again.

"Yes." It was an answer to the question.

"And I assume they didn't work."

"They didn't." Athena's eyes fluttered shut. "Can I have silence?"

"Yes." Monti pressed her lips together hard, but she stopped asking questions. Especially intrusive ones, despite the fact that she kept thinking about them.

Every time she ended up in Athena's presence, she wanted to know more. She wanted to figure out why Athena ticked this particular way, why she was so resistant to any kind of touch. Monti used some more oil as she enticed Athena to turn onto her front.

Her shirt shifted in the process, the tank top sliding farther over on her shoulder. Monti frowned at the skin, the sharp bright white line that was without a doubt a scar. One that had been deep and long, and another one that was quite old. She avoided touching it, especially without permission, and moved to sliding her hands up the nape of Athena's neck as she leaned over her.

The silence was deafening because normally Monti was used to talking through these sessions. She beckoned Athena to turn back over, starting on her scalp and the craniosacral massage again. Her fingers slid through Athena's hair, slicking it with the oil still on her fingertips. The scent wasn't strong. In fact, it was barely there, but Monti knew it should help relax Athena even more.

Athena's breathing deepened. It slowed. Her legs and arms twitched as she slowed into a light slumber. Monti continued the massage until she was sure that Athena was deep in sleep. Finally she pulled away, silently stepping back from the sleeping woman.

Wiping her hands on the towel in the bathroom after washing them, Monti waited to see if Athena would wake up. Still she rested. Monti couldn't leave her here alone, not with the way she had woken up the last time. She would need some sort of care afterward.

Monti pulled a throw over Athena's body, making sure that she was covered. Then she turned around the room and tried to figure out what to do next. Three books were stacked on the corner of the desk. With nothing else to do, Monti snagged the one on top and smiled at the familiar cover. She slid into the desk chair and began reading. She would wait until Athena woke.

Then they could start the real work.

eight

Warmth.

Athena was cocooned in it. The fingers of sleep surrounded her and pulled at her, trying to keep her under their spell. Yet at the same time, sunlight brushed across her skin, and she could feel the warm rays tickling her flesh and teasing her into wakefulness.

Is this what it was like?

Turning on her side, Athena reached for her pillow to pull it under her chest and maybe catch a few more minutes of slumber. But when she stretched out her arm, she was met with nothing but her cold comforter. Wrinkling her nose with dissatisfaction, Athena stretched her fingers out. The bed was cold. But she was so warm, so filled with rest.

On her back again, Athena blinked her eyes awake and stared at the ceiling above her. It took her more time than she cared to admit to clear her vision and focus on the pattern of the molding. Her breaths were deep and slow still, and she felt a sense of peace within her in a way it hadn't ever been before.

Athena ran through her body, stretching her muscles starting with her toes and working her way up. She felt amazing. Energy coursed through her. She wouldn't even need that extra cup of coffee for the jolt of caffeine that morning. Maybe she could do without it entirely? She smiled at that. Who was she kidding? She'd never do without that.

Stretching her arms above her head, she teased the muscles in her back into submission. Who was she and what had she done with the person who couldn't sleep? This was exactly what she'd needed. She would have to send Monti something as a thank you or give her the world's biggest tip when she told Fallon to pay her.

Athena lifted herself up, her hands planted on the mattress behind her. Halfway sitting, she looked at the bed and frowned. She must have fallen asleep in the middle of the massage again. That was so unlike her. But then again, it had been so long since she'd properly slept—

"I'm glad you're awake."

Athena jerked with a start. She swiveled her head toward her desk sharply, pain searing through her neck and chest with how quickly she moved. Monti was still there? What the hell time was it?

Monti put her hands out in front of her, but she stayed in the chair at the desk. She shook her head, worry etching across her face. "I didn't mean to scare you. I'm sorry."

She was scared. Athena's heart ran wild in her chest, and her entire body was on high alert. She hadn't been able to stop that from happening. "What time is it?"

"Almost nine."

"In the morning?" Athena nearly screeched, but she caught herself just in time. Fallon was going to kill her. She was beyond late, and she was someone who was never late.

"Yes." Monti relaxed slightly, still staying in the chair but shifting so it was easier for Athena to see her. "I already texted Fallon to let her know."

"What did you tell her?" If Monti had revealed anything, Athena would kick her out of the house before she could say anything else.

"That we were still in a session." Monti looked exhausted.

Deep dark bags were under her eyes, her skin was pale, her dark brown short hair was askew atop her head.

"Did you sleep in that chair all night?" Athena dug her fingers into the covers on the bed. It was the only thing keeping her rooted to the spot right now, and she needed it.

"I think sleep is too kind a word." Monti stood up then, pressing her palms into her lower back and stretching. Her breasts jutted forward, her nipples peeking through the fabric of her shirt.

Athena hadn't noticed that before. She hadn't seen that Monti wore nothing but yoga pants and a thin t-shirt, and clearly no bra underneath it. Not that she necessarily needed it. Her breasts were small, well-rounded, and her nipples looked—what the hell was she thinking? Her cheeks flushed with heat—this time burning, unlike the warmth she had woken up with. Immediately, Athena dropped her gaze to the covers and tried to find herself again.

With sleep, she must have lost what was left of her sanity.

Monti groaned, and the sound sent a thrill through her body, taking that heat from her cheeks and putting it in places Athena had long thought to try and kill off. She couldn't do this. She could not handle this. Not this morning. Hell, not any morning.

"How are you feeling?" Monti asked.

Athena held back her groan of despair, but barely. She clenched her eyes shut tight. Monti wasn't asking about the thoughts racing through her brain. She was asking about the sleep and nothing else. About how the massage had gone the night before, the one that had relaxed her so much that she had somehow allowed Monti to stay in the room with her, completely vulnerable, for the entire fucking night.

"I'm fine," Athena croaked out.

"Try again." Monti smiled at her and moved closer to the bed. She gestured to it. "Do you mind? That chair isn't very comfortable."

Athena looked down to the mattress and back up at Monti,

those dark brown eyes pulling her in. She couldn't resist. She couldn't stop the words from leaving her lips. "Feel free."

Monti sat on the edge, still giving Athena a lot of space, which was something Athena would be forever grateful for. Pulling her knees to her chest, Athena wrapped her arms around her legs and rested her chin on her knees. When was the last time she had allowed herself to sit like this? When was the last time she'd allowed herself to become this weak?

"How are you? Really?" Monti asked pointedly. "And don't avoid the question again."

Athena wanted to push against her, wanted to avoid, wanted to refuse to answer simply because she wouldn't be forced into anything. But Monti was just trying to check in and make sure that she was okay. With a deep breath, Athena straightened up and slid to the edge of the bed. She wasn't sure how long she could stand to be here.

"I'm fine."

"What does fine mean to you?" Monti rubbed her eyes, using one finger to pull the sleep from her lashes.

"Did you sleep at all?" Athena asked, her palms on either side of her as if she was ready to get up and leave. But something chained her to that mattress. Some unseen force kept her there, staring into Monti's dark eyes, her ashen and weary face.

Was it compassion?

"Not really. I don't think you can count the few times I drifted off only to jerk awake when my chin met my chest." Monti gave her a half smile.

"You should have slept."

"Perhaps." Monti ran her fingers through her hair again, raising her gaze to meet Athena's. "But my job was to ensure you a safe space. I don't take that job lightly."

Athena's heart stuttered, her breathing became ragged. There was that heat again, that same warmth she'd woken with and the heat from before. Monti was trying to create a safe space for her, and somehow, in the three times they had met, she had managed to do that. At least enough that Athena had put some trust in her.

"Is that okay with you?" Monti asked, her voice gentle. "That's always my intention when I'm with clients."

Client.

Right. Athena was nothing more than a client. She knew that. But why did she seem to want more than that? Why did it feel like more than that? Rubbing her lips together, Athena stayed put, her chest rising and falling with her steady breathing.

"Yes, that's okay," she answered in a whisper.

"Good." Monti scratched her scalp. "Good, I'm glad. I hope that we can continue on this trajectory."

"Continue?" Athena posited, her brow wrinkling. "You're not my therapist."

"No, no, I'm not." Monti winced and ran her fingers through her hair again. "You'll have to forgive me. I'm quite exhausted, and my brain isn't as sharp as it should be for this conversation."

"What conversation?" Athena tightened her grasp on the edge of the mattress, waiting for whatever shoe was going to drop next. Because it always did.

"A reflection and a check-in. That's all this is." Monti pressed her full palm to the bed. "I wanted to make sure you had as much uninterrupted sleep time as possible. I wasn't sure when your husband would be in."

"My..." Athena stopped herself. Monti didn't know. No one knew, not really. Not even Fallon. Athena had never allowed any one of her staff to get the full picture of her marriage, and that had been on purpose. Kevin had done the same. They were so well-practiced at it by that point that it was second nature. But for some reason, some unspeakable reason, Athena wanted Monti to know. Because maybe next time she wouldn't hurt herself to stay awake the whole night just to protect Athena.

And that was what she'd done, wasn't it?

Protect Athena from any interruptions so she could get exactly what she needed. And the cost had been Monti's lack of sleep. Athena's heart clenched at that thought. Too many times she'd allowed her own issues to hurt others, and she hated when that happened. She had to rectify it.

"My husband doesn't sleep in this room," Athena answered, her voice somber and dry. "He has his own room."

"Okay." Monti seemed curious, but she didn't push for an answer either.

Who did that?

They fell into a silence, the awkwardness filling Athena's chest with raw emotion she hadn't expected. But she wasn't quite ready to pick through it yet. Not when Monti was still in the room. "If you're too tired to drive, Fallon can drive you home."

Monti frowned. "I am too tired to drive. But my home is my van, Ms. Pruitt."

"Your van?" Why hadn't she realized that before? Surely Fallon had said something about that. Monti was a drifter, that much had been clear, but how had Athena missed that her entire life was in the vehicle that she drove?

"Yeah. So if you don't mind me sleeping on your property, that'd be preferred. I can drive it off in a few hours after a good nap."

Athena shook her head slowly before she realized that was what she was doing. She leaned in closer to Monti, the scent of her skin filling Athena's nostrils. It was a mix of body odor, though not strong, and something else that she couldn't place, something that made her head spin with delight. "Stay here."

"What?" Monti stilled.

"I mean stay in a guest room. I'm sure the bed is more comfortable than what you have in the van."

"My van is pretty comfortable. But anything is better than that chair." Monti's full cheeky smile was beautiful—stunning.

Athena was knocked back by it, her stomach twisting with odd sensations. She shook her head again. "Stay in a guest room. It's not a bother at all. We have all these rooms that are never used. You might as well find one to sleep in for a few hours."

"Hours?"

"Or all day if you need it."

Monti canted her head to the side, raising her chin up and narrowing her eyes down at Athena. Monti was judging her, that much Athena knew, but it wasn't one of those mean judgmental looks. It was as if Monti was just trying to figure out exactly what was going on through her brain, the ins and outs of what she meant.

"It's the least I can do."

"It's not a requirement for a massage," Monti answered. "I'll be fine in my van."

Once again, Athena shook her head and rejected Monti's attempt. "Sometimes, Monti, you just have to accept the gift. Even if you don't want it."

"All right, then. Where am I sleeping?"

Athena stood up, finally. She walked in her socks toward the door to her bedroom and waited as Monti stumbled after her. Damn, this woman really was tired. Not wanting to parade her through the entire house, Athena walked straight to the closest guest room, which was a few doors down from her own. She opened the door and allowed Monti to walk inside.

"Stay as long as you like."

"Thank you." Monti ducked her chin, her cheeks suddenly red.

Athena wanted to reach up and touch her. Actual fingers-to-cheek contact. The feeling scared the ever-living shit out of her, so she clenched her fingers hard into a fist to prevent herself from doing anything stupid. She needed to get out of there. She needed to clear her head and think straight.

Without another word, Athena turned on her toes and walked out of the room and back to her bedroom. She shut the door—and locked it—leaning against the cold wood to catch her breath. Her heart raced. Her body was still so damn hot that it was hard to focus. She closed her eyes, and all she could feel was Monti's fingers on her skin, pushing into her muscles, teasing out the knots. Monti's hands in her hair as she massaged her scalp, the way Monti's breathing changed to match hers.

What the hell was she thinking?

Shaking her head wildly, Athena gathered herself. She pushed off the door and walked straight to her en suite. She needed to get ready for the day, which meant she had about an hour to figure out just what was going on with her. She stripped off her clothes after turning the water on to let it warm up.

As soon as she stepped under the hot spray of water, Athena sighed and relaxed. The water pounded onto her shoulders, wetting her hair and her body. She ran her fingers over her body, the oil still making the skin slick on her arms and neck where Monti had touched her.

What was it with Monti that Athena couldn't resist?

Maybe Monti was right.

Maybe she really did just need a safe place for once in her life.

Athena's fingers hit the ripples of scars along her back and her stomach as she ran soap over herself. She'd gotten so used to those, but to think of Monti touching them, to see the look of horror on her face when she finally saw them? Athena couldn't imagine it. She'd seen it before, and she couldn't imagine witnessing that again.

Holding back her tears, Athena found the longest scar on her body. It ran from the center of her chest down to her belly button, and it was raised and stark white. She sucked in a sharp breath and dropped her hand, turning into the spray of the shower to wash her feelings away.

No.

She wouldn't allow that to happen again.

Monti deserved to live in the world without Athena's pain.

If there was one thing Athena had learned in the last twenty-two years, it was that she was way too damaged for anyone. Not friends, not family, not lovers. Leave all of that to Kevin—he at least deserved it. She was just a burden and too dirty for any type of relationship, romantic or otherwise. Her darkness would instantly taint whatever came near her.

And Monti?

She was too young and innocent to deserve that. She had her whole life ahead of her.

Shivering even though the water was hot, Athena pushed away all thoughts of allowing Monti to give her that safe space again. She just wouldn't do it. She started to wash her hair, and along with it, she washed any glimmers of hope from her chest.

nine

The bed Monti woke in was heaven. The mattress cocooned her in a warm hug that she hadn't felt in ages, sleeping in her van. Athena hadn't lied when she said this bed would be more comfortable than the van. If this was the same one Athena had on her bed, Monti could understand why she fell asleep so hard.

She checked her watch and her phone, finding a message from a long-time friend she hadn't seen since they were in school together. She smiled and sent a swift message back to see if they could get together that evening.

Monti left the room after refreshing herself in the en suite and went in search of Fallon. She should probably tell at least one person that she was leaving the property so that they didn't think she was still sleeping.

Fallon was sitting at her desk, the bright light from her computer reflected on her reading glasses as she still squinted at the screen. Monti shook her head to herself and stepped inside, crossing her arms in the process.

"You really should get your prescription checked again."

Fallon jerked with a start, her lips parting, before she realized it was Monti standing there. "Jesus, I didn't think you were still here."

Furrowing her brow, Monti stepped inside farther. "Ms. Pruitt pretty much ordered me to sleep in a guest room. I crashed hard."

Fallon smirked. "Whatever you did, it worked."

"Oh?" Now Monti was curious. What difference was Fallon seeing? Because this was always about more than just sleep.

"I've never seen her this relaxed."

Interesting. Monti kept that thought to herself. She nodded toward Fallon and then the door to the interior office. "Is that one hers?"

"Yes, but she's out at a meeting right now."

Monti pressed her lips together. "I'm going to dinner with a friend tonight."

"I thought we were going to see Mom."

Tensing, Monti tried to push down the feeling of unease that swamped her. Peace. That was what she needed, not this sensation that the world was going to collapse in on her. "We can go some other time."

"Monti..." Fallon trailed off. She finally pulled her reading glasses off and set them on top of the desk. "The weather's going to get really bad soon, and you're going to leave. If we want to go see her, now's the time."

You. Monti corrected in her head. Fallon was the only one that wanted to go, and the fact that she kept talking about their mother like she was alive was ridiculous. But Fallon had always been that way. Nostalgic and stuck in the past. Monti couldn't live like that. She didn't have those memories that Fallon had.

"I was going to have lunch with Tia on Saturday when she's off work."

Fallon frowned. "That's it?"

"Yeah, that's it." Monti let her anger lash through her. She was tired of the pretense that she was so unaffected by Fallon's pushing. Surely she had to know by now that Monti didn't want to go to their mother's grave.

"She raised us."

"She did," Monti agreed. "And she did a damn good job at it. But I don't see what that has to do with me getting lunch with her."

"You don't want to stay with her?"

"No." Monti tightened her arms crossed. "No, I don't."

"I don't get you."

"I know," Monti answered softly. Fallon had always tried, and she'd never managed to. Changing the subject away from the conflict, Monti shifted her stance. "Did Ms. Pruitt want to meet with me again?"

"She didn't say," Fallon answered, flicking her gaze up and down Monti. "But I'm all for it."

Probably because Fallon was under the illusion that the job would keep Monti around longer. Well, that simply wasn't true, but Monti would continue to work with Athena while she was in town. "Okay. Schedule it in. If she wants to cancel, just let me know. I've got to meet up with Zoe."

Monti left the office with a sharp nod toward Fallon and went to her van. As soon as she was inside, she relaxed her shoulders. She would park her car and change before meeting up with Zoe. For right now, she just needed to clear her head from that intense conversation.

"Peace," she whispered, her voice not echoing through the vehicle.

Why was peace so hard for her to find?

She understood it wasn't just difficult for her, but she'd spent years searching for it and never finding it. Sighing, Monti started the engine and left the house. It took her thirty minutes to get to downtown Seattle and find a parking garage that could handle her vehicle.

Crawling in the back, she slipped out of her yoga pants and wrinkled shirt. The entire time, she ran through a meditation, checking in with her body and her emotions. She needed to know that she would be okay when all of this was through. She needed to know that Fallon wouldn't be any more hurt when she left—because she would leave.

She was tired of leaving a trail of pain behind her.

That wasn't her purpose in life. It wasn't good for anyone. Monti ran her fingers through her short hair and spiked it up on the top with a little bit of product. She rubbed deodorant under her pits and then sat cross-legged on the small bed along the far wall. Resting her palms on her knees, Monti tried in vain one last time before she had to leave, to find some type of peace.

Athena had clearly found it the night before, so why couldn't she?

She was so good at helping others find their center, and yet she was left with nothing for herself. Steadying her breathing, Monti focused her mind. She didn't want to run away. She didn't want to leave. She didn't want to stay. She wanted to simply be exactly who she was born to be, and find peace in that.

So why the hell couldn't she?

Her phone chirped next to her.

Zoe: You coming still?

"Fucking hell." Monti snagged the phone, her jacket, and a bag. She raced through the motions as she left her van and walked toward the little restaurant in the center of downtown where they were meeting.

Zoe sat in a small chair right up front when Monti got there. She held out her arms for a hug, and Monti walked right into them, grinning. "Fuck, it's been a while."

"Do you think you could ever show up on time?" Zoe laughed lightly and squeezed Monti right back. "You'll have to tell me all about where you've been."

"Definitely."

They walked to the table that had been waiting for them.

Monti relaxed, an ease falling over her that she had missed. Zoe had always been astute and understanding. She was someone who could never do anything wrong in Monti's book.

"So where have you been?" Zoe leaned forward on the table, ignoring the menu in front of her. Her dark brown eyes were lit with energy and excitement.

Monti had missed that too. "All over. I spent some time up in Vancouver and the BC area. Drove up to Alaska for a few weeks."

"Oh! I've never been there!" Zoe laughed lightly and leaned back into her seat. "Was it cold?"

"I went in summer." Monti pulled the beer she'd ordered closer to her. She spun the chilled glass in her fingers, not taking a sip yet. "Tell me what you've been up to. Still working with that hot boss?"

Zoe's cheeks turned bright red. "Um. Kind of. *Working with* is a good way to say that. We started our own company together."

"Did you?" Monti raised an eyebrow and leaned back into her seat, finally sipping her beer. "I sense there's more to that story."

"It's a long story." Zoe drank her own beer, her gaze falling to the tabletop.

This was something shameful, that much Monti could tell. She didn't want to push, though. She wanted to know what Zoe was thinking, everything that she'd been through in the last year since they'd seen each other. Monti licked her lips and leaned into the silence. Zoe was never one who dealt well with the quiet. If Monti waited long enough, Zoe would spill. Most people did.

Although she suspected Athena was very comfortable with quiet.

Where had that thought come from?

Monti dug her fingers into her thigh underneath the table. Athena was a client, and she had to keep reminding herself of that. She might not have a practice anymore, but there was no doubt in her mind that she wouldn't have met Athena if she hadn't been seeking some sort of therapy—massage or psychological.

"Earth to Monti!" Zoe teased.

"Sorry." Monti shook the thoughts of Athena from her mind. "I was thinking about this new client I'm working with. She's taking up a lot of mental space for me."

Zoe hummed like she understood, but how could she? "Do you remember that girl who lived next door to you in the dormitories?"

"Jazz?"

"Yes!" Zoe's eyes lit up. "I had such a crush on her, and you kept telling me to stay away from her."

"You didn't, did you?" Monti wrinkled her forehead in concern.

"I did. Once. I was super drunk, and I just wanted to know what all the fuss was about."

"Did you even get anywhere?"

"I puked all over her boots." Zoe giggled.

Monti laughed. "You never could hold your liquor."

"No, I couldn't." Zoe fiddled with the napkin in front of her. "Seems that hasn't changed much over the years. I thought for years that just working with Gwen was going to be enough for me, but it really wasn't."

"Glad you finally realized that." Monti's beer was halfway empty before the waiter came over to take their food orders. Zoe was a much slower drinker, and rightfully so. "So what did you figure out about yourself?"

"I can do anything I want. And I'm not completely wasting my business degree now that Gwen and I are actually working together. Technically she owns the company, but I'm far more a partner than her personal assistant now."

"That's good. You seem happy, anyway." Was that jealousy slipping into Monti's voice?

"I am!" Zoe grinned broadly. "She proposed."

"*She?*" Who exactly was Zoe talking about? Monti felt as though she had missed out on a large chunk of her friend's life.

But that was par for the course when she never stayed anywhere long enough to form deep connections.

But that was also the point.

She didn't want those deep relationships because once she left—which she would—that person would be left with a wake of ripples from her departure. And that was something Monti didn't want to happen. That was beyond what Monti could permit in terms of harm to others. She rolled her shoulders and eyed Zoe across the table again.

"Gwen." Zoe laughed and then pushed her hand across the table, the diamond winking in the light from the bar as she showed off her new ring.

"Wow!" Monti took hold of Zoe's hand and gazed at the ring like she was interested. It wasn't that she was upset about Zoe doing exactly what she wanted. It was just that much more of a reminder for Monti that this wasn't what she wanted.

Ever.

She couldn't believe that these types of relationships were for the best. She'd seen too many of them fail in her lifetime. And fail spectacularly they did. Monti ran her hand through her hair. "Congratulations!"

"You'll have to come to the wedding."

"Sure. Just send me an invitation." Monti would show up if Zoe wanted her to. But she would leave in much the same way she would this time and had the time before that: quietly, without taking a piece of Zoe with her. "I'm so happy for you."

"It hasn't been easy. But what's a relationship without work?" Zoe grinned as she took another sip from her beer.

She was right about that. But Monti still wasn't sure that it was something she'd want to put in effort for. Rubbing the back of her head, Monti moved to change the topic of conversation again. She needed to ease them away from the personal. She knew she was in the midst of that part of her life when everyone would be getting married and having babies, and that just wasn't for her. She'd seen how much that could be torn apart firsthand.

She wouldn't allow herself to relive that.

More importantly, she wouldn't allow herself to be the cause of it either.

Perhaps Athena was the same way. She'd made comments about her odd relationship with her husband, yet they were still married. What exactly did that mean for them? Athena clearly still had her independence, and a lot of it. Maybe Athena had found her peace in that.

"Monti!" Zoe was laughing again. "I don't think I've ever seen you this distracted before."

Sighing heavily, Monti apologized. "I'm sorry. It's…" She trailed off, not quite sure how to explain it. She wasn't even sure she'd been able to put words to what she was feeling yet. But ever since she'd come back, she'd felt so unsettled. "Being home is harder than I thought it would be."

"Oh, that's right! You're from here. I forgot that."

"I am. Born and raised." Monti lifted her beer in a sarcastic toast. Zoe didn't lift her glass to clink, sensing the unease Monti had allowed into the conversation.

"So are you visiting family while you're here?"

"I've met up with my sister several times. Do you remember Fallon?"

"Yeah. She's a few years older than you, right?"

"Seven." Monti's shoulders tightened, and she had to purposely work to lower them back down to where they were supposed to be. Why was that a trigger for her tonight? It shouldn't be at all. "My aunt still lives here too. We're having dinner on Saturday."

"That'll be nice, I bet. I always love going home and visiting all my old haunts."

Monti hummed her agreement even if she didn't agree. In fact, she avoided most of her old haunts from high school. She didn't want to run into anyone from her past if she could avoid them. They wouldn't be of any use to her now.

"Well, I hope you have fun with them."

"It'll be a good visit, I'm sure."

"So you're leaving again?"

Monti raised an eyebrow at Zoe, her lips thinning. She'd never been so sure of something before. "Always."

"I don't know how you do it. I'd miss Gwen too much."

"It's not that hard, honestly. Friends are everywhere, and there's always someone new to meet. The bonus is that when I leave, no one will miss me in the long run. We're friends when we're together, but as soon as we're apart, it's like I was never there."

Zoe frowned, a line forming in the center of her forehead as she contemplated what Monti had said. Then she shook her head wildly. "That sounds incredibly sad."

"It's peaceful." Monti tapped her fingers on the tabletop. At least, she kept telling herself it was. "So, I'll leave, head on to the next adventure. I was thinking about going to Belize for a bit in the spring. Maybe bring Fallon with me."

"I bet she would enjoy that."

"She would." Monti finished her beer and set the glass down heavily. "Maybe I'll go to Thailand."

"You always were such a traveler."

I am. Monti didn't say it out loud though. She didn't want to make Zoe feel any worse than she already had. They should enjoy this time they had together, the quick conversations and joy they could bring to each other. "You should try it. I'll go with you if you ever want to explore somewhere fun."

"I'll take you up on that offer! I'll need a long vacation somewhere sunny with a beach after this year."

"Oh? What's been going on?"

Zoe sighed, her face fell. "That, my dear friend, is a very long story."

"Then I'm all ears."

ten

"Where is she?" Athena stood at her doorway, staring Fallon down, as if her personal assistant had all the answers.

Fallon shook her head. "I don't know."

Holding back her scoff, Athena walked into her office and shut the door. She'd paced the room for the last fifteen minutes, waiting. Monti was supposed to be there an hour ago, and there was still no sign of her. It had thrown Athena into a loop of chaos. It shouldn't have, but it did. She stopped by the window and stared out into the forest again, the frustrated energy coursing through her without stopping.

The respite she'd gotten had given her enough clarity to be able to think. Athena had immersed herself in work all day, focusing more than she had in weeks. She stretched her neck and her back. Kevin being home wasn't helping things. As much as she loved him, his very presence disrupted her routine.

The knock on her door startled her. She'd expected Fallon, but when she turned and saw Kevin, Athena winced.

Speak of the devil...

"I wanted to check in on you," he started, stepping inside and shutting the door behind him.

Athena sighed and dropped her hands. "I'm fine."

"You're not."

Rolling her eyes, she leaned against the edge of her desk.

"When's the last time you left this house?"

"A few hours ago." Athena waved him off.

"For something other than to go to your other office."

She wrinkled her nose. He knew her too well. Which had been a huge part of why they'd agreed to this arrangement in the first place. It benefitted both of them. "How's Clayton?"

"Don't avoid my question." He gave her a flat look, and she knew she was going to have to answer.

The problem was, she didn't honestly remember. She'd have to check with Fallon, because all dates in the last year seemed to vanish from her mind. Gnawing on her lip, she looked at him. He already knew. So why was he even asking?

"This isn't healthy, Athena."

"Nothing in my life is healthy," she mumbled, crossing her arms again in the best protective move she could muster. "How's Clayton? Truthfully."

"Same as always." Kevin sat next to her, leaning on the desk and mimicking her position. "Mad I won't divorce you. Deeply in love with me. I don't want to marry him. I'm happy with our arrangement."

Athena snorted. "You'd think it'd be easier, wouldn't you?"

Kevin shook his head. "No. I never thought marrying you would be easy."

Laughing lightly, Athena tilted her head into his shoulder and closed her eyes. Kevin uncrossed his arms and settled his palm on her thigh. He was the only one allowed to do this. He always had been. "Perhaps I thought we'd be better at it by now."

"I think we're pretty damn good at this." Kevin's voice was a deep rumble in his chest, and it brought her such comfort to hear.

"Maybe." Athena breathed in his familiar scent, relaxing slightly. It was one of the few times she let him touch her, though if anyone was going to do it, Kevin and Simon were the only two allowed without asking first. She leaned in and kissed his cheek. "When do you leave again?"

"Few days. I think I'll go to that gala with Simon while he's home, let you out of that responsibility." He wrinkled his nose. "Have to make sure that the house is running properly, you know."

Athena avoided the subject of Simon. It hurt too much to talk about him some days, and others to even think about him. Most days, Athena was certain Simon would have had a better life growing up if she hadn't been a part of it. Tapping into the humor she knew Kevin adored, she said, "Oh yes, we need a man here to keep everything in order and explained properly."

He laughed loudly. Good, her tone had landed, and he hadn't noticed her shift into the depression and back out of it. Athena applauded herself for that side step. Now if she could keep it up until Kevin left her alone again.

Kevin relaxed as he added, "I was working on Simon's birthday bash. I'm taking him to Vegas."

Athena jerked sharply. She tried to cover it up by shifting her stance. Just the very mention of that place took her immediately back to twenty-two years ago. And she hated going there. Sucking in a slow breath, Athena pushed down all those uncomfortable emotions and focused on the here and now as best as she could.

Why did they have to go there? To the place that was the center of all her pain, to the place she had... She shut that thought off immediately. With her anger already raging, she couldn't let herself go down that path.

"Really?" Athena wrinkled her nose. Kevin knew she hated that place. He *knew* what memories it held. Why would he even let this be a possibility? "Couldn't think of anything better?"

"It's where he wanted to go." Kevin wrapped an arm around her shoulders and dropped a kiss into her hair. "You're welcome to join us."

Had he gone off his rocker and completely forgotten the main reason they had gotten married?

To cover it up.

To make sure no one knew what happened.

Athena steadied herself, trying to find the best way to answer without being offended. But she was. She couldn't believe he didn't remember. Or worse yet, that he didn't care.

"No, thank you. That can be a father-son excursion that I will gladly not be a part of." Athena covertly slid from his grasp and stood up, walking toward the window. She crossed her arms and protected herself again. Because she had to. Kevin wasn't doing it this time like he normally would. "When will you go?"

"Next week."

She nodded to no one in particular and tried to push the memories back in the locked box where they belonged. She grasped at straws for something else to talk about. "Did Fallon talk to you about Shiloh's Home?"

"I can't go."

"What?" She spun on him, anger flaring in her chest. She couldn't do this without him. A room full of people without him there to calm her? It would be impossible. But this was something she could grasp onto. This was a place that was safe where she could put her emotions.

He put his hands up in defense. "I've already booked the entire week for a trip to Tahoe with Clayton."

Athena held in her worry, but it was getting harder to do that by the second. That was something for her future self to figure out, since the event was months away still. She wasn't going to be able to do it, especially not with the state she was in lately. And that would only add to the turmoil she was already feeling.

"Call Simon, will you? Figure out what you two will do for his birthday. It's his twenty-first, and he needs to know you care about him."

"Yeah." Athena's shoulders dropped. She wasn't a good mother. She'd never been. It wasn't that she didn't love Simon, but she hadn't been made to be a parent. Kevin was much better at it than she was, but she wasn't even sure that he had been made for it. And with the way he was conceived…

"Athena."

"I promise," she added, locking her gaze on his. "I'll call him."

"Good." Kevin gave her a discerning look before leaving her office.

Plunged back into the quiet, Athena only had one thing on her mind to distract her now.

Monti.

Where the hell was she? Because she could already feel the tension from before sneaking back into her and making it impossible to focus again. It wasn't awful now, but in another day or two, she would be right back where she'd started.

She gave it another five minutes—at least, she thought it was five—before standing in front of Fallon, arms crossed, and rage in every fiber of her being. "Where is she?"

"I—I don't know." Fallon shrugged, glancing from Athena to her cell phone and back again.

"She was supposed to be here an hour ago."

"Yeah, but the thing about Monti is that she's a free spirit."

She was quickly learning to hate that phrase. Athena narrowed her gaze, the muscles along her neck and shoulders tightening intensely. "I don't care if she's a free spirit or a dead one. I pay her to be here. Where is she?"

Fallon's jaw tightened, her lips thinning to the point they were barely even there. She glanced at her phone again, but even Athena could see that there were no messages on it. "Look, I love my sister dearly. She's my baby sister. I helped raise her. But ever since she's been on this quest, time and responsibilities are something else to her. She used to be so good at showing up to everything she had to, always ten or fifteen minutes early."

"Now she's an hour late."

"I know," Fallon pleaded. "And I've called and texted, and she's not answering. What I'm trying to say is that Monti doesn't really pay attention to time anymore."

"Who would do that?" Athena gave her a flat look, not understanding any of what Fallon was saying. The words made sense. The actions didn't. "If you have a job, you show up on time."

"Yeah. Yeah I'm with you. I understand that. But Monti is often in her own little world, and through most of the day, she doesn't know what time it is."

"How does she get anything done?" Athena narrowed her gaze. "How does she not get fired?"

"Well, she doesn't have a job."

Athena knew that, but she still didn't quite understand how it all worked. "How does she afford to live?"

"That's a complicated answer, but she finds a way to earn cash when she needs to."

"Like this?" Athena pushed. She wanted to understand Monti better, because this person she was imagining was nothing like the person she'd seen in her bedroom a few nights ago. She was nothing like the woman who had checked in with her after staying awake all night to make sure that she was well enough to be on her own. Her heart raced at that thought. Monti had sacrificed something she needed for the betterment of Athena. At least that was her intention.

"Yeah, like this." Fallon sighed heavily, again looking at her phone. "I'll call her again."

"Don't bother." Pursing her lips, Athena walked out of the office. When she reached the door, she called over her shoulder, "Go home, Fallon. Get some rest."

Without looking back, she left her work for the day.

Athena went to the one place she knew she could find some peace, at least the one place she usually could. The library brought a gentle calm, something that she had complete control over. Except she wasn't finding that calm.

The library door opened, and Athena turned, expecting to find Kevin. Instead, she came face to face with the one person she wasn't sure she wanted to see today. Not after everything that had happened.

"I'm so sorry," Monti started, clearly seeing the anger in Athena's eyes. "I lost track of time."

"Fallon assures me that's a normal problem with you."

Monti sighed, coming in and shutting the door behind her. Now it was just the two of them and no one else. No one would interrupt them. No one would save either of them by stopping the argument that Athena knew was coming. "It is."

"I don't understand you."

"Not many people do." Monti shrugged slightly.

Which only infuriated Athena even more. People weren't that hard to understand. Everyone had their own quirks, but they were either trustworthy or they weren't. Monti stepped forward, and Athena immediately stepped back, her hand out in front of her.

Monti froze on the spot. "I'm not going to hurt you."

"I know that." Athena's heart raced, clogging up her throat in that age-old feeling she knew would never leave her. It had been with her for decades. As much as she hated it, it was the most useful thing she'd gotten from the entire experience.

"Do you?" Monti's voice was gentle, her eyes pleading with compassion. "Athena, relax."

Athena shook her head wildly. Her throat was so clogged up that it was getting hard to speak. "I am relaxed."

"You're not." Monti's voice wavered.

Athena could barely hear her. She faced the small window in the library, putting her back to Monti. She hated doing that, but she needed to collect herself. If Monti could see her sliding down into the bowels of panic, then surely she must already be well on her way there. One deep breath. Then another. Athena counted them. The air in the room was too hot, too sweltering.

Where was Kevin when she needed him?

He was the only one who could calm her down from these things. He'd managed to do it earlier, so why wasn't he here now to talk her down again?

"Where were you?" Athena threw out into the room. She didn't really need the answer. She didn't even want it. But it was something for her to focus on, something other than what was going on with her own body.

"It doesn't matter. I missed our appointment time." Monti came a little closer. "You're not breathing well."

"I'm breathing fine," Athena ground out. She hated that Monti was so damn observant. Why had she even allowed Monti into her life like this? Why hadn't she held that line more firmly?

"Athena," Monti said.

That balm.

Athena breathed it in, allowing it to expand in her lungs before she exhaled. But it didn't leave her like she had anticipated. Instead, that balm stayed with her. She breathed it in again. "It's unacceptable for you to be late."

"I understand." Monti took one more step closer.

Athena could feel her over her shoulder, but they didn't touch. She breathed in Monti's scent. Rain. Grass. That same oil that Monti had used on Athena's skin. It was all there, just under the fragrances that blended so well into what she would describe as Monti's scent.

When had she thought about what Monti smelled like?

"I can't do this," Athena whispered, the vehemence gone. This was something else entirely. Resignation. "I can't..."

"You can," Monti countered. "We're just talking."

It was so much more than that. Yes, words were exchanged, but how did Athena tell Monti that this was so much more? This was connection and compassion in ways that Athena had never experienced before. There was something about Monti that drew Athena to her like a moth to a flame. She took another deep breath filled with nothing but Monti's scent.

Athena's eyes fluttered closed.

She listened deeply. First to her own breathing, to the white noise that raged through her ears and was her typical companion even late into the night. But she found Monti's breaths. They were deeper than Athena's, purposeful.

In and out.

In and out.

Athena latched onto those breaths, onto the rustle of the fabric as Monti shifted her body, to the hum of the electricity through the lights in the library, to the rush of wind outside along with the patter of rain against the window. She'd missed that sound.

She couldn't remember the last time she'd heard it so clearly.

It was as if everything was new, as if the world had just opened up in front of her and laid its blessings bare for Athena's taking. Her breath rattled in her chest when she turned and faced Monti. Those dark brown eyes glued to her face.

"Athena?"

"I can't do this," Athena repeated.

She meant to step off the landing and walk around Monti. She meant to leave the library and never see Monti again. Instead, she wrapped her fingers around Monti's wrist, rough fingertips to smooth, hot skin. Athena's heart jumped. Her shoulders loosened. She stared down at their physical connection.

Why had she done that?

She never willingly touched anyone.

Looking up into Monti's gaze, she saw the exact same confusion she knew was swimming around in her brain. But it was swimming through a fog, and she couldn't see it clearly. What had gotten her so upset?

Las Vegas.

"What are we doing tonight?" Monti asked gently.

Athena shook her head. She had way too many thoughts going on at once, and she couldn't filter them out enough to even begin to answer Monti's question.

"Do you want to sit?"

"No," Athena answered firmly. "I want you to leave."

Monti didn't falter. Her face remained stoic. She held Athena's intense stare for a few more seconds before her damp lips finally parted. "If you want me to leave, then why are you still holding me here?"

eleven

"Athena."

Monti's mind ran wild. Athena was touching her. Her fingers were wrapped so tightly around Monti's wrist that Monti was pretty sure she couldn't pry them off if she wanted to. But this wasn't about that. It was about the fact that Athena had initiated trust.

No, touch.

Shaking her head, Monti corrected her thought. Athena had initiated touch. Their eyes locked, and that panic that Monti had sensed dissipated a little bit. Monti softened her tone, eased her own body so she'd be less threatening. This was progress. Although Athena probably would see it as anything but.

"Focus on my voice, okay? Use that to stay here in the room with me."

Athena swallowed, the muscles in her neck straining. But she looked up, meeting Monti's eyes. Hers were so blue, depths of oceans that contained so much. Everything was perfectly in place —her hair, her makeup, her jacket that covered almost every inch of her body.

"Can you do that?"

Athena paused, a little breath escaping her lips. "I'm here."

"Good." Monti smiled a bit. This was progress. "What are you thinking about?"

Athena's face hardened, the lines pulling taut, her brow dropping. Athena slowly moved her head from side to side, telling Monti that this was pushing it too far. Monti changed her plan quickly. Athena took time to ease into these things—she had to remember that.

"Okay," Monti sighed. "Let's start with an apology. I'm so sorry that I wasn't here when I was supposed to be. I let you down. I failed you."

That changed something in Athena. Monti wanted to know what it was, what had clicked in her brain to allow this slice of openness that they needed. Monti stayed completely still, not wanting to scare that part of Athena away.

"I didn't realize how much you needed me." The words died on her lips. She had worked so very hard to never be that integral to someone's life. For Athena to have that tight a connection with her already was beyond what Monti had ever thought possible. It wasn't unusual for clients to feel safe with her. That was her job, after all, but so quickly? Did Athena even realize what was happening?

"I don't need you," Athena answered, that hard sheen coming back across her features.

This push and pull of control between them was exactly where they needed to be. This was where true work happened and meaning was made. Monti spun through what to say next, which question to ask, where to lead the conversation. But Athena's eyes were so bare.

"What do you need?"

Athena's face crumbled. Her grip on Monti's arm tightened sharply, her nails digging into Monti's skin. But Monti ignored the pain. It was nothing compared to the actual progress that they were making. Monti allowed silence to fall between them, using it for discomfort and peace at the same time.

"I needed you here two hours ago."

"I'm so sorry," Monti whispered. "I'm so sorry that I wasn't here for you."

Athena released Monti's arm, bringing her hand up to pinch the bridge of her nose and close her eyes. Did she even realize that she'd been holding on to Monti with a death grip?

"What happened today?"

"Nothing." Athena crossed her arms, her shoulders squared.

"Look, I'm here. At least let me help."

"Nothing happened today." Athena tightened her jaw, the muscles bulging at the sides. She looked down at the ground, an obvious sign of shame.

Monti was going to have to take this one step at a time. She couldn't skip through anything, and she needed to follow the circular pattern that Athena had created to protect herself from whatever it was that had triggered this panic.

"Tell me about your day then."

"I woke up. I went to work. And then I waited hours for an appointment." Athena's glare was sharp, but she was still talking to her. That was a bonus.

"You woke up?" Monti raised an eyebrow. "Does that mean you slept?"

Athena's lips parted, as if that realization just dawned on her. "Yes."

"That's good. How long did you sleep for?" Monti slid her hands down her hips, realizing at the last minute that she was searching for her pockets. She stopped herself and relaxed her arms by her sides. It wouldn't do to send Athena into another panic accidentally.

"A few hours." Athena waved it off as if it was no big deal.

"That's huge." Monti looked directly at her. "How did you manage to relax enough to fall asleep?"

"I..." Athena trailed off, looking over Monti's shoulder toward the door. "I don't know."

"Okay. Do you want to maybe figure that out?" Monti clung onto the hope that Athena would agree. It would make this whole process so much easier if she did. "I can give you a massage to help work on the muscles while we talk."

Athena sucked in a sharp breath, her gaze dropping decidedly to Monti's hands before trailing back up and over Monti's chest, her mouth, and then her eyes. Monti's heart skipped a beat, because that didn't look like fear. If she wasn't mistaken, *that* was a look of longing.

"Athena?"

"Yes. Yes. That sounds good." Athena stepped around her and toward the door.

Monti paused, not sure what that interaction had been, but it felt awkward. And it sparked that curiosity deep inside her. What was Athena thinking just then? What had gone through her mind? Stumbling on the step down from where the shelves were, Monti caught herself before she landed flat on her face—but barely.

Athena had stopped in the doorway, her gaze lingering on Monti as she righted herself. Again that look was there, and Monti wanted to know exactly what she was thinking. Perhaps that was what they needed to tease out during the massage.

No.

That wasn't it.

They needed to talk about why Athena had been so panicked, why she had nearly gone into a full-blown panic attack all because Monti was late. Monti trailed Athena to her bedroom, and Athena shut and locked the door this time.

"Kevin won't be interrupting us. No one will."

"All right," Monti answered, her voice quieter than she expected it to be.

Athena gave her a tight-lipped smile before nodding and walking toward the bed. "I'll be right back."

Monti stood awkwardly in the center of the bedroom while Athena disappeared into the en suite. It wasn't until the bathroom door clicked shut that Monti snapped back to reality. Right.

She should be preparing for this massage, not standing there trying to figure out why Athena was acting so odd today.

She'd gone from pissed off, angry, to panicked, and now to what? Because Monti wasn't sure she could quite put her finger on what Athena was feeling at the moment. Monti snagged a pillow from the head of the bed and put it at the foot, where she'd be more easily able to reach Athena's body. She set her satchel on the chair she'd slept in and riffled through it until she found the oil they'd used before.

She wished she had her whole setup. It would make this so much easier. Then again, Athena might be more resistant. It had a more clinical feeling, and was far less relaxed. Since Monti wasn't massaging the entire day this way, it shouldn't kill her body too much in the process.

Athena stepped out of the bathroom, her jacket and shoes off. Her pants were loose fitting, as was the tank top she wore now. She was much shorter without shoes on, but she also seemed so much more relaxed.

Was this really the same woman she had met before?

"I set the bed up, if you're comfortable with that?" Monti asked, checking in like she always did.

"I am." Athena sidestepped toward the bed, sliding onto the edge of the mattress.

Monti followed her, sitting next to Athena for a moment. "Only when you're ready," Monti murmured. "I brought the same oil as before."

Athena nodded, but didn't say anything. She leaned forward slightly, the buttons on her blouse parting to reveal the pale skin of her breast, the curve shadowed by the dim light in the room. Monti averted her gaze immediately. She would give Athena as much privacy as she could.

"What do you think would be most comfortable for you?" Monti watched Athena carefully, looking for any sign that something was wrong.

"Nothing is ever comfortable," Athena muttered.

"Something has to be."

Flicking her gaze up, Athena bit her lip. "Not today."

"Why today?"

Sighing heavily, Athena pulled her body backward on the bed, her legs straight out in front of her. Her toes were painted a dark maroon, and she wiggled them. Monti smiled at the move. Athena was already more comfortable with her than she had been before.

"My son is turning twenty-one in a few weeks," Athena said, though her tone didn't bely any emotion.

She was masking. Monti was sure of it. But she had successfully pointed out the problem, which was a step in the right direction. "That's a big milestone."

Monti filed away the information that something major had happened twenty-one years ago. Athena had brought up that number multiple times, although she was pretty sure that it was more than just having a baby. Which was also odd. Athena had failed to mention her husband and her son more times than not when they should have come up in conversation.

"It is," Athena answered, her voice trailing off. "Are we going to start?"

"Sure. If you want to." Monti gestured to the bed. "Where would you like me to start today?"

"No preference."

Athena lay down, her body not quite relaxing into the pillow. She stared up at the ceiling, her long lashes moving every time she blinked. If Monti wasn't careful, she could get lost in those lashes, in Athena's eyes, in her bod—nope. She really needed to stop that line of thought.

Immediately.

"I'm going to move your hair." Monti put her hands next to the pillow, standing behind Athena's head.

Athena lifted her head slightly so Monti could pull her hair out from under her head. Monti combed her fingers through Athena's hair gently. "I'll start with your scalp, if that's all right."

"It is." Athena dragged in a deep breath and let it out slowly, finally relaxing a little more.

Monti started with her fingers gently pushing into Athena's scalp. She bided her time, trying to figure out a way to ask a question that would get Athena thinking and talking. She could already tell that Athena was closed off, probably as a way to protect herself. But what exactly happened twenty-some-odd years ago that would cause that.

"So what are you doing to celebrate?"

"Celebrate what?" Athena tightened her jaw.

So that was a touchy point. "Your son's birthday?"

"Kevin is taking Simon to Las Vegas."

"All right." Monti moved down to Athena's temple and then her jaw. "But what are *you* doing to celebrate?"

Athena sighed, and Monti could distinctly see her heart thudding hard in her chest. Was she that anxious? Did she feel that threatened?

"Tell me if you want me to stop something, okay?"

"We're not doing anything."

It took Monti a moment to realize that Athena wasn't talking about the massage.

"Why wouldn't you?" Monti asked back, keeping her tone soft.

"We don't have that kind of relationship." Athena folded her hands over her belly, wrapping her fingers tightly together.

Monti needed to fix that. She'd caused too much stress already. She was just working through how to ease the conversation in a different direction when Athena sat up sharply, her back to Monti. Her shoulders dropped, pulling toward each other. She moved her legs and crossed them. Her breathing was loud and ragged.

"Athena?" Monti rounded the corner of the bed, the front of her thighs pushing into the mattress and the fluffy comforter. "Athena, what's going on?"

Athena shook her head. She reached up and brushed her

hands over her face, her hair curtaining her face and making it impossible to see. A sob tore through her, shaking her shoulders. Compassion overwhelmed Monti, and she slid onto the mattress, keeping as much distance as she dared between them.

"Oh, Athena." Monti rested her hand over Athena's knee and waited to see what would happen.

Sucking in a sharp breath, Athena shook her head and brushed her fingers over her cheeks again. "I'm not crying."

"Sure you're not," Monti said lightly with a smile. "It's okay to cry, you know."

"From a massage?"

"I believe I told you once that a lot happens in the body that's affected by the mind. I'm betting this is just a big release of whatever you've been holding onto." Monti squeezed her fingers tightly, but didn't move them any more than that.

Athena said nothing, but she slowly pulled herself together. The sniffles became fewer between, the shaking of her shoulders eased up. Monti stayed right where she was, offering whatever support she could. They needed this. It was a connection, a pain point uncovered, and Athena was working through whatever her past was that needed to be worked through, even if it was in silence, and even if it was only a little piece of the puzzle.

Monti stayed right where she was when Athena took a sharp, bolstering breath. Everything happened in slow motion. Athena tilted her chin up, her eyes red and puffy from the tears, her cheeks stained with tears that weren't quite dried yet. Monti's breath hitched at the look of utter agony in Athena's gaze.

"I'm here for you," Monti murmured.

Athena dropped her gaze to Monti's lips, then locked their eyes together. She swallowed hard, her breathing picking up. Monti's entire body was on fire, telling her one thing while she forced it to do another. She wanted to lean in, to wrap her arms around Athena's shoulders and hug her, to remind her that she wasn't alone through any of this.

"Monti..." Athena's voice trailed off, the whisper barely there.

What was that look? Athena's eyes were back on her lips. Athena's cheeks were red, but Monti was pretty sure it wasn't from crying this time. Panic swelled in Monti's chest, pushing up into her throat and constricting her airway.

This was common.

This wasn't outside the normal behavior patterns for a client.

Monti had created a safe space. She had allowed Athena to feel and to know that she could do that in an environment where she would be supported. But it had been so long since Monti had dealt with something like this. It had been ages since she'd thought it was even a possibility.

And yet...

As much as she was scared, realizing what Athena was thinking, she wanted to close the gap. She was just about to move when she managed to stop herself. Closing her eyes, Monti did the only thing she knew that could save them from this.

"What happened twenty-one years ago?"

The silence was so loud.

When Monti opened her eyes again, Athena's glare was unmatched. Her gaze was clear, righteously full of anger and hurt. Guilt was a brick in the middle of Monti's stomach, and it just kept getting heavier and heavier with each passing second.

"Get. Out."

twelve

"Hey, Mom."

Athena tensed, the phone pressed to her ear. She hadn't expected this reaction to Simon. She'd experienced it before, but it had been years. Shouldn't she be better by now?

Then again, she always asked herself that question.

"Hello, Simon." Athena snagged the pen on top of her desk and flipped it through her fingers in a well-practiced habit.

"Has Dad talked to you?"

Athena's grasp on the pen faltered, and it clattered to the desktop. She didn't immediately grab it, wanting to focus on Simon for once. "About what?"

"Vegas."

"Yes, he did. I think it's a wonderful idea." Athena snagged the pen again as the lie slipped through her lips. They were back on even territory now, where Kevin and Simon had their special bond and Athena lived just on the outside of any deep relationship with them. She never should have been a mother, that much was for certain.

Kevin could at least fake it better than she could. And he'd wanted this. Athena had no choice in the matter.

"I wasn't sure how you'd feel about it."

"Why's that?" She frowned and turned to her computer screen, pulling up the file she'd been working on an hour ago. She needed to get it done so she could submit it to the courts, but she'd been dragging her feet. Which wasn't her norm. Then again, nothing seemed normal lately.

"Because you hate Vegas."

Athena wrinkled her nose. She did, in fact, hate Las Vegas, and it was for one very specific reason. Which Simon had no idea about. She'd never told him. Kevin had never told him. And that wasn't something anyone needed to share. Rolling her shoulders, Athena focused on her computer screen even though she wasn't actually seeing anything. The words blurred in front of her gaze, lights flashing and darkness invading her vision.

Fuck.

What was that?

Athena swallowed and focused on Simon's voice again.

"So I wasn't sure how you'd feel about it."

"Dad and I talked, and I'm fine with him taking you. It's your twenty-first. You should do something fun and exciting. Whatever you want to do." Athena closed her eyes and rested back in her chair. She took deep slow breaths because her heart raced.

"Are you sure?"

"Do you think I'm lying?" The accusation in her voice was sharp. But she hated when people didn't believe her. She never said anything she didn't mean.

"No." Simon's tone dropped before it lifted in a question. "Are you okay, Mom?"

"I'm fine." Athena clenched her fist sharply, digging her nails into her palm. "I hope you enjoy your trip."

"Right. Guess I'll talk to you later, then."

Athena didn't wait as she ended the call. She pressed her forehead to her arms as she leaned against her desk and continued to take slow, deep breaths. She needed to calm herself down. There was nothing wrong with what was happening. Her son was an adult, and he deserved to live his life doing whatever he wanted.

Something she'd never been able to do.

But she and Kevin had agreed early on in their marriage that when Simon was born, he could take or leave any family obligations. She didn't want to force him into anything the way they had been.

Standing up sharply, Athena paced her office. Energy coursed through her, and it wasn't a good kind of energy. She knew she was slipping into the past, and that it would be a monumental task to pull herself out of it. Moving to the front of her desk, she pressed her hands flat against the cold wood. Closing her eyes, she leaned forward and tried to focus, but the memories kept coming back.

One after the other.

Tears slipped from the corners of her eyes, dropping onto the desk. Athena hated the stinging and burning in her nose. She hated the scratchy feel in her throat, the inability to take a full deep breath. Clenching her jaw hard, she stayed as much in the room as possible.

But the memories...

Fuck.

They pulled at her, grabbed her, drowned her.

It was Simon. It was always Simon who brought these, and it wasn't his fault. It wasn't anything he had done. She hated that she couldn't look at him without these damn memories. Cringing, Athena pushed herself to stand, but the room swam. She had to sit on the edge of the desk to keep from collapsing to the floor.

She held herself up, barely. She warded off as many memories as she could, but they came at her so fast that it was next to impossible. In the recesses of her awareness, she heard the knock on the door. She heard Fallon's voice. But she couldn't focus on it long enough to even comprehend what she was saying.

She couldn't see Fallon's sweetly rounded face.

Athena dragged in a breath of cold air, hoping that it would clear her mind enough to think. But she was wrong. All it did was bring the memory of the first breath of fresh air that she could take after... She froze. Gripping onto the desk for dear life, she tried her best to stay in this year. In this moment. In this reality.

But the fingers of the past kept dragging her back.

Yet, she wasn't kicking and screaming.

Athena was quietly waiting for those memories to arrive and consume her whole. That's how this always happened. Purely accepting what was about to happen was the best way for it to take her. She'd come out the other side faster.

"Athena." Kevin's voice shocked through her body.

But was it then?

Or was it now?

She couldn't look. He'd been there in the hospital with her. He'd been the only one to come and check on her, to stay with her and navigate her healing. He'd brought her home. He'd been her savior through it all.

"Athena, come back to me."

Tears streamed down her cheeks. The cold trails they left against her skin were markers of the path of destruction as they dripped hotly off her cheeks. Why was she crying so much lately? Why couldn't she just let it all go?

Usually it was just the emotions. Just the god-awful feelings of what had happened, of being trapped. Suffocated. True flashbacks were so rare these days.

"Athena!" Kevin's voice was stronger.

Finally, she opened her eyes and cringed.

Fallon stood in the doorway, her eyes wide with fear. Kevin right in front of her, but giving her space. She focused on him, the length of his beard. He hadn't had that twenty-one years ago. He'd been clean shaven. He'd been young. Those wrinkles weren't around his eyes.

"I'm fine," she managed to mumble. But the sound was so far from her ears that she doubted if she'd even spoken out loud.

"Liar," Kevin spoke softly.

Which meant she had said it out loud.

Athena shuddered, finally feeling her fingers clutching the

edge of her desk. They hurt so much, yet it took more effort than it should have to pry them off.

"Can I sit next to you?" Kevin took a step closer.

Athena jerked back. She stared at him with wide eyes, her voice caught in her throat. She couldn't speak. Her heart hammered in her chest. Her entire body was on high alert. It was going to take her weeks to come down from this, to ease the triggers to the point that she could pretend to function again.

Pretend.

That's all she'd done for two decades. If not more than that. She'd pretended even when she was little. And she'd never fucking stopped.

"Athena." Kevin's voice broke through her thoughts.

She looked him directly in the eye, finally seeing him truly for the first time. This was better. This was more where she should be.

"I'm fine." Her voice sounded so far away.

"Don't lie again."

She gave him a flat look and stood up, smoothing her hands down her thighs as she glanced toward Fallon—who still looked scared. Fallon had never seen her like this before. But Athena wasn't going to address that—not yet. Not if she could avoid it.

"I'm fine," she stated again.

Without hesitating, she walked directly out of her office, holding her breath as she passed Fallon. Athena didn't turn around to look. She didn't need to know what Fallon was thinking or what Kevin was wondering. Neither one of them would follow her, that much she knew. Rolling her shoulders, she walked through the house and straight to her library.

This was her safe place.

There was no other place in the world she would rather be than right here. Sighing, Athena shut the door, pressing her shoulders against it. She slid to the floor, her knees folded and pressed against her chest. She closed her eyes and let go, completely.

In here she was safe. No one would invade her space, no one would ask her questions, no one would be watching her. She didn't cry, but she did have to work hard to settle herself into a calm enough state that she wouldn't mind leaving the room.

Until then, she was stuck here. Butt against the hardwood floor, back against the door, and body not sure what to do. Her heart was still beating a mile a minute, and her head was still cloudy to the point she couldn't really think straight.

What she needed was Monti.

Where the hell had that thought come from?

Athena opened her eyes and stared at the bookcase across from her, all the hardbacks and paperbacks neatly in their place. It was orderly. It was perfect in here. Sealed off from all the outside worries and fears. Athena swallowed the lump in her throat, but it came right back up. She'd never told anyone what had happened that night, not fully.

No one else needed to experience what she had even in the smallest way.

Pursing her lips, Athena blew out a breath. She was much calmer now than she was before. Alone. That was the way to go. Never with someone else, always on her own.

So why was she thinking about Monti?

Because she was such a calming presence. That had to be it. Her entire energy was calm, cool, and collected. Which probably meant she was an absolute mess underneath it all just like Athena was, but still, Athena craved that sense of peace. Monti had shown her that lately. Beautiful insights into the possibility of peace.

Sighing, Athena relaxed and pressed the back of her head into the door. Monti had shown her serenity. And that moment the other week had been so much more than that. Athena shivered, her body reacting in a new and different way. The boomerang effect—from the intensity in her office to this—was impossible to keep up with.

Monti would be so gentle with her. She'd calm her down.

She'd talk but not expect answers. Except—she had. She'd asked directly what had happened twenty-one years ago, and Athena had tossed her out.

Maybe that was what had triggered this entire episode. It wasn't Simon. It was Monti and her damn questions, her damn massages, her damn fingers. Athena nearly groaned at the memory of Monti's hands on her shoulders and her neck. Shivering again, Athena scooted around and pulled her phone out of pocket.

She pulled up Monti's contact and stared at her name. After all of that, after Monti pushed her and Athena had pushed back, why did she want Monti there? Why did she want Monti's hands on her again? Why did she want to hear Monti's voice, her smooth calm tones, the gentle place that Monti created?

No. Not gentle.

Safe.

Athena breathed out relief.

Monti was safe.

thirteen

"You about ready for lunch?" Monti stepped into Fallon's office, expecting to find her sister nose deep in work like she always was.

Fallon jumped up and immediately started scratching her arms. She rounded the desk and stood right in front of Monti. Her eyes were wide, her lips thin, and anyone could see that she was obviously stressed.

"What's wrong?"

"Did Ms. Pruitt call you?"

Monti wrinkled her nose and shook her head. "No? Did I miss another appointment?"

"No. No, you didn't."

"After last time…" Monti trailed off, not sure if Athena had told Fallon about that or not. She bit the side of her tongue to try and figure out how to phrase what she was going to say next. "I didn't think we'd scheduled another appointment, but you never know."

"You didn't. But she needs… fuck." Fallon scratched her arms again.

"Okay, seriously, what's wrong?" Monti touched Fallon's arm lightly, offering her what comfort she could. But when it came to the two of them, she was never very good at this. That whole baby sister thing really got in the way.

Fallon closed her eyes and shook her head, staring down at the floor as her cheeks reddened. Whatever this was, it was bad. Fallon hadn't been this disturbed by something in a long time, at least that Monti was aware. It wasn't like they talked all that often anymore.

"I don't know what happened. I've never seen her like that."

"Like what?"

"Like she wasn't even there. I tried to talk to her, but she was just kind of spouting gobbledygook. I went and got Mr. Brock, but he couldn't help her."

"Mr. Brock?" Monti tried to figure out what was going on, but it was clear she was still missing a good portion of the story. Her stomach twisted hard. What if she'd missed something? What if she'd allowed her own reaction to Athena to get in the way of caring for her? She shouldn't have forced the conversation the way it had gone last time. She should have stayed to make sure that Athena was okay.

"Her husband. He's in town right now. I went and got him, and she started to make some sense, but then she just kind of walked out, and I don't know, Monti. I've never seen anyone act like that before." Fallon's nails dug into her upper arms, red marks left in their wake.

That was a nervous habit she'd always had. Monti was so glad that she hadn't inherited that one. Sighing, Monti took Fallon by the arm and moved her to one of the empty chairs in the room. She sat down and leaned her elbows on her knees.

"She seemed more with-it when she left?"

"Yeah, but she couldn't even answer a question when I came in." Fallon frowned.

Monti nodded, processing what she knew of the situation and what possibly could have happened. "And Kevin came in?"

"Yeah, but like I said, he wasn't much help."

"How close are they?" It was the easiest way Monti could think to ask that question without setting off any warning bells for Fallon.

"What do you mean? They've been married for over twenty years."

She must not have gotten her point across. Monti rubbed her palms together. "Right, but how close are they? He was on a trip when I got here. Does he do that often?"

"Yeah, but she also goes on trips a lot."

"Does she?" Monti furrowed her brow. That surprised her. She figured Athena would be pretty much a recluse, considering she never seemed comfortable anywhere.

Fallon nodded. "She used to, anyway. He loves her."

"Is their marriage a good one?" Monti shifted the topic a little. Love didn't necessarily make a relationship work or make it healthy, and she wasn't about to point that out to Fallon who was already upset and clearly needed something to focus on.

"I think so?" Fallon said it like a question, as if she was digging deep to find an answer. "I don't see them together all that often except at events or right before events, and Ms. Pruitt doesn't talk about him all that often."

"What about her son?"

"Simon?" Fallow scrunched her face. "She never really talks about him."

"Never?" Monti raised an eyebrow at that. Usually parents were ecstatic about anything their children did. Even if Athena seemed disassociated from life on a good day, Monti had expected her to at least seem like she cared.

"She's a very private person."

"Right. Okay."

"You have to talk to her," Fallon added, her tone pleading.

"Talk to her?" Monti's entire body tightened. She hadn't come here to help Athena—again. She'd come to have lunch with Fallon to make up for their argument the other day.

Fallon nodded. "Please. I'm so worried about her."

Leave it to Fallon to always worry about her boss, or really anyone in her life. She was the big sister through and through, and she always wanted to make sure that everyone was taken care of before herself. Monti leaned back in the chair. "I'm not sure that's a good idea."

"You've gotten through to her. I know you have."

"I'm not so sure about that."

"Please, Monti. You have to try. Someone has to help her."

Fuck.

She hated when Fallon used that tone on her. She was powerless against it. It was the same tone of voice she'd used when she called the first time to see if Monti would give her sleepless boss a massage to help her relax.

"I don't think this is a good idea."

"Helping someone isn't a good idea?" Fallon fired back. "Who are you and what have you done with my sister?"

"Damn it, Fallon. I don't want to be a therapist anymore."

"This is different!" Fallon was back to pleading. "This is someone I care about, and she's hurting."

Monti narrowed her gaze. She sat in silence, contemplating her options. Fallon wasn't going to give this one up, and if Monti didn't agree to it, she knew Fallon was going to be angry with her for a long time. If there was one thing that Fallon did well, it was hold a grudge.

"Fine." Monti clapped her hands together. "Fine, I'll help. Where the hell is she?"

"Library, I think."

"Of course." Monti should have known that, and if she'd thought about it, she would have. But she'd wanted to avoid Athena and the awkwardness that had come between them the last time they'd been in a room together.

Standing up, Monti looked down at Fallon. "Lunch another day then?"

"Yes."

"Fine." Crossing her arms, Monti walked to the library.

When she got there the door was shut, but she could feel Athena's presence on the other side. She had that understated power that drew Monti to her at every turn. Licking her lips, Monti pressed her palm to the door and steadied herself.

She could do this.

She could go in, figure out what the hell was wrong, get Athena back on even ground, and extricate herself from the situation as fast as she'd gotten into it.

That's all she needed to do.

Reaching down, Monti turned the knob and pushed the door open. But it didn't budge. Pushing harder, she stopped when Athena grunted and the door finally gave way. Furrowing her brow, Monti slipped inside and stared down at Athena, curled up into herself, sitting on the floor, wide eyes staring up at her. Immediately, Monti dropped to her knees.

Fuck.

This was bad.

Fallon hadn't lied.

Monti shut the door, and Athena shifted back to lean against it. Her shoulders were so tightly drawn that she looked like she was trying to crawl in on herself. Monti shifted to lean against the door as well, stretching out her legs in front of her and staring at the window.

Instead of saying anything, she stayed there in silence. She was going to have to approach this issue delicately. And it was going to take every ounce of patience and strength she had to keep Athena on the right track.

"I love this room," Monti finally said, keeping her tone light and calm. The last thing Athena needed was to feel her own anxiety pulsing. "I think it might be my favorite room in your house. I haven't seen your whole house, but I imagine this would still be my favorite."

Athena took a deep breath, her lungs expanding and collapsing as she blew the air out. That was at least a good sign.

"It's mine, too," Athena murmured before reaching up and brushing her eyes. The tear stains were clear, but they were already dry. So it had been a while since she'd stopped crying.

Monti wondered if Athena knew how long it had been.

"Why? Why do you like it in here?" Monti scooted a little closer, hoping that Athena wouldn't pick up on just how close she was.

"It's calming." Athena dragged in a deep breath and let it out slowly, her eyes fluttering shut as she pressed her head into the door. "No one else comes in here."

"So it's only for you?"

"Yes."

They fell into a comfortable silence. Monti watched Athena carefully while Athena sat there quietly with her eyes closed. Monti moved her toes in her shoes, biding the time as she waited for Athena to calm down even more.

"Are you okay that I'm here?" Monti finally asked. "I know we didn't end on the greatest note last time."

The question hung in the air, the tension taut from finally being asked. Monti was seeking permission and forgiveness, needing it before she could move forward with anything else. She shuddered and waited.

Athena didn't answer her. Instead, she released her knees and straightened them out, mimicking Monti's posture. Athena rubbed her thigh, the heel of her palm pushing hard into the muscles three times before she stopped. She lifted her hand and reached over, setting it on top of Monti's. Athena curled her fingers around Monti's hand. She relaxed, her shoulders dropping even more.

Curious, Monti scooted a little closer. "I take it that you're not kicking me out of the room this time."

Athena turned her head, looking directly into Monti's eyes. She looked so wary, so broken and vulnerable. Her lips parted and quivered as if she was trying to speak but couldn't find the syllables to make the words. Monti waited patiently, giving

Athena whatever time she needed. Fingers tightened around Monti's.

"Stay," Athena whispered.

"Are you sure?"

"You're the only one making this better."

"Athena," Monti murmured, covering her hand and rubbing the edge of her thumb along Athena's skin. "You must be so lonely."

Athena choked, fresh tears falling down her cheeks. "You have no idea."

"Tell me." Monti bit her lip.

Shaking her head, Athena tilted it onto Monti's shoulder and sighed. "No."

"Can I take a guess as to why?" Monti continued the sweet pattern against Athena's hand, hoping it would keep the same calm quality.

"Sure."

"Something happened twenty-one years ago—"

"Twenty-two," Athena interrupted. She flicked her gaze up to Monti's. "It's been almost twenty-two."

Monti smiled. That was more information than she'd anticipated getting out of Athena. "Thank you for trusting me to share that."

Athena nodded, the movement so subtle that Monti would have missed it if Athena wasn't still resting against her.

"You don't have to tell me what it is, but almost twenty-two years ago, something happened. And that something shut you off from the world. You haven't let anyone in since. Including Simon." Monti trailed off as she said his name, realizing for the first time that *that* was the reason for the distance between them. "I think you let Kevin in but only because you knew him before and only so much."

"Touché," Athena answered, relaxing even more.

Monti moved her hand up Athena's wrist to her elbow and then back down. "They're all worried about you."

"I know. But I can't..." Athena turned her face into Monti's shoulder, burying herself. "I can't deal with them today."

"You don't have to." Monti moved her head, catching a full whiff of Athena's scent. Tingles ran through her body. This closeness was almost too much. She was there to hold a safe space for Athena, and yet, there was so much more going on in this undercurrent. More than she could possibly put words to right now. "I'll do it."

"Kevin will be fine. But Fallon—"

"Worries about anyone and everyone."

Athena hummed her agreement. "She's very sweet with her concern."

"You can only say that because you're not her little sister."

The small chuckle that left Athena's lips was promising. It meant they were on the right trajectory. Athena was easing back into this world from her triggered state, and Monti was keeping her rooted here.

"Trust me. Having a big sister who is all up in your business isn't a fun experience."

"Let me guess, she tried to parent you."

"Every day."

Athena looked up into Monti's eyes, her lips curling into a gentle smile. Then her look faltered, the smile falling away, as those tears filled her eyes again. "In three months, I'll celebrate my twenty-second anniversary."

Another piece to the puzzle of this woman.

Monti loved that Athena was willing to give her these little tidbits of information, even if it was like pulling teeth to get it out of her. She folded her hand around Athena's. "Is it the anniversary that's bothering you? Or is it something else?"

Athena shook her head back and forth slowly. "I honestly don't know."

"That's okay. We can figure that out later."

They settled in next to each other again. Monti was going to stay here as long as Athena possibly needed. Monti continued to trail her fingers across Athena's skin, admiring the softness, the warmth, the feel.

"I'll stay here as long as you need."

Athena hummed. "Thank you."

"Of course."

fourteen

"Glad to see you're on time."

Athena stood at the door to the library, where she'd wanted to meet with Monti. Two days and she was far calmer now than she had been. Monti had sat with her for hours. They hadn't talked much, mostly listening to the quiet and steady breathing coming from each of them.

It was the closest she had felt to anyone in a long time.

"I made a point of it," Monti answered, clearly a little nervous still.

Athena enjoyed that look on her, the slightly awkward but still confident gaze. She held in her smile and ducked her chin. "Good to know you can do that."

Monti snorted lightly, a chuckle leaving her lips. "And I'm glad to see that you're almost back to your icy, distanced self."

Athena paused at that. Because she actually felt anything but. She was still raw from the other day, but worse than that, any time Monti was near her, she felt more than she should. More than she had in ages. Stepping in close, Athena stopped shoulder to shoulder. She looked Monti directly in the eye when she answered. "I secretly think you like it."

Monti's eyes widened, her cheeks reddening, and her lips

parted. That was exactly the reaction that Athena had hoped for. Instead of moving away like she usually would, she leaned in, their arms brushing. The fabric of her jacket pressed into her skin, scratching it. Athena sucked in a breath and bit the inside of her cheek.

"I think I'm right."

"Athena."

"Shall we?" Athena stepped away, giving her space. What was she even doing? She hadn't intended to make this into some sort of game that neither of them could win. But she had also been thinking about Monti more and more lately, about the calm presence she had, the way it was so easy to talk to her.

"Uh. Sure." Monti followed behind as they walked through the house and directly to Athena's bedroom.

This had become the routine, that was for sure. And Athena loved her routines. She left Monti as she went into the bathroom, slipping off her jacket, her bra, and her shoes. She'd never thought she'd feel comfortable with someone like this.

She didn't have to talk herself into it anymore—or out of canceling the whole thing. When she stepped back into the bedroom, Monti had already fixed the bed in the way she wanted it, closed the curtains to dim the light, and stood with her bottle of oil in her hand.

"Are we ready?" Athena folded her hands in front of her.

"Do you mind if we work on a chest massage today?"

Athena halted in her step toward the bed. She met Monti's gaze.

"It's not your breasts, I promise. It's all around them, but when there's a lot of back and neck tension, we need to release those muscles as well." Monti sounded so confident, like she'd done this a thousand times before.

Athena couldn't remember the last time anyone had touched her chest.

"We can leave your shirt on still. I don't need you to take it off."

Mulling through the comment, Athena held her breath. Eventually she gave a sharp nod of affirmation and then climbed onto the bed. Monti pulled the clip from her hair and threaded her fingers through the strands. This was how they always seemed to start lately, a gentle pattern to get used to the touching.

Athena's heart raced.

She knew what to expect now. The gentle brush of Monti's fingers in her hair, the slick feel of her hands against her neck, the scent of the oil reaching her nostrils and relaxing her even more. Dragging in a deep breath, Athena closed her eyes and pushed into the mattress.

"Do you want to talk more about the other day?" Monti's voice was quiet.

For some reason she couldn't put her finger on, Athena wanted to say yes. But that damn sensation clogged her throat again. She wanted the words to spill from her, she really did, but it was next to impossible to work past that sensation.

"You're so tense." Monti pinched her way down the muscles in the sides of Athena's neck, easing them.

Suddenly, Athena was able to breathe better. She dragged cold air into her lungs and settled even more. Monti used her thumbs along the side of Athena's neck, easing the tightness there one stroke at a time. As much as her neck muscles were relaxing, the rest of her body tensed.

No, that wasn't right.

Athena closed her eyes and felt through her body. It was so rare that she did this, that she took the time to see what she was feeling physically. She followed the sensations from Monti's fingers, the firmness, the tingles they created. Her breathing became shallow as she tracked the tingles from her neck into her chest, where they seemed to almost multiply.

Now that hadn't happened ever. Not with anyone before. Athena bit her lip, keeping her eyes closed. She couldn't look at Monti while she did this. She couldn't think about the fact that

Monti was touching her, and not really in the way that she wanted.

Athena stopped at that.

Not in the way she wanted.

Was that what this was? Was this arousal? The tingles continued to build in her chest, and her nipples hardened. But that could have been from the cold in the room, right? Her breathing steadied as Monti moved to the other side of her neck, pulling and manipulating her body to stretch the muscles.

It felt odd at first, but Athena couldn't deny how it felt afterward. She kept her eyes closed while Monti moved her fingers back into Athena's hair, thumbs down her forehead and against her cheeks. That sweet tension—and it was definitely sweet, not painful—increased in her chest again. Athena allowed it to grow, wanting to test it out and see what it was.

She liked Monti touching her.

"Did you want to talk?" Monti asked again, her voice a stark reminder that she was still in this room.

Not that Athena needed it. She was viscerally aware that Monti was in the room with her. She was aware of every fingertip that Monti moved against her, the way her body reacted to the touch. Heaving a breath, Athena tried to get ahold of herself.

"It's not easy to talk," Athena finally answered, her voice breathy.

What was happening to her?

"I don't imagine it is." Monti didn't stop moving. Athena would never have expected a skilled massage could be the one thing to turn her into this blubbering puddle.

Athena relaxed again, the tingles floating through her chest and moving into her stomach and then lower. She let them go, curious if they would lead exactly where she thought they would. She'd read about this, in her books of course, and she wasn't ignorant about what people felt when they were aroused. But she couldn't remember ever feeling like this.

She'd thought she was broken.

She'd thought she was too destroyed for this.

They had taken everything that was her essence and ripped it to shreds right in front of her eyes. Athena swallowed the lump in her throat, her shoulders suddenly cold when Monti's hands left her. Opening her eyes, she looked up to see Monti staring down at her with concern written all over her face.

"What?" Athena asked, her throat thick with mucus.

"You're crying," Monti said, so matter-of-factly. "I wanted to be sure you were okay or if I'd done—"

Athena shook her head, reaching up and wiping her cheeks. She hadn't realized she was crying. "No, it's fine. I'm fine."

"Just another release of those pesky emotions?" Monti's lips pulled up to one side, quirking in hope.

"Or something like that," Athena mumbled, clearing her cheeks again. "You can continue."

"Are you sure?" Monti pressed her palm fully on Athena's shoulder, her dark eyes boring directly into Athena's.

"Yes," Athena whispered. Whatever was happening to her, she knew she didn't want to give this up.

"It's not abnormal, you know." Monti started back on Athena's shoulders, working the muscles in her neck and then around to her collarbones.

"What's not?" Athena asked, again breathy and unable to control it. This slow slide out of control was the only way she could possibly do this—whatever this was, because she wasn't even sure yet. But even though she was losing control, something about it felt right.

And good.

"The release of emotions, the tears. We hold a lot of emotion and trauma in our bodies, and as we start to work through it, our physical reactions can be explosive and odd and almost random." Monti leaned closer, her breasts directly over Athena's face.

Athena gulped.

"Do you mind if I start on your chest now? I didn't want to move there without asking."

"Uh... sure." Athena held her breath as she waited to see what Monti would do next. Instead of standing at the edge of the bed like she had before, Monti climbed onto the mattress, the weight of her body dipping Athena toward her.

"Sorry. It's the only way I can really reach under your arm since I don't have a table anymore."

Athena's heart raced, but not for the reason she'd thought it would. Monti was so close to her. This was far more intimate than it had been the other day in the library. This was the closeness that she had longed for, that she'd read about, that she'd seen with others all around her. And yet, Monti was only there because she was paid to be there, because Athena hired her for a job.

"You don't mind, do you?"

"No," Athena answered quickly.

Warmth seeped from Monti's body into hers even though they weren't touching. Athena held her breath until Monti was settled next to her, looking her over as if to check and ask if this was all right. Athena nodded before she could even ask.

"This is fine."

"Okay." Monti smiled, her lips curving fully this time. "I'm going to move your arm in some awkward ways, and I'm going to massage here—" she pointed to Athena's side "—and here—" she made a circular motion right around the tops of Athena's breasts and across her ribs. "I promise I won't touch you anywhere else."

"I understand." Athena waited for the first touch, for the first caress of fingers against skin, for that moment when Monti would be right against her and those tingles would coil tightly between her legs again.

Because yes, this *was* arousal.

Athena knew that now.

And she needed to see if it would continue to grow or if this was a fluke.

Monti started slowly, checking multiple times about the amount of pressure she was applying and if it was too much or too little. Athena answered the questions succinctly. As the massage continued, her cheeks heated, her chest tightened deliciously as she tried to keep herself contained. Monti didn't need to know what she was thinking about, or hell, what she was feeling.

"Do you know what you were releasing?" Monti asked, that same balm in her voice that Athena had come to know and love. "You don't have to share if you don't want to. I'm just asking if you know what it was."

"Yes," Athena said before she could stop herself. She'd always known what the problem was. Her life growing up had been benign. She'd had two parents, and while it wasn't always the most loving environment and she knew what the expectations were, she never felt slighted by them.

Her job was to marry, have an heir, and keep the money in the family. It had always been that. And she'd done that, for the most part. She'd done exactly what they asked. Only she and Kevin knew the truth, and they'd sworn to never tell anyone.

"I was raped." The words were gone before she could stop them.

Tears pricked her eyes, her nose burning again. Athena held it back, focusing on Monti's fingers that didn't even miss a touch. She blew out a breath and looked directly into Monti's gaze.

"I haven't said that out loud in nearly twenty-two years."

"How does it feel?"

Athena scrunched her nose, pushing a few tears over the edge of her eyes to fall down her cheeks and vanish. "Good and bad at the same time."

Monti nodded slowly. "I get that. It's an uncomfortable emotion, but it's a relief to not be so alone in the discomfort."

Swallowing hard, Athena nodded. "Spot on."

"Thank you for sharing with me."

"I wanted to." Athena furrowed her brow, not quite sure why she'd finally opened up about it. It certainly wasn't everything her life had become, but it was the tip of the iceberg. Relief flooded her, as if an afterthought to it all. She sank deeper into the mattress and smiled up at Monti. "I really did."

"I'm proud of you."

Monti's words swelled in Athena's chest, as if every woman in the world who had experienced something similar was holding her up in this one moment. Was this what true support felt like? Athena waited while Monti shifted around her body to the other side and started the same massage on her right side. This silence was comfortable. It was filled with understanding instead of pain.

Finally, it hit her why Monti hadn't been surprised. Athena snagged Monti's hand, holding her loosely to get her attention. "You knew, didn't you?"

"I took an educated guess." Monti raised an eyebrow and dropped her hands to her knees. "No one told me anything."

"The only person who knows is Kevin, and he wouldn't say anything."

Monti nodded. "I worked with some trafficking victims when I was going through school. While the traumas are different, some of the responses can be tracked as patterns. That's all I picked up on."

Athena understood. As much as she didn't like that Monti had figured it out, it made sense that she had. Athena pushed to a sitting position on the bed so they were almost face to face. With Monti still on her knees, they weren't quite on even ground, but it didn't feel as though Monti had the upper hand.

In fact, it had never felt like that.

Monti had always given her the grace to find her own way. That's exactly what this had been all along, hadn't it?

"Everything okay?" Monti asked, touching Athena's upper arm lightly.

Athena stared down at the connection before closing her eyes and focusing on the touch. She was so comfortable with this, so connected to another person in ways she'd never been before. Athena looked directly into Monti's eyes, into the dark browns that seemed darker in the dim light. The slight wrinkles around her eyes and lips, her lips that were so different from Fallon's. Athena lost herself in her study of Monti's features, the slight things that made her exactly who she was.

"Athena?" Monti tried again.

"Everything is good," Athena finally replied, understanding that Monti needed that reassurance more than anything. It wasn't about what she felt, but about communicating that with the person who was there to provide the safe space. "I'm good."

"Okay," Monti whispered, a hint of confusion in her voice still.

"I think I want to be done for today."

"I understand." Monti gave her a small smile. "I want you to take care of yourself when I go. Don't go back to work, please."

Work hadn't even been a thought in Athena's mind in all honesty. A long vacation was, perhaps to her beach home for a week. She could manage it. Dropping her gaze to Monti's lips again, Athena breathed out as another thought of touch crossed her mind.

A kiss.

They'd been so close to that the other day, and Monti had retreated. Which again, Athena understood, and she stood by those rules and boundaries Monti was putting into place. Yet as much as Athena didn't want to think about it, she couldn't stop herself. Not after the arousal that she'd fully allowed to course through her body, to have free rein in her for the last hour.

Just what would it be like to be that close to someone again?

"Athena," Monti chastised lightly. "Promise me you won't work."

"I promise I won't work, not today." Athena touched Monti's hand, curling their fingers together again.

Why did this feel so right?

"Should we continue this tomorrow?"

"If that's what you want."

"It is." Athena nodded, finally looking back into Monti's eyes.

"Then I'll see you tomorrow." Monti scooted off the bed as if escaping.

That was something Athena couldn't blame her for. She watched as Monti quickly collected her things in silence and nodded firmly at Athena as her goodbye. When the door was shut, Athena collapsed onto the bed again, her hands resting on her hips as she closed her eyes, imagining Monti's hands, her fingers, her lips. Just what would it be like?

A kiss.

A touch.

A hope of something different.

fifteen

Today the rain was oppressive.

Monti wanted the sunshine on her face, the warm breeze as it blew across her skin, and the feeling of sand between her toes. She smiled at that thought. Maybe she really did need to take that trip with Fallon to Belize sooner rather than later. Rolling her shoulders, she closed her laptop as she stared at the house in front of her.

She'd been parked in Athena's driveway for the better part of two hours, just waiting for their appointment time that day and killing the minutes in between. Since Monti had given up her job and gone on the road, this was the longest she had stayed in any one place. The itch to move was strong, and she had learned over the years that she needed to follow it.

Scratching the back of her head, Monti stretched her legs out on her bed and rolled her shoulders. She had fifteen minutes before she needed to go in. And she was mostly avoiding Fallon. They hadn't rescheduled their lunch date yet, and as much as Monti wanted to spend time with her sister, she didn't want to get caught up in even more of the drama of their family.

Eventually, Monti got out of the van and went inside. She was let in by a staff member who led her straight to the library. Instead of finding Athena there, she found a tray with tea. Frowning, Monti sat down in a wingback chair and steeped her tea bag as she waited. This was odd, even for Athena, who hadn't shown any sign of knowing how to relax or even pause.

Monti rubbed her temple and closed her eyes. Where was that peace again? If she was going to have a few extra minutes, she might as well try a quick meditation. She followed her breathing, the gentle flow in and out of her lungs. She checked in with her entire body from head to toe, and then she stilled.

And waited.

The silence was deafening.

Which was the part she hated the most. She'd grown up with so much silence in her life that she'd become used to it, but those first few years had been loud. She might have been young when her parents died, but she vividly remembered the fights, the arguments, the yelling and thuds of fists being thrown against solid bodies.

She shuddered.

"Monti."

Jerking with a start, Monti looked up into Athena's curious gaze. Athena had her hands folded together in front of her, like she was just as scared of what Monti was capable of in the silence as Monti herself. Shaking her head to clear the memories from it, Monti forced a smile onto her lips.

"Sorry. I was lost in thought."

"Glad to know I'm not the only one who does that."

Monti shrugged and glanced down at her tea, which had no doubt steeped too long. She took it anyway and sipped the no longer hot liquid. Athena sat next to her, making her own tea and holding the mug as she stared out at the window.

Guess they weren't diving headfirst into a massage today.

"Kevin and I got married shortly after it happened."

"Oh?" Monti didn't ask a question. She hadn't expected Athena to just come out with information, but perhaps they had broken the dam that had clogged her up for so long and now everything was going to spill. She was going to have to maintain proper boundaries for Athena then, because it was clear she was struggling with doing it herself.

If last night was anything to go off.

They'd almost kissed. Again.

Or rather, Athena had almost kissed her. Monti just hadn't pulled away. She hadn't moved to put distance between them, but had held that sweet tension firmly. Her heart raced at the memory, because she had wanted to lean in and kiss Athena, see if her kisses were as sharp as her words. Monti doubted they were. In fact, she was willing to bet that Athena's kisses were desperate.

"He's been my best friend since I was five."

Monti smiled at that. Kevin would be the perfect person to marry then. She assumed they were engaged before *the event* as Athena has called it, which would make sense. Sipping her tea again, Monti relaxed into the chair. If Athena wanted to talk today, then that's what they would do. Monti wasn't there to force her into anything or to make her do what Monti wanted. She was there to allow Athena the space for whatever it was she needed.

And if what she needed was to talk, then Monti would listen.

"Kevin left this morning."

"For Simon's birthday?"

"No." Athena slid Monti a look, but it was sharp. It was imploring, as if she expected Monti to be able to figure out what was going on by reading between the lines. Except Athena had once again failed to give her the lines to read between.

It wasn't the first time, and Monti doubted it would be the last. She kept quiet, hoping that Athena would continue on her own. Monti crossed her ankles and stretched them out in front of her. Athena had become quite comfortable since they had started working together, and until she was told otherwise, Monti was going to see that as a success.

"Kevin left to be with his long-term boyfriend, Clayton."

"Oh." Monti halted the cup as she moved it to her lips and stared directly at Athena. "How long have they been together?"

"Eight years, I think." Athena stared into her cup, as though the tea leaves held all the answers to the questions she wasn't willing to ask. "He stays there most of the year."

"And when he's here?"

"It's for appearances."

"Ah." Monti's heart sank, the understanding settling into her chest. "So did this begin as a marriage of convenience or become that?"

Why had she asked that? It wasn't any of her business, not really. Athena and Kevin could live their lives exactly as they wanted. Then again, she was pretty sure that she wasn't asking because of judgment. She was genuinely curious. Just what was their arrangement?

"It's always been that." Athena frowned, as if Monti should have understood that from something she'd said before. "He's my best friend."

"Right," Monti stated, finally clicking with what she'd missed. "So if he has a partner, do you?"

Athena chuckled. "Can you imagine me with a partner? That's amusing."

Ah, the disparaging conversation that Monti had with herself so often. Except Athena's belief of her own brokenness seemed to go even deeper than Monti's. Monti wasn't broken. She just didn't want to break anyone else in the process of living.

"Have you wanted that with someone?"

Athena's breath hitched. She settled her cup onto her thigh, but she didn't raise her gaze to meet Monti's. In fact, she didn't even turn to look at Monti. She held still aside from rubbing her lips together, a clear sign that she was thinking through something.

Finally, Athena whispered, "No."

Monti nodded her understanding. Athena had completely

closed herself off from everything. "Does your marriage work for you? Or do you want something different?"

"It's worked for decades." Athena finally took a sip of her tea, her throat moving as she swallowed. But she immediately relaxed again. "We agreed to this before we got married."

"That doesn't mean it isn't hard to watch him find love."

Athena narrowed her gaze, her fingers tightening on the mug. "I wouldn't want it any other way."

What if this really was working for them? At least as they needed it to for now. Casual relationships were a thing, and they both got something out of the marriage even if it wasn't sex or romantic love. Monti had worked with polycules before and had always been fascinated by their ability and desire for open communication when it came to wants and needs. She'd just never quite felt the pull toward that beyond the communication.

Well, that and the fact that she wouldn't be permanently attached to any one person in particular.

Monti ran her finger along the edge of the mug, listening to Athena's regular breathing. Kevin and Athena must have found their own little way toward happiness. Even if Athena wasn't truly happy or experiencing joy, it wasn't because her marriage was on the rocks.

"We did it for Simon, you know."

"Did what?"

"Got married." Athena toyed with the tea bag, as if she was distracting herself from the conversation. "We needed a child, each of us, to carry on the family name. Why not have a child together?"

"But you said Kevin is gay, right?" Monti reached over and touched Athena's arm lightly.

Athena glanced toward the door to the library. When she saw it was closed, she turned back to Monti. Her cheeks were pale and sunken. Was this *the event* that was haunting her again? Because she seemed comfortable with her marriage.

"He is."

The silence this time was almost palpable. Monti waited for Athena to break it, realizing far too late that she wasn't going to say the words. She wasn't going to spill the last secret that she held.

"How many people know?" Monti held on to Athena's hand, lacing their fingers tightly so Athena would know she was there.

"Two." Athena sounded so small.

"I assume you lied on his birth certificate."

Athena didn't answer, but her lips thinned, and she stilled. That was as much confirmation as Monti needed. Monti stroked her thumb across the back of Athena's hand, using the touch and the repetitive movement to keep the two of them connected.

"You do know that I'm bound by confidentiality. Anything you tell me, I won't share."

"There are ways around that." Athena canted her head to the side. "You just have to know the right lawyer."

"Would that be you?"

"Some days." Athena drank her tea, but she turned her hand, facing their palms together so they truly grasped onto each other.

Monti shivered, her entire body wanted this. Hell, her mind wanted it too. Connection was what every human being craved, and to deny herself that basic need wouldn't do her any good. It would leave her in an unbalanced state.

"Do you think your current case is affecting you?"

Athena chuckled lightly, and the sound sent a thrill though Monti. Her nipples hardened, and with the hand holding, she felt like she was really in a relationship. At least, if she allowed herself that fantasy for a few brief seconds it felt like that. "I wouldn't be a good lawyer if it wasn't."

"Why do you take cases like that?"

"Because they deserve better than what I got."

Monti hummed understanding. "So you think you got shafted."

"Think?" Athena shook her head slowly, her eyes lighting

with mischief. "I know I didn't get justice. If I can help someone else find that, I'll work my ass off for it."

"So now you're a modern-day Robin Hood." Monti used her nail this time instead of the side of her thumb, adding a different sensation. Athena's breath hitched, and her gaze dropped to their joined hands.

"Absolutely not."

Monti was curious about that. How did Athena view herself if not the hero of this part of the story? She was clearly overcompensating for some things, but what did that mean to how she saw her role when it came to her career? Because she didn't have to work, from Monti's understanding.

"I imagine it's similar to why you studied psychology," Athena added.

"Why do you think I studied psychology?" Monti was intrigued now. Rarely did she hear people's opinion on this. They would ask her, but they never blatantly assumed they were correct in whatever assumption they would make.

"Because you're never completely broken and you're never completely fixed. But you always have hope that there's something better out there." Athena locked their gazes together.

Monti's stomach twisted in a knot, her heart racing. How the hell had Athena put that so succinctly? She was right. Without hope, Monti would never be where she was today. She just couldn't figure out where that hope came from. And unfortunately, her hope never led to peace. Which was what she really craved.

"Tell me I'm wrong." Athena looked almost giddy, as if she wanted Monti to confirm just how right she was.

But did Monti really want to do that? Did she want Athena to have that satisfaction? With a sigh, Monti shook her head. "I can't."

"Then we're not so different after all, are we?"

"Somehow, I think we're more similar than either one of us originally thought."

sixteen

"Are you ready to start?" Monti's voice was back to that confident calm that Athena always admired.

They'd spent the day before just talking, and that had been as much a balm to Athena as anything. Athena had never expected that. The talking had been so easy. It was never easy. Athena brushed her fingers against Monti's arm, sliding them up to Monti's shoulder as they stood in the doorway to the library.

Why had touching her become so easy?

Why couldn't she seem to stop doing it?

Athena pressed her lips together and dropped her hand, her finger pads sliding against Monti's hand before she put some distance between them. She hadn't actually answered Monti's question yet, and she knew that holding the silence wasn't going to move them any closer to why they were there.

She knew eventually Monti would ask her again, needing permission before anything else could happen.

But Athena wanted to do things differently today. She wanted to take this a step further than they had before. With renewed vigor, Athena touched Monti's hand again and slid their palms together with a squeeze.

"Yes, I'm ready."

"Good." Monti's cheeks tinged a light pink.

The reaction sent a thrill into Athena's chest. She held onto that sensation, to the closeness, the intimacy.

Athena stopped.

Hard.

Intimacy.

Is that what this was? She let go of Monti's hand and folded her arms across her chest, but she could still feel Monti's warm skin in hers. She could still imagine Monti's skin brushing against her fingertips. Athena shuddered and closed her eyes, her breathing becoming ragged.

What the hell was happening to her?

Athena moved up on her toes before dropping back to her heels. They still hadn't moved from the doorway to the library. They should have moved already, right? Athena stepped toward the door and said nothing as she walked through it with the assumption that Monti would follow her.

When they got to her bedroom, Athena walked straight to her en suite and stripped out of her shoes, socks, jacket, and bra. She caught sight of herself in the mirror and paused. Biting her lip, she looked herself over: her breasts that sagged a little lower than they did a few years ago, the smooth lines of her arms that were littered with freckles.

The shirt hid what was underneath. The scars on her skin that she'd hated to look at. She could picture them if she closed her eyes, but she didn't want to do that. She wanted to have smooth, flawless skin like Monti did. She wanted to be young and carefree again, without all this baggage that weighed her down and made it impossible to do anything.

Today she would do that.

Or at least take one step closer to being the person she wanted to be.

With a steadying breath, Athena stepped out of the bathroom to find Monti had already set everything up. Athena walked silently and stopped in front of the bed and Monti. "I thought today we might do things a little differently."

"Oh?" Monti raised an eyebrow and flitted her fingers over the pillow.

Athena stared down at Monti's hands, that clog in her throat starting again. But she wanted to do this. She really did. She *needed* to become the person who wasn't so afraid of living. "I thought I might take my clothes off today."

When had she decided her pants were included in this?

"Are you sure?" Monti's voice was firm, and her hand was on Athena's upper arm. Warmth. Comfort. Safety.

It was exactly what Athena had needed to answer. She nodded, lifting her gaze to meet Monti's eyes, those deep brown eyes that held so much, so tightly wound. Were they really so different from each other? Athena's scars were just visible. Monti's were so well masked no one would see them if they weren't looking deep enough.

"Yes."

"Okay." Monti smiled, tightening her grasp on Athena's arm before letting go. "I'll get a blanket. Then I'll go to the bathroom while you change, get under the blanket and we'll go from there."

Athena clenched her jaw, expecting anxiety to rear its ugly head in the center of her chest, but it didn't. She felt around for it, waited for it, prepared for it. But it never came. Monti was gone before Athena realized it. Shaking her head, Athena sat on the edge of the mattress and took a moment for herself.

She was really doing this.

She hadn't been willingly naked in front of someone other than a medical professional since she was in her teens. Tears brimmed in her eyes, and she blinked them back. She could do this. She just had to remember that she wanted this. Pulling her shirt off, Athena folded it carefully and set it on the nightstand. The cold air in the room caressed her skin, raising goosebumps along her chest and arms.

Her nipples hardened, pulling to tight little points, but

without clothes or a bra on, she could feel the tightening all the more intensely. Athena slowly let out a breath, raising her hands to her breasts to warm them briefly, the scars such a different texture than the rest of her skin. She hated them.

Cringing, Athena dropped her hands to her waist and stood up. She was sure Monti would be knocking on the door and asking if she was ready at any moment. She pulled off her pants and folded them, setting them on top of the shirt. Athena climbed into the bed, laid on her back, and pulled the sheet and blanket over her chest and up to her chin.

"I'm ready," she called, hoping that Monti would hear her. If they didn't start now, Athena was going to chicken out. She was going to run away and never come back into this room. That or she was going to lock herself in the closet until Monti left.

It seemed like hours before the door to the en suite opened and Monti stepped into the room. But suddenly the entire feel of the room changed. It was warmer than before, and Athena's comfort level eased back to where it had been before when she'd made this decision. Pressing her shoulders into the mattress, Athena stared up and waited for Monti to appear over her.

Monti put a hand on Athena's shoulder. "How are you doing?"

"I'm fine."

"Don't brush it off, Athena."

Athena sighed and held back the cringe. "I'm doing good."

"Are you comfortable?"

"No," Athena answered honestly. "But I am as comfortable as I can be." She pursed her lips, looking up into Monti's eyes. She wasn't lying. Something about Monti's presence comforted her, and she couldn't even explain it.

"If you're ready to begin, I'm going to lower the blanket a bit, just to the top of your chest."

Athena's heart jumped, but she nodded her agreement. Monti waited another second before moving swiftly and pulling the blanket to adjust it. She touched her hand to the top of Athena's shoulder gently.

"I'm going to check in with you as often as possible, okay? If you want me to stop, just say so."

"Okay," Athena whispered.

"You mentioned some scarring before, and I can see the start of it. Have you ever had red light therapy?"

Athena's brain spun. She had no idea what Monti was talking about. Athena bit the inside of her cheek.

"It's just a little red light that I wave over your skin. It'll help heal the scar tissue."

"There's something that can do that?"

"It can help." Monti smiled down at her, her beautiful lips curling up.

Athena's heart thundered. "Then let's do it."

Monti shifted, but she didn't walk away. She grabbed something out of a bag that Athena hadn't even seen on the bed. She must have been so distracted by everything else. She was never this distracted. Watching every move Monti made, Athena waited to see what would happen next.

Monti did exactly as she said, and she waved the light directly over the scars at the top of Athena's chest. But Athena had so many more scars than that, so many that Monti hadn't even begun to see yet. But Monti put the light down and grabbed her oil, rubbing it between her hands.

"I'm proud of you," Monti murmured.

"What?" Athena bit back the word with a moan as Monti dug her thumbs directly into a very stiff muscle in her neck.

"I'm proud. I never thought I'd see the day when you'd do this."

"Do what?" Athena swallowed the lump forming in her throat again and tried to relax. But Monti's gentle words, her firm hands, the smooth glide of her fingers slick against Athena's skin —it all pooled between her legs, stirring Athena in ways she'd started to feel before. But this time it was so much more intense.

Athena focused on it, using it to distract herself from the fact that she was almost completely naked with another woman touching her.

"When you'd willingly start to take off your armor."

Athena tensed, clenching her thighs together when everything was suddenly so hot she almost couldn't stand it. It felt slick and wet. She swallowed hard as Monti continued to work her body, teasing the tension right out of her. Athena's cheeks heated, her chest tightening. Was this really happening now?

"Let's turn you onto your stomach," Monti murmured.

Monti held the blanket at an angle and turned her head away. Athena closed her eyes and flipped over, shifting until she was settled. Monti folded the blanket down to Athena's lower back, tucking the flat sheet into the waistband of her underwear.

Athena waited for the comments. She waited for Monti to say something about the scars like everyone who saw them did. But she was met with silence, then the warmth of what she could only assume was the red light. Eventually it stopped, and Monti's warm hands were on her again. Monti told her everything that she was going to touch and do, checked in multiple times to make sure that Athena was comfortable with it.

When she started on Athena's legs, working up to Athena's thighs, that same hot sensation as before came back instantly. It was a force to be reckoned with. Athena took deep breaths and closed her eyes, trying to figure out what was going on, but she couldn't. Her entire body felt like it was electrified, and every time Monti moved her hands up and then down, that sensation intensified.

Athena struggled to stay still, her hips wiggling each time Monti stroked her.

No.

Not stroked.

That wasn't what this was.

Biting her cheek again to keep everything at bay, Athena clenched her eyes. Monti's movements slowed, and Athena's heart rapped hard against her ribcage, like she couldn't keep any of it in. She was just about to make Monti stop when the sheet was pressed over her skin again. Athena breathed out relief. Maybe they were done and Athena could crawl back into her hole.

"Is everything all right?" Monti's voice was gentle.

Athena lifted up, her elbows under her so she could look up into Monti's eyes. "Yes."

"Why don't you turn over. I'd like to work on your chest again."

Fuck.

Athena clenched her jaw hard. But she did exactly what she was told. Once she was on her back again, Monti shifted a towel to cover Athena's breasts before scooting the blanket off her chest and down to her hips. More exposed than ever, Athena blinked tears again.

"I'm sorry about the scars," Athena whispered.

"Never apologize for something you didn't cause and can't control." Monti sat on the edge of the mattress. "Do you want me to continue?"

"I don't know." Athena clenched her fists.

"All right, then we'll pause here for a minute." Monti scooted onto the bed even more, stretching out so Athena could see her completely. "We'll let you figure this out."

"Figure what out?"

"Whatever put your brakes on."

Athena wrinkled her nose. She'd never been so comfortable naked in front of someone before, her scars on display for everyone who walked in to see. But Athena knew, without a doubt, that Monti wouldn't let anyone come in there.

"I know what it is."

"Want to share?" Monti took Athena's hand, lacing their fingers together and stroking her thumb along the top of Athena's hand. "I'm here to listen."

Athena had to push back that lump in her throat again. She

wanted to know if this was normal, if what she was experiencing would continue. Because the last time…

"Athena," Monti gently prodded.

"I don't know if what I'm feeling is normal." There. The words were out, her uncertainty was there for the whole room to hear.

"All feelings are normal."

Athena rolled her eyes and then closed them, her cheeks heating again with embarrassment. Her nipples hardened even more. Athena crossed her arms to protect herself. Monti moved and skimmed her hand from Athena's elbow to her wrist and back again.

"What are you feeling?"

She couldn't say it. Athena grimaced. This was too embarrassing. She knew what was happening. Deep down in her chest, she knew exactly what her body was telling her, but she wasn't sure she wanted to share that with Monti.

"Anything you say in this room, stays here. Judgment free zone." Monti flashed another smile, and Athena believed her. Monti had never once judged her or any of her odd quirks.

"I'm feeling aroused." Athena whispered the words, unleashing them. She couldn't bring herself to say it any louder.

Monti's eyes widened slightly, her lips parting before she sighed. Her hand stopped its gentle movement on Athena's arm for just a brief moment before picking back up again. "Oh."

"You said…"

"Yeah, I did. It's not impossible or abnormal, Athena." Monti looked at her directly, leaning in.

Athena's heart skipped. Was Monti going to kiss her? Athena had thought about that. The last time they were this close, when the intimacy between them was scorching. Her breath caught in her throat, but the block that was normally there was gone.

"To me it says that you're comfortable with me. Perhaps that you trust me." Monti stopped her gentle motion, curling her fingers around Athena's wrist.

Why did Athena want Monti to hold her wrist like that as Monti pressed her face between Athena's legs? She had to hold back the moan as the image and the sensation flashed through her mind. It had been so long since anyone had done that.

"If you're uncomfortable, we can stop," Monti murmured. "But I'm comfortable with continuing if you'd like."

"I…" Athena paused, her heart racing so much.

"It's rare anything beyond some physical discomfort happens."

Physical discomfort? Did Monti even know what Athena was feeling? The way her labia tingled with imagined touches and licks, how they were damp and desperate for Athena to reach down and just see what they felt like. Or better yet… Monti—

Nope.

Athena sucked in a breath, locking her gaze on Monti's. "And if more does happen?"

"Then that's normal, too. When you feel relaxed and close to someone, when all those walls fall down that you've been holding up, it's normal to feel connected."

"But you're my massage therapist."

"I am." Monti grinned. "Which is why I'm comfortable with continuing if you'd like."

"It's an ethical issue for you," Athena pointed out the obvious.

"Not if you understand our roles."

"I'm a lawyer, Monti. It's an ethical issue."

Monti sighed heavily and squeezed Athena's arm again before letting go. "We can stop if you want. There's no need to argue it."

Athena clenched her jaw. She didn't want to stop. And she didn't like women this way. She never had. Kevin was the gay one. "Let's finish."

Monti grinned, her stunning features lighting up as that moment of joy hit her. Athena relaxed as Monti sat up and adjusted herself again. She started with gently applying pressure to Athena's chest, the muscles that seemed to always be tense beyond her control. As soon as Monti started touching her, though, the same sensations floated through her body.

Athena couldn't stop herself from moving. Her hips wiggled side to side. She stared up into Monti's eyes. She'd been right earlier. Monti had so many secrets to tell. Athena gasped, her entire body lighting with the fire of pleasure. She hadn't expected that. She'd trusted what Monti had told her, that it wouldn't get to this point. But she was so close.

"Monti," Athena murmured, closing her eyes as she arched upward.

"Does that hurt?"

Athena groaned and shook her head. This wasn't pain at all. This was pure unadulterated pleasure. Athena dug her fingers into the sheets, gripping onto them to hold herself as still as she could.

Monti hesitated. Athena could tell. Her hands waited a moment before she started to massage again. A groan ripped from Athena's lips, louder than she'd ever heard herself before. Monti took in a deep breath, the sound loud in Athena's ears. She couldn't concentrate on anything except Monti's body next to hers, the firm feeling of Monti's fingers on her skin, her steady breathing.

"Athena, don't hold back. It's not good to keep everything bottled inside."

She wanted to say something back. She wanted to have Monti's fingers between her legs, her mouth against her, anything. Athena jerked suddenly, gasping. What was she supposed to do with this? But Monti didn't stop. She kept up the slow movements against Athena's body, tenderly pushing her muscles, brushing fingers against skin.

No.

Athena cringed. Monti wasn't doing that to her. That was her mind running away with fantasies that would never happen. She didn't like Monti like that. All of this was because Monti was safe.

She listened. She didn't judge. She showed up when Athena needed her.

Pleasure stole over her in an instant. Athena reached up and clutched Monti's arm, her nails digging into Monti's skin, but she couldn't stop herself. She'd completely lost control. But fuck, this felt so good. Athena clenched her eyes tightly, her breathing so ragged that she couldn't keep up with it. Her head spun.

But Monti was right there.

Gentle fingers running through Athena's hair and over her shoulders. Monti's sweet voice as she spoke words that Athena couldn't hear because the rushing in her ears was too much. Athena's entire body was hot, oversaturated with pleasure.

"Ease your way through it," Monti's voice was a balm again. "Don't worry about anything."

Athena wasn't. The embarrassment didn't show up. The fear was gone. For the first time in as long as she could remember, she was actually relaxed. Athena sucked in a sharp breath, and she pulled Monti's hand against her cheek. Monti's fingers were cool against her clammy skin.

"Thank you," Athena said. She held the quiet tension, but this time it was perfect. It was exactly what it should be. Athena looked up into Monti's eyes. "I'll see you on Monday."

"Oh. Okay." Monti's face fell. She stayed still for another moment before shifting off the mattress. "I'll clean up real quick and let you get dressed."

Athena stayed put while Monti packed up her bag. As soon as Monti was gone, Athena did what she'd longed for since the massage had started. She slid her hand down her body and pressed her fingers between her legs.

Fuck.

This feels amazing.

seventeen

Monti didn't want to go inside.

Whatever had happened during her last session with Athena had been so out of bounds. And yet, the entire weekend, she hadn't been able to stop thinking about it. About *her*. Athena had managed to weasel her way into Monti's life, so that every other thought she had was about Athena and what they would discuss next.

Their visits were typically short, but their connection was so strong. And when they actually talked, not just about whatever Athena was avoiding, but about anything, Athena was flat-out brilliant. And she had a dry sense of humor that Monti was fairly certain most everyone missed. Especially Fallon. Because the one time Monti had made a comment about Athena's humor, Fallon had stared at her like she'd completely lost it.

But she hadn't.

At least not again. She very much had control of her faculties right now. Well, for the most part, because she was still sitting in her van, hiding out in front of Athena's house. She was even early for their scheduled appointment time, and she wasn't sure she wanted to go inside.

She should have booked that flight already.

Or she should have filled up her gas tank and left town.

She'd been there way too long, and the itchiness to leave and explore was eating away at her. But she still couldn't decide where she wanted to go next. It wouldn't be the first time she had left without knowing where she was headed, but for some reason, she was filled with a sense of unease when she thought about it this time.

Which was ridiculous.

She'd done this so many times before that she should just be able to pick up and leave. So why couldn't she? And why couldn't she stop thinking about Athena and the way her face pinched in pleasure, the beautiful flush that rose to her cheeks and chest, the way her body writhed against the mattress. Monti hadn't intended for that to happen.

She'd honestly thought Athena would stop herself before it ever got to that point.

But she had been wrong.

So very fucking wrong.

Slapping down the lid on her computer, Monti heaved a breath of frustration. She really needed to go inside because staying out here wasn't getting her anywhere. She'd broken the rules, and she needed to turn back now. She needed to escape and put boundaries back up between her and Athena.

Yet she found herself walking into the house with her bag in her hand. Rolling her shoulders, Monti stopped in front of the office suite her sister shared with Athena. Not for the first time, Monti was struck by the fact that she wasn't there to see her sister, and she didn't really want to see Fallon. All her thoughts had been on Athena.

"Hey," Monti said in greeting as she stepped inside.

Fallon sighed heavily and nodded toward her. "Hey."

Monti sifted through Fallon's mood, trying to figure out what she was missing. Something was wrong, but Fallon was often moody, especially when it came to something Monti didn't understand. Something Fallon thought she should. But for the life of her, Monti couldn't remember.

"Did I forget something?" Monti asked as delicately as possible. Lay the blame on herself for forgetting whatever it was and hopefully Fallon would forgive her all that much sooner.

"Of course you did." Fallon's voice was full of venom.

And it hurt. Monti tried to shove the sting off, but it was next to impossible. She wanted the fight. Anything that would distract her from thinking about Athena was just what she needed right then.

"Would you stop with the attitude and just tell me what I did this time?" Monti dropped the bag next to her and put her hands on her hips. Her voice was louder than it should be, but at the same time, she couldn't bring herself to care.

"My attitude?" Fallon stood up, her hands flat on her desk as she leaned over it with narrowed eyes. "You don't even have a clue what I'm mad about, do you?"

"Nope. Not one clue." Monti huffed and rolled her eyes. "But you seem to fly off the handle at the littlest thing lately, so what do you expect? Me to be a mind reader? Sorry. No can do. I'm a trained psychologist, not the next Miss Cleo!"

Fallon scoffed. "You're an idiot. Do you know that? You flit around this world like no one gives a shit about you. And then you have the audacity to be mad when we show that we care!"

"Yelling at me is caring?" Monti's shoulders tightened. This was hitting too close to home. "What if I told you that I don't want you to care. I don't want you to even think about me!"

"You don't believe that." Fallon came around the corner of her desk.

Suddenly, Monti felt backed into a corner. She stayed put, but if Fallon were to get too close to her then she wouldn't be able to control herself—not that she was doing a good job of it now anyway. "I do."

"You don't!" Fallon's voice rose. "You can't live without relationships, Monti. You would know that if you'd even pay one minute of attention to your family."

Family.

Right.

That's what this was always about. Fallon wanted Monti to be closer to the family, and Monti had exactly the relationship with everyone that she wanted. Never deeper than necessary. She should have known that Fallon would bring it back to this. They always hit this argument point whenever they were in the same city. Usually it was within a week. Monti had mistakenly thought they'd actually worked through some of the conflict by now and grown into civilized adults.

Apparently, she was wrong on both counts. They were both still idiots.

"You don't need me, Fallon. You've always relied on me to be the center of your world, but give it up already." Monti's tone was low, dangerous. They were about to head straight into the territory that would send them both spiraling, and as much as Monti could see it happening, she didn't want to stop it, either. She needed this fight.

"We all need you!" Fallon nearly screeched. "Why don't you see yourself as part of our family?"

"Because I'm not." Monti threw that out there in a way she'd never said before. "I'm not a part of the family."

"Of course you are."

"No. I'm really not." Monti ran her fingers through her hair and sighed heavily. "You still consider them your parents. I don't. I don't remember them. I remember her, barely, but that's really only from stories you and Tia have told me. They aren't my parents. Tia is my mom."

"Then why don't you call her mom?"

Monti's jaw dropped. She tried to find words to explain it all, but she couldn't. They'd always just called their aunt Tia. Monti had asked once when she was in fourth grade if she could call Tia "mom" and she'd been shot down immediately. But she didn't remember their mom. She didn't believe their mom was in that coffin. She didn't want to visit...

Fuck.

She'd missed the anniversary.

That was what had set Fallon off so much. Monti had completely spaced it, as she normally did, because again, it didn't make a lick of difference in her life. They weren't her family. Softening, Monti tried to come at this from a different direction. If she could just apologize for that—again because this certainly wasn't the first time this had happened—then they could move on.

"I'm sorry I forgot." It was the best Monti could do.

"How can you be so callous?" Fallon's voice was barely above a whisper, but the venom was back.

"I'm not callous. Like I said before. They're not my family. She's not my mom."

"Of course she is!" Fallon yelled. "She gave birth to you. I was there! I was in the room with her when you were born."

"Jesus Christ, Fallon. Everyone knows that damn story by now. Give it up already. You aren't some saint who raised me after she died. You were a kid. Tia raised us." Monti's heart raced, and she glanced toward Athena's office door, which creaked open. Of course she would be in there and not in the library waiting for Monti to arrive. Of course she would witness this disaster that was about to unfold.

"Because I've been there for every part of your life! I will be there for every part moving forward."

"You don't have to be!" Monti shouted back. Her cheeks reddened as embarrassment pulled through her. Athena was going to see everything unfold. The line of ethics was going to be broken even more. Monti should have known this was going to happen, that working with Athena who also worked with Fallon was going to come full circle in a pit of hell at some point. Well, today was the damn day.

"Yes! I do!" Fallon's chest rose and fell sharply, her cheeks red with anger, her eyes wide with fury. "I'll never let you down like they did."

"For fuck's sake, they didn't let me down. It's not like mom chose to die!"

"Fallon," Athena's voice was quiet.

Fallon didn't even hear her as she bulldozed her way to the next point of her argument. "You can't even bring yourself to visit her."

"She's not fucking there!" Monti flung her hands out at her sides, wincing when she saw Athena jerk back in surprise. Fuck, she hadn't meant to trigger Athena in the same moment that she was fighting with her sister. Why couldn't she have just left well enough alone and not taken the bait into an argument?

"How can you say that?" Fallon's eyes teared up. She was about to snap. Monti had seen it happen so many times over the years that she knew exactly where this was headed.

"Fallon." Athena stepped closer, standing right in the middle of them. There was no way Fallon could avoid seeing her now.

"Shit," Fallon mumbled. She brought her hands up to her cheeks and brushed away the tears that freely fell.

Monti wanted to step in and give her a hug, give her the support Fallon needed, but she couldn't bring herself to be that compassionate person right now. Not when all of her wires were crossed and telling her to fire insult after insult until they just blew up and didn't talk for the next six months like normal.

"Take a walk if you need to," Athena suggested. "We can talk when you get back."

Fallon shook her head. "I should really get to—"

"Take a walk, Fallon." Athena's words were sharp and direct, but when she spoke, she was looking directly at Monti.

Fallon pursed her lips, her eyes wide as if Athena had never talked to her like that. Monti knew otherwise, though. Athena could be cruel to her sister, especially when she was stressed. Fallon had told her about it several times over the years.

Monti stayed put as Fallon snagged her jacket from the hook and shoved her arms into it. She was still pissed off. Monti could see that from a mile away, and she knew Athena was no idiot either. Perhaps a walk was exactly what Fallon needed right now. But that would leave Monti alone with Athena, which was exactly what she didn't want right now.

Fallon stalked past Monti, bumping purposely into Monti's shoulder as she headed for the door. Monti cringed but said nothing and barely even moved as she waited for the door to slam behind her. When it didn't happen, she opened her eyes to look directly into Athena's pale blue ones.

Her heart stuttered.

"I guess we all have it in us to be petty."

Monti snorted loudly. She shook her head, her lips curling upward. Raising her hand to her mouth, she tried to hold back her laughter, but she couldn't manage it. Laughing loudly, Monti did the only thing she could think of. She snagged Athena's hand and squeezed it hard before letting go. "Fuck, yes."

"I've never seen Fallon that upset before."

"Clearly you don't know what buttons to push." Monti winked. "Little sisters are the best for that."

"Hmmm." Athena glanced toward Fallon's desk as if she was still sitting there. "I'll have to take your word for that. I don't have a sibling, and since Simon is an only child..." Athena trailed off with a small shrug of her shoulder. "What were you two arguing about?"

Monti sighed heavily. She really didn't want to talk about it, especially not here. Besides, how much of it was her story to tell and how much of it was Fallon's? If Fallon hadn't told her, then Monti didn't want to be the one to break that silence. It would change Athena's view of both of them. And if Monti were the one to share? It would break even more ethical boundaries that really needed to be in place right now.

"It's not important."

"I'm pretty sure you would tell me otherwise if positions were reversed."

Positions.

Athena naked on the bed, staring up at her with complete vulnerability in her eyes before she writhed to orgasm flashed through Monti's mind. She really didn't need that memory to pop back up now. She needed to end this relationship—quickly. Monti needed to move on and find somewhere else to explore immediately.

"Don't like it when the tables are turned?" Athena's tone had a teasing quality to it, one that Monti wasn't used to hearing. Was this woman someone else entirely now?

Monti took a deep breath. How was she supposed to get out of this one? She wished she'd been allowed to follow Fallon. As much as their argument would have continued, it also would have been resolved much more quickly without this break in the action.

"Monti." Athena stepped in closer to her. "Do you want to talk here, in my office, or in my library?"

"Is there a fourth option of not at all?"

Athena grinned. She was so beautiful. Her body so light and carefree in ways Monti hadn't seen her before. This must be who she was beneath all of that stress, and since they'd managed to unload some of it, Monti was finally able to see who Athena really was. Who she wanted to be.

"No," Athena answered, her lips still curled upward. "All feelings matter."

"Fuck you," Monti said with a laugh. On instinct, she threaded their fingers together and stared down at them. When had their lives become so tangled together that she struggled to separate them? Because it wasn't like she was in love. It wasn't like she wanted a relationship. Athena was married.

"Where are we going?" Athena reminded her of the original question.

Giving in to the inevitable, Monti looked into Athena's eyes. She found clear strength reflected back at her, confidence, but also compassion. Monti's breath caught in her throat, and she struggled to form an answer.

"Library."

eighteen

"Is this where the tables turn?" Athena smiled at her question before taking a sip of her tea. Ever since they'd come into the library, Monti had been stunningly quiet. However, she was anything but at peace. Athena could see that a mile away.

"Meaning you become the therapist and I become the unwilling victim?" Monti winked, her lips curled up slightly.

That had to be a good sign, right? Athena chuckled lightly, enjoying this alternative storyline to their acquaintanceship. "I'm not sure I'd call you unwilling."

"I meant you." Monti took her own mug of tea and brought it to her lips. They pursed as she gingerly took a sip, no doubt to test the temperature. Then Monti put the mug on her knee and sighed heavily. "What has Fallon told you?"

"About?"

Monti stared out the window. It was a tactic Athena was quite familiar with. The debate over what to say, the search for the right words. Athena gave her the time, not prompting even though she really wanted to. Resisting her nature was hard.

"About our mother."

"I know she passed when Fallon was young." Athena took another sip, enjoying the way the floral notes blended together.

This was one of her favorites, and she was so glad that's what had been brought when she'd requested it.

"I was two when our mother died. Fallon was nine." Monti spun her cup on her knee carefully, the liquid not sloshing over the side. Still Monti wouldn't look at her.

Was she embarrassed?

How could she be? It wasn't like it was her mother's fault that she died. Or was it? Athena spun through the possibilities, but she'd never looked into it. She'd left Fallon alone when she'd mentioned it.

Monti sighed heavily and rubbed her palm over her forehead. "You can't treat her differently. I know you'll see her differently than before, but if I tell you this, you have to treat her the same."

Athena's lips parted, the rejection of whatever Monti was thinking on the tip of her tongue, but something in Monti's eyes made her stop. There was that carefully guarded pain again. Monti blinked and the spell was broken.

"I'll try my best," Athena answered honestly. "But I assume what you're going to tell me is going to change the way I see her."

Monti grimaced.

"I can tell from your reaction that it will." Athena put her mug down. "Go ahead."

"Fallon and I were raised by Tia, our aunt, after our mother died. I don't remember much from before. You'd have to ask her for details, but I'd suggest not doing that. She doesn't like to talk about it."

"Does anyone like to talk about their trauma?" Athena answered dryly.

Monti smirked. "You might be surprised, but some people do. Or at least they like the release they get afterward."

Athena hadn't thought about it that way before. She'd seen people in the aftermath of trauma so many times. She'd never thought that perhaps it was freeing. She'd only ever seen justice be freeing, and since she'd never had it... Athena snapped back to the room and the moment.

"You're avoiding," Athena mumbled softly.

"I know." Monti gave a wan smile and shook her head. "I don't remember it. But Fallon does, and she expects me to remember it or to be as affected by it as she is. And sometimes I just want to tell her to fuck off, you know?"

"No, not really." Athena furrowed her brow in confusion. Monti still hadn't told her what had happened. In fact, she'd only gotten more vague by the moment.

Monti groaned and dragged her fingers through her hair, ruffling it. She put her mug on the side table between the chairs and leaned down, elbows on knees. Athena pressed her lips together and did the unthinkable. She reached over and trailed her fingers up and down Monti's back. Monti visibly shivered before she shrugged off Athena's touch. Giving up, Athena pressed her hand back into her lap and waited Monti out.

"Our dad killed our mom."

"Oh." The wind rushed from Athena's lungs. She hadn't seen that one coming, and she should have. Monti stayed bent over her legs, hands cupping her face.

"Then he killed himself."

"Monti—I'm so, so—"

"I don't want to hear it." Monti jerked her chin up, shaking her head. She looked Athena directly in the eye. "I don't. I don't remember them. They weren't my parents."

"But it still affects you."

"Not really. What affects me is the fact that Fallon expects it to affect me the same as it does her. And it doesn't. I just don't care. And I don't believe in heaven like she does, so I don't believe I can just talk to them—not that I'd want to anyway. And I don't believe that anything but a shell of her body is in that coffin."

"What do you believe, then?" Athena kept her tone calm, trying to use it to soothe Monti's obvious upset.

"I believe she moved on. I'd like to think she did anyway. That now she's free from an abusive drunken asshole." Monti turned, looking directly into Athena's eyes, and tears streamed down her cheeks. "I believe she found peace." Monti's voice broke on the last word.

Athena's heart shattered right along with her. Monti was just as broken as she was. They hid it in different ways, but they were equally broken—smashed by the realities of the world. "You can tell me all you want that this doesn't affect you, Monti, but you're crying. It might not be the same as Fallon's pain, but it's there. Deep within you. Justice wasn't served."

"It couldn't be." A deep line formed in the center of Monti's forehead. "He killed himself."

"But without that closure—"

"I was two!" Monti's voice rose. Her fingers clenched the side of the chair tightly, turning white from the force.

"Yes, you were." Athena folded her hands together, running her thumb against her palm. "Ten years ago I worked on this case where a young woman had been brutally murdered and the investigation was botched." Athena waved her hand in the air. "The woman had a brother who was five and her mom was pregnant with another on the way. Different dads from the first to the last. It doesn't really matter."

"What's the point, Athena?" Monti's voice was sharp.

"The point is that even though the second brother wasn't born at the time of the murder, he still grew up with the ghost of his sister. There is no getting rid of that pain. It wasn't like his brother's or his mother's. But it was still there. Whether or not you and Fallon have different beliefs about the afterlife, you are two individuals. Each and every person experiences things differently, but our past traumas and the family trauma that we come from affect us even if we don't want it to."

Monti gaped. She stared wide-eyed at Athena for a brief second before shaking her head and letting out a soft chuckle. "Who's the psychologist now?"

"Let's just say, I'm a quick learner."

"Sure." Monti closed her eyes and scratched the back of her head. "Some massage today, huh?"

"This is more important."

"Refereeing arguments between siblings?"

"Learning more about you." Athena said the words before she could stop them. She should have stopped them. Because the look Monti gave her now was pure fear. This was what she'd been afraid of. The last time they'd been in the same room, something had happened. Something that altered the state of their relationship. Athena wasn't sure they would ever be able to go back to the way it was.

She wasn't sure she wanted to.

"I'm sorry. I shouldn't have said that."

"No. No. We do need to talk about *that*."

Monti's emphasis on the last word set Athena on edge. She didn't know what to say. Was she embarrassed? Yes. ...And no. Did she want it to happen again? She wasn't entirely sure about that. But they hadn't talked about it. Athena had avoided that like she normally did.

"We really don't." Athena stood up and walked to the window, abandoning her tea and Monti. She knew it was a defense mechanism, but she couldn't stop herself. She needed space. She needed to avoid Monti.

"We do." Monti was right behind her.

Athena gasped and spun around, nearly coming nose to nose with Monti. Moving from Monti's troubles to Athena's wasn't what she'd planned for this conversation. Hell, they weren't even supposed to be talking. Monti was supposed to be massaging. Athena's heart was in her throat, and it was so difficult to breathe, especially with Monti standing this close to her. But it wasn't a scared fear, not a run-for-her-life fear. This was so different than that.

"I don't want you to be embarrassed about what happened." Monti's words were meant to calm, however they did anything but.

All Athena felt was the same all-over-body warmth that she'd had when Monti was touching her. But not touching her like that. Not like Athena had actually wanted her to. *Damn it.* When had she wanted that? Athena's heart raced. Monti took Athena's hand lightly.

"It happens sometimes," Monti added.

What was she even supposed to say in response? Athena bit the inside of her cheek, something that was becoming a bad habit lately. She broke the touch from Monti and faced the window, crossing her arms and staring out at the forest outside. Fallon was out there walking somewhere. That or she was already back at her desk, working. Probably that. Fallon wasn't someone who would leave the office for long, and Athena had no doubt that she was still upset about the argument.

"You should go talk to Fallon."

"And apologize?" Monti asked.

Athena nodded.

"I will. Don't worry." Monti put her hand on Athena's elbow, cupping it. "Right now, I'm here to talk to you."

"I think we're not doing that today."

"No, we're not having a massage today." Monti stepped in even closer.

Athena's heart doubled its rate. She was sure of it. Because what else was this feeling? She turned her head, lifting her chin and looking directly into Monti's eyes. "You should talk to Fallon."

"We need to talk about the other day." Monti dropped her gaze down to Athena's lips, then moved them back up to her eyes.

What was that?

Athena moved onto her toes. She was getting closer. She needed to stop herself. But she'd never been this comfortable with anyone before. She'd never thought something like this would happen. She closed her eyes, wishing they were anywhere else but here. But if Monti was involved, she was pretty sure they would have ended up here anywhere. They'd almost kissed twice before.

Athena had thought about it so many times in the intervening weeks that she couldn't stop. She didn't want to stop. Groaning, Athena shook her head and faced the window again. "No."

"No?" Monti asked, moving in even closer.

"No." Athena's fingers quivered. Her heart raced. She didn't want to talk about anything. She wanted to escape to her bedroom, away from all of this. She wanted Monti to leave her alone. No, that wasn't right. She wanted to see what it was like. If all those dreams were anywhere close to reality.

"Athena, we need to put some boundaries in place now that—"

"Now that we've crossed them," Athena interrupted. She was sure that's what Monti was going to say. It was what she would say in this situation if the roles were reversed. Athena should be terminating their contract. She should be refusing to hire Monti any longer. But the problem was that in the short time they had known each other, Athena had discovered she couldn't leave. She could demand Monti did, but right now, staring into those deep brown eyes, Athena couldn't find the words.

"Now that we've crossed them," Monti repeated, her voice dropping at the end.

"I don't want to talk about it." Athena tried to make her feet move, but she couldn't do it.

"You haven't told me to leave yet."

Damn Monti for being right.

Athena bit her cheek again. What were they doing here? They'd come to the library to talk, to have it out over the argument that Monti was having with Fallon. And how had they ended up here? Fingers clasped together. Toes inches apart. Athena's heart racing. Her entire body telling her to close the gap.

"Monti," Athena whispered, wishing that Monti would stop whatever was happening. That she would know just how hard this was for Athena.

"Athena," Monti answered, a tease in her tone. Which was the exact opposite of what Athena needed right now. "You say my name in five hundred different ways and each one has a different meaning. Did you know that? I don't know you well enough to decipher them all."

"Fuck," Athena mumbled before moving in. She pressed their mouths together, holding her breath. She kept her eyes closed and waited for her brain to catch back up.

What am I doing?

Monti dropped Athena's hand and slid her fingers behind Athena's neck and dragged her in closer. She backed up for a second before moving in again, this time with her lips pursed as if she was ready for it. Athena hummed, wrapping her arm around Monti's side and splaying her fingers along Monti's back.

Monti's lips parted in an open-mouthed kiss that Athena readily accepted. Her body was right back to where it had been before—on fire, heated, wet, and ramped up. Athena groaned as she flicked her tongue out against Monti's lower lip. She tasted like the tea, a slight bitter note but mostly floral, the hibiscus coming in full force a second later.

Athena was just about to slide in for more when Monti pulled away. She shook her head and put space between them. Suddenly everything they'd done felt wrong. Athena's stomach twisted hard, the hot tea sinking and churning to the point that she wanted to throw up.

"I'm so sorry," Athena whispered, stepping back. "I shouldn't have done that."

"You're a beautiful woman."

"I don't need an easy letdown, Monti." Athena put that wall firmly in place. She couldn't take the usual comments. Not from Monti. Not when everything between them had been so pure and authentic. Not when she was safe, when Monti had never lied to her before.

Monti's lips quirked up slightly, and she pulled Athena back to her. "Not what I was going to say." Monti trailed fingers over Athena's cheek, then her shoulder, down her arm, lacing their fingers together again in a safe way. "You're a beautiful woman, Athena. And yes, it's been hard to resist your beauty. What's on the outside, but also what's in here." Monti lifted her free hand and pressed her palm directly over the center of Athena's chest.

"I'm not fragile. I can stand you telling me no."

"Everyone's fragile." Monti kissed Athena's cheek before she stepped away fully and went back to the chair. She slid into the seat and held her mug of tea like nothing had happened. Like they hadn't just kissed.

Athena stared at her completely in awe. Was this what peace was like?

She'd never experienced it before.

Monti smiled at her. "Your tea is getting cold."

Athena held her breath. She'd just done the unthinkable and Monti wanted to have tea with her? "No. I think we're done for today."

She stepped off the upper level of the library and toward the door. She couldn't even look at Monti. She hadn't been embarrassed before, but now she was. And this feeling wasn't something she wanted.

"See you Thursday?" Monti asked, her lips still curled up in a sexy grin.

Athena stuttered. "Y-yes."

"Good. We can finish talking then."

Panicked, Athena walked right out of the library and back to her office. She passed Fallon on her way inside, shutting the door behind her and leaning against it. She blew out a breath and clenched her eyes shut, lifting her hands to her mouth.

What had she just done?

nineteen

The text was sent, and Monti didn't know what else to do. But she was pretty sure Fallon was already back at her desk, and there was no way she was walking through the halls of the house with Athena on the loose. She needed to clear her head and think about what a fucking idiot she was.

She had kissed her client.

To be fair, Athena had kissed her. But it wasn't like Monti had stopped her. It wasn't even like Monti had tried to break up that first kiss. She'd dove right back in and deepened everything. She'd moved with her heart and not her head. And it had felt amazing.

Monti was so used to being alone on the road that she hadn't realized how much she longed for that particular connection. She hadn't noticed how lonely she really was. But being with Athena was no different than anyone else. Athena was nothing serious. The connection they felt was manufactured by the nature of their relationship.

That's all this was.

At least that's what Monti kept telling herself. When the door opened, Monti jerked with a start. She sighed when Fallon walked in and closed the door behind her. "What the hell did you say to her?"

"Nothing!" Monti was immediately on the defensive. She'd nearly forgotten their fight in the middle of all that had happened with Athena. She really needed to find an exit plan soon because she was messing everything up here. It wouldn't be easy to leave if she stayed much longer.

"You said something. She stormed through there and holed herself up."

"Oh. That." Monti wrinkled her nose, guilt swimming into her belly like it owned the place. "That has nothing to do with our argument."

Fallon narrowed her eyes, judging whether or not Monti was telling the truth. This was almost too much. Monti's head was spinning, and she was longing for that one thing she never seemed to find. Peace. Would she have it if she left right now?

"What the hell did you say to her?" Now Fallon was mad, but it wasn't filled with hurt anymore. She was justifiably angry, even if she didn't know what it was over yet.

Monti sighed heavily and ran her hand through her hair, pulling at the roots. No way in hell was she going to tell Fallon what had happened. "I didn't say anything to her. We rescheduled for Thursday."

"Thursday?" Fallon gave her a disbelieving look and plopped into the chair Athena usually sat in. "I don't believe you."

"I don't know what you want me to tell you." Monti eyed her over.

"Oh my God, you like her!" Fallon's voice raised up sharply.

Monti couldn't lie. Fallon knew her too well and lying would be too hard, and damn it all to hell, Monti didn't want to lie. "She's gorgeous and I'm a lesbian. Can you blame me?"

"She's my boss!"

"I like how that's your go-to objection. Not that she's *my* client." Monti pressed her thumb to her chest. "I understand the boundaries." But did she? "I'm not planning on crossing them." Again. Definitely not again.

Guilt ate away at her stomach even more.

She wanted to. Monti wanted to hear Athena scream her name, and it wasn't until that day that she fully allowed herself to acknowledge it. Those almost kisses—Monti had wanted them. And the one today? It filled her soul.

Fallon narrowed her eyes. "Why don't I believe you?"

"Because you grew up with distrust in your first relationship which causes you to automatically think the worst in everyone."

"Shut up!" Fallon said with a wave of her hand. "I don't want a psych lesson today."

"Good." Monti blew out a breath. "Because I'm all out of them for now."

Fallon fiddled with Athena's half-filled cup on the tray, spinning it around. Oh how they were so similar and yet so very different. Monti had used exactly the same tactic only minutes before with Athena in the room.

"I'm sorry about earlier," Monti mumbled, hoping the change in topic would give her a few more minutes to think.

"About what exactly?" Fallon slid her gaze up to Monti before dropping it again.

"About everything. I'm bad with remembering to begin with, but since I was in town, I should have taken special effort to make sure I didn't forget. And I really shouldn't have gotten so defensive when you confronted me about your feelings."

"Damn straight you shouldn't have." Fallon's tone was angry, but her face said she was teasing.

Monti was glad to see it because she'd needed this easy calm again. "Want to go to the cemetery still?"

"Yeah. Let's go."

"Now?" Monti nearly choked again.

"Sure. Why not?"

"Don't you have to work?"

"I'm pretty sure Athena will give me the afternoon off if I ask for it. Especially if I take you with me, because I'm not convinced something didn't happen yet." Fallon pointed at Monti. "And we have a whole car ride to the cemetery to talk that one over."

"Uh, no we don't. We have two cars here."

"You can drive!" Fallon grinned. "Come on, Sis."

What had she just gotten herself into?

Groaning, Monti dragged herself up. They were in her van before she could find another excuse. The last thing she wanted was to go to an empty grave site. She just had to keep telling herself that this wasn't for her. It was for Fallon.

"So what did you actually say to her?"

"You know I can't tell you that." Monti stared at the road in front of her, trying to remember exactly how to get there. Fallon interjected directions. "She's a client."

"Somehow I don't think what you two were talking about today had anything to do with HIPAA."

Monti clenched her jaw. That had been her best reason to not share and Fallon was already poking holes in it. "I told her about our parents."

"You didn't."

"Well, I figured you had by now, to be fair." Monti took a turn to end up on the highway.

"It never came up."

"You made sure it never came up." Monti knew it was a low blow, but it was the truth. Fallon had avoided that one just like Monti did. They hated talking about their parents, but it was for entirely different reasons. Monti never felt connected and all Fallon felt was grief and confusion. She sighed heavily. "Anyway, so now she knows."

"She's going to research the hell out of that case now. You know that, right?"

"No. Why would I know that?" Monti frowned. Would Athena be sitting at her computer doing that? Would she be looking through the news reports that were on television and in the papers? Would she see Monti's name in there amongst the survivors? The date of the funeral for their mother? The fact that there hadn't been one for their father?

"Because she's obsessive about these things. She's probably going to try and figure out why there wasn't a trial."

"It's obvious why there wasn't one." Monti pinched her face.

"No, I meant why no one sued the cops or the social workers or something like that. She'll want to know everything."

That didn't sit well in Monti's stomach. She'd never considered that there had been other people who could shoulder some of the blame for what had happened. She'd never really asked either. Monti kept her mouth shut as she turned off the highway and toward the cemetery.

When they pulled up by the grave, Fallon still leading the way with practiced directions, Monti parked and sighed. She really didn't want to be here. But she was doing this for Fallon and for their relationship.

The rain was unpleasant, cold and biting against Monti's skin. She walked around the van and followed Fallon's footsteps through the incredibly soggy grass. Her shoes were soaked in seconds, the water already seeping up the edges of her pants to her ankles. That was going to take forever to dry if she even managed it before bed that night.

"Why are there flowers here?" Fallon asked as she stopped in front of the headstone. Her brow was furrowed as she bent down and lifted the bouquet up.

Roses, white and red, were in a spray of greens with small white flowers next to them. Monti should know what they were called, but the name slipped through her mind. The vase was glass and still mostly full of water. Not that that meant anything since this was Seattle and it rained almost constantly this time of year.

Fallon held the bouquet out to Monti. "Did you do this?"

"It took a huge argument and you reminding me the anniversary was this week for me to even remember, and you think I paid to have flowers brought to an empty grave?" Monti pinned Fallon with a disbelieving look.

"You're right. That was stupid." Fallon put the roses back down. "Then who brought them?"

"No clue. Maybe Tia did it."

"Maybe..." Fallon trailed off. "Except she said she hadn't been to visit yet."

"When did you talk to her?"

"Few days ago." Fallon shoved her hands in her pockets.

Monti stood next to her and stared down at the flowers before reading her mother's name. Carla Montgomery. They'd buried her under her maiden name, wanting absolutely nothing to do with their father. Fallon drew in a shuddering breath, and Monti knew what was coming next.

They'd come every year growing up. Monti had started avoiding it as soon as she was old enough to voice her hatred of it, and Tia would let her stay home. Still, Fallon usually managed to drag her down here at least once a year until Fallon had moved out of the house.

Fallon would cry, sob, and she'd probably mumble something like *I love you, Mommy* or *I miss you, Mommy*. Then they would stand there in awkward silence for what felt like an eternity before Fallon would agree to leave after Monti had whined enough.

It was always the same.

Every time.

"I didn't tell her to hurt you." Monti stepped up next to Fallon, not able to tear her gaze away from her mother's grave.

"I know you didn't." Fallon sighed heavily. She grabbed Monti's arm, wrapped her hands around it, and rested her head on Monti's shoulder. "You told her because you like her."

"I told her because we were in the middle of a huge argument. I couldn't really avoid it."

"Sure you could have. You're brilliant at avoiding. You just didn't want to."

Monti held back her retort. Fallon was wrong. She had to be. Because if she was right, that would mean there was way more between her and Athena than there should be. Athena was her client and nothing more.

Except that was a lie.

One of the biggest that Monti had ever told herself.

She backtracked and closed her eyes, listening to her body first and then her emotions. There was definite attraction there. The kiss, while awkward and stymied, had been good. Monti had been the one to stop them because she had to. For so many reasons.

Athena was married.

They had a complicated relationship.

Athena wasn't ready to trust.

Monti would be leaving soon.

Frowning, Monti played over those objections again. The marriage thing hadn't seemed to be an issue for Athena. At all. And if Kevin was allowed extramarital affairs, why wouldn't Athena be?

"Has Athena ever dated someone?"

"What?" Fallon turned on her sharply. "We're at our mother's grave and that's what you want to talk about?"

"Sorry." Monti wrinkled her nose. "Just a thought that popped in my head."

But it wasn't the only one. The complications were only there because of the fact that Athena had hired Monti to do a job. One that was going to create this sense of connection between them. One where Monti was required to provide a safe place for Athena. And yet that entire relationship had been twisted into something else, something that Monti had never allowed before.

Because she was a professional.

She hadn't left the business because she had done something wrong or because a client had. She'd left to find her own sense of peace. Yet here she was, wondering if peace was this elusive thing that might not actually exist. How could she tell clients that they should want to find it if she didn't believe it actually existed in the world? Or perhaps it only existed for them and not her.

Athena was clearly ready to trust. But the question remained whether she would trust knowing that Monti wasn't her therapist or that they were deliberately crossing those ethical lines. Athena should understand the conundrum that put Monti in, shouldn't she? Did she even care about that? She'd seemed truly remorseful when she'd apologized. But Monti had still wanted to feel Athena against her again, the touch of her mouth, the taste of her lips. Their kiss had been nothing but brief. And Monti wanted it to be so much more.

But that left the fact that Monti would be leaving soon. She needed to leave and see if she could find peace. Whatever that was and wherever it was. Because with it, she couldn't do what she wanted to. She couldn't be a therapist. She couldn't help others through their traumas and their hurts. Because if peace didn't exist, what was the point?

"Do you think it'll ever be easy for you?" Monti asked this time, wondering if Fallon even understood what the question was without context.

"Being here?" Fallon responded.

"Living." Monti looked Fallon directly in the eye.

Fallon sighed lightly. She wrapped her arm around Monti's shoulder and pulled her in for a side hug. "I'm not sure living is meant to be easy."

"But do you think you'll ever have peace over what happened?" Monti rephrased, still not quite having the answer she was after.

"I think peace is found in having hope."

"What do you mean by that?" Monti drew in a deep breath of her sister's hair. She worked through the scent of the damp rain, her shampoo, and focused on the base that was Fallon. She remembered Fallon holding her tightly to her chest, hiding in the bottom of the closet. The loud bangs. Fallon as she jerked as each pop echoed through the closet door.

"You have to have hope that it can be different. I think that's all that peace is."

Monti frowned. That didn't seem so hard. It was something Monti had too, so why didn't she feel at peace yet?

Fallon shivered. "Come on. It's fucking freezing out here, and I want coffee."

"Sure thing." They stayed a few more seconds, standing shoulder to shoulder and staring at the stone.

"I miss you, Mommy," Fallon whispered as if Monti couldn't hear her. She blew their mother a kiss and then turned to walk back to the van.

Monti canted her head to the side, reading their mother's name again. She nodded her head to no one but herself and followed Fallon's footsteps. Hope that something could be different. It wasn't that simple. Monti knew it.

But she wanted it to be.

Maybe that's what Athena had found. Maybe she could answer Monti's unasked question. Monti had until Thursday before she could ask. And she had no doubt that she was going to ask it. She and Athena had a lot to talk about, and Monti had a lot to decide. Because that kiss...

It was enough to feed her dreams for days.

twenty

Athena drew in a staggering breath as she waited for Monti to come back into the room. She was already stripped down to her underwear, under the sheet Monti had placed on the bed, and she was waiting.

But she wasn't entirely sure for what.

Monti had seemed off since she'd shown up that day, and Athena had felt just as awkward as soon as Monti had arrived. They hadn't talked about the awkward kiss, about the very obvious ethical lines Athena had forced Monti to cross, about the fact that they probably shouldn't even be doing this today.

But Athena couldn't stop herself.

Pressing her lips together, Athena closed her eyes and tried to steady her racing heart. Monti was going to make her talk today. She'd all but promised it as Athena had left her in the library. They were going to bare their souls again, and all Athena wanted to do was curl up into a ball and pretend the other day hadn't happened.

But she couldn't.

Because the memory of Monti's lips against hers, of the warmth that spread through her body, was too prevalent. Athena couldn't get the sensation off her skin. She couldn't make it go away, and she'd spent far too many hours thinking about it, analyzing it, dreaming about it. She'd been so distracted that it had been a struggle to work again, although not as hard as before.

"Are you ready?"

"Yes," Athena's voice wavered as she answered.

Monti stepped into the room and that warmth was back. It crept up Athena's body from her toes to her crotch to her chest to her neck. But it wasn't oppressive. It was a nice warmth, and she loved the feeling as it wrapped her in its intensity as soon as Monti stood over her.

"Right, so we'll start with your hands today." Monti sounded nervous. It was the first time Athena had ever heard that from her.

She winced, knowing that she was the cause of the discomfort. Not that she was unaccustomed to causing that with clients or a court, but to see it written so clearly on Monti's face when she had done it unintentionally was another thing entirely. Athena waited for Monti to take her hand, her fingers slick with oil.

"We need to talk about the other day," Monti started.

So they were jumping right to it, then. Good. Athena pressed her shoulders into the mattress to ease the tension and awkwardness. "It was inappropriate of me."

"It was." Monti's voice had a singsong quality to it, but she didn't sound mad. "I'm not offended by it, if that's what you're thinking."

It had been, at least a little. That comment eased the tension in Athena's chest a little more.

"I'm actually flattered in a way. It means the work we've been doing has been in the right direction."

What work were they doing? Athena bit her lip, staring over at Monti as she slid her fingers up and down Athena's arm. "Again, I'm sorry."

Monti sighed, but she didn't say anything else.

Athena's defenses started to go up. What was Monti thinking?

Was she trying to figure out a way to end this relationship as much as Athena wasn't? Did she feel forced to be here? Touching her?

"You said you and Kevin were married only for convenience."

"Yes. We come from families where particular kinds of marriages are expected. It was easy for us to make this decision and it's worked well for the last twenty-one years." Athena relaxed when Monti moved away. That was until she shifted onto the mattress, kneeling, and starting on Athena's other arm.

"And you don't mind that he has relationships outside of marriage?"

"No, and he wouldn't mind if I did."

"If you *did*?" Monti flicked her gaze up to meet Athena's. "So you haven't."

Athena pressed her lips together hard. "No. I haven't."

"Have you ever been with a woman?"

"What are the twenty questions for?" Athena pulled her hand away from Monti. That space was so important, because these questions weren't like any that Monti had asked her before. These all had a particular bent to them, and they felt so personal. Which was ironic considering what else they'd talked about.

Monti bit her lip and shook her head sharply before holding her hand out for Athena's again. "I'm sorry. I shouldn't be asking those things."

Athena paused. Her entire body was still on fire. It seemed to be every time Monti touched her, and it was more than just being relaxed. She was turned on and aroused. It was so much more than being safe. If anything, what Athena should have taken away from that awkward kiss was that she was attracted to Monti. So why had it taken her until now to understand that?

Maybe it wasn't understanding she'd needed.

Maybe it was simple acceptance.

Licking her lips, Athena reached out and took Monti's wrist in her hand. She wrapped her fingers around Monti's soft skin and gripped onto her. "Why are you asking?"

Monti's lips parted like she was going to answer, but she

stopped. Athena raised Monti's hand up, bringing it to her mouth. She took a deep steadying breath as she pressed her lips against Monti's knuckles in a tender kiss.

Why did this feel so right?

Athena turned Monti's hand, kissing her palm, the scent of the oil overwhelming her for a moment before she moved to the inside of Monti's wrist. Monti dragged in a staggering breath. "Athena..."

"Why are you asking?" Athena repeated, pressing Monti's palm to her cheek for a brief second before she moved to sit up so they were facing each other. Athena held the blanket against her chest and dropped Monti's hand into her lap. She wanted to see everything Monti wasn't saying, and she needed to be this close to see it properly.

Monti canted her head to the side. She dragged her gaze from their joined hands up Athena's body to her mouth, where she lingered, and then back to her eyes. "I don't stay in one place for long."

"I'm not asking for forever." Athena couldn't believe she'd said that, but she had no doubt that she'd spoken the truth. "I'm married, and I'm not planning on getting a divorce."

Monti's head moved side to side. "You're married."

"Legally, yes. But Kevin and I have never...romantically isn't why we're in a relationship. It's never been that way." Athena traced her fingers over Monti's hand. "I've never been with a woman before. I remember wondering and being curious when I was younger, but after..." Athena drew in a sharp breath to steady herself. She could say this word again. She could name the elephant in her life. "...After I was raped, I was more concerned with other things. I just assumed that I was too broken for anyone."

Tears brimmed in her eyes, and when she met Monti's again, all she saw was pity. That was the look she hated. The one that made her want to turn away and disappear.

"Everyone is broken, Athena. Everyone. We're broken in

different ways, but I want you to remember this. We're never completely broken, and we're never completely fixed."

Athena nodded slightly. "I think I'm starting to believe that now."

"Good." Monti smiled, her eyes lighting up and cheeks flushing. "And I'm asking because I can't stop thinking about the other day."

"You can't?" Athena couldn't stop the smile from lighting up her face.

"But I'm not here for that. You hired me to help you."

"I know," Athena whispered, the breath sucked from her lungs. "I don't want you to think that I expected something different from you, that I expected *this* to happen."

"If anything, it's the opposite." Monti winked and leaned back, stretching her shoulders and back, which jutted her breasts out.

Athena couldn't help but stare. Monti always wore tighter fitting shirts, and the way she was positioned wasn't helping Athena's imagination any. She wanted to move forward and touch, caress, tease. But she held herself still, moving her gaze up finally. Monti was laughing at her.

"Did we break the glass so now it's impossible to hide feelings anymore?"

"Perhaps," Athena answered with a sigh. She wasn't doing a good job at holding back. Because she didn't want to. Smiling freely at the realization, Athena touched Monti's knee in a small challenge to herself. "Maybe I just don't see the point."

"Oh, are you a forward lover?" Monti teased lightly.

"The possibilities are endless." It was the easiest way to get out of answering the question, because Athena didn't know if she was a forward or a timid lover. It had been so long since she'd allowed anyone to get this close. "What about you?"

"What about me?"

"Are you a forward lover?"

Monti hummed, this time purposely dragging her gaze all over

Athena's body. The difference was stunningly sharp. Athena's entire body was on fire just from that one simple look, and she wanted Monti's fingers to follow the same path. To touch. To tease. To soothe.

"I love to take control," Monti finally answered, her voice raspy. "I don't suppose you like to give it up."

Athena had no doubt that their previous conversations led to that conclusion. Was that why she was being so forward now? Was that why she wanted to pick Monti's hand up and press it to her breast, show Monti how to tease her nipple? Athena held back her moan, but barely.

"What are you thinking about right now?" Monti's voice was soft, a balm again. As if Athena could say anything and there would be no judgment. Monti had proven that time and time again to be true. Why would today be any different?

With her heart in her throat, Athena did exactly as she imagined. She wrapped her fingers around Monti's long, slick ones and started to lift her hand. "Let me show you." Athena dropped the sheet she held against her chest and pressed Monti's palm directly against her. She used her thumb against Monti's and moved it in slow circles against her already peaked nipple.

The rush that went through her was a thrill she'd never felt before. Every single swipe of Monti's rough thumb sent shockwaves of pleasure through her, ending right between her legs. Athena removed her fingers from Monti's hand, glad when Monti took over the tender motion on her own. She danced her fingers up Monti's arm to her shoulder and back down again.

"Are you sure?" Monti asked. "Because we shouldn't be doing this."

"I understand the rules we're breaking." Another thrill ran through her. Was that what part of this was? Breaking the rules was erotic. Athena had lived according to the expectations of others her entire life, and here she was, breaking every single one of them. "I want you to touch me."

Athena could see the moment Monti gave in, the switch that

flipped and made her completely okay with whatever was happening. Athena had seen that look on so many faces before in courtrooms. But seeing it here, in the intimacy of her bedroom, when they were talking about sex and pleasure, an entirely different sense of satisfaction ran through her.

Their mouths touched. This kiss wasn't unexpected, not like their first one. Athena leaned into it fully, the pressure of Monti's lips against hers warm and inviting. Monti's tongue was slow as she peeked it between her lips before exploring. Athena moaned and cupped Monti's cheek, keeping her as close as possible.

Athena sank into the embrace, losing herself in it and creating new memories to draw back on. She slid her hand through Monti's soft hair, tugging lightly to see what kind of reaction she could get. The growl was so welcome, and it sent another thrill through her. Monti shifted closer, sliding her hand from Athena's breast to around her back and pulling Athena in toward her.

Moving up onto her knees, Athena changed the angle on everything. It was awkward and odd as she walked on her knees on the mattress until she could straddle Monti's lap. She was higher now, more in control, and she loved this feeling. She slid her hands through Monti's hair, as they continued to kiss.

Athena was completely bare except for her underwear, pressed into Monti's body, and she didn't even care. Monti touched her, fingers dragging from Athena's upper back to her lower back, her hips, her ass. She squeezed. Heat rushed through Athena, an inferno burning so hot that she wasn't sure she could control it. She was certain it was about to consume her.

"Stop," Athena mumbled. Her heart was racing so fast that she couldn't keep up. She pressed her forehead into Monti's shoulder, clinging on for what felt like dear life. She clutched her hands to Monti's upper arms and clenched her eyes shut. "Stop."

Monti barely moved. She held Athena, her fingers making circle patterns against Athena's back. Focusing on that, on the way the circles didn't change, on the pressure of Monti's hands against her, Athena took deep steadying breaths.

"You've got this," Monti whispered into her ear. "You're in charge."

Why was this so much easier when she was by herself? Touching herself was one thing, but Athena didn't understand why adding another person into the mix made it damn near impossible for her to fully relax and let go.

"We're not doing anything you don't want to. I promise you."

Athena whimpered and clenched her eyes closed a bit more. She kissed Monti's hot neck, then her cheek, then her lips, but she kept the touch brief. "I don't know why this is so hard. Masturbating is so easy." God, why had she said that?

"Are you masturbating?" Monti asked, but again, there was no judgment in her voice.

"Yes."

Monti smiled and leaned back slightly to look Athena in the eye. "Masturbating is easy because it's trusting just yourself. Which I'm glad to see you're doing. That's the first step." Monti palmed Athena's thighs, her thumbs moving back and forth just below the crease of Athena's hip. "Sex is trusting someone else, and that's a hell of a lot harder."

"Oh."

"Yes, oh." Monti brushed a strand of hair behind Athena's ear. "We'll never do anything you don't want to do."

"But I'm sure you're ready—"

"Even if I am, masturbation is a thing for a reason." Monti lay on the bed, her hair fluttering as she landed. "And if you'll let me, I'd love to masturbate to memories and fantasies of this and beyond. But if you don't want me to, I'll choose something else."

Athena paused. No one had ever asked her that. She'd never even thought about it. "You want to masturbate to me?"

"Of course." Monti grinned broadly. "I wasn't lying the other day when I said you're beautiful. You're fucking hot."

Athena laughed lightly. "I don't understand you." She bent down on all fours and pressed a kiss to Monti's lips. This felt right.

"We don't know each other," Monti murmured against her mouth. "Who knows if we'll ever have the time to properly get to know each other."

"Come to the Keys with me."

"What?" Monti stiffened.

Athena lay next to Monti, covering herself with the blanket before she scooted against Monti's side and relaxed. "I always take a trip before I have to start a trial. I have one coming up in the next couple months and I need a week or two of respite before the real work begins."

"You want me to go with you?"

"Yes." Athena slid her hand along Monti's stomach and then inched her way up slightly. She wanted to touch Monti's breasts, see how soft they were, if Monti's nipples were as hard as hers, but she hesitated and then lost her gumption.

"Am I going as your masseuse, your therapist, or..." Monti trailed off.

Ah. That was the real issue, wasn't it? They had no clue what was going on between them anymore. Athena picked through the options carefully, choosing the most open-ended answer she could give. "Come as someone I want to get to know better, and as someone whose company I enjoy."

"What does that mean?"

"It means whatever we want it to mean." Athena stayed still, waiting for Monti's answer. "You said you were thinking of leaving soon. Think of this as a free way to explore somewhere new."

"I've been to the Florida Keys before."

"Of course you have." Athena smiled, not quite sure she wanted to look into Monti's eyes.

But Monti didn't give her a choice. She raised Athena's chin with a finger until their gazes locked. "You realize I can't play the role of your therapist now, right?"

"Did you ever?"

"Yes." Monti gave her a firm look. "Yes, I did."

"It's not what I hired you for."

"It's not." Monti bit her lip. "But I'm making it thoroughly clear now that our relationship can't be that anymore."

"I understand."

"Good."

Monti slid in and pressed their lips together. She deepened the embrace, and Athena allowed it. Athena moved her tongue against Monti's, moaning when Monti nipped at her lower lip and held the back of her neck. Athena could stay like this for hours. Something about being in Monti's arms was so comfortable.

"I'll go to the Keys with you."

Athena grinned. "Perfect."

"But for now, what are we doing?" Monti traced one finger down Athena's cheek to her neck. "Am I leaving?"

"Only if you want to. I'd love to stay here for a while longer." Athena kissed Monti again. "If you're amenable to that."

"Seems I have the time."

twenty-one

"Did you have sex with her?"

"Oh my God. What?" Monti froze in her tracks as soon as she walked into Athena's house.

"She's taking you on her trip. Did you have sex with her?" Fallon crossed her arms and stood up on her toes, trying to make herself taller than Monti, but that hadn't worked since Monti was sixteen.

"I didn't have sex with her." Monti ducked her chin, because it had been damn close. And if Athena hadn't stopped them, she would have. She would gladly have sunk between Athena's legs and not stopped until they both came.

"That look. Right there." Fallon pointed at her sharply. "What's that look?"

"It's nothing." Monti tried to push past Fallon so she could walk to Athena's office. Their flight was in a few hours, and the car was supposed to pick them up here. Athena had told Monti she could leave her van at the house while they were gone.

Fallon snorted. "You said the same thing when I caught you with a hickey on your neck after a night out with Rosie Gruber."

"Jesus," Monti muttered and shook her head. "Athena is a client. There's nothing—"

"Even though it's been twenty years since your night with Rosie, you're still a shit liar." Fallon grabbed Monti's arm and dragged her toward the library, slamming the door shut. "What happened?"

Monti sighed heavily and dropped her duffel bag on the floor. "You know I can't talk to you about anything."

"Bullshit. You like her, and you can talk to me about that." Fallon poked a finger into Monti's shoulder. "You're falling for your client."

Monti groaned. She sighed heavily and tugged on her hair sharply. "It's unethical."

"It is." Fallon crossed her arms, eyeing Monti over thoroughly. "Why is she taking you to Florida?"

"I don't know. She asked, and I needed to get out of here, and it was a way to escape."

"Escape?" Fallon's voice cracked. "What could you possibly need to escape?"

Monti couldn't say *you*. That would send Fallon into another spin. That was the last thing Monti needed before leaving for two weeks. She dragged in a sharp breath and blew it out. She was going to have to walk a very careful line on this one.

"I need to move on. I've been here long enough. This was a way to do that. I'll come back and get the van in a few weeks and head north for a bit." Monti rubbed her thumb against her finger pads, hoping her reasoning was going to work out for the best. "It's really for the best. I mean, we've had our big blow up. It's time to leave before we have the next one."

Fallon narrowed her eyes, canting her head. Fear ratcheted up a notch in Monti's stomach. Were they about to have another fight? Because she wasn't sure she could handle that and then leave the state.

"When will you ever believe that I want you here?"

"Fallon," Monti said with a whine. She had no response to that. She couldn't even figure out what to say. It had nothing to do with Fallon wanting her there or not. It had everything to do with finding her peace.

"Why do you hate me?"

"I don't hate you!" Monti wrapped her arms around Fallon's shoulders and pulled her in for a hug. "Oh God, I don't hate you at all."

Monti didn't want to let go. They'd never been close. But that didn't mean they had to be distant either. Monti had thought all this time that she was trying to put distance between them so it was easier on Fallon, but maybe she'd been wrong the whole time.

"Why won't you stay?" Fallon mumbled into her shoulder.

"I'm not someone who stays in one place. I'm just not." How was she supposed to explain to her sister that she was on a quest for peace? She'd tried so many times and never managed it. "You know that."

"I know." Fallon moved back and wiped her cheeks. "I just miss you when you're gone."

This had been what Monti wanted to avoid. She'd managed it with everyone else except Fallon. Her sister had always had some kind of unhealthy attachment to her. "I'll be back."

"You don't know that."

"I'll be back in two weeks." Monti straightened her back. "I promise."

"Fine." Fallon gave her a hard stare. "I'm still not convinced that you two aren't sleeping together."

"Oh my God. She's *married.*"

Fallon snorted. "You say that like I'm an idiot. I've seen the way she looks at you. And I think she's called you more in the last month than she's called me ever. Definitely more than she's called Mr. Brock."

"You work for her. Why would she call you outside of the job?" Immediately Monti knew she'd said something wrong. The look in Fallon's eyes was too gleeful, too self-serving, too excited.

"I knew it!" Fallon shouted. "You *are* sleeping with her!"

"I'm not!" Monti clenched her fist and glanced at the door to the library. "I swear we haven't had sex. But if you don't let me get to the office, I'm going to be late, and we know the fit of rage she'll have if I'm late and we miss our flight."

"If you haven't had sex...yet...then you *want* to."

Monti pressed her lips together hard. They rarely talked like this. But something in Monti told her this was the time to confide, the time to lean into that sisterly bond they had. "We've kissed, yes. But I don't..." Monti paused, again trying to find the right words. "I don't know if anything will happen. Something just doesn't feel right."

"Feel right?" Fallon checked her watch. "We have ten minutes."

Fallon dragged Monti into the library and pointed at the chairs in a command.

Giving in, Monti sat in the chair she'd unofficially claimed as hers. Fallon took the other one. Where was this going? Was Fallon going to divulge everything Monti had been waiting for? Did she even know? Based on what Athena had told her, no one knew.

"Look, our parents fucked us up."

"What?" Monti jerked her head back. She hadn't been expecting that twist.

"They did. You can deny that they affected you until you turn blue, but the fact is, they fucked us up. Dad by killing mom and then himself. Mom because she stayed with him too long, but then I guess we wouldn't have you and that would be a tragedy."

"Where are you going with this?" Monti curled her fingers around the edge of the chair, clinging onto it for dear life. She'd been down this road so many times, and she really didn't want to go down it again.

"They fucked us up. What if the reason it doesn't feel right is because you were born into the worst kind of wrong?"

"I don't want to psychoanalyze my own life any more than I already have." Monti put her hands on her knees and prepared to stand up and leave. She didn't have time for this conversation. "Mom made some bad choices in her life. We can't go back in time and change those. But I don't remember what it was like in that house."

"Our bodies have memories. Aren't you the one who told me that?"

Monti scrunched her nose. She had told Fallon that. And she'd believed it at one point too, but she'd never managed to remember anything specific. No matter how many types of therapy she tried, it just wasn't there. "That is true."

"So you remember some of it, whether you remember it up here or not." Fallon pointed to her temple. "Maybe that's why this doesn't feel right."

"What doesn't feel right?"

"You and Athena."

"I don't think that's it." Monti rubbed her thighs, all her nervous habits coming back. She thought she'd gotten rid of those. "She hired me for a job, and I'm here to do that job."

"By going to Florida with her?"

Monti shrugged. "I go where I want to, and sometimes that's where the work is."

"Give me a break." Fallon rolled her eyes. "Am I happy you're interested in my boss? No. But I'm not going to stop you either. You both deserve a little bit of freedom from the oppression you seem to live under."

"What do you mean by that?" Monti's chest tightened. What the hell was Fallon getting at? This conversation was taking all sorts of odd twists and turns.

"Do you really not see how similar you two are?" Fallon raised an eyebrow. "I can't believe you."

"What do you mean *similar*?"

"You really don't, do you? You both avoid your feelings with the best of them. You shut down at any sign of emotion. You refuse to admit you need help. You run away from your problems. You both have hearts of ice."

"I do not." Monti rolled her eyes and stood up, walking to the window. Was there any truth to that? She'd spent hours with

Athena and she'd thought they were alike, but not to that extreme. Monti cursed. Damn Fallon for being right. She sighed heavily and turned back around. "What the hell do I do about it?"

"It looks like you're handling it well."

"Handling what well?"

"Being cracked open." Fallon stood, swaying her hips saucily as she followed Monti's path toward the window. "Or maybe the better metaphor is your ice is being chipped away one sliver at a time."

"What ice?"

"The ice you put around your heart."

"I'm a trained therapist. All I do is help people and have compassion for their plights. I'm not made of ice."

"Sure you aren't." Fallon grinned cockily. "You let us mere mortals play around in the shallows, but no one ever gets to the deep. Maybe my boss has the stamina to make it there."

Monti scoffed. "You're really full of yourself right now."

"And you are in like."

"I'm attracted to a beautiful woman, yes. I'll admit that."

"You kissed her."

Putting her finger up in the air, Monti locked her eyes on Fallon's. "To be fair, she kissed me. Twice."

"Twice?"

Monti shrugged. She really didn't want to fight that one because she'd wanted more kisses. She longed for more touches. That deepening of a relationship would be so nice right now. Maybe the world wouldn't seem so lonely then.

"Oh, you're thinking about it!" Fallon teased.

Monti really didn't want to talk about it right now. She shoved her hands into her pockets and gave Fallon a serious look. "Your ten minutes are up."

"Fine, fine. I hear you. But just listen to me on this, okay?"

Monti waited, and when Fallon didn't continue, she pushed. "And...?"

"Athena has to be handled carefully. I don't want you to screw this up."

"Because you'll lose your job?"

"No, she's not that kind of witch." Fallon put her hands on her hips. "I don't know what's been happening this year, but something's been off with her for months. And it wasn't until these last few weeks that she's seemed more herself. The only difference is you."

"It's not me who's making the difference." It was all the work that Athena was doing, the processing, the thinking, the sharing. Monti was willing to bet that she hadn't done that in twenty-two years, which meant telling even one person in a safe environment was a weight off her shoulders. It wasn't because of Monti. It was because Athena was finally willing to let go. But it wasn't like Monti could tell Fallon that. She would never betray Athena's secrets.

"Well, I think it is. Just be careful. I don't want you to love her and leave her. Wait, that wasn't quite the way I wanted it to come out." Fallon pressed her lips together hard. "I don't want her to be as devastated when you leave as I am."

Monti's heart broke a little. She hated that Fallon felt that way. If they weren't so close, if Fallon wasn't so attached to her, it wouldn't be that bad every time. Monti held her breath for a minute before she blew it out. "I won't love her and leave her, as you so *eloquently* put it."

"Good." Fallon smiled. "Then I guess I shouldn't tell you that you're late."

Monti looked at her watch and cursed. "Damn you."

Giggling, Fallon waved as Monti raced to grab her bag and leave the library. She was so throwing Fallon under the bus for this one.

twenty-two

"I hope you and Fallon have worked your argument out." Athena had no idea where to start a conversation, but considering they had barely spoken since leaving the house and arriving at the airport, she had to start somewhere. Monti seemed distracted in a way Athena had never seen her before. She'd always been focused.

"We always do," Monti mumbled as she shifted in her seat on the plane. They'd been in the air for twenty minutes, finally flying smoothly after takeoff.

"Good." Athena looked across Monti to the window. She hated sitting next to the window. It was always cold and cramped there. Though now she could probably identify that it was because it was confining and not as easy an escape if she needed to run. Thankfully, Monti hadn't minded switching seats since Fallon had forgotten Athena's preferred placement.

They sat in silence for another five minutes, during which Athena checked her watch several times. Monti barely moved, staring at the back of the seat in front of her as if it held the world's most interesting book.

"Have you read Bristol Flyte's newest book?"

"I'm sorry, what?" Monti shook her head, blinking wildly as she tried to catch her bearings.

Athena sighed. "What did I say?"

"Something about a book." Monti frowned.

"No. That's not what I meant." Athena folded her hands together in her lap. "If this is about the other night, when I invited you, I hope you didn't feel obligated to come with me."

"Obli..." A deep line formed in the center of Monti's forehead. "No, I didn't feel obligated. Why would you think that?"

"You've been..." Athena waved her hand over Monti as if indicating something, but she struggled to put a word to it. "...distant."

It was the best she could come up with.

"Oh. That." Monti reached over and took Athena's hand, setting it in her lap as she covered it. "How much does Fallon know about your relationship with Kevin?"

"As much as she needs to know." Athena pushed her shoulders into her seat, the odd turn of the conversation putting her more on edge than she'd been before.

"Does she know about Kevin's partner?"

"No."

"Does she know about why you two are married?"

"Why would she need to know that?" Athena winced at her tone. It was so sharp. She hadn't meant to come off as so defensive, but she could barely hold herself together right now. Monti was prying in ways she didn't need to. How many times could Athena explain this? It wasn't the norm in society, but it wasn't unheard of either.

"I'm asking because of something she said. Well, something she asked me." Monti trailed one hand up and down Athena's arm, still gripping her fingers with the other. "I'm not explaining this well, I'm sorry. Fallon asked if we'd had sex."

Athena's lips parted, but no words left them. She stared wide-eyed at Monti, her brain already spinning in a thousand ways. She hadn't talked to Kevin yet. She'd meant to, but the thought of even starting that conversation had her blood running cold. They'd agreed to have those conversations before any relationship, and as far as she knew, Kevin had honored it. But for Fallon to know...

"She's my big sister, Athena, and as much as I would love to hide things from her, sometimes she can read my subtleties."

"I don't understand."

"She's not stupid when it comes to me being attracted to women and particularly what type of women I like. She made the leap before I did."

"Before you did." Athena bit the inside of her cheek, her stomach twisting in knots. This wasn't how she'd wanted the conversation on the plane to go. She wanted to escape immediately, but she was stuck on a plane somewhere between Seattle and Dallas. "If you don't want this—"

"I do. Athena, I promise you I do. I wouldn't be here if I didn't." Monti lifted Athena's hand to her lips and pressed a delicate kiss to her knuckles. "I told you about how our parents died, but what I didn't really talk about was Fallon. She fancied herself as a substitute mother to me, as much as I despised it."

Athena could see that. Monti would hate being coddled, and Fallon would want nothing but to coddle. Fallon was such a mother hen, even when it involved Athena. She should have realized that Fallon would have picked up on the nuances of her marriage with Kevin. Fallon had been there nearly every day for years, and while she and Kevin were familiar, it was clear to anyone who had insight that they weren't romantic.

"Fallon cornered me in the library today. That's why I was late."

"Cornered you?" Athena faced Monti, quickly dropping her gaze to their still-joined hands. This felt so good. Yet the conversation was tense and confusing. She couldn't follow the logical path that Monti was taking.

"She wanted to know if we'd had sex." Monti tightened her grasp on Athena's hand. "Normally, if it was anyone else, I'd avoid telling them anything. But she's my sister."

"And she's my personal assistant."

"Yes." Monti kissed Athena's knuckles again. "And I told her that we'd kissed a few times."

"I don't understand why you're telling me this." Athena hated that she was suddenly so tense. Was this the breakup? Was this Monti realizing what they were doing wasn't for her? Did Fallon convince Monti to run the opposite direction?

"Because Fallon had a point to make, and I think it's a valid one."

"That we shouldn't be kissing because I'm a married woman?" Athena gritted her teeth. She kept waiting for the other shoe to drop, and it was finally time for that to happen.

"No. No, she didn't even mention that." Monti waited until Athena looked into her eyes before continuing. "I'm trusting that you're telling me the truth about your relationship with Kevin. You've never lied to me. Why would you lie about that?"

"Because I've lied about it for over twenty years," Athena whispered.

"Have you? Or did you simply bend the truth to suit the situation?"

Athena wanted to argue. But when she thought about it that way, she hadn't lied. She did love Kevin. Just not the way most people thought she did. He was her best friend, and he had been the best support she'd ever had. "You might be right about that one."

"Trust me that I am." Monti smiled, a lightness to her face that she hadn't had all day. "I have a degree or two for a reason."

Athena chuckled lightly. "What did Fallon notice?"

"Oh, that we're not all that different from each other." Monti kissed Athena's knuckles again. This time, however, Athena turned her hand and presented Monti her wrist. Just what would Monti do with that offering? Monti lifted an eyebrow, made eye contact, and then lowered her lips again, pressing them delicately against Athena's skin.

Athena drew in a raspy breath, her heart skipping a beat or two. "How are we the same?"

"We both run from tough emotions."

"You're a therapist," Athena commented.

"Which is a really convenient way to talk about someone else and not myself." Monti kissed Athena's wrist again.

Athena's breath caught in her throat. She wavered on what to pay attention to—Monti's mouth against her skin, or the words she was saying. The words whose impact Athena was avoiding through distraction. "So what are you not telling me?"

"I'm on a journey to find peace."

Monti kissed again, this time against the fabric of Athena's jacket. But Athena swore that she could feel it on her skin. That Monti's lips were really touching her. She held her breath, wishing they weren't on a plane full of people, that it was possible to find somewhere a bit more private.

"It's a long journey because I haven't made very much progress." Monti kissed her again, this time on the inside of her elbow. "I was in the middle of a therapy session when I figured it out, when I realized that I shouldn't be a therapist until I'd done the work myself. Unfortunately, and I think you'll agree with this, old habits die hard."

"Mmm...yes." Athena was completely enraptured with Monti's mouth, the way she moved, the soft and tender touches. She tried to focus on what she was saying, but it was so hard.

"So I've continued to avoid the real problem." Monti kissed her shoulder.

Athena slid in closer, wanting desperately for Monti to continue right on up. Her body was warm, ready for the touches, for the caresses. "What's the real problem?"

"I might not remember my parents, at least not very well. But my body remembers them. My body holds the arguments, the violence, the chaos that I was born into." She kissed Athena's neck, her lips so hot against Athena's skin that it felt almost like she was burned.

Athena whimpered and tilted her head ever so slightly to give Monti more access. Because she wanted more. She wanted to feel everything that Monti was offering, not just the touches and the kisses, the pleasure. She craved that peace.

"If I want to find peace..." Monti kissed her chin. "Then I can't avoid what happened any longer."

"S-some conversation." Athena swallowed hard, facing Monti. "Seems Fallon has a way with words like you do."

"Big sisters are useful for some things, aren't they?"

"Fallon is very useful." Athena dropped her gaze to Monti's mouth, from the gentle rise of her upper lip to the bottom curve of her lower one. Monti's pink tongue peeked right at the edge of her mouth before disappearing again. Before she knew what she was doing, Athena leaned in and captured Monti's mouth in a generous kiss.

Monti wrapped her fingers around Athena's neck, pulling her in closer and deepening the embrace. This time they were on even footing. Athena leaned over the armrest, cursing the seatbelt that pushed against her hips and forced her to stay put. She nipped Monti's lower lip and then slid her tongue across the slight injury to soothe it.

The sound of a throat clearing caused Athena to jerk back. But when she finally got the courage to look, no one was there, or at least whoever had interrupted them was back to doing whatever they were doing before. The two businessmen across the aisle from them didn't seem to pay them a lick of attention. Athena shifted in her seat, her underwear damp and her skin flushed. She'd never wanted to take her jacket off more than she did at that moment.

"We're both in prisons of our own making," Monti finally said, settling back into her seat with Athena's hand in hers again. "Your house is yours. The lack of a house is mine."

"I suppose," Athena murmured, her brain struggling to catch up.

"You don't think you hide away in your house?"

"My house is safe," Athena answered honestly.

"Sometimes it's necessary to take risks." Monti kissed Athena's knuckles.

Would Monti start the same path back up to her neck again? Athena would love that. The kiss against her wrist brought back the memories from moments before. A flush washed through her, and Athena smiled.

"What risk are you taking?"

"Many." Monti winked and kissed Athena's forearm, over the cloth of her jacket again. So they were playing this game. The real question was whether or not Athena could wait for the inevitable or if she wanted to skip straight to the good parts. "Did you know that Monti isn't my real name?"

"What?" Athena blinked hard, suddenly tossed straight back into reality.

"Fallon's always called me that, ever since our parents died. Dad named me after his mother. No one wanted to be reminded of who we were related to. So they started calling me Monti after Mom. Her maiden name was Montgomery." Monti kissed Athena's shoulder and then her neck.

"So are you avoiding or are they avoiding for you?"

"Astute question, young grasshopper." Monti's tongue dashed across Athena's neck, flicking against her skin.

Athena gasped, curling her fingers into Monti's hand and tightening her grasp sharply. Moving in, Athena kissed her quickly before pulling back and remembering the clearing of the throat from before. She didn't want to experience that again. "Monti..."

"Five hundred and one ways to say my name. What does that one mean?" Monti scraped her teeth across Athena's skin.

Athena bit back the groan, closing her eyes as her underwear was nearly soaked through already. If Monti continued this, she'd have yet another orgasm without being touched. And fuck, she wanted Monti to touch her this time. There was no doubt in her mind about it now.

"It's a warning," Athena answered, meaning her tone to be sharp and commanding. Instead it came out breathy, and she barely held back a second groan.

"A warning or a siren's call?"

"Damn it, Monti," Athena muttered and kissed her quickly. "We still have to get to Florida."

"I thought the vacation had already started." Monti's grin was outright cocky. "No one here knows who we are. Why are you so concerned about what they think?"

Why was she? All Athena had done her entire life was try to live up to the expectations that were placed on her. Since the moment she was born, people expected her to be someone, and she'd lived those prescribed roles with every breath she had.

But Monti had none.

No, that wasn't true.

Monti expected her to be no one but herself. Free. Authentic. Pure. Honest. Staring into Monti's eyes now, all she saw reflected back at her was curiosity and gentleness. Athena had gone to school, she'd gotten married, she'd had a child—everything she had done was to fulfill someone else's expectations.

But what expectations did she have?

What did she want?

In that moment, she could only come up with one answer. Pulling Monti forward by the back of the neck, Athena kissed her hard. All doubt had left her. Their lips moved over each other, teasing and pleasuring. Athena hummed as her eyes fluttered closed, and then she pulled away.

She smiled, and she knew it was cocky.

Athena pecked Monti's lips, her grin broadening.

Without a word, Athena undid the buckle on her belt and slid out of the seat. She couldn't stop smiling. Why had it taken her so long to figure this out? Why had it taken twenty years of a self-made prison for her to understand that she didn't have to live up to anyone else but herself. She grinned at Monti as she walked down the thin aisle of the airplane toward the bathroom.

This was it.
This was what she wanted.

twenty-three

What is that look for?

Monti curled her fingers around the armrest between their seats, holding on for what felt like dear life. She kept her gaze on Athena's retreating form, the curve of her lips, the lines around her mouth, the pink in her cheeks. Athena paused a step, biting her lip as she raised her hands to her front and slid open the buttons on her jacket and then slid it off her shoulders.

She stepped back to the seat and plopped her jacket into the chair, her eyes completely alight in a way Monti had never seen before. Athena leaned over, holding still for one brief moment before smiling again.

"Almost forgot to take that off."

Monti's voice caught in her throat when Athena walked away again toward the back of the plane when the closest bathroom was in the front. Monti had no doubts what that look was all about now. Athena didn't look back. She didn't send Monti another hint as to what she was expecting. Monti stared across the aisle at the two gentlemen who had interrupted them before and winced.

She'd never done something like that. But Athena just seemed to take all those proprieties away, and Monti had to work to keep her hands off her. She blew out a breath and relaxed into her seat.

Athena really wanted to do this here? Now? Of all fucking places to fuck...

Monti rubbed her thighs, her hands flat on her knees. Her entire body was cued up and ready to go, just like it had been the last time they'd almost...fucked. "Oh, damn it."

Monti ran her fingers through her hair. She had held back for so long. Not on her feelings for Athena or the fact that she was interested, but she'd held herself back in life. What was she doing here other than running away again? Athena had offered her the perfect out. Escape to Florida for a bit and avoid the real problem even more.

Except this time Athena had come with her. And Monti had underestimated the fact that they had a commonality. *Fallon.* Cringing, Monti stood up and walked toward the back of the plane. First class seemed so far away from everything. The line of people was long, and she had missed which bathroom Athena had gone into.

Bouncing on her toes, with her hands shoved into her pockets, Monti waited. She kept her face turned toward the bathrooms, counting how many people went out of each one. It was the third person when she was sure that Athena had gone into the bathroom on the left. No one had gone in or gone out.

Two more people.

Just what was she going to find when she knocked on that door? Athena naked? Monti snorted at that idea. It was enough that she'd taken the jacket off in a plane full of strangers and then paraded her way from the front to the back. She'd never be naked.

Monti licked her lips. What would they do? It would be quick, dirty, and fuck, would Monti even get off? She flat out didn't care. So long as she got to taste and touch Athena, see her come undone—what little was left to unravel.

One more person.

Monti tapped her toe against the floor. Why was she nervous all of a sudden? It wasn't like she hadn't known they were headed this direction. Athena had invited her on a trip, a vacation to the beach. They'd cuddled for hours in her bed. They'd kissed so many times already. They had a connection.

One that was undeniable.

Wetting her lips, Monti stood at the ready. What would she say when she first walked in there? *Hey there, sexy. Waiting on someone?* Monti's heart raced. She was nervous. Of all things for her to be, nervous wasn't it. But this was so different than with anyone else before. Monti had never shared so much with someone, opened up to them. And she hadn't even realized she was doing it at first.

She'd let down her guard unexpectedly, meeting Athena right where she was. The person in front of her went into the bathroom on the right. Monti held her breath as she knocked rapidly on the door to the left.

"It's me, Athena."

Immediately the lock clicked, and the door slid open. Athena's bright face greeted her for a brief second before Monti stepped inside and locked the door behind her. She didn't even care if anyone had seen her. All she wanted was to get her hands on Athena, to touch and taste and smell and bask in the glorious woman in front of her.

But fuck, she forgot how small these damn bathrooms were.

Monti maneuvered around, pressing against Athena unexpectedly because there was literally nowhere else for her to go. And this was a bathroom. One that she had no doubt many other people had already used today.

"Hey," Athena said, her voice light and high-pitched.

Was she just as nervous?

"Hey," Monti answered. "The plane, really?"

Athena shrugged. "You're the one who wouldn't stop touching me."

Monti laughed lightly. "Sometimes you're irresistible. What can I say?" Leaning in, Monti kissed her softly. "Are you sure you want to do this?"

"Beyond sure."

"Then how? Because there isn't exactly a lot of room in here."

"I don't know." Athena shook her head. "I've never had sex with a woman before."

"Right." Monti blew out a breath. "Well, first things first, since we're definitely in a bathroom." She took hold of Athena's hips and flipped them so Monti was in between the sink and Athena. With one more kiss, she turned around and started washing her hands. The last thing she wanted was for someone to get sick.

Athena didn't touch her. Instead she leaned against the wall, her shoulders stiff and her look guarded as she watched Monti dry her hands and toss the paper towels. Was the heat of the moment gone already?

"We don't have to—"

"I want to, Monti." Athena looked at her directly, and Monti saw no doubt in her gaze. "I'm tired of waiting. I just don't know what to do."

"Okay. I hear you." Monti placed a hand on Athena's hip and bent slightly to kiss her cheek. She moved slowly to kiss the other one. "As much as I'd love to take this slow, I don't know how much time we'll get."

Athena shivered.

Monti kissed her lips, taking her time but not deepening the embrace. She pulled away slightly and slid two fingers along the edge of Athena's shirt. "I love touching you like this."

Athena sucked in a breath sharply, but her hands remained firmly at her sides. Monti fully slid her palm against Athena's side under her shirt. It felt like possession, but also willing submission. Stepping in closer, Monti whispered into Athena's ear.

"Wrap your arms around me."

Athena did as she was told, tilting her head up to capture Monti's lips. This was going to be an adventure, one that neither of them had ever experienced before. Monti deepened the kiss, sliding her tongue against Athena's. This was comfortable for them. They'd done this before. Athena knew how to kiss. What she didn't know was how to touch or move or trust her body.

Monti nipped Athena's lip, and then pressed small kisses all along Athena's jaw to her ear and sucked on her earlobe. Athena hummed, digging her nails into the small of Monti's back. It sent a shiver through her, the desire that Athena showed even if she didn't realize that was what she was doing in the moment.

"I love when you hold onto me," Monti whispered, kissing her way down Athena's neck. "Will you let me kiss your breasts?"

"Yes," Athena answered, already moving her hands to her shirt to pull it up.

Monti reached behind Athena's back and flicked the clasp of her bra, swiftly loosening it. Monti didn't care if Athena got her clothes off or not. She pulled the shirt up and the bra down and pressed her closed lips right against Athena's skin. She smelled heavenly. Athena's skin was so warm and inviting. Monti kissed her again, taking as much time as she dared to make sure that Athena got exactly what she wanted.

Athena clutched at Monti's back again before she dragged her hand up into Monti's hair and pulled Monti against her. Smiling, Monti parted her lips and covered Athena's nipple. She flicked her tongue against the hard little nub and grinned when Athena let out a small grunt. She'd noticed that her breasts were sensitive before, and she was finally getting more of them. Not everything she wanted, but enough to keep both of them satisfied until they landed in Florida.

The sharp tug against Monti's scalp was enough to make her back up. But Athena pushed her right back down onto the other breast. Monti had pegged her right from the start. Athena might not know what she was doing, but she knew exactly what she wanted, and she wasn't willing to give up that control.

Using the flat of her tongue, Monti licked Athena's breast before sucking her nipple and scraping her teeth as light as possible against the underside of her boob. Athena whined, holding Monti's head to her.

"If you keep that up, I'm going to come again without you touching me," Athena whispered, her voice disappearing in the noise from the plane.

Monti repeated the tease. If she could keep Athena on her toes, not knowing what was going to happen next, then she could figure out exactly how they were going to do this. Athena let go of Monti's head and moved her hands to the front of her pants, pulling the belt and the button. Monti covered her hands to stop her.

"I want to make sure that you want this."

"If I didn't want this, we wouldn't be here." Athena clasped Monti's hand, lacing their fingers. Her cheeks were red with arousal, her eyes glassed over. "If you don't touch me, then I'm going to touch myself."

Monti's lips curled upward. "Aye aye, captain."

"Touch me."

Putting her hands on Athena's hips, Monti pushed her pants down. On instinct, Athena spread her legs. The scent of her arousal was unmistakable, and Monti's knees nearly buckled as it hit her full force. "God, you're sexy."

"Touch me, Monti."

Monti slid her palm against Athena's thigh, easing her way from Athena's leg around the side to right between them. Athena's curls were long, wild, and so fucking wet. Monti pressed her mouth hard against Athena's, the kiss out of control. She breathed deeply, her eyes closed as she did everything by feel and let herself get lost just a little bit in this amazing woman who was so willingly opening for her.

Athena jerked slightly, and Monti halted all forward motion. She slowed her kisses, pulling Athena's lip between her teeth as she kept her hand as still as possible. "You okay?"

"Fine," Athena said, her voice tight.

"We don't allow *fine* as an answer."

"I'm impatient." Athena dropped her hips down, pushing Monti's hand more firmly against her.

Monti laughed. "If that's all it is."

"That's it."

"Then will you let me touch you?"

"I told you to already."

"Testy, are we?" Monti kissed Athena's neck. "Can I put my fingers in you?"

"That's probably the least sexy way to say that. Couldn't think of anything else with your word magic?" Athena dropped her hips again, as if she was trying to grind against Monti's open palm. And maybe she was. Maybe that was her solution to the fact that Monti was insisting on directions.

"Sometimes clarity isn't sexy. And it was a nicer way of asking if you don't mind penetration." Monti moved up, looking into Athena's eyes. She couldn't tell just from her voice if this was an avoidance tactic or simply Athena's odd way of flirting. Monti waited as Athena's eyes cleared and her mouth opened.

"Oh. No." Athena brushed her fingers against Monti's cheek, then her lips. "That's exactly what I want."

"Tell me if you want to stop."

Their mouths pressed together hard. Monti kept her fingers flat against Athena, bringing them back into the moment and out of the technicalities of sex for the first time with someone new. She deepened the kiss, sliding their tongues together, pressing their bodies tight. When Athena relaxed, when she dropped her hips and moaned, Monti finally made her move.

She dipped her fingers between Athena's hot and swollen lips, finding her slick and wet. She pressed slowly, backing away on a tease and then pressed again. Athena keened, her arms tightening in a grasp around Monti's shoulders as she bit Monti's earlobe and then her neck, sucking hard. Monti swallowed, wetting her thumb.

Slow circles. Teasing circles. Monti counted to ten, then fifteen, then twenty before Athena bit her neck hard.

"Stop teasing already," Athena said into Monti's shoulders. "I told you what I want."

"You did," Monti answered, biting back her smile. She started with one finger. She pushed slowly inside, past the tight circle, and straight to her second knuckle.

Athena bucked her hips. "Yes."

Monti kept the motion with her thumb, making sure that she was teasing and distracting in every way she possibly could. This was only the beginning, she knew that, and it was such a glorious way to start.

"More," Athena demanded. "I need more."

Monti moved her finger in and out, but Athena clenched her eyes and shook her head back and forth.

"No. Another finger."

Doing as she was told, Monti slid in a second finger. Athena groaned and pressed their mouths together in a sloppy kiss as if she was drunk off the pleasure. Maybe she was. Maybe Monti had found the last key that Athena needed to unleash everything. Athena dug her nails into Monti's shoulders as she clutched her back.

Monti stroked Athena's clit as she slid her fingers in and out. She watched with rapt attention as Athena closed her eyes and bit her lip.

"More."

She added a third finger, the tight circle of Athena's body straining under the intrusion and hugging Monti's fingers. She moved slowly, not wanting to cause any pain or harm. Athena's hips jerked sharply, only this time Monti had no doubt it was from the pinnacle of pleasure Athena was about to reach.

Athena's breathing increased, her lips parted, and she was lost. Monti held her here to reality, but that was it. The one thread that could send her away and pull her back. Monti pressed her body in, keeping as tight a hold as she dared. Athena jerked again, then again. She cried out, her chest coming forward as all that pleasure that had been building pulsed through her.

Monti stayed with her. She eased her through everything, pressing kisses against her neck and cheeks and lips as she waited.

When Athena opened her eyes, when she looked directly at Monti, she shook her head with a loud laugh, one that was completely free.

"You stopped running," Athena stated so simply.

"So did you," Monti answered.

Laughing again, Athena kissed Monti fully on the lips. Monti kept her fingers firmly inside Athena for as long as she could, enjoying the way Athena moved against her, not confined, not weighed down.

"What's next?" Athena answered, eyes bright with curiosity.

"We land in Dallas." Monti kissed her quickly. She finally pulled her fingers away and put them in her mouth, cleaning them. Her eyes fluttered shut as the flavor blossomed on her tongue. Damn, they would have to do that next. When she opened her eyes, Athena gave her a curious look.

"Do I taste good?"

"Like heaven." Monti winked. She shifted away, uncomfortable, especially knowing they had at least another four hours before they landed in Florida and got to Athena's beach house and she could take care of that very poignant discomfort. "Fix up your clothes, and I'll meet you back at our seats. We should be landing soon."

"Monti?" Athena snagged Monti's fingers.

"Yeah?"

"Don't give up on finding peace yet."

Monti's breath caught in her throat at the serious expression in Athena's eyes. There was nothing she could say or do that would alter this moment. Nodding slowly, Monti let go of something. She wasn't quite sure what it was yet. But Athena took it away so easily.

"I'll see you in a few minutes," Monti said, needing to escape. She wasn't ready for what she saw in Athena's eyes. Neither of them were.

twenty-four

"Do you mind if we go on a walk?" Athena asked as she wrapped her arm around Monti's back.

She'd been doing that more and more lately, especially since she'd fallen asleep on Monti's shoulder on their flight from Dallas to Miami. The drive to Marathon had been easy, and Athena had gladly let Monti take the wheel on that one. She'd never quite enjoyed driving, and spending hours navigating traffic was stress she loved avoiding.

"Sure." Monti slid her arm along Athena's shoulders.

They walked like that, as if it was so easy and had always been that way. Athena adored it. Things were so simple with Monti in ways they shouldn't be. But feeling with her, trusting her, being with her was easy. Athena sighed and nuzzled her cheek against Monti's shoulder and let Monti lead the way onto the beach.

It was so easy not to be in control when Monti was there. Well, at least this kind of control.

"You seem more relaxed here," Monti commented.

"I'm not sure if it's the place or the company," Athena answered, trying to be as honest as possible. She hadn't been able to decide which it was. Either way, Monti was right. She was relaxed. She was happy. And for the first time in as long as she could remember, she was enjoying herself.

"Well, I do like to hear that." Monti dropped a kiss into Athena's hair. "I'm glad to be off the plane and out of the car."

Athena chuckled. "I used to enjoy traveling. I still do, but it's a lot more stressful now than it used to be. Well, before everything happened."

"Where did you travel?"

"All over." Athena smiled, her foot sinking into the rough sand of the beach as they stepped toward the sunset. They'd gotten there just in time to see the sun fall below the horizon. The air would start to chill them soon and they'd have to go inside, but listening to the quiet waves on the beach was idyllic.

"What was your favorite place?"

"Kathmandu." Athena smiled. "I only went there once, and I didn't get to explore for long. I wish I'd been able to climb up in the mountains and explore the surroundings a bit more, but I was short on time."

"When were you there?"

"I must have been twenty. Kevin and I went for a late summer trip." Grinning, Athena turned and glanced up into Monti's eyes, but Monti's look faltered slightly. Her face seemed to fall. "What did I say?"

"I'm glad that Kevin has been able to be there for you throughout your life. It must be wonderful to have a friend like him."

"He's family." Athena slid her hand down Monti's arm and twined their fingers together. "He's always been family."

They walked a few more paces down to the beach, just feet from where the water was rushing toward them, and stopped. Athena shivered slightly and sidled in closer to Monti.

"Don't you have someone like that? I just assumed Fallon..."

"Fallon liked to pretend she was my mother. That caused a lot of arguments." Monti frowned. She stilled, staring out into the ocean in front of them.

Athena watched everything she could about this intriguing woman. They were both going through a magical transformation, but Athena had no idea where Monti was in the midst of hers. Was she toward the beginning still? Athena's had seemed to take off like a slingshot and it was impossible to stop it now.

"I hated her, growing up." Monti laughed. "She was always trying to boss me around, tell me what I could and couldn't do. I was so happy when she was going to go to college, and then she decided to go to University of Puget Sound and commute. I was so mad."

"You thought you had your getaway."

"I did!" Monti laughed again. "God, she was a terror."

"I can see how that might have happened." Athena ran her fingers up and down Monti's arm. "She commands my office, and most of my life that I'll allow her—"

"Which I assume isn't a lot," Monti chimed in.

"My schedule primarily. But she's very good at keeping everything orderly and on track."

"Did she tell you that she lies to me about what time our appointments are so that I show up on time and you don't know that I'm late?"

"What?" Athena's eyes widened, shaking her head. "No, but I suppose that does make sense. She would think of something like that."

"I can't wait for the day she ends up in love with someone who's perpetually late and flies by the seat of their pants. She'll never hear the end of it." Monti turned, facing Athena. She reached forward and cupped Athena's cheek. "Thank you for bringing me on this trip. I needed a bit of an escape."

"An escape from Fallon?"

"Some of it was that. Some of it is just someplace new to explore." Monti moved in for a swift kiss.

"But you said you'd been to the Keys before."

Monti narrowed her gaze. "There's always somewhere new to find an adventure. Don't you think so?"

"I suppose." Athena hadn't thought about that before. Ever since the event, she'd only ever gone to places she was familiar with, where she knew her surroundings and where the fastest exit was. She wasn't ever comfortable elsewhere. She'd managed to calm her fear enough to function in society, but she'd become a recluse, when before she'd always been the first to hop on a plane and visit someplace new.

"We should go in. You're shivering."

"Yeah." Athena led the way into the house through the patio doors.

She showed Monti around the first level before bringing her up the stairs to show her the bedrooms. She'd specifically chosen Monti's room to be right next to hers. When she opened the door, she leaned against it and waited for Monti to walk inside to check it out.

"I didn't want to assume anything." Her cheeks were flushed, the memory of the plane ride coming back full force. She'd wanted to find some place in Dallas to sneak away, but the conversation they'd been having was so good that she didn't manage to bring the idea up. And then they were here and driving.

Monti touched her shoulder. "I get it."

"Right. My room is next door if you need something." Athena kept her back plastered to the door, her hand on the knob. She had no idea what to say or do or how to even begin a seduction to the level that Monti had earlier that day.

"Oh, I'm sure I'll need something at some point." Monti stepped in closer, pressing Athena against the doorway. Their breasts touched through the fabric of their clothes.

Athena's eyes fluttered shut, the ghosting memory of Monti's caresses filling her mind. She drew in a shuddering breath, wanting that as much now as before. But surely Monti would expect her to touch in return at some point, wouldn't she? Sex was hardly ever just one way, but more than that, Athena wanted to reciprocate.

Monti pressed a kiss to Athena's cheek, then along her jawline to her ear. "I think I could use some help with this." Monti put her hand against Athena's jacket, the one she'd promptly put back on as soon as she'd returned to her seat from the bathroom. The buttons came undone in seconds, and Monti slid her hand around Athena's side to her back. "Oh would you look at that, I didn't need help."

"Cocky," Athena mumbled. She moved slightly, pressing her mouth to Monti's cheek, then her neck. She scraped her teeth much like Monti had and settled into what teasing she could do in that moment, what she was comfortable with. Athena sucked, sliding her tongue against the skin at the base of Monti's neck while she trailed her hands up and down Monti's sides.

"I think you like me that way." Monti moaned lightly. "That feels so good, by the way. Not just your mouth, but the way you're touching me."

The compliment spurred Athena on. Were they really going to pick up right where they left off?

"Monti?" Athena finally managed to ask.

"Yeah?" Monti pulled back to look Athena in the eye, the curiosity and timing precisely what Athena needed in that moment.

How did Monti always seem to know that? How did she always seem to follow the cues Athena wasn't even sure she was giving? "I think I'd like to freshen up first. I always feel so dirty after flying."

Monti chuckled. "I get it." She leaned in and kissed Athena, tangling their tongues in a quick, heated kiss before she backed away with a few more touches of lips to lips. "Go, do whatever you need to do. I'll be waiting for whatever you're ready for."

"Whatever?" Athena pushed, cascading her hand purposely down the front of Monti's body, over the swell of her breasts, to the curve of her waist, and the slope of her hip.

"Yes, whatever. Whether it's sex, kissing, cuddling, massaging."

"I can always go for another massage."

Monti laughed, the sound freely echoing through the room. "I'll give you a massage whenever you want."

"What if I want one in the middle of the night?" Athena pulled Monti back to her by the belt loops in her pants.

"Well, then definitely." Monti's voice dropped, the tones seductive and arousing.

Athena bit back her smile, but barely. She was enjoying this side of Monti, and of herself. She'd never been the flirtatious type, at least not in recent memory. She was almost coming back into the person she used to be.

"What about at dawn? On the beach?" Athena trailed her fingers up Monti's stomach, reaching for her breasts and circling them.

"On the beach? Don't you think that's a bit public?"

"And the bathroom on the airplane isn't?"

"That has a locked door."

"True." Athena looked up into Monti's eyes. "Are you sure you won't mind?"

"Anywhere and whenever, Athena. The choice is always yours."

"Good to know." Athena dragged Monti back in for another kiss, humming her pleasure so Monti would know exactly what she was feeling and how much she was loving this. Eventually, she slowed the embrace and nipped Monti's lower lip, sucking a little, before finally releasing her. "I should go shower."

"Probably. Otherwise you might not make it there."

"Is that a threat?"

"A fun one." Monti put her hands up by her sides and took a step backward. "Go on. I'll be here waiting when you're done."

Athena debated whether or not to actually leave. She was enjoying their time together so much that she didn't want to break the spell. With one last kiss, she slipped from Monti's hold and walked to her bedroom. Closing the door with a definitive click, she locked it and put her forehead against the cold wood.

What was going on with her?

It was like she'd never had sex before in her life. She couldn't get enough of Monti, of the touches, of her kisses, or the teasing. Smiling, Athena shuddered. She was ready to go again and again if only Monti would let her. And for some reason, the fear she'd had before about what to do and where to touch was mostly gone.

Although she was pretty sure that it'd come back full force as soon as she was put into the situation that sex, real sex, was actually going to happen. Athena dragged in a slow breath, steadying herself. She really needed to get into the shower.

Stripping off her clothes, she folded them as she went. Settling them into the laundry basket in the en suite, Athena started the water and let it warm up. She studied herself in the mirror. She almost didn't even recognize the woman she'd become. She'd aged since the last time she'd truly looked at herself, the wrinkles around her eyes and lips far more prominent.

She was a middle-aged woman, no doubt about it. Her father had retired when he turned fifty-five, and she only had ten more years to reach that. Though she hadn't planned on retiring any time soon. She was happy with her workload, but more importantly, she was happy with the work she was doing.

Helping people find justice.

Athena sucked in a sharp breath. Perhaps her justice was simply living and finding joy in the life she'd been handed. That would certainly tilt her whole world on its axis in a new way. But today she'd been touched, and she had enjoyed every single moment of it. Every single glide of fingers against skin. She'd loved having Monti inside her, consuming her, possessing her.

Closing her eyes and leaning over the counter, Athena let the lingering sensations float through her. She hadn't even been self-conscious about what she looked like. The thought hadn't even flown through her brain that Monti would care or that it would make a difference.

Athena straightened her back, this time seeing herself in the mirror anew. She didn't want to be who she'd become over the last twenty years. She wanted to be that girl from the past. Maybe not that girl exactly, but she wanted to experience life with such joy and excitement and fervor as she had. Rubbing her hands together, Athena stopped.

Why was she still wearing her wedding ring?

She'd rarely ever taken it off, but it wasn't like Kevin wore his. She frowned at it, sliding it from her finger and staring at the large diamond that had been passed down through six generations after being won in a gambling match. She'd never liked it. Never appreciated the family significance behind it. Spinning the ring in her fingers, Athena dropped it into the small jewelry bowl on the counter.

Enough was enough.

It was time for her to become someone new.

Someone she'd always wanted to be.

Someone who made her own rules.

Athena showered quickly, drying off and slipping into loose-fitting and comfortable clothes. She walked out of her bedroom barefoot and immediately went next door, only to find Monti asleep on the bed. Her hand was tossed over her head, one leg dangling as if she was about to stand up, but her gentle breathing and soft snore were sure signs that she was fast asleep.

Grinning from ear to ear, Athena snagged a throw blanket off the end of the bed and laid it gently over Monti's sleeping form. They had two full weeks together. They'd find the time to figure out what they were doing. Bending down, Athena brushed a kiss into Monti's hair before heading back to her bedroom.

twenty-five

Monti woke with a start, her entire body jerking as she sat straight up in bed. Her heart was in her throat when she looked around the unfamiliar room as her eyes cleared. For a moment she'd thought she was at home.

No. Not home.

Sucking in a sharp breath, Monti tried to remember exactly where she'd thought she was, but now that she was awake, she couldn't bring the dream to her memory. It was as if she was grasping at smoke, trying to catch it between her fingers as it slipped away and became impossible to see anymore.

Monti plucked the thin blanket off her legs and stood up. She was in Florida with Athena. And she must have fallen asleep before Athena had gotten out of the shower because she couldn't remember her coming back into Monti's bedroom. And the door was shut. And the blanket.

She'd never fallen asleep quite like that before, not unless she was under the stars. Sighing, Monti wrapped her arms around herself and rubbed her hands up and down. Why was she still chilled?

Taking a quick shower, Monti unpacked her bag and headed to the kitchen. She wanted coffee. Maybe that would warm up her bones like the shower had failed to do. She made a pot of coffee and stared out the window as the sun rose and lit up the sky. If the house faced the other direction, she would have been able to see it. But this way, all she got to witness was the way the light painted the sky and the clouds, creating a masterpiece of its own body.

Monti stayed put, mesmerized by the beauty that was so natural to the world. It was peaceful here. Wait. What was that thought? Monti pursed her lips and took another sip of coffee, letting the caffeine rip through her and wake her up even more.

It was peaceful here.

She breathed in that blessed feeling, allowing it to settle into her chest. That had been what she was searching for. But why was she finding it here of all places? Was it because this was somewhere new? Or was this just the newness tricking her into thinking that it was peace?

"Morning," Athena singsonged as she stepped into the kitchen.

"Morning." Monti smiled as Athena leaned in and kissed her cheek.

"You were asleep when I went to find you last night." Athena brushed her fingers along Monti's hand as she reached for a mug, intentionally teasing.

Athena had become a whole new person overnight it seemed. Monti glanced at the clock on the stove, surprised to find that hours had passed since she'd come downstairs. She'd always been one to lose herself and forget about time, but this seemed different.

"Do you need a refill?"

"Uh. Sure." Monti handed her cup over and waited as Athena filled it. "Just milk."

Once she had her second cup between her fingers, Monti leaned against the counter and looked out the patio doors again. "You missed a beautiful sunrise."

Athena hummed. "Did I? I guess I was worn out from all the...travel."

"I'm sure it was the travel." Monti picked up on the flirting instantly and played right into it.

They finished their coffee, setting the mugs in the sink before walking out onto the deck. It was already warm outside, and the breeze was gentle as it caressed Monti's skin. She was impressed to find that Athena wasn't wearing her normal buttoned-up outfits, but a loose-fitting shirt that showed off her arms. More than that, her hair was pulled back in a ponytail, giving her face a much younger look.

"Was there anything you wanted to see while you were here?" Athena asked.

Monti took her hand, lacing their fingers together. When Athena stopped on the deck, Monti continued forward, taking Athena with her. If they were going to be here, then Monti didn't want to be cooped up in the house all day. She stopped at the bottom of the deck and toed off her shoes. The sand was cold against her feet, but it was a glorious contrast to the warm sun that was hitting her skin.

"Take your shoes off," Monti said, her voice so soft. She wasn't sure that Athena would agree or not, but it would be interesting to see if she did. Athena would probably think this was childish, but Monti loved the beach. She loved the woods. She loved any type of nature that she could find, including the world made by the hands of humans.

"What are we doing?" Athena asked, holding Monti still.

"Exploring." Monti knew that single word was a statement.

"What are we exploring?" Athena canted her head to the side in the most adorable look of confusion.

Leaning in, because she couldn't resist, Monti kissed Athena's nose and grinned. "Everything."

This time, Monti didn't wait. She dropped Athena's hand and walked away. She headed straight for the surf, and when the sand was wet against her toes, she sighed with relief. She needed the comfort of it, the contrast of the cold to the warmth of the day. Yet she still felt cold inside, like something wasn't quite sitting right within her.

Turning back around, Monti was surprised to find that Athena had followed her into the surf, her feet bare and her pants rolled up to her knees. The flash of skin was absolutely enticing, and if Monti had her way, they'd pick up right where they left off the night before. Neither one of them would likely regret it, and they'd both be satisfied.

"The water's warm today."

"The gulf usually is, especially when the water's coming in from the east instead of the south," Athena answered.

"Don't take the fun out of it." Monti laughed, her voice carried in the breeze as she went farther into the water, the waves brushing against her pants and wetting them. She was going to have to change, but she didn't care. She was more fascinated by the fact that Athena was actually doing this, willingly.

She was standing in the middle of the ocean, her hands on her hips, with only a slight scowl on her face. The intrusive thought came to her without a moment's hesitation. Monti shook her head once before giving in. Bending down, she flapped her fingers into the water, bringing it up to splash against Athena.

"Monti!" Athena screeched, but her lips were curled upward.

"Yes?" Monti straightened her shoulders, playing off the role that she'd been caught red-handed. But she'd intended it, completely. She wanted to see if Athena would play into this light-hearted game that she'd set up.

When Athena didn't say anything else or scold her again, Monti bent down and scooped up even more water, splashing it at Athena.

"Monti!" Athena shouted again with a laugh.

Giggling, Monti bent down just as Athena did. Water flew between them, catching their clothes, their skin, their hair. Monti eventually stepped forward, grabbing Athena by the waist and spinning her as the waves hit against their thighs. They kissed.

Athena moved in, deepening the embrace. Her fingers cupped

Monti's cheeks and pulled her in closer. Monti wrapped her arms around Athena's back, tilting her slightly to change the angle of the kiss. Athena gasped.

"Are we going to spend all day frolicking in the water?"

"Only if you want to," Monti answered, kissing her again. "But I suppose we have to eat at some point."

"And have tea."

"And read books as we bask in the sun," Monti murmured against Athena's neck. "I know you despise electronic books, so did you bring a suitcase filled with paperbacks?"

"What makes you think I don't have my own mini-library here?"

Monti laughed wholeheartedly. She should have guessed. She should have figured that Athena would have prepared for that, especially since this was—according to her—her second most favorite place on earth. Monti tugged her in for another long kiss.

"When's the last time you played in the ocean?"

Athena shook her head, biting her lip. "When I was sixteen or seventeen?"

Monti spun her around, holding her as they stared out into the vast expanse of the ocean in front of them. They rocked side to side as the waves lapped against their thighs. "If you could go anywhere, where would you go?"

"I'm loving where I am," Athena answered. "Really. I don't want to be anywhere else."

Something tightened in Monti's chest, something that she couldn't quite name. But it hurt. She knew Athena had meant for those words to be kind and comforting. Athena was being honest. They were enjoying each other's company so why would Athena want to be anywhere else. And yet, it pained Monti to think about that.

If Athena clung to her presence too much, holding on to her as if she was the solid rock Athena could stand on now instead of her own two feet, then Monti would be exactly where she didn't want to be. Hurting someone when she did finally leave.

Because she would go. The world called to her, that quest for peace.

Monti paused.

She sucked in a deep breath, pressing her chin against Athena's shoulder as she held her tightly in a hug. Athena was choosing to be here, and here was where she was finding comfort and peace. Perhaps there was something to that. Perhaps Monti was missing the biggest point of Athena's statement.

Clenching her jaw, Monti kissed Athena's neck. "Let's go in and dry off."

"You get me all the way out here and now you want to go in?" Athena raised an eyebrow at her, questioning Monti.

"What do you suggest?"

"In a low tide, we can walk pretty far out."

"It's not a low tide, Athena." Monti kissed her cheek. "But where do you want to walk to?"

"Anywhere so long as I'm with you."

There was honesty there, but something underlying it—or perhaps underlying only Monti's hearing of it—turned it against truth and into something akin to fake. She wished she could point her finger at exactly what was wrong. But Athena seemed so happy and relaxed. This was what they'd worked at for months now, and if she had to stay in this moment, if she had to ignore her instincts because Athena had finally found her peace, then Monti would do that.

It was her job after all, wasn't it?

Help her clients find what they were looking for, work through their problems, make headway and steps forward—that was what she was paid to do. And that was exactly what she'd agreed to when she had taken the job with Athena. Tracking her hands down Athena's arms, Monti laced their fingers.

"Come on. Let's go inside."

She helped Athena walk through the surf and back to the house. Instead of going inside, however, Athena stopped them on the deck by sitting in the lounge chairs that were there. It was close enough. Monti sat next to her, lifting Athena's feet into her lap and massaging them. Athena moaned, tossing her head back into the chair and rolling her shoulders as her eyes fluttered shut.

"This is perfect," Athena murmured.

Monti smiled. "Perfect isn't real."

"Sure it is." Athena looked Monti directly in the eye. "Perfection is whatever we make it. If I want this to be perfect, then it's perfect."

"Do you try that in the courtroom?"

Athena snorted, then she giggled, no doubt in response to her unintentional reaction. "No."

"You should." Monti got hold of Athena's hand and brought her fingers up to kiss her knuckles again. "I bet the judges would eat that up."

"Oh my God."

"What?" Monti winked. "I think it'd be sexy to see you argue in court."

Athena laughed, the sound low in her throat. "Well, you're welcome to come to my next open trial if you want to. Until then, you'll have to make do with your imagination."

"Then I'll let my imagination go wild." Another wink and Monti settled into the day. This was something she could handle. That feeling from before? Like everything was going to shatter around her? That she needed to run full force from, all the way back to Seattle. She just had fourteen days to survive and then she could.

twenty-six

Athena had watched the beach fastidiously since Monti had left for a run over an hour ago. The sun had set on their first day there, and Athena couldn't be happier. She couldn't be more satisfied. Her entire life up until that point had been filled with the tension of keeping everything hidden and under wraps, but with Monti, she had none of that.

The door snicked open, and Monti stepped inside. Her cheeks were flushed from the exercise, her hair no longer slicked back in the ponytail she'd left with. Flyaway hairs sprung out by her ears and temples, and she tried in vain to put them back before giving up and grinning at Athena.

"Good run?" Athena asked. Her stomach clenched at the sight of Monti, the curve of her lips, the way her body swayed as she walked closer.

"Best in weeks." Monti walked straight to her, cupping her cheek and pulling her in for a deep kiss.

Athena gasped. She fell into the embrace, allowing herself to be swept away in it. She wrapped her hands around Monti's back, her skin slick with sweat and small granules of sand that were rough against her skin. Humming, Athena parted her lips and slid her tongue against Monti's. She'd been wanting this all day.

They'd been so close all day, talking, laughing, enjoying each other's company. But this time, Monti didn't pull back in a rush. Instead, she got on her knees, parting Athena's so she could be nestled right between them. Athena moved in, trailing her fingers up and down Monti's shoulders and back. She didn't want to let go.

Something about this moment was so pure. Athena pulled the tight elastic holding Monti's hair up. Her sweat-dampened hair fell around her shoulders, and immediately, Athena tangled her fingers in it. Monti was so real. She was someone who was built of hopes and dreams instead of nightmares and fears.

Sucking Monti's lower lip into her mouth, Athena moaned. She wanted all of Monti tonight. She wanted their bodies entangled and full of pleasure. She wanted Monti inside her, against her. Athena dove in to deepen the kiss, trying to work her way through exactly how to ask that, how to tell Monti that she was wanted.

"Why don't..." Monti said, her lips against Athena's as she smiled "...I go upstairs and take a shower, clean up a bit, and you can choose if you want to join me or wait until I'm done."

"That's a tough decision."

"But it's all yours." Monti kissed again, dragging in a sharp breath and groaning as she pulled away. "If I don't leave now, I'm not leaving."

"I'm not opposed to that."

Monti laughed, but she moved to stand up. "I'm a sweaty mess."

"Pretty sure that comes with the territory." Athena stayed exactly where she was, feet flat against the floor, knees spread. She gave Monti a teasing look, dragging her gaze down Monti's tight body and then back up, slowly and deliberately. She wanted this to be just as hard for Monti as it was for her. She wanted there to be tension between them.

Anticipation.

"Oh, I have no doubt you know what you're doing." Monti

took a step backward, narrowly missing the side table that held Athena's tea and the book she'd been pretending to read while she waited for Monti to come back. "I can't wait to see what you decide."

Monti disappeared upstairs.

Athena clutched the sides of the lounger she was in, holding her breath as she waited. But what the hell was she waiting for? Monti had literally told her this was her decision, and she'd been thinking about it all day. She wanted to have sex. And she wanted to have sex with Monti right now.

Standing up, Athena didn't even bother to clean up. She walked immediately up the stairs to Monti's bedroom. She shut and locked the door behind her before stripping her shirt off and then her pants. The water was already running in the shower, the sound calling to Athena.

When she opened the door, Monti smiled from the open glass door to the shower and stepped inside. Athena's heart jumped. Monti was stunning. It hadn't even occurred to her that she hadn't seen Monti naked yet. That in every encounter they'd had, Monti had remained fully clothed.

Athena's heart ran rampant. Her body begged her to move and do something, but she stood still in the doorway, stunned speechless. Monti was young, her muscles taut, her skin tight and smooth. She didn't have scars or weird dimples on her ass or legs or stretch marks on her breasts from pregnancy. She was perfection wrapped up in long legs and stunning curves.

"Shall I start without you?" Monti called through the door. "Because I don't mind."

Snapping to attention, Athena unhooked her bra and slid her underwear to the tile floor. Her voice was caught in her throat, and she wasn't sure she was going to be able to speak. She shook as she reached for the shower door and popped it open. Steam filled the small shower, but through it, she found Monti with her shoulders against the wall, and fingers firmly planted between her legs.

"We can always start with some mutual masturbation if you'd like."

"No," Athena said, though she wasn't sure she was loud enough for Monti to hear her. Placing one foot into the shower, she stepped inside, her decision firmly made. One more step and they were plastered together.

Skin to skin.

Breasts to breasts.

Mouth to mouth.

Athena ran her palms over Monti's front, over her breasts, her hard nipples, to her hips and her thighs. She was doing this. And she wasn't going to be scared or worried about anything. Because she trusted Monti. She trusted that what they had together so far was true and real. Athena followed Monti's hand down between her legs, matching Monti's fingers with her own.

"See?" Monti's voice was breathy. "You know what to do."

The confidence boost was exactly what Athena needed. She pressed more firmly, sliding one finger inside Monti. She was so hot, her body slick and wet.

"That's it," Monti cooed. "Deeper."

Athena loved this side of Monti. She was demanding, bluntly so. But as her confidence grew, she didn't need Monti to tell her what to do anymore. She pressed the heel of her hand against Monti's clit and started to slowly slide her fingers in and out. Monti shuddered, digging her nails into Athena's sides as she clutched onto her.

"Don't be afraid to make noises," Athena muttered into Monti's ear. "I want to hear what you're feeling."

"Yes," Monti hissed. She tossed her head back into the wall with a light thud.

The heat from the water started to make Athena dizzy, but she wasn't going to stop. She pressed forward, pushing herself into Monti's body.

"Fuck," Monti muttered, her hips jerking sharply. "Right there."

Athena listened to the understated direction, keeping the pace and positioning of her fingers. She pressed their mouths together, the kiss becoming sloppy as Monti's movements became uncoordinated. Athena held onto her, keeping her upright. The control Athena had in this, the power to give Monti pleasure or not, to keep them both upright and moving—it was addicting. Athena nipped at Monti's neck.

"I don't know what—" Monti swallowed hard "—you were worried about."

Athena scraped her teeth against Monti's collar bone and then used her tongue to chase after the droplets of water that slid across her skin and over the tops of her breasts. She should have spent so much more time there. She should have started with these perfect boobs. Moving her hand from between Monti's legs, Athena palmed Monti's breasts, rubbing her thumb across her nipples. Monti whined her protest and tried to grab Athena's hand and push it back down.

Athena froze.

Monti's eyes snapped open, and she let go of Athena's hand instantly. "I'm so sorry."

"For what?" The tension was back in between Athena's shoulders, tightening and pulling until her chest started to hurt. "You didn't do anything."

"Nope. I did." Monti put her hands on Athena's shoulders, tightly. "Will you look at me?"

Athena had to blink hard to focus her eyes, but she finally found Monti's in the steamy haze. "What?"

"I will never force you to do anything you don't want. I should have asked."

"Asked what?" Athena leaned in, their breasts pressed together again.

"For you to touch me." Monti raised her eyebrows. "How are you doing?"

"I'm fine. Why—"

"You're shaking, and you're so tense I'm pretty sure you could smash through a concrete wall." Monti smiled, though it didn't quite reach her eyes.

When Athena looked at her, she could definitely see the worry in her gaze now. Blinking, Athena stepped forward and pressed her forehead to Monti's shoulder. She wrapped her arms around Monti's back and sucked in a long deep breath. She checked in with her body, and Monti was right. Her back was rigid, her leg muscles were tense. She didn't want that right now.

"I'm fine."

"Fine isn't acceptable, remember?"

"I'm okay," Athena corrected. She refused to move her body from Monti's. She used the touch to center herself and bring herself right back into this moment. "I'm good. I promise."

"You didn't even notice."

"Yes, well, as we've established, I'm not good at that." Athena leaned back slightly and smiled. "I don't want to stop."

"Are you sure?" Monti slid her fingers down Athena's arms to her hands. "Because we can definitely stop."

"I don't want to." Athena slid in and kissed Monti on the lips. "Only if you do."

"I'm good." Monti pulled Athena in for a deeper kiss. "But I think we should get out of the shower. I'm starting to get overheated."

"Oh um... sure." Athena bit her cheek and stepped back. Something about the mood had shifted, and she wanted it back where it was. She held her breath while Monti dipped under the spray of the water and cleaned herself off quickly.

Giving Monti some privacy, Athena stepped out of the shower and snagged a folded towel. What had she done that was wrong? Everything seemed to be going so well until it wasn't. She knew she'd been the one to mess that up. Wrapping the towel around her chest, Athena left the bathroom and picked up her clothes as she went. Would Monti want her to leave?

She sat on the bed and was starting to pull her shirt over her head when Monti's voice stopped her. "What are you doing?"

"I thought..." Athena frowned, looking over Monti's very naked and very wet body. Her breath caught in her throat. "I don't know what I thought."

"Did you think I wanted you to go?"

"Yes," Athena admitted, shame sitting at the top of her chest right where all that tension had been.

"Oh no, no no no no." Monti came forward immediately, getting down on her knees and putting her hands on Athena's legs. "I don't want you to leave, not unless you want to and even then, I won't want you to leave."

"I thought..." Athena trailed off. She held her breath, staring down into Monti's dark eyes. "I thought I had ruined it."

"You ruined nothing." Monti lifted Athena's hand and kissed her knuckles. "I just wanted to check that you were okay and comfortable with what we were doing and give you a few minutes to collect yourself. That's it."

Collect herself? Athena dragged her hand through her damp hair. They'd barely gotten started and had to stop already. Now everything was awkward, and she was pretty sure the last thing Monti wanted was to have sex. Her cheeks burned with embarrassment. She should have known better than to think that this was going to happen.

"Athena," Monti said sharply.

Snapping her eyes back to Monti's, Athena found her center again.

"Stop riding the shame train, okay?"

"Easier said than done."

"I know," Monti murmured. "Don't be ashamed of who you are. Ever." Monti kissed Athena's bare knee. "I want to be with you, exactly as you are today in this moment."

"I'm not someone worthy of that."

"Of course you are." Monti kissed her knee again, then a little higher. "Everyone is worthy of love."

Athena's entire body warmed, a pleasant sensation seeping into her, something she had long forgotten. She breathed it in, enjoying it, loving it, reveling in it. Doing the only thing she could think of, she bent down and pressed their lips together. She dropped the towel she'd been holding up and dragged Monti closer to her.

She wanted this. Desperation clawed its way through her, clinging to that warm sensation she wasn't willing to give up. Monti's wet hair was cold against her fingers, and Athena tugged sharply and smiled when Monti grunted in response.

"I want to touch you," Athena mumbled against Monti's mouth. "I want to touch you everywhere."

"Perfect."

Confidence restored, at least as much as it could be, Athena stood up and took Monti by the hand. She walked around the edge of the bed and sat on the mattress. Monti moved in and kissed her. Hands skimmed, lips touched. Before she knew it, they were in the middle of the bed and Monti was on top of her.

Athena loved the weight and feel of her. She put her knee up, cradling Monti's naked body between her legs and tenderly running her hands all over Monti's back and ass. She scraped her nails lightly, and when Monti groaned, Athena did it again.

"I want to know what it feels like..." Athena trailed off as Monti pressed kisses down her neck and across her breasts, teasing her nipples with the tip of her tongue. Athena arched her back up, shoulders pressing into the mattress and giving Monti as much access to her body as possible. Her heart was racing, pounding so hard.

Monti pressed open-mouthed kisses down to Athena's stomach, kissing her scars as she went. Athena wiggled, encouraging Monti to move even lower. Because that was exactly what she wanted. She'd thought about it more times than she could count at this point, and the fact that they were so close, that this was actually going to happen.

"Yes," Athena murmured, clenching her eyes shut as she allowed her body to just feel everything that was happening. This was so nice, but she still wanted to be able to touch, to know that she could give just as much pleasure as she could receive. "Yes, your mouth."

Athena put her hand on the top of Monti's head and pushed. Monti was immediately face first between Athena's legs. Athena lifted her hips up, begging for Monti to put her mouth against her. Monti nipped the inside of Athena's thigh.

Squeaking, Athena wriggled. "Enough of that."

"The tease is the best part sometimes."

"Not tonight," Athena muttered back.

Laughing, Monti kissed the inside of her thigh again. "I love when you demand."

"I demand all day."

"Yes, yes, you do." Monti scraped her teeth.

Athena clenched her legs against Monti's head and groaned. She wanted Monti's mouth on her right now. She wanted to feel her entire body in tune with what Monti was doing. Athena wrapped Monti's wet hair around her fingers.

"Now."

"Yes, ma'am." Monti moved in immediately. She pressed her tongue, hot and wet, against Athena's clit. She sucked and pulled back and did it again and again.

Athena groaned, bucking her hips up. "Yes. Finally."

Monti didn't stop there. She pressed in tighter, nose deep in Athena's curls. Athena looked down, their eyes locking together as Monti teased her. That was sexy as hell. No one had ever done that with her before. Monti snuck her hands around Athena's hips and up onto her stomach, reaching up to caress her breasts.

"Fuck," Athena said. Monti played with her nipples, intensifying every sensation that floated through her. This was so much more than she'd ever imagined. She held onto Monti's hair, using the cold wet strands to keep her rooted in the moment. She rocked her hips up into Monti's mouth. "That feels amazing."

Monti didn't answer. Not that she could when her mouth was doing such delicious things. Athena cried out as her orgasm unexpectedly swept through her. She was so flushed, her skin sweaty and damp, but definitely not from the shower.

"Get up here."

"Yes, ma'am." Monti crawled up her until their mouths could touch.

Athena tasted herself on Monti's lips, the wet from Monti's cheeks rubbing against Athena's face. The scent was unmistakable arousal, and the taste so tangy compared to what she'd always assumed it would be like. Not that she'd done a whole lot of thinking about that either.

Bringing her leg up, Athena pushed into the bed and flipped them over so that she was on top of Monti. She deepened the kiss and slid her hand between their bodies, caressing Monti's breast before sliding her hand even lower. She wanted to pick up right where she left off. She wanted Monti to feel her inside just like Athena had in the plane.

"I want what we were doing before."

"Yes. Do that," Monti answered, already parting her legs to give Athena the space.

Their mouths were pressed together again, and Athena slipped one finger inside Monti. She teased her, sliding her thumb back and forth. Monti keened before pulling Athena in for another kiss. Athena wasn't going to stop this time. She kept her fingers between Monti's legs, teasing.

Monti held Athena, arms around her back, tightening her grasp. Athena didn't stop. She rocked harder, pressing deeper. "Do you like this?"

"Yes," Monti breathed her answer. "Yes, I love it."

"Good." Athena kissed down Monti's neck to the top of her chest, licking her collar bone and tasting her damp skin. She scraped her teeth and kissed again.

"Athena." Monti's voice cracked.

Athena could tell that Monti was close, that they were about to reach the pinnacle, that they were about to do everything they had been waiting for since that last massage in Seattle. Athena held Monti close, twisting her hand and her wrist.

"Let me see you fall apart."

Monti gasped, her body tensing. She breathed hard and pressed her face into the crook of Athena's neck and held on. Athena didn't want to let her go either. In fact, she wanted to stay here all night, cocooned in the safety of Monti's arms. And that was exactly what they were going to do.

twenty-seven

"Fuck!"

Monti sat straight up in the bed, her entire body ready for flight. She blinked back the weariness as she figured out where she was and caught her bearings. She missed her van, the small confinements made nights like these so much easier. There wasn't as much lurking in the shadows because there weren't as many shadows.

A rustling startled her, and when she looked down, she found Athena curled up on her side with the covers across her hips, fast asleep. They'd stayed up most of the night, touching and talking, kissing and listening. Monti brushed her fingers lightly over Athena's temple and moved her hair away from her face.

Athena was fast asleep.

Monti sighed in relief as she leaned against the pillow and attempted to relax. She stared up at the ceiling and did what she'd told so many clients to do—took slow deep breaths. One after the other. Push away negative thoughts. Settle into the emotion.

But it wasn't working.

Despite how long she lay there and tried to catch her bearings, she couldn't manage to do it. All of her nerves told her that something bad was going to happen, that someone was going to come into the room, that she would be covered in darkness and wouldn't be able to see, that the panic she'd felt wasn't going to go away.

After an hour had passed, Monti slid from the bed as quietly as possible. She slipped her clothes out of the drawer and dressed in the bathroom. Before she knew it, she was downstairs. The pot of coffee brewed quickly, and she immediately made herself a cup.

Monti finished her coffee, but she couldn't stay still. She bounced on her toes as she paced through the kitchen and then the small living area where she and Athena had spent a considerable amount of time reading. But she couldn't stay there.

With her heart in her throat, she walked out onto the back deck and stared at the waves lapping in the dark water. That was what her soul felt like. A black abyss. Why did that thought hurt so much? Empty tears fell down her cheeks. She crossed her arms and hugged herself, trying to ward off the chill in the air.

Or rather, the chill in her soul.

Monti blew out a breath as more tears joined the others. Why on earth was she crying? She swiped at her cheeks and stepped off the wide stairs of the deck and into the sand. Small grains of sand. They could be molded in so many ways, transformed into beautiful things.

Not unlike people. All it took was time and effort and energy. Monti had wrongfully assumed that all her time on the road she'd been doing that, but she couldn't have been more wrong. All she'd done was hide effectively in plain sight.

She walked aimlessly, moving down the beach as she allowed her emotions to guide wherever she needed to go.

What was she doing here?

It was fun coming on this trip, a more extravagant one than she'd pay for herself, with someone she cared about and enjoyed spending time with. Monti bit her lip and smiled. Since when had they shifted from client and therapist to friends with some benefits? That slide had been almost easy, but it felt right. Monti walked along the edge of where the waves came up onto the sand, wetting her toes but not her feet as she followed the curve of the water.

"What are we doing, though?"

Athena was probably more invested in the relationship than Monti was. She had to be, right? Which would mean at some point Monti was going to hurt her as she shifted the parameters of the relationship when she left.

That thought sent a physical pain through her chest. Monti frowned and stopped short, staring out at the dark waters. It was nearly pitch black out there, but the light from the moon and the stars gave enough that she could make out the different shapes.

Leaving was painful.

Since when?

Monti dragged her fingers through her tangled hair. Because she didn't want to leave this time. Not like she had before. Something had shifted inside her, and she wanted to stay and see how Athena made out. She wanted to go to Zoe's wedding and maybe be around when Fallon finally started dating someone. She wanted to know if Athena would ever take her jacket off in public again.

That last thought made her smile.

Damn, that woman was sexy. She hid it all, buttoning up and hiding with the hope that the world wouldn't see her. But it was impossible not to see her. Monti warmed slightly as the sun started streaking across the sky. Monti had noticed Athena the moment they'd met, and she hadn't been able to stop.

"Well, I'm definitely in like with her." Monti told the ocean. "What do you think?" She kicked at the water, cold lingering on her feet as she stepped deeper into the surf. Bending down, Monti put her hands in the water as it raced up toward her. Then she dug her hands into the wet sand, grabbing hold of it.

As the water moved away, it took the sand with it, leaving only a small amount curved in her palm. In the center was a small white shell, the whorls spiraling up toward a point. Monti rinsed it off in the water as another wave came up and studied it.

"There you are!" Athena's voice shocked through her.

Monti stood up, startled, her heart in her throat. She clutched the shell tightly in her fist.

"You scared me." Worry marred Athena's features.

Monti stepped closer and grabbed Athena's hand with her free one. The sun was already over the horizon and making the sky bright. It painted gentle hues over Athena's face, though the shadows of doubt were still there. "Sorry, I didn't realize I'd been gone so long."

"Long?" Athena moved in closer. "When did you leave?"

"I don't know. I didn't look at a clock." Monti pressed a kiss to Athena's cheek. "I'm sorry I worried you."

"You left the deck door open." Athena's voice wavered, and Monti definitely noted the fear over the worry.

"You don't like open doors." Why had that thought never occurred to her before? Monti had to open every single door every time she'd walked into a room. Athena always closed the door behind her or them when they went somewhere. She really should have noticed that. "Athena, I'm so sorry."

Monti wrapped her arms around Athena's shoulders and pulled her in, hugging her and kissing her head. She breathed in Athena's scent that was so familiar now. She closed her eyes and basked in it and in Athena's steady breathing.

"I should have been more careful."

"It's okay. You're safe," Athena mumbled into Monti's chest. She finally wrapped her arms around Monti's back and held on tightly. "You can't leave me like that."

"I needed some space to think."

Athena sighed heavily. "What's going on?"

"It's nothing." Monti kept her tone calm. She pulled back and slid her hand down Athena's cheek and her thumb over Athena's lips. She leaned in and pressed their mouths together quickly.

"Please don't coddle me."

Monti's heart sank. She had been doing exactly that. Athena had shared with her so much over the last few weeks. It was no wonder that she was looking for Monti to share as well. Kissing Athena again, this time lingering a little longer, Monti pulled back. She turned and started to walk toward the house.

"I had a nightmare."

"Oh." Athena gripped Monti's arm tightly.

Intuitively, Monti knew that Athena would understand those. She'd already deduced that had partially been why Athena wasn't sleeping. Monti laced their fingers together and dropped a kiss onto the back of Athena's hand.

"Do you ever sleep more than a few hours in a night?" Monti asked.

"No. Do you?"

"No," Monti responded, lifting Athena's hand again. "But I'm not used to nightmares. I don't dream much either. It is a trauma response, but I used to just ignore it."

"Used to?" Athena ran her fingers up and down Monti's arm.

"I don't want to ignore it anymore." Monti stopped walking. She looked into Athena's eyes and canted her head, slowing her breathing. She could do this. She could explain it to Athena in a way that she'd understand. "I realized that it's not about finding peace. It's not just somewhere out there in the next best place."

"No, it's not." Athena furrowed her brow. "You have to find it."

"I have to *make* it," Monti corrected. "But until this week, for some reason, I didn't realize that."

Athena rested her head on Monti's shoulder. They were filled with a comfortable silence, the only sound the lapping of waves and nature all around them as the world started to wake up.

"How do I make it?" Monti's voice was thick with emotion, and she was very well near tears again. She winced and buried her face into Athena's neck, using her to calm down. "How do I deal with a past that I don't remember?"

"Aren't you the one who said our bodies remember things? So you do remember it."

Monti let out a wry laugh. "Yeah. You're right."

Letting that knowledge settle into her chest, Monti stayed put. She closed her eyes, breathing it in and breathing it out. Just admitting that was harder than it should be. Fallon had been telling her for years that she remembered it, that it affected her, but now it was real. Now she didn't want to ignore it.

"All right, so I remember." Monti clenched her fist tighter, the shell digging into the center of her palm. It was a reminder of life and death, and the beauty in the world through all of it. "Now that I remember, I get to deal with it."

"How will you do that?"

"I don't know yet." Monti grinned and kissed Athena loudly on the cheek. "What do you think? Maybe we can just have sex so much that I'll forget it even exists."

Chuckling, Athena shook her head. "I'm pretty sure that's the exact opposite of what you just said you wanted."

"The sex?"

"No." Athena slapped Monti's arm lightly. "The avoiding with sex."

"Oh, because I'm all about sex." Monti kissed Athena's jaw. "Last night was fantastic."

"Are you sure?" Athena tensed, but she did tilt her chin up and turned her head, which gave Monti the exact access that she'd been looking for.

Monti took the opportunity, pressing another kiss to Athena's jawline. "Oh yes. In fact, I'd love a reprise."

"Already?" Athena whipped around to look at her.

"Yes. Do you?"

"I..." Athena paused, looking deep into Monti's gaze, as if trying to judge just how truthful Monti was being. "I don't know."

"Then let's spend some time figuring that out." Monti looped Athena's arm through her own. They started back toward the house. While Athena had definitely closed the door on her way out to find Monti, this house didn't feel like a prison. Not like the one in Seattle anyway.

"Fallon's worried about you," Athena murmured as they stepped onto the deck.

"Did she call you?"

"Of course." Athena opened the door and let them in. "I talk to her every day."

"Really?" Shock ripped through her. "What do you talk about?"

"Work." Athena shut and locked the door. Then she gave Monti the most *no-duh* look Monti had ever seen. "I have a trial coming up."

"You're on vacation."

"The work doesn't stop." Athena curled her hair around her ear and crossed her arms. "I still need to file some petitions, do some interviews, and get my files together."

"I guess I just assumed when you said a vacation to rest that you actually meant no work." Monti walked toward the kitchen. One more cup of coffee and maybe she could keep up with Athena. But the lack of sleep the last couple of days was starting to kick her butt. "I guess that does mean no sex, then. If you have to work, that is."

Athena hummed, and she moved right into Monti, kissing her. "I don't know about that."

Monti ran her hands up and down Athena's sides. "I'm sorry I scared you earlier."

Athena pursed her lips before shaking her head slowly. "You did scare me."

"I'm so sorry." Monti smiled. "I'll make it up to you later."

"I'll hold you to that."

twenty-eight

Monti had fallen asleep on the couch, her feet resting next to Athena's thigh and the book she'd been reading flat against her chest. Athena trailed her fingers up and down Monti's calf muscle, smiling at her gentle breathing. They'd been sitting there for a couple hours now, and it had become their routine.

Morning coffee and a walk on the beach, a little bit of work for Athena while Monti entertained herself, then they'd spend time in the afternoons reading in the quiet out on the deck. Athena had never been so relaxed in her life, so calm. Even with the intensity of the work that she was doing, the case she'd taken on, she'd managed to not be disturbed by it.

The only problem was that over the last few days, Monti had closed in on herself more and more. Athena started circle patterns with her thumb right under the inside of Monti's knee. Monti twitched, her entire body jerking with a start, but she still seemed to be sleeping.

She'd been doing a lot of that. Athena had noticed it both at night and during the day. She kept up the pattern on Monti's leg and settled back into her book, but the words were harder to focus on. What did her future mean? So much had changed in the last few weeks, and there was one thing Athena knew for certain. She didn't want to go back to the way it had been.

What was the point of going back?

Except to change where she was.

Athena brushed her fingers over her lips, remembering the way Monti had pressed against her, the lightness it had created deep within her. She smiled. She'd never felt that with anyone else, and she'd never thought she would feel that with someone. She had thought she was too broken for love, at least love that was this deep. Because this wasn't just love.

It was understanding.

Vulnerability.

Compassion.

Connection.

This was intimacy at its finest. And she knew Monti didn't feel the same way. But for some reason, that didn't matter. Athena wasn't looking for reciprocation so much as she was looking for acceptance. She wanted to be believed, and Monti had done that every second of every breath. She'd never questioned Athena's experiences. She'd never denied Athena her truth.

But where did that leave her? Because she hadn't once thought to call or text Kevin. Simon's birthday was in a couple days, so she'd need to call him, but that wasn't for support. Kevin was the one she usually ran to for those kinds of things, but the entire time she'd been here all she needed was Monti. All she'd needed was to pause and remember that life was different now. That she could be at peace.

"What have you done to me?" Athena murmured, keeping up the pattern on Monti's leg when she twitched again.

Athena rested her head against the back of the outdoor sofa and closed her eyes. The rays of sun warmed her skin. She enjoyed that feeling. She'd locked herself up for too long. It was finally time to come and play. Yes, play. Because Monti had shown her how to have fun this week, and it was something Athena didn't want to live without again.

What kind of parent would she have been if she'd known how to play with Simon when he was little? What kind of adult would he have grown into? God, she hoped she hadn't screwed him up too much. She'd tried to avoid all the mistakes of her parents and her past as best as she could, but there was no way to completely ignore them.

Monti jerked again, this time a little grunt at the end. Athena looked over at her, frowning. This seemed to be a little more than just restless sleep. But she wasn't sure what to do about it. Simon had nightmares when he was a kid, but she'd mostly let Kevin handle those. Biting the inside of her cheek, Athena waited to see if Monti would do it again, but she didn't.

Kevin was the perfect parent, and if she could help it, no one would ever know that Simon wasn't his biologically. It wouldn't matter in the long run. Because Kevin had been the perfect parent. He'd been more of a parent than she had. Athena sighed. What had she dragged him into?

Sure, he'd agreed to marry her, to play a role that wasn't his, and to be there for her. They both got the protection of a marriage out of it. She could finish law school and start a career, and Kevin could find a lover who could truly love him. Athena dropped her foot to the ground, the ball of her foot rubbing against the sand on the deck.

But it wasn't the early two-thousands anymore. They didn't *have* to be married for that protection. Kevin could legally get married to his boyfriend, and Simon would still inherit everything. She couldn't imagine Kevin ousting him, ever. They were two peas in a pod, which left her squarely where?

Monti jerked, this time her entire body tensing and voice crying out shrilly.

Okay. This wasn't just sleep.

Athena rubbed her full palm up and down Monti's calf muscle to try and wake her up. But it didn't work. Monti twitched again, her voice getting louder. Athena shifted, pushing Monti's feet away from her thigh and reaching up.

"Monti, wake up." Athena's heart was in her throat.

What was she supposed to do? She'd never been with an adult who had a nightmare. But this was a nap, and most people didn't get nightmares from naps. Athena tried again, increasing the pressure on Monti's leg.

Monti flung upward, her chest heaving, her eyes wide open, her lips thin and her face pale. Athena jerked back, her shoulder hitting the back of the outdoor sofa and scraped her skin. Her throat clogged up instantly, but Monti didn't move. She continued to breathe heavily as if she was unseeing.

"Monti, it's just me."

Shaking her head, Monti turned and planted her feet on the deck. She rested her elbows on her knees and hung her head. Athena was scared to touch her, scared to say anything to her. What was she supposed to do? She wasn't trained for this. Hell, she could barely take care of herself most days.

"Give me a minute," Monti mumbled. She sounded so down.

Athena's heart broke. Just what was Monti going through? Had bringing her here been too much? Monti dropped her hand onto Athena's knee and sucked in a sharp breath.

"I'll be fine, just give me a minute."

"What happened?" The question was out of Athena's mouth before she could stop it.

She didn't want to pry. She didn't want Monti to think that she had to share when she didn't. Athena bit her lip and clenched her fingers into a tight fist. Her gaze dropped to Monti's hand still on her knee, and after another moment of hesitation, she lifted her hand up and set it right on top of Monti's. She curled her fingers under Monti's palm and tightened her grasp.

"Take all the time you need," Athena corrected herself. "I'm right here."

Monti flipped her hand up and laced their fingers. She took deep breaths and tried to relax, but her nerves were on edge. Monti was normally the calm one, but right now she was anything but. The muscles in her back tightened almost painfully as she tensed and waited for Monti to say something, do something. Because Monti was the one who knew what to do in situations like this.

"I just need a minute," Monti repeated.

Athena didn't answer this time, because she was pretty sure that Monti wasn't hearing anything she said. Instead, Athena held Monti's hand tightly in hers and waited. When nothing happened after another five minutes, Athena moved on instinct. She wrapped an arm slowly around Monti's back, sliding her fingers from one shoulder to the other, and she pulled Monti into her chest.

Dragging in a deep breath, Athena closed her eyes and breathed in Monti's scent. She dropped a kiss into Monti's hair and simply held her. Monti had done the same thing to her when she'd needed it. Maybe that was all Monti needed right now. Maybe this would be enough, because it was all Athena could offer.

She was too broken to give anything else.

Monti's shoulders shook. Her breathing was sharp, and Athena couldn't pretend she was hearing anything but Monti trying to prevent herself from crying. Athena's heart shattered a little more, and she threaded her fingers through Monti's hair, pressing kisses to her head as often as she could.

What were they doing here?

They were both broken and shattered. They were both falling apart right in front of each other.

They could never work. Athena held Monti close to her, keeping Monti pressed to her chest and tightening her hold. They could stay like this a little bit longer. They could stay here in the cocoon of this trip and pretend that they might come out on the other side without any more scars to show.

These ones might be invisible to the naked eye, but they ran deep. They weren't easy to stitch closed.

Athena pulled Monti's mouth up to hers and kissed her. Monti fell into the embrace, the first sign that she was focused and feeling, that she was present in the here and now. Athena kissed her hard before slowing down and closing her eyes.

"It was a bad nightmare," Monti whispered. "I'm sorry if I scared you."

"Your nightmare didn't scare me," Athena answered, curling the loose hair behind Monti's ear. "Will you talk to me?"

"I don't know what there is to say."

"Whatever you want to say." Athena pulled Monti in for another kiss, this one tender and full of compassion.

"I remember him beating her. Kind of, anyway. I remember what it sounded like." Monti pressed her face into Athena's neck. "It sounded like a dull thud."

Athena remembered that sound. But it wasn't from someone else being beaten, and she remembered what it felt like to have knuckles pound into her skin. Shaking the memory wasn't easy, but she wanted to focus on Monti. "I know what it sounds like."

Monti tightened. "I didn't realize. I'm sorry."

"Stop apologizing for your own experiences." Athena pulled Monti's face up to look into her eyes. "You can't control what happened to you."

"Who's the therapist now?" Monti gave her a weak smile, but it was the first sign in days of the person Athena had come to know. And she clung onto that. "I keep remembering it."

"Flashbacks are a bitch."

"Athena Pruitt!" Monti laughed lightly. "I never thought I'd hear you talk like that."

"Oh, I've said worse." Athena leaned back into the outdoor sofa and relaxed. She finally felt as though they were balancing the chaos of their lives. At least it felt that way for a moment. Athena was pretty sure that balance was impossible to find, but at least she was looking for it now. At least she could be a little closer to it.

"What have you said?" Monti rested her arm along the back of the seat, playing with the ends of Athena's hair.

She was acting like nothing had happened, like she hadn't woken from a nightmare in a panic, like she hadn't just confessed to remembering her dad beating her mom. Athena couldn't keep up. Was this Monti avoiding or was she really just that good at getting over her trauma quickly?

"I've told people to fuck off before."

Monti snorted.

"There are quite a few judges I had choice words for. Though I did not say it to their faces. That would have gotten me thrown out." Athena tried to figure out what Monti was doing when she leaned away. She felt so distant, as though she was shutting back down again. The brief window into who Monti really was had already closed and Athena was left with this awkward tension between them.

She didn't like it.

She'd thought they could come here and get closer to each other, and yet, ever since they'd arrived, everything had gone the complete opposite direction. Then again, perhaps this was her lot in life. Athena ran her fingers over Monti's arm and gave a sweet smile.

"Do you want to go out to dinner tonight?"

"You want to eat out?" Monti looked confused. "I'm assuming that's not a euphemism for anything."

"Monti!" Athena laughed, the sound bubbling up in her chest. "No, I meant go out."

"Do you eat at restaurants?"

"Yes." Confusion swam through Athena. "Why wouldn't I?"

"Because you don't like people putting their hands in their pockets, you're always looking for the exit, and you never relax in a room full of strangers."

"Oh." Athena pressed her lips together hard. She hadn't realized her neuroses were that obvious. Did that mean Monti didn't want to go out that night? Because she was more than willing to put up with the extra stress in order to enjoy time out of the house with Monti. She wouldn't ever consider this if she was alone.

"We can just stay in." Monti walked her fingers along

Athena's shoulder to her neck, cupping the back of her head and pressing their mouths together in a kiss. "I'm going to go for a walk on the beach."

Monti stood up. Where Athena expected there to be an invitation to join, there wasn't. And she didn't feel as though she could invite herself along. She stayed put and watched as Monti walked down toward the beach. The distance between them increased, the chasm widening. Perhaps this was all there was to them.

Perhaps it hadn't ever been deeper than that.

Athena waited until Monti was out of her sight. She'd thought they had something special, but she was wrong. Monti had been hired for a job and that's what she was doing. She didn't want or need Athena's help, not that she'd been able to give any. She was hopeless when it came to things like this—too broken to even attempt to help someone else through their brokenness.

Sighing, Athena stood up and walked inside.

It was better this way.

They were too broken for this to work.

twenty-nine

Hours meditating on the beach had only soothed the memory. Monti found as the sun fell over the horizon that it hadn't settled her soul. Once again, she was left with the choice as to whether or not to make peace. Sighing, Monti stood up, her toes digging into the cold sand.

What was she doing out here?

Monti wanted to be inside. She wanted Athena's arms around her again, holding her, keeping her together the same way she had earlier that day when Monti had woken up so scared. She grimaced. She was screwing all of this up, wasn't she?

She'd never allowed herself to get close to anyone, and that had left her exactly where she found herself now. Alone. But that wasn't what she wanted anymore, and Athena had offered to give her exactly what they both needed.

Turning around, Monti headed back to the house, the sun at her back as she found her way to the back deck. The door was closed, but it was unlocked, thankfully, because she'd forgotten her key in her haste to escape.

Athena was inside, a wine glass in her hand and a book on her lap. Monti smiled, warmth threading its way through her as she closed—and locked—the door behind her. She really should have taken Athena up on the offer for dinner out, but she hadn't thought she would be able to stand people staring at the two of them. And they would stare. They didn't look like they belonged together at all.

"Hey," Monti said, sliding into the seat next to Athena and taking Athena's foot. She started a gentle massage out of habit, using the repetitive pattern to bring herself into this moment and stay here. "Thanks for giving me some time."

"Didn't realize that's what I was doing." Athena put her book down and snagged her wine glass. "Did you want a drink?"

Monti shook her head. Normally she would have agreed, but not tonight. She didn't want to stand up again and potentially lose her gumption to do what she'd come in here to do. She was going to take this a step further. She was going to share what needed to be shared.

"Do you need anything?" Monti asked, cursing her habit to avoid her own personal issues. She was so good at it some days.

"No, I'm good. Thank you." Athena settled her drink onto the ground and hummed when Monti hit a particularly tender spot.

The sound sent a shiver straight through Monti. She could so easily fall into distracting both of them by seducing Athena again. But that didn't seem like the right choice to make. Monti switched feet. The silence was so comforting. The problem was that Monti knew she had to get uncomfortable in order to do this the right way.

Earlier that day, she'd tried to put Athena's comfort over her own. She moved her hands up Athena's calves, digging her thumbs into the tight muscles there. Again, she elicited another moan from Athena.

"You're so good at that."

Monti chuckled. "Well, I did study it for years. I wasn't always good."

"I'll have to send your instructor a thank you note." Athena groaned again, her back arching slightly.

"I'm sure she'd appreciate it."

"Did you seduce her like you did me?"

Monti tensed. Is that what Athena thought all this was? "I never slept with her, no. And for the record, Athena, I've never slept with a client before either—a massage client or a therapy patient."

"Ah." Athena didn't look at her though. And Monti couldn't tell if she really understood or not.

She'd been told for years during her training and practice that starting a relationship with a client was impossible, and this was why. The power dynamics, the trust—everything was all wrapped up in a formulated relationship. There was nothing natural about this.

"Fallon used to hide us when our dad beat Mom. I didn't remember that until today, but she used to pull me out of the crib and into the closet to hide." Monti found every ounce of courage she had and used it to open her eyes and gaze into Athena's.

What would she see there?

What did she need?

Athena, however, gave her a whole lot of nothing. The pleasure from the massage had gone, and her face wasn't much more than a simple blank stare.

"I didn't realize how much I remembered, and it's difficult to remember it." Monti moved her hands farther up Athena's leg, to her thigh. It was an awkward angle to massage in, but she really didn't want to move either. "I'm not very good at this."

Monti was going to add more, but when Athena didn't respond, she struggled to find the words. She'd never thought she'd be met with silence when sharing. It wasn't something she was used to, but then again, she'd been trained in what to say. Athena hadn't.

"I assume he was never arrested."

"He's dead."

"Before that." Athena shifted, wiggling slightly when Monti hit a particularly hard knot along the outside of her thigh.

"I don't know." Monti's brow creased as she thought. "It never came up, and I don't remember those kinds of specifics. I was young when he died."

Athena nodded. "Our justice system doesn't work for the victims."

"No, it doesn't," Monti agreed. "But that sounds like something you can change."

"Only one case at a time." Athena crossed her arms. "Doesn't seem to make much of a difference."

"Then why continue?" Monti moved her hand to Athena's hip, pressing into the muscles and teasing them out of their tension. Athena hadn't told her to stop yet. And Monti was going to continue as long as Athena was okay with it.

"Why would I stop?" Athena covered Monti's hand and pulled it from her hip. She set it gently back on her thigh, but held her fingers there so they couldn't move. "I'm sorry you never got justice."

"It's not about justice. It's about peace." Monti covered Athena's hand with her other one. "I've been searching for peace my entire life. I didn't realize how long it had really been until recently. But it's kind of been my quest since I could name it."

"What does peace look like?" Athena asked, her eyes fluttering closed.

Monti wished they could look at each other, that she could see Athena's reactions to what she was saying. Then again, maybe it would be easier to speak if she didn't have to look Athena in the eye. "I don't know."

"It would be nice to have that answer."

"Wouldn't it?" Monti smiled slightly, but she wasn't getting the response she needed. Athena was so disassociated from the conversation, like she couldn't be there in the moment to even hear what Monti was saying. Perhaps this wasn't the best time for the conversation to happen, but Monti needed it to be now.

She hadn't told anyone these things. Ever.

"I've believed for a long time that if I can reduce my impact on the people I love, then they won't be hurt when I leave."

"Why would you leave?" Athena still wasn't looking at her, but her cheeks paled instantly.

"I always leave." Monti ran the edge of her thumb along the side of Athena's hand. "I've always left, I guess. I've never stayed. College, grad school, finishing my practicals and hours to get licensed. I always move on to something else."

Monti clenched her jaw. As much as she loved to travel, something about being here with Athena this week made her not want to leave. At least not in the same way she had before. She missed Fallon and Tia. She loved them. She wanted them to love her.

Sucking in a sharp breath, Monti rolled her shoulders and leaned into the couch. "You hide in your house, and I hide out there. We're really not that different, are we?"

"I suppose not." Athena frowned. She played her fingers over Monti's hand and upper arm. "That probably makes us incompatible."

"It might." Monti tried to find Athena's gaze, but again she failed. "It might not." Was Athena thinking of a longer-term relationship than just these couple of weeks? She was married, and while Monti understood the nature of that relationship, being married to someone else and being long term with a third party didn't typically go hand in hand. Monti would never be able to go to a gala or a party with Athena and walk in with Athena on her arm. She would never be able to say publicly they were together.

She didn't want a relationship that was hidden.

Hiding her pain from the world was typical, but she had never hidden her happiness or her love. That was something Monti wasn't interested in doing. So she'd assumed that long term the two of them wouldn't work. But she didn't want to bring that up, not right now, not when Athena didn't really seem to be an active participant in the conversation.

"I think I'm going to head up for the night." Monti pushed Athena's legs off her thighs and stood up.

She looked down at Athena, understanding the confusion and not having the energy to deal with it. Athena was going to have to do this work on her own.

"Night," Monti added, trying to make it clear that she still wanted time alone. If she couldn't get what she needed from Athena, then she would have to find it herself right now, and that meant quiet. Monti walked up the stairs and to her room. She took the longest and hottest shower that she could manage, and when she stepped out of the bathroom, steam billowed around her.

Monti collapsed naked on the bed and stared up at the ceiling. All she had to do now was to find that peace. Monti fell into the emotion that she was feeling, finding it and holding it in her chest. That feeling was one she needed to follow. It was the unease from her childhood, the pain from instability. She let it settle, she let it take over her body, and then she let it go. At least as much as she could. It would probably take many repeated sessions of this.

Monti sighed heavily when she heard Athena on the stairs. Athena stopped just outside of Monti's door, and Monti knew she was debating what to do next. But she didn't have the energy to stand up and end Athena's misery. She held her breath until Athena walked by. The door of the bedroom next door shutting was exactly what Monti had expected to hear.

What she had told Athena earlier was true. She needed to stop holding back from her relationships with those she loved. She needed to talk to Fallon. That was a must, and something she would work on when she got home. They needed to meet in person for that conversation.

Allowing herself to be loved wasn't going to be easy. Because she knew it would come with pain. She knew she would screw up and hurt someone. She knew that with that good came hardship. Monti groaned and turned on her side, facing the window.

She would wake up early in the morning, go for another run, and do some meditation. That would help her figure out where her next step was. Until then, she would attempt to get some sleep—preferably without nightmares.

Though she had slim hope that would happen.

thirty

"Hey, you got a minute to talk?" Athena's voice wavered as she sat down in the den in one of her favorite chairs. She'd spent all night thinking about it, and it was time to finally make the call. She just wished she didn't feel so awful about it.

"Yeah, what's up?" Kevin's voice was confident, as he always was.

"Are you alone?"

"Yes? What's going on?"

She knew, intuitively, that he was worried she was sick or even dying. But she couldn't figure out a better way to say this, and the words kept getting stopped up in her throat like they always did.

"Athena? Are you okay? Are you safe?"

"Yes." She swallowed the lump, answering him swiftly. "Yes, I'm okay, and yes, I'm safe."

"I've been worried about you." She could hear soft music in the background. He always had something playing if he was alone. Kevin hated the silence.

"Don't be."

"I'll always worry about you. Simon said something about it too."

"Did he? How was Las Vegas?" She asked, sidestepping her

son's worry and moving straight into a conversation she was far more comfortable with having.

"It was good. We had fun, lost a lot of money at the tables."

"A lot?"

"No. You know me, I hate gambling." Kevin clicked his tongue at her. "Simon lost money. Enough to feel like a man, not enough that he's going to suffer for it later."

That was also true. She'd never known him to take a risk if he could avoid it. Kevin would have worked to teach him how to gamble and stop. Athena brushed her fingers through her hair, finding knots tangled in the ends, knots she knew were there from Monti. Her cheeks reddened. She'd never been able to talk to Kevin about sex—well, not since that night. Before then? Absolutely. But so much had changed when she was raped, and it had never gone back to the way it was before.

"Why did you call, Athena? I don't get the sense that this is a check-in."

She sighed and pulled at the small knots, untangling her hair. How was she supposed to tell him everything that had happened? Everything she realized that she wanted? She rubbed her lips together, crossing her arms and walking to the window to stare out of it at the beach.

"Athena?"

"I'm okay, I promise you. I don't need you rushing out here."

"You know I will, right? And you saying that doesn't exactly make me feel like I don't need to be there."

"I actually don't need you here." A tremble ran through her. Athena turned around and stared at the den. Why did the world look so different now than it had before? The simple answer wasn't that the world had changed but that she had. "Do you remember graduation night? When you, me, Dennis, and Evelyn got really drunk and started listing all the expectations our parents had of us?"

"Vaguely?" Kevin was no doubt frowning, his brow furrowed

as he tried to remember. Athena could see his face now, pinched in concentration.

"I'm tired of living up to what other people expect of me. Aren't you?"

"I'm lost on what we're talking about."

Athena swallowed the lump. The words were on the tip of her tongue. Why couldn't she just say them already? Why couldn't she just tell him what she wanted? "We got married because it was a way for us to do what needed to be done and still be able to live our lives."

"Yeah. What's your point?"

"I love you, Kevin, so much." Athena fisted her hand and then relaxed it. She rolled her shoulders before walking back to the chair and sitting down. Immediately, she stood up, not sure what to do or say next. But she had to get this out there. She *had* to tell him what she'd been contemplating. "I don't want to be married anymore."

The silence was deafening.

Athena waited for him to say something. She waited for him to speak, to yell, to scream, to agree or disagree. Anything! But she got nothing except that silence.

"You love her," Kevin murmured.

"Who are you talking about?" The hair on the back of Athena's neck stood up.

"That woman who was giving you massages."

"It doesn't matter if I do or I don't," Athena answered. "I think you deserve to live the life you choose, and I deserve to live mine. We don't have to pretend anymore."

"Who was pretending?"

There was that hurt she'd been expecting. Athena pressed her lips together firmly. She wished she was better at this part of life, but she wasn't. She never managed to get it right the first time. She pinched the bridge of her nose to concentrate. "We both were pretending in this marriage, not in our love for each other. You know that, and I know that."

"Why now?" Kevin sighed heavily. "Jesus, Athena, we've been married for twenty-two years almost. Why are you deciding you can't do this anymore?"

That really was the ultimate question, wasn't it? She had spent years doing what everyone else around her wanted, and she was done with it. But what had flipped that switch for her? What had been the thing that pushed her over the edge?

"It was Monti," she said simply.

"Because you're in love."

"Not because I'm in love." Was that even a denial? She was getting weaker with it every passing moment. "Because she helped me get my head on straight. I haven't been myself for decades, Kev."

"I know." He sniffled. "I've missed you."

"You are the most patient man on this planet." She smiled to herself, wishing he was here in person for this conversation, but knowing it had to happen this way. She couldn't wait for it, and it was easier if she didn't have to look at him. "I want you to be free to be happy."

"I am happy."

"You're not." Athena swiped at the tear that trickled down her cheek. "You haven't been in a long time. You're satisfied."

"You really have had your eyes opened."

She smiled at that. "I have."

Standing at the window again, she stared outside, wishing she could see Monti now. What would Monti tell her? What would they talk about if Monti knew she was doing this? Athena rubbed her fingers over her lips, remembering their kisses, their caresses.

"I don't want this life anymore," she murmured. "Not that what we've had hasn't been good, but it's not what I want anymore."

"What if it's what I want?"

"Do you?" She hadn't honestly thought that was a possibility. Athena had always assumed that when she was ready to call it quits, he would walk with her hand in hand to sign those papers.

He'd never been someone who would resist her requests. It had been how she'd convinced him to marry her in the first place.

"I want what's best for us, all of us."

"And Simon?" She had to ask. She needed to know what he was going to tell Simon, what they needed to share with him.

"He's always going to be my son, Athena. I couldn't give him up even if I wanted to."

She breathed out relief, and it flooded her chest and into her fingers and toes. Athena pressed her head to the window frame and reveled in the cool wood as it touched her skin. "I worry about him so much."

"He's an adult. He's going to do what he's going to do."

"No, not that." She stood up straight. "I'm worried that he'll become them."

"Oh, baby, he'll never do that." She could almost feel the hug he'd no doubt give her if they were together in person. "You are so much a part of him, and that sense of justice and love and compassion is what made him from the moment he breathed life."

She sobbed, the sound tearing from her lips. All that pent-up fear released. She had done well in raising him. They had worked together brilliantly for years, and Simon had become a wise young gentleman, someone who was enjoying life in ways Athena never had the ability to do.

"He's *your* son, and that's what matters."

Athena had no idea what to say to him, where to even begin to take the next steps and share everything that had flitted through her brain in the last month. She needed Kevin like she needed water, but she needed Monti like she needed air.

"We'll still be the way we always have been, right?" He sounded so timid now.

"Yes, of course!" She rushed to reassure him. "You're my best friend. I love you."

"Then that's all I needed to hear." He sighed lightly, but it wasn't in stress, it was in relief. "Will you get everything set up?"

"Yes. Yes, I can do that." She wiped her cheeks again as she spotted Monti on the horizon. "It'll take a while to get all the paperwork together."

"Take your time. It's not like we're in a rush."

"Yeah, no rush." Except it didn't quite feel that way. Monti meandered up toward the house. Athena needed to end the call. She smiled. "I love you, Kevin."

"Love you, Athena. Since I'm assuming your love just walked in—"

"Kevin..." Athena said in a warning.

"I'm not taking that one back. I'll let you go so you can be with her."

"Do you even know her name?"

"Does it matter if she makes you happy?"

Athena's smile faltered. He would be the most supportive person on this planet. How she'd ever been so lucky as to find him and love him and grow up with him, she'd never know. But she couldn't have made it through life without him. "I'll call you soon."

"You do that. Remember, Athena, don't be afraid."

He had told her that countless times over the years. But for the first time, she believed that it might be possible.

"I'll try," she whispered, knowing it was the answer he expected. "Talk to you soon."

Hanging up, Athena slid her phone into her pocket. She left the den and met Monti at the door. Monti looked wind worn, her hair wild around her face as if it had battered her along her walk. But she'd never looked sexier. With the pink in her cheeks, the sweat clinging to her skin. Athena sucked in a sharp breath when Monti's eyes locked on hers.

Damn Kevin for being right.

But even if he was, that didn't make this relationship the right one for both of them. Athena's mouth went dry, and she wet her lips as best she could as Monti started toward the kitchen. On instinct, Athena followed her.

Monti had a glass of water in her hand while Athena pulled over a half-full bottle of wine she'd drunk earlier that day. "How was the run?"

"Not as useful as I'd hoped," Monti answered, setting the glass on the countertop. "It's beautiful here, though."

"I've always loved it here." Athena took one sip of her wine before putting the glass down next to Monti's drink. "I never found running useful. Well, physical running."

Monti laughed lightly, her lips curling upward. "I'm glad you can joke about your trauma. That's a good sign, actually."

"Is it?" Athena raised her eyebrows.

Struggling slightly, Monti snagged her glass again. "For you I think it is."

"I'll take that as a compliment."

"I'm proud of the work you've done and the progress you've made. You should be proud of yourself too."

Narrowing her eyes, Athena tried to figure out why Monti was talking like this, as if they were back to therapist and client. Sidestepping, as she did best, Athena slid in closer to Monti. The scent of her body, sweaty and sun-laden, hit her first, and Athena was so intrigued by it.

"Maybe you can teach me to like running someday."

"Spoiler alert," Monti teased back. "I don't like running. Don't get me wrong, I do love what it does for me, keeping my body in shape, and how it makes me feel when I'm done, but I much prefer a long walk in the woods to a run on the hot sandy beach."

"Me too." Athena looked up into Monti's eyes. She dared herself to do the first thing that came to mind, so she reached forward and covered Monti's hand with her own. She brushed her thumb back and forth in a gentle caress. "Maybe we should take that walk someday."

"We can, if you want to."

Was she just not being clear enough? Athena stepped in closer, their bodies brushing in the heat of the moment now. She pressed her palm to Monti's hip, holding her close as she lifted up on her toes and touched their lips together. The kiss was sweet, full, and filled with tenderness.

"Come upstairs with me." There, the words were out. Athena kissed her again, intensifying the moment. Monti cupped the back of her head, tilting her slightly as their tongues swept against each other.

"Not tonight, Athena," Monti murmured. But Monti kissed her again and again, as if the words she was saying didn't quite match up with what she was doing. Which left Athena very confused about what they were doing and why.

With one last kiss, Monti stepped away. "I'm going to take a shower and then hit the sack."

Athena said nothing as she watched Monti walk away from her. She'd put so much on the line to try and make that seduction happen, to work through all the walls that she typically had in place, only to be rejected? Confused, Athena took her wine glass and went back to the den.

She sat in her favorite chair, crossed her legs, and stared out the window as the sun settled fully below the horizon. What were they doing there?

Kevin may have been right, but that didn't mean Monti felt the same.

Disappointment hit Athena first. Then on the back end, she was overwhelmed with a sense of stupidity. She should have known better. She really shouldn't have just switched the expectations she'd lived with onto someone else.

Finishing her glass of wine, Athena took a new book and started reading it. For now, she could at least get lost in a fictional world. She could find a way to deal with her feelings in the morning.

To avoidance it is.

Athena smirked.

thirty-one

"I can't do this."

Monti paced the small bedroom so many times it was impossible to count. She stared at the phone on her bed, debating whether or not to call Fallon. It was a long time since she'd been this worked up, and having that outside voice from someone who understood—

Fuck, when had she started thinking that Fallon understood?

Monti paced again. Straight to the window, then to the door. Energy coursed through her veins, making it impossible to settle. She wasn't going to get any sleep that night. What had she been thinking? This was impossible.

Picking up her phone, she called Fallon. She needed someone else to calm her down, and she couldn't put that weight on Athena. Not when Athena was still struggling with figuring out her life at the moment. This was why she should have never started this kind of a relationship with a client. Although, to be fair she didn't start it.

"Monti!" Fallon's voice was sharp through the phone.

"Yes. Hi. Sorry." She hadn't realized that Fallon had picked up already. Her panic was overwhelming, and no matter how many runs she'd taken that week, she hadn't managed to figure out how to calm it down for longer than a few hours. She knew Athena was worried, that she was wondering why Monti had changed so much in the last few days, why Monti was pushing her away, but she just couldn't bring that down on their budding relationship or the way that Athena was finally opening up.

"Monti," Fallon said in a warning this time. "You're scaring me."

"I'm sorry. I..." Monti trailed off, locking her eyes on the curtain by the window, the one that was moving because of the breeze outside. If she could concentrate on that, then she could focus enough to talk to Fallon. "I needed to talk to you."

"Then talk, because this awkward start-and-stop silence is starting to freak me out."

"I'm so sorry."

"Stop apologizing! Tell me what's wrong."

"That's what I'm saying is wrong," Monti growled. She'd at least gotten this far in her internal debate of what to do and not do that week. She owed Fallon the explanation of a lifetime. And she hated that it was going to happen over the phone, but at this point, it was better sooner rather than later. Get one thing off her chest and then maybe she could focus on the next problem at hand.

Her relationship with Athena.

And how she'd managed to screw that one up in the short time they'd actually been together.

"I'm so confused," Fallon's voice shocked Monti back to reality.

"I know." Heaving a sigh, Monti collapsed onto the bed and stared up at the ceiling. She'd practically memorized what it looked like at this point. And that was another problem she was going to have to deal with. She needed to calm the hell down already. "You've wanted to be closer to me for years, and I haven't let you."

There. It was out there in the universe. They could now talk about the elephant that had trampled on their lives for the last thirty some-odd years.

"What?" Fallon's voice quivered.

Monti knew that she was blindsiding her, that this was going to be out of the blue, but she had to know, didn't she? "I haven't gotten close to you on purpose. I haven't let myself be loved by you."

"*This* is what you called about? Tonight of all nights?"

Monti ran through her memory to try and remember what the significance was that she was missing.

"It's Mom's birthday."

Her blood ran cold. She was such an idiot. She never remembered dates like she should. Groaning, Monti turned onto her side and clenched her eyes tightly. "I hate that I keep doing this."

"Why do you keep doing it?"

"Because I never cared before."

"Before?" Fallon paused. "Do you care now?"

"I care because it matters to you." Monti flipped onto her back again. "I should be there for you, and instead, I've pushed you away at every turn because I don't want to hurt you if something were to happen to me."

"If something—"

"If I died." Monti trembled. She stared at her door, seeing Athena's feet in the shadow from the light in the hall. She swallowed hard, her heart in her throat. Was Athena going to come in? Was she going to listen in from the doorway and see if Monti was okay? Because she wasn't okay. She was definitely not all right.

"How can you think like that?"

"How can I not?" Monti fired back. She debated whether or not to keep talking since she knew Athena was out there, but what else did she have to lose? "They died and left. Mom died and you've been broken ever since. I couldn't add to that."

"So instead you just closed yourself off?"

"Yeah." Monti bit her lip, watching as Athena's feet disappeared. She relaxed. "Yeah, I did, because I don't want to hurt anyone like Mom hurt us."

"It wasn't her fault that she died."

"No, it wasn't," Monti agreed. She toed off her shoes and heard the plops as they fell to the floor. "But it is her fault that she didn't do something about it sooner. And I get it. I've worked with victims of domestic violence and abuse before. I get that she was scared and didn't feel like she had a choice, but a part of me still blames her for not doing something."

"Monti..." Fallon trailed off, sighing. "I blamed her for years too. But at some point, I had to stop."

"What difference would it even make?"

"All the difference."

Monti held her breath, like Fallon was going to tell her some secret that she'd been waiting for that she couldn't let through her grasp.

"It allowed me to just love her."

Was it really that simple? Monti swallowed back the worry and the fear, the discomfort at being so close to someone. If she pushed past the blame, could she love her dead mother? Could she learn to love Fallon and let Fallon love her? She took in slow breaths, that pent up chaotic energy dissipating just a little.

"It allowed me to love you," Fallon added. "Because you know that's not always easy. Especially when you're off gallivanting around the world and not talking to me."

"I never ignore you on purpose, you know that, right?"

"Not intentionally. But I do think that you limit contact because you're scared of allowing me in."

Why did her sister have to be so astute tonight? Then again, that had been why Monti had called. She'd needed a swift kick in the ass. One that would get her on the right path again. "I don't do it with just you."

"I know." Now Fallon sounded like she was smiling. Which she probably was, because she was getting exactly what she'd wanted from Monti for years. Openness. Vulnerability. Actual deep conversation. "You do it with everyone."

"How do I stop?"

"One step at a time."

Well, what the hell did that mean?

Monti looked back at the door, wondering if Athena's feet were still there. She knew they wouldn't be, that Athena would be hurt by what had happened downstairs, but that hadn't been Monti's intention. Or had it? She pressed her lips together hard as she thought that one through. No. It hadn't been to hurt her, although that had been the result. She'd wanted to protect Athena, and in that protection, all she'd done was harm.

"I think I love her," Monti murmured out loud, not even sure if the words were actually going to leave her lips or not. "I don't want to push people away anymore."

"Then don't," Fallon replied. "Now is as good a time as any to stop."

"But I don't know what to expect."

"You'll figure it out. You're a smart woman, Monti. I've never had any doubt about that." Fallon seemed much lighter already, her tone not as concerned as it had been before. "And if you love her, then you need to tell her that. I'm pretty sure that Athena needs to feel loved more than anything in her life."

"Kevin loves her."

"He does. But it's not enough."

Monti continued to stare at the door, wishing that Athena would try again. Because if she did, then Monti would hang up and go to the door. She would fall into Athena's arms and not look back. Wouldn't she? Who was she kidding? She'd be looking back for a long time and wondering if she'd made the right decision. That was what she was known best for.

"She needs you," Fallon said gently.

Monti's heart kicked up a notch, pounding hard, and it was becoming difficult to breathe. What was she supposed to do now? "I don't know what to do."

"Yes, you do."

"Nope. I'm all out of ideas."

"Get out of your own way," Fallon chided. "You've got this."

"Yeah, I guess." Monti didn't like what she was hearing, but who would? She loosened her grip on her phone. "Thanks, Fallon."

"I do love you. You know that, right?"

"I've never doubted that." Monti smiled, genuinely for the first time in what felt like forever. "I love you too."

"You have no idea how good it feels to hear that."

Monti relaxed, settling into the knowledge that what she'd done was good. What she'd wanted wasn't out of bounds. And Fallon was right. She needed to get out of her own way for anything to move forward and to get any of what she wanted.

"I'll call you soon, I promise," Monti said, already preparing to hang up. She needed to get the rest of the energy out, and there was only one way coming to mind.

"I'll hold you to that. And for the record, Monti, good luck. I want her to be happy as much as I want you to be. You both deserve it."

Monti smiled as the call ended. She lay on the bed for a while longer, listening to Athena putter around in the room next door. It hadn't been a wise choice for her to allow a relationship between them to flourish or even begin. She should have put a stop to it ages ago.

But they were here now.

Athena was relying on her, and Monti had better figure out a way to get her shit together so she could take care of Athena. Because that was what she was hired to do. This could potentially be one more step for Athena, one more way of breaking out of her shell.

Standing up, Monti left her bedroom and went immediately next door. She rapped her knuckles against the door and waited. Athena appeared, looking disheveled. That was all Monti's fault. She'd been so caught up in her own chaos that she hadn't been able to focus on Athena, which was the whole point of being here.

"Come with me," Monti said in a rush, her voice breathy.

"It's late," Athena protested.

"I know." Monti held out her hand, waiting for Athena to take it. It was the only way this was going to work. Athena had to choose this. If she didn't, then they wouldn't move forward. Athena would continue to stay stuck in the hell of her own making.

"What are we doing?" Athena's bright blue eyes locked on hers.

"Trust me."

That's what all of this was about in the end, wasn't it?

Trust.

Athena dropped her gaze, staring at Monti's outstretched hand. Her breathing slowed, her lips parted. She was about to protest again. Monti could feel it in her bones. She held still and sucked in a breath.

"All I'm asking is that you trust me. One last time."

"One last time?" Athena flicked her gaze up to meet Monti's eyes. "I don't want this to be the last time."

"Then you have your answer, don't you?"

One more brief moment of hesitation and Athena pressed her hand into Monti's waiting one. "What are we doing?" This time her question was filled with confidence.

"You'll see." Monti folded their hands together, lacing their fingers.

With full conviction, she walked down the hallway and the stairs. She went straight to the back deck and outside. Athena followed her without a protest. Their toes were bare in the sand, digging into it. Monti walked straight for the ocean.

She'd always been fascinated with the water and the way it moved, the metaphors it held, the darkness and unexplored depths but also the lightness and familiarity. She let go of Athena's hand and tugged off her shirt.

"What are you doing?" Shock rippled through Athena's tone.

Monti chuckled as she reached for her waistband. "I'm going to clear my head of all the bad thoughts. And I'm going to come back up a whole new person."

"What?" Athena held onto Monti's hand tightly, preventing her from pushing her pants off her body. "You're getting naked."

Monti grinned wickedly. "Don't feel like you have to though. The rebirth will be the same whether you have clothes on or not. I just want to be as close to the water as possible."

Monti stepped back and finished undressing. She walked into the water, letting the waves hit her ankles and then her knees and her thighs before she turned around and faced Athena on the beach. "Don't you want a new lease on life?"

"Yeah, but not like this!" Athena called back. "This is insane!"

"Maybe!" Monti kept walking backward into the surf. Athena became smaller on the beach the farther she went out. She knew she wouldn't go that far. She'd be able to stand no matter what so that she could get back in, but she craved this freedom. "I need to start over in the best way possible!"

"Monti!" Athena nearly shouted, but there was no command that came with it.

Not that Monti would have listened. Raising her hands above her head she looked up at the moon and the stars, a full smile blooming on her lips. Fallon had been right. She just needed to get out of her own way, and that was exactly what she was doing. Sinking to her knees first, Monti let the water cover her shoulders. Then she dipped her head under the cold water, closing her eyes and getting lost in the sea.

The water rushed over her, caressing her, encompassing her. Monti held her breath until she couldn't anymore, and then she pushed up, breaking through the water. Brushing her hair out of her face, Monti looked back at the beach to find Athena still watching her.

What would it be like to have Athena there with her? Naked in the water?

What would it feel like to press against each other, touch each other, kiss in the moonlight?

Magical?

Intimate?

Like peace?

thirty-two

Monti was crazy.

Never in her wildest dreams had Athena thought to go skinny dipping in the ocean in the middle of the night. Anyone could walk by and see her. Anyone could stumble across their clothes and steal them. Anyone.

Athena crossed her arms, watching as Monti dipped below the surface again. Her heart caught in her throat as she waited to see if Monti would resurface. If she'd have that same giddy expression on her lips when she did.

Because *that* Athena did want.

It was this pure child-like joy that Monti seemed to have since they'd arrived. At least in moments like this. Then there were the other moments, when Athena had seen the weight of the world on her shoulders and had been unable to pry Monti loose from that responsibility.

Still, the call to wade into the water and join her was strong.

Just what would it feel like to have the water carry away everything she didn't want to think about?

Athena stepped a little closer, her feet freezing as the water rushed over her skin. Would she do anything for Monti? She wanted to be the person who would. Another step into the water, and her pants started to get wet. Athena sucked in a sharp breath.

She couldn't get naked, not like Monti did. She couldn't make herself do that, but she could walk in. She could do this part of the way. But would that be enough? Was she whole enough for this? Gnawing on her cheek again, Athena went in a little farther.

Kevin would think she was a lunatic for this. He wouldn't even recognize her. Or maybe he would. Twenty-five years ago she might have thought about this. All before she'd been broken. All before she'd been shattered into a million little pieces. Athena stepped in even farther, her shins getting wet.

Monti laughed as she dunked herself under the water again.

Just how freeing was it?

Athena stopped hesitating. She walked into the water and followed Monti's path. Monti came up from the waves just as Athena got there and snagged her hands. Monti wrapped her arms around Athena's waist and held on tight in a hug.

"I'm so glad you came," Monti whispered. "The water feels amazing."

Athena's breath was loud in her ears as she pressed her cheek into Monti's. She struggled to remember how to breathe properly, Monti's naked form pressed against her, the dampness seeping through her clothes.

"How do you want to change?" Monti murmured into her ear. "What do you want to leave behind?"

"My mistakes," Athena answered immediately. "All of them."

"Down you go."

Athena held her breath and dipped below the surface of the water. It was freezing cold. It bit at her skin, feeling like her flesh was being ripped from her muscles. Athena gasped as she stood up. Monti gripped onto her elbows, holding her upright.

"What else?" Monti rushed.

"My pain."

Without being asked, Athena dropped back into the ocean.

The water was loud as it rushed over her head, but this time the biting cold wasn't so bad. When she resurfaced, she was expecting Monti to be close to her this time. And instead of waiting for a breath, Athena pressed their mouths together. Monti hummed, cupping her cheeks.

Athena sighed into the kiss, longing for it to be deeper than this. But she wasn't quite ready yet, and intuitively, she understood that Monti wasn't either. Without being asked, Athena offered up the next thing she wanted to erase from herself. "My belief that I'm not worthy."

Monti's lips parted in surprise. Athena locked their eyes together as she lowered herself slowly into the water and below its surface. This time when she came back up, she knew she was ready. She wanted this. She wanted a relationship with Monti. She wanted to believe that she wasn't too broken for love.

Their mouths touched again.

Athena slid her tongue along Monti's lips, praying that Monti would let her in just a little more. She shivered as their wet bodies pressed together, as they melded even closer. Athena enfolded herself around Monti. She wasn't going to go under the water again, not without Monti this time, not without the hope that when she came back up something would be different.

Slipping her hand across Monti's breast in a tease, Athena tested to see how open Monti would be to seduction this time. It was as though she'd gone into the bedroom and come out a completely new person. Whoever she'd been talking to on the phone must have helped her. Athena only wished she'd been able to do that. But she wasn't good at the interpersonal.

Monti hummed, deepening the kiss and pulling Athena in even closer. Athena closed her eyes, focusing on the feel of their bodies together. She felt so free with Monti. She was unconfined by everything that had kept her imprisoned before. She had peace and joy and hope and love. Monti nipped at her lip.

"No matter how much I try to stop touching you, whenever

you get close, I can't stop myself from wanting this." Monti's words sounded almost foreign.

"Stop touching me?" Athena asked, still keeping her hands on Monti's body, sliding her fingers from her waist to her hip. "I don't ever want you to stop."

Monti kissed her neck. Athena tilted her head to give Monti better access, to encourage her to do more than she was already doing. She knew that at some point she was going to have to be more forward, but she wasn't sure today was the day. Athena hugged Monti closer.

"Please don't ever stop," Athena murmured.

Why was she saying that? Why was she pushing this relationship when Monti so clearly was still struggling with it? Athena slid her hand against Monti's ass, holding her firmly. Their mouths locked together in a furious, desperate kiss.

Despair clawed at her. If this was their last chance, then Athena was going to take it. If she could feel any of this freedom, then she wanted to hold onto it for as long as possible. Athena arched her back, pulling Monti with her as a large wave came up and pounded against their thighs. They were going to have to go in soon. But to get a few more moments, Athena held on.

Finally, Monti pulled away. "Let's go inside."

"Come with me," Athena begged. She hated and loved the whine in her tone at the same time. Because she was desperate. She didn't want this little oasis they had created to disappear, not yet. She loved it too much. "Come to my room with me."

Monti pulled back slightly, looking at her directly in the eye. "Are you sure?"

"Yes." Athena brushed her wet fingers over Monti's lips and repeated herself. "Yes."

One of the few things she'd doubted this entire journey was Monti. She wanted Monti to be near her, whether it was in her bed or in her vicinity, she didn't care. But she wanted the joy that Monti brought, the comfort, the safety that Monti created for her.

"I want you," Athena responded.

"Then you have me."

As sure as Monti sounded, there was an undercurrent of trepidation. Athena picked up on it instantly, but she didn't know what to do with it. She didn't know how to bring it up and hoped that it would resolve or that they could talk about it. Because in a few days, when they left, Athena knew that she was going to return home and Monti would leave for her next adventure. They were going to go their separate ways.

She just hoped the work they'd done together would last.

"Are you sure?" Athena asked, needing one last confirmation.

"Yes." Monti kissed her again. "Come on."

They trekked through the water until they reached the beach. Monti bent down and picked up her clothes while Athena pulled her wet ones away from her skin. It was so cold out here now that they were out of the water. Her nipples pebbled, goosebumps ran over her skin, and chills ran up and down her spine.

Monti led the way back inside, the same way they'd left. Was it really that simple too? The same way but in reverse? Athena had always been a joyful and happy person before everything had hit the fan. But that was who she wanted to be again. Someone who was free from the shackles she'd been put in.

Once the door was shut, Athena was on Monti. She pushed their bodies together, mouths melding. This was her time and her moment. First she had to get out of these damn wet clothes. Athena pulled at her shirt, but it stuck to her skin, clinging to her stomach and her breasts uncomfortably. It felt like a straitjacket, tightening against her until she couldn't breathe.

"Slow down," Monti mumbled as she stilled Athena's hands. "It's stuck."

Athena glanced down at Monti's hands, finding that the extra button on the inside of her blouse was caught on the loop of her slacks and every time she tugged it just made it worse. Monti's nimble fingers worked it carefully and quickly until she had it loose.

"There." Monti reached up and started on the buttons on Athena's blouse, undoing them one at a time. "Is that better?"

"Yes." Athena watched, entranced with the way Monti's hands moved so confidently. She wished she had some of that confidence. When her blouse was undone, Monti pushed it off her shoulders and spun her around to drag it down her arms. The blouse dropped to the floor with a heavy plop.

Monti's body was covered in goosebumps, her arms, her chest, her breasts. Athena delicately ran her fingers over the tops of Monti's breasts, feeling the small bumps on her otherwise smooth skin. She left off by flicking Monti's hard nipple.

"I never thought anyone would like looking at me," Athena whispered. "I don't even like looking at my own body."

"Because of your scars?" Monti asked, reaching behind Athena's back and flicking the clasp of her bra. "There we are. Have to get you out of your wet clothes before you catch a cold, you know."

Athena's lips curled upward into a sly smile. She loved that Monti was playing flirtatious when she didn't have to, that she was taking the lead on the seduction even though Athena was the one who had started all of this. Athena stepped in closer, pressing their chests together and kissing Monti swiftly.

"You make me feel wanted," Athena said, trailing her fingers up and down Monti's back. Now that they were almost skin to skin, Athena felt like she was ready to go to new heights. She wanted that connection with Monti, what they'd shared the first time they were together, the passion when she couldn't wait to keep touching her again.

"You are wanted," Monti answered, kissing the side of Athena's neck.

Athena shuddered. She swayed from side to side before moving in and kissing Monti's cheek and closing her eyes. "So are you."

She could feel the moment Monti shifted, when her tense shoulders relaxed. Monti let out a startling breath and buried her face in Athena's neck, saying nothing. Athena wanted to keep whatever was happening between them going. She reached between them and palmed Monti's breast, teasing her nipple again as she waited for Monti to answer her unasked question.

"Pants," Monti choked out the word, dragging Athena's pants over her hips. When had she managed to get the zipper and button undone? Athena pushed her pants the rest of the way down and stepped out of them.

Monti crashed their mouths together, but Athena didn't want these first moments to be self-serving. She wanted to find that streak of confidence she knew she had somewhere, and she wanted to lose herself in figuring out Monti's pleasure.

Lowering herself to her knees, Athena ran her fingers up and down Monti's thighs. Their eyes locked together, and Monti raised an eyebrow at her. "Are you sure about this?"

"Yes." Athena hadn't done this yet. In their one night together, she'd avoided it, scared that she wouldn't know what she was doing, but it was now or never. Athena ran her fingers down to Monti's knees and back up. "Are you?"

"As sure as I'll ever be." Monti brushed her fingers through Athena's wet hair.

Athena moved in, pressing a delicate kiss to the front of Monti's thigh. Then to the other thigh. She breathed in deeply, her heart hammering away as she readied herself for this exploration. Monti's skin tasted like salty water, still damp from the ocean and whatever free-willed baptism they'd given themselves outside.

Using her teeth, Athena scraped a trail and hummed when Monti groaned in response. That was exactly what she wanted to hear, the sounds of pleasure, the soft quiet moans of a woman enjoying herself. Athena wrapped her hands around the back of Monti's thighs as she held on and pressed in closer. She nuzzled her nose through Monti's damp curls.

"Yes," Monti breathed the word. "Athena..."

This might be the most beautiful thing she'd ever experienced.

Athena breathed deeply, steadying the final nerves that ran through her. Reaching her tongue out, she tasted. Flavor blossomed on her tongue, Monti's unique flavor and her scent, the taste of the water they'd bathed themselves in. Athena's heart calmed, and she dug her fingers into the backs of Monti's thighs, not letting go.

"Oh God," Monti mumbled.

When Athena looked up, Monti's eyes were closed, her head thrown back, her chest heaving as she dragged in a breath.

"You've barely even touched me," Monti murmured, her voice disappearing as she sucked in a sharp breath. She parted her legs and planted her hand on the top of Athena's head. She curled her fingers into Athena's hair. "It feels so good."

Athena said nothing as she pressed her face in closer. She wanted to do this right. She flicked her tongue in a tease, happy with the resounding gasp Monti gave her. Rejuvenated with hope, Athena intensified her teasing. She held on as tightly as she could and closed her eyes, focusing on doing everything she could to pleasure Monti.

"I have to get on the floor." Monti dropped to her knees and then her butt, her eyes wide as she blew out a breath. Her cheeks were flushed, her skin no longer chilled. Monti sent her a cocky grin as she leaned back on one hand.

Athena canted her head to the side, not quite sure what to make of Monti's sudden move. And once again, words caught in her throat.

"You made my knees Jell-O," Monti said with a slight laugh. "Please, don't stop."

Athena warmed at the compliment, the little boost to her confidence exactly what she needed. Monti lay onto her back and spread her knees. Athena climbed on top of her, kissing her lips and then trailing a path down her neck to her chest.

"You make me have hope," Athena whispered, glad she was able to talk again. She could do words. She could say anything to sway people to her argument, but to actually say words that had meaning, meaning from what she was feeling, was so difficult. And yet, here she was, once again telling Monti exactly what her heart desired. "You help me find peace."

"Make peace," Monti corrected.

"Yes." Athena scraped her teeth over Monti's hip bone before dipping between her legs again. She didn't want to give this up, not for anything. What she'd found here made her exactly who she wanted to be.

Athena covered Monti's clit with her mouth, sucking gently. She moved her hands up and down Monti's legs, down to her ass, and then she shifted. She slid her fingers deep inside Monti's body, curling them, pressing in a slow tease of exploration. Monti gasped, her hips rising up as she pressed her body harder against Athena's mouth.

Athena doubled down in her focus. They were so close, weren't they? Close to finding each other, close to breaking down those last barriers? Except it still felt as though something was holding Monti back. Athena didn't stop. Monti's gasps got louder, little grunts and noises became more frequent.

She was doing this, and she was doing it right. Athena kept going, pressing in more as Monti rubbed against her. Once again, Monti's fingers dug into her hair, tugging and pulling as she writhed. Then she clenched, her body jerking as her voice reverberated through the room. Monti chuckled as she relaxed. She pulled Athena up as she sat up. Monti moved their mouths against each other.

"You are amazing." Monti said it with so much care.

Athena cupped her cheeks and deepened the embrace. She fluttered her eyes closed and settled into this moment. She danced their tongues together, completely surrounded by Monti in ways she'd never been before. But this was exactly what she wanted. It was what she needed.

"I can't get enough of you," Athena said, cringing as she heard the words out loud. She was so very close to saying exactly what she didn't want to say. They weren't ready for that yet. Monti no doubt didn't feel the same.

"You're just as addicting." Monti skimmed a hand behind Athena's neck and pulled her in more, falling back onto the floor. "But we're not done yet."

thirty-three

Monti coaxed Athena up her body until Athena straddled her face. Smiling, Monti shook her head. Now this was bliss. Screw the cold nighttime dive in the water, finding herself planted in between a beautiful woman's thighs was exactly the peace she wanted for tonight.

"This is my favorite position," Monti murmured, turning her cheek to press a kiss to Athena's inner thigh. "I can smell your arousal. It's heavenly."

Athena rocked up slightly, as if expecting Monti to go straight for it. But that's not what this was about. Monti wanted to take her time, to share everything she'd figured out in that cold dip outside. Closing her eyes, she kissed Athena's thigh again. Her skin still had a slight chill to it, as if she hadn't warmed all the way up yet.

"You are so much stronger than I am." Monti loosed her first confession, and she felt as though there was a click in her heart unlocking something she wasn't even aware was hidden away.

"What?" Athena asked, her voice wavering.

When Monti looked up their eyes locked together. "You are. If it hadn't been for you, I think I would have kept running."

"Running?" Athena looked so confused, and it was adorable.

It didn't surprise Monti that Athena was lost. This conversation was coming out of nowhere for her.

Monti hummed her assent. This time, instead of a kiss, she licked Athena's thigh, chasing the salty flavor from her legs as she went. Monti wrapped her arms around Athena's thighs and held on. She was losing her own patience to hold them within this moment.

"I'm really good at avoiding things." Monti licked her again, this time getting ever closer to the apex of Athena's legs, the one place they both wanted her. But the conversation was so important, and for once, Monti wasn't going to avoid it. She was going to dive right into the depths of sharing that she needed to experience, that Athena needed to be receptive to. "I thought I was doing everyone a favor, you know."

"No, I don't know," Athena answered, awkwardly shifting on her knees. That probably was getting uncomfortable. The floors were hard stone, and as much as the cold was welcome against Monti's back, she couldn't imagine kneeling on them for too long.

"By keeping my distance." Monti kissed Athena's clit before pulling back and looking up into those stunning blue eyes. This was the moment of true confession, the real reason she had held back for years. Athena deserved to know why Monti had held back on whatever was between them. "I thought I was protecting them."

"Oh." The word came out on a breath.

"But I was protecting myself from feeling my pain."

Monti kissed Athena's clit again, this time adding in a teasing flick with her tongue. She groaned as her eyes fluttered shut. Controlling herself right now was one of the hardest things she'd ever done. Moving her knees up, she pressed them into Athena's back to knock her forward slightly. She was so ready to have her mouth against Athena. She was tired of waiting for this moment of clarity to hit. It was there. Monti licked her fully, and Athena let out the softest moan in existence.

"In order not to feel it, I couldn't feel anything else," Monti added before diving back in. She sucked Athena gently, slowly building the pressure until she stopped again. "I don't want to do that anymore."

"You're not making any sense." Athena leaned back, twisting half her body and pressing her hand to Monti's knee as if to hold herself steady.

The idea hit Monti hard, and she sent Athena a wicked grin. "Touch me if you want. I love feeling your fingers inside me just as much as I loved your mouth."

"Do you?" Athena raised an eyebrow at her.

"Yes." Monti started sucking on Athena's clit again. She was going to make this the hardest orgasm Athena had ever experienced, one that was dragged out until she couldn't stand it anymore. At least that was her intention, but she knew herself well enough to know that she would get impatient soon enough. Still, intentions counted for something, didn't they?

Monti reached up and covered one of Athena's breasts, flicking her hard nipple with the edge of her thumb while she continued the same damn sucking pattern. Athena's hips rocked before they twitched. Satisfaction rolled through Monti. She was doing something right.

"I don't want to be alone in this world." Monti took a breath and went right back in.

Athena cried out. She slid her hand between Monti's legs, fumbling as she found the right position to slide two fingers inside her. Monti instantly tensed at the intrusion, the lingering sensations from her earlier orgasm building up quickly. Damn, Athena was good with her fingers. For someone who'd never done this before, she was a fast learner.

Throwing her head back, Monti gasped when Athena hit a particularly sensitive spot. "Fuck."

"Being alone is so hard," Athena murmured.

"It is." Monti met Athena's gaze. "But we're not alone anymore, are we?"

"No."

"I want you, Athena. I really do."

Athena looked like she wanted to move and bend down and kiss Monti senseless. But they were far from any position that would allow them to do that. Monti didn't give her a chance either. She pressed her face right back between Athena's legs, teasing her with sucks and kisses and flicks. She pulled Athena closer, ignoring her own pleasure if only to have Athena fall apart on top of her for a change, all that power directly above Monti.

Hissing, Athena moved her hand as she clenched her eyes in concentration. Monti knew Athena was close now. She redoubled her efforts, teasing Athena's nipples while sucking on her clit. Athena's legs trembled, the physical reaction a sure sign she was about to shatter. Monti maintained, keeping everything just perfect as Athena unraveled.

Her hips undulated into Monti's mouth, rocking hard and firmly as her stomach clenched tightly. Monti kept the pressure up, waiting for a sign from Athena that she wanted it to stop, that she wanted a break. Without warning, Athena shifted off her knees and fell to the side. She collapsed onto the tile floor, her hand on her stomach and her arm over her eyes as she tried to catch her breath.

Monti climbed closer to her, lying against her side and running soothing fingers over her arms and chest and stomach as she waited for Athena to speak again. They stayed there for a long time, the silence that had become their comfortable companion taking up the space all around them, wrapping them in its safety. Finally, Athena lowered her arm so she could look up at Monti.

"What do you want?"

"So many things." Monti smiled, but nerves hit her full force in the chest. "But I need you to be more specific about what you're asking."

Athena's lips parted as if she was going to ask a question and then stopped herself. Monti played her fingers over Athena's breasts, not quite teasing, but definitely letting Athena know that she was still there.

"For yourself," Athena finally clarified. "Where do you want to go from here?"

"I want to work on things with Fallon." Monti's brow furrowed. That hadn't really been what she wanted to say. But until she knew where Athena stood, if they were both in the same place, she wasn't ready to confess that maybe some sort of relationship between them would be the way to move forward. And that would take a lot of talking. Dating a married woman wasn't something Monti had done before, and it didn't matter if Athena and Kevin had full comprehension of their relationship. Adding in another person to that mix was going to shake things up.

"You want to be a better sister," Athena added.

"Yeah. I've been a really crappy sister, honestly." Monti shifted, resting her head on her hand so she could stare down at Athena. Monti found herself following the path of Athena's scars one after the other all across her chest and breasts and stomach. She'd thought about counting them but wasn't sure what good that would do either of them. "I know you don't like your scars, but I love that you seem to have accepted them."

"What do you mean?" Athena paled as she stilled suddenly.

Monti cringed. She hadn't meant to change the topic like that. Again, she was damn good at avoiding when she wanted to. Now she just had to figure out how to get back on track. "Your confidence in your body has skyrocketed since I met you. I love seeing that side of you."

Athena softened at that. "Oh."

"That's all I meant." Monti bent down and kissed Athena's lips. "I haven't allowed Fallon to get close to me. For that matter, I haven't allowed anyone to get close to me, but I feel that I need to correct that with Fallon immediately. She deserves better."

"She does," Athena agreed. "She keeps up with all your travels. Some map she has at her desk where she marks off the different countries you've been to."

"Does she?" For some reason, that thought brought so much joy to her. Monti sighed at it. "Would you do that for me?"

"Probably not," Athena smiled and pulled Monti back down for another kiss. "I'm not very sentimental."

"Ah." Still, the fact that Athena wouldn't wasn't what Monti had wanted to hear. And she wasn't quite sure why that was. She'd wanted to know that Athena was thinking about her when she was gone, that there was some hole left in Athena when she wasn't nearby. In some ways, that would be intentionally causing pain, which Monti never wanted to do. But it was a good kind of pain, wasn't it?

It would mean that she'd allowed Athena into her heart. Or perhaps it was the opposite of that. It would mean that Athena had allowed her in. And that was really what Monti wanted, wasn't it? She wanted Athena to care. She wanted Athena to love her. And with everything they'd done up until now, Monti couldn't say one way or another if Athena thought of her beyond the current state of their relationship.

Sliding her hand down Athena's body, Monti slipped her fingers inside her. "Are we done for the night?"

Athena gasped. "I guess not."

Monti sent her a wicked smile. "Do you want me to take you here or do you want to go upstairs?"

Moaning, Athena threw her arms over her head and spread her legs wider. "Why not risk it?"

"What are we risking?" Monti asked, starting a slow pace of her thumb against Athena's still-damp clit. She rolled circles gently. There were so many ways she could ask the questions she was avoiding, but this way seemed like they would both get a lot out of it. At least Athena would get another orgasm before they parted ways for the night.

"People walking in on us?"

"Who's coming?" Monti asked, daring herself to keep her eyes on Athena and not look up at the glass doors to the deck. "Because I'm pretty sure we're alone here."

Athena laughed nervously. "We are. It's just a constant fear of mine."

"That someone's watching us?"

"That someone will see me."

Monti stopped, a deep crease forming in her brow as she once again looked into Athena's eyes. She debated for a quick second before asking the question she knew Athena wasn't expecting. "Are you talking physically or metaphorically?"

Athena stilled, her lip pulled between her teeth. Her cheeks slowly started to redden. Had she meant to say that? Did Monti just call her out on something she hadn't wanted to think about? Again. It seemed to be a trend in their relationship thus far.

"Both," Athena whispered, the word carrying straight to Monti's heart.

"Which one are you afraid of me seeing?"

"All of me." Athena reached up and cupped Monti's cheek. She pulled Monti down for another kiss, this one deep and slow.

Monti allowed herself to get lost in the embrace, in the soft touches, in the slide of their tongues, in the warmth of their bodies touching. Monti started the circle on Athena's clit again. Monti wanted to see all of Athena, and she knew she'd only gotten a small piece of her so far. They were just scratching the surface of getting to know each other, of learning the depths of who they were.

Athena lifted her hips up, and Monti pushed in deeper, adding a second finger. "You see so much already."

Monti moved in and took Athena's lips, offering whatever comfort and safety she could. Because this was hard work. To admit this, to allow Monti to see more of her even in this one moment—this meant everything to her.

"You see so much of me," Monti answered, kissing her way down Athena's neck to the tops of her breasts. Monti covered Athena's hard nipple, flicking her tongue over the hard little nub. Athena's voice reverberated through Monti's body, spurring her on.

"Don't ever stop," Athena murmured, her eyes shut tight.

Monti wanted to ask her what she wasn't supposed to stop. The movement of her fingers? Asking the hard questions? Being there for her? The massages that had landed them in this position? But Athena was clenching around her, tightening as she cascaded through another orgasm and slyly wrapped her arms around Monti's shoulders, pulling Monti down on top of her.

The kiss was sloppy, wet, and full of raw emotion. Monti leaned into it. This was where she wanted to be. At this moment, they were nothing more than two women exploring. They were finding themselves and each other, and they were learning how to face the world. But Monti wanted to do that together. She wanted to take Athena by the hand and look whatever came next dead in the eye.

Monti slipped back and pressed her forehead against Athena's. She listened to her steady breathing, to the quiet in the room. And she whispered the only thing that she could think of, the one thing she'd always held true in her heart.

"I never want to hurt you."

thirty-four

Athena spent the morning in her office at the beach house. She managed to get some work done for the upcoming trial, but more than that, she'd hired a divorce attorney. The last few days with Monti had given her new life, and she didn't want to wait any longer.

She wanted her life to be different.

Immediately.

She'd lost so much time keeping the world away from her, and it had left her nothing but lonely. And that night with Monti…she smiled at the memory. She'd never have done something so crazy on her own. Monti had pushed her to take chances and think about the world in different ways.

Something had changed that night. Athena had never felt so close to someone before, even with Kevin. He knew everything there was to know about her, but Monti had reached in and tenderly caressed her soul with all the hope she had alive in her. It was contagious.

Athena sent off the text to Kevin, updating him on the fact that she'd retained a lawyer and the divorce was underway. She then added one last thing.

•　•　•

Athena: I'll tell Simon.

It was the one thing she hadn't wanted to do, but someone had to. And since she was the one who had initiated the separation, it was her responsibility. All she could hope was that it wouldn't throw Simon too hard off track. He was such a good kid.

Which was something Athena was glad about. Simon had advantages she hadn't had growing up, and hopefully that would make him a better person in the long run. She received Kevin's response, his sweet wish of good luck and to call him after if she needed, and she called Simon.

If she waited any longer, then she would just put it off. Rubbing her lips together, Athena held her breath as she waited for Simon to answer.

"Hey, Mom."

"Hey, baby." Athena smiled, but the nerves reared their ugly heads. She wished she was better at this. Talking with Monti had helped, but that still didn't make any of this easy. She sighed. "You got a minute to talk?"

"Sure?" Simon sounded nervous now.

She hated to put him in that state, but there was no good way to deliver this news. There were better ways than others, but no matter what, Simon was going to be shaken. She ran her fingers through her hair, remembering the way that Monti had threaded her fingers through the tangles, pulling on them.

"This is serious, and I know it's going to disrupt your day," Athena interrupted her own thoughts. She needed to keep focused on what was important, and that was first and foremost always Simon. "So I want to make sure that you're not rushing off to go somewhere."

"Okay?" He was scared now. She'd recognize that tone of voice anywhere.

Athena wasn't doing a good job at this. She was already regretting doing it over the phone instead of in person, but with school in session, she wasn't sure when she'd see him next. Swallowing that lump that clawed its way up her throat, Athena chose her words. She played with a pen on her desk, distracting herself.

"Mom?"

"Your dad and I have been talking a lot lately about our relationship moving forward." She bit her lip and cringed. "We're getting a divorce."

"What?" It was an accusation, and it rang through the phone and deep into Athena's soul. "But nothing's changed."

"Yes and no." Athena picked up the pen and dropped it loudly on top of her desk. "Your dad and I are best friends first, you know that. And even with this divorce, that's not going to change. I can promise you that."

"Have you met someone?" Simon whispered it, like he was too scared to ask the question but like he had to know the truth.

And the truth was yes, she'd met someone. But it wasn't like he was thinking. Or was it? No, it wasn't like that at all.

Athena's face pinched. Honesty. That was what she had to use for this conversation. "I did, but not like you're thinking. I've been seeing a therapist."

That much was true at least, or at least as true as she was willing to admit. It wasn't why she hired Monti, but that had certainly been the turning point in their relationship.

"Are you serious?" Everything on the other end of the phone was silent save for Simon.

Athena wished she was there in person, to assure him that nothing would change, that all of these things were happening for the right reasons. "Yes. I know I wasn't the best mother to you. I've struggled with some things in my past and I let them affect my relationship with you."

"Mom..." Simon trailed off. "I don't even know what to say right now."

"You don't have to say anything. But your dad and I have been married a long time, and we've never been under the illusion that our marriage was anything other than what it was." Athena started playing with the pen again, drawing circles and flowers lazily on whatever piece of paper she could find. She needed to distract herself from avoiding any more of this conversation.

When the energy coursing through her was too much, she stood up and paced her office. From the window to the wall to the door and back again. She made circles around her desk. Athena listened for any sign from Simon that would tell her where to head next with the conversation.

"Your dad and I got married to appease our parents and to make a life for ourselves that we wanted to make. We both knew exactly why we were getting married and what our marriage would look like. But times are different now. We don't have to do this anymore." Athena's voice wavered. Was she really going to tell him? Was she going to tell Simon the one thing she'd kept hidden for years?

"So you got married just to shut other people up?"

"Yeah." Athena hated admitting that. She wished she had been stronger when she was younger, more like him. She ran her fingers through her hair again. "I was different back then. There was a lot going on. Your dad and I have been friends all our lives, and I knew he would take care of me. He saved me."

"No offense, Mom, but that sounds like the most selfish thing on the planet."

"It was." Athena nodded in agreement. She hated to think about it like that, but Kevin did get something out of their marriage too. His parents never would have accepted him being gay. They never would have allowed him to inherit anything or carry on the family name. He would have been ousted in two seconds flat. But they were dead now, and Kevin could have far more freedom. "But Dad got some things out of it too, I promise. You'll probably want to talk to him when we're done talking. He's expecting your call whenever you're ready."

"Are you really doing this?" Simon asked again. He sounded like a lost little boy, afraid of the monsters under his bed again.

Oh how Athena wished she could wrap him up in her arms

and hold him tight. It didn't matter if he was twenty-one, he was still her little baby. She smiled as she stopped in front of the window, seeing Monti read a book outside. Her legs bare in the sunlight as she soaked it all in. Athena would love to kiss her way up those legs, between them.

"Mom?"

"Yes. Sorry. Yes, I'm really doing this. Dad and I talked about it." Athena bit the inside of her cheek. She crossed her arms. She really needed to focus on Simon right now. "I guess you could say that I met myself again."

Simon groaned. "What does that even mean?"

She knew she was overwhelming him with information. "It just means that I've been doing a lot of thinking and a lot of intro-spection. I'm ready for some changes to happen, and so is your dad. We both want this."

"I don't know what to say," Simon responded. "I didn't think you'd ever drop this bomb on me."

Something in his phrasing caused Athena to pause. She furrowed her brow and thought through the words again. "What do you mean by ever?"

"You and dad have never really been happy."

"We're very happy with each other."

Simon groaned. "That's not what I mean." He sucked in a sharp breath and blew it out. "I mean you two were never really married. You always just kind of did your own thing."

"Yeah, that's what we agreed to when we got married."

"Right, so I guess...I guess what I'm saying is this doesn't really come as a surprise. I mean it does, but it doesn't." Simon finally finished, and she could hear the relief now that it was out in the open.

Athena plopped down in her desk chair, still staring outside, but now she couldn't see Monti. "You're right."

"Did you meet someone?" He sounded so hesitant in his question.

Athena couldn't lie to him. She'd never done that before, and she didn't want to start now. She couldn't get Monti's image out of her mind. Her sweet smile, her firm hands, but it was so much more than that. It was the way that Monti made her feel so utterly safe. Athena had never experienced that before.

"Yes."

"Really?" Simon asked, his voice raising up loudly.

"But it's not like you think it is, I promise. Monti has helped me see the world in a new way. She helped me deal with some of the issues in my past—or at least start to. And I realized that I can't keep living like this. Your dad deserves so much better than what I can give him."

"So do you, Mom."

Athena's heart stuttered. He was always such a sweet kid. He'd always had everyone else's best interest in mind. Athena held her fingers over her mouth. "We all deserve better."

"So who is this Monti?"

Athena smiled. "She's wonderful, really. She's Fallon's younger sister, actually."

"Oh yeah?" Simon got excited, and Athena chided herself. She'd always forgotten that he'd had a secret crush on Fallon for years now and had never managed to get over it.

"Yes. She practices holistic therapy. I've been seeing her for a little bit now." *Seeing her.* Those words echoed in her mind. They were having sex, yes. They were sharing their life stories. But they weren't together, not in the way those words could imply. But she wanted that. Athena desperately wanted Monti to be right there with her through whatever the next step was. "She's been very helpful."

Athena missed what Simon said next, because she was still so caught up in the fact that she wanted Monti. And it was about more than what Monti could do for her. She wanted to help Monti. She wanted to be there when Monti finally decided to open up and let love in. She wanted to be the one who loved her.

But she wasn't sure it would ever work. Even if Monti visited more often than she had been, she was such a free spirit. Athena couldn't imagine her ever being tied to one place for longer than a month at a time. It wouldn't work. They could have a fling, they could share moments together when Monti was in town, but that's all they would ever be together.

Athena would have to decide if that was enough.

"Hey, Mom. I'm going to call Dad. Okay?"

"Sure thing, baby." Athena brushed her fingers over her lips, that sense of dread she'd done so well to avoid settling into the pit of her stomach. "Call me if you need to talk this through more, okay? I'll make sure to answer. And I do want to talk to you more about some things, maybe explain where I'm at right now when you have time."

"For sure. I love you, Mom."

"Love you too, Simon."

He hung up first. And Athena dropped her phone onto the desk. She brushed her fingers over her face and then through her hair. She was in love. And Simon, her son who had never met Monti, seemed to pick up on that fact.

She was in love.

The only problem was what was she supposed to do about it?

thirty-five

Monti handed Athena the tea and sat next to her on the couch. The number of books they'd consumed in their first ten days there was immense. Athena was going to need a whole new library for next time. Monti smiled at the thought, but then it sent a scared little chill through her.

Did she really want there to be a next time?

"I wanted to talk to you about something." Athena didn't sound so sure either.

Monti rubbed her lips together as she put down the book she'd just grabbed and turned her full attention to Athena. At the very least, Athena deserved that, didn't she? It didn't matter if Monti was having internal turmoil. She had to be there for Athena.

"I spoke with Kevin earlier this week, and I talked to Simon a couple days ago."

Okay, well that wasn't that odd. Monti kept her mouth closed, waiting for Athena to find whatever words she was looking for. Monti ran her fingers along her thigh, using the gentle movement to soothe herself. There was no reason for her to be upset or hypervigilant.

"Kevin and I are separating."

The words slammed Monti in the chest. Her entire body tightened. Her chest constricted, making it difficult to breathe. There was only one question racing through her mind, and she didn't even know how to ask it. She couldn't ask it, could she? Because this was Athena's turn to share. Monti clenched her fist around the arm of the couch, using the feeling of the fabric under her palm to keep her rooted.

But it wasn't working.

"I retained an attorney, and we'll be working on filing for divorce shortly. It shouldn't take too long since we kept everything separate to begin with except where it concerned Simon, but he's an adult now." Athena was rambling.

Monti understood that, but she still couldn't get herself to focus. Panic clawed its way up her chest. Hadn't she just been thinking that she was ready for this? That she wanted to have deeper and more meaningful relationships?

"Anyway, not much will change for me going forward, I should think." Athena touched Monti's arm, dragging Monti's mind fully back into the moment. "I'm doing this for me, you know."

The ringing in Monti's ears came to a sudden halt. When had that started? She sucked in a sharp breath, filling her lungs as the constriction in her chest loosened just a little bit.

"I love Kevin, fully. But we've never been in a romantic relationship. And you showed me, though I don't think that was your intention, that we both deserve to live. I'm tired of living under someone else's thumb—and I'm not talking about Kevin's. I don't want to be someone who gives in to the demands of others because it's easier than fighting for what I want."

Monti wet her dry mouth, swallowing hard. When she raised her chin to look directly in Athena's eye, she asked the only thing she could think of. "What do you want?"

"I want to live life." Athena's smile became sheepish, as if she was almost embarrassed to say this out loud.

Monti's heart shattered for her again.

"That's all I want, and I don't even know what life is right now, but I know it's not this."

Maybe Athena wasn't pushing this in the direction Monti had originally thought. She took Athena's hand and folded their fingers together. She raised Athena's knuckles to her lips and pressed a delicate kiss to her skin. "So you're taking steps to get what you need."

"Yes." Athena's lips curled upward in sweet surrender. "Yes, I am." This time, Athena took Monti's hand and kissed the back of it. "And what I want is to explore."

"Explore what?"

"Me, this world, us."

That last word sent a shock wave through Monti. But niggling under all of it was exactly what she wanted. It wormed its way closer to the surface, past the fear and the worry, and right into the center of her chest.

"I want to see what will come of us," Athena repeated in more detail.

"I don't do traditional relationships. If you're thinking that we're going to get married—"

"What? No." Athena shook her head, laughing lightly. "What would make you think that?"

"Because you're getting divorced, and let's be honest, you can't say it's not because of me."

"Well, it's because of your influence, yes. But I wouldn't put you at the heart of that decision. I've wanted to release Kevin from any obligation he may have felt toward me for years. You helped me finally have the courage to do it. He can go be happy with Clayton now."

Monti's chest tightened again, almost painfully so. Why couldn't she just get over herself for this? "I'm proud of you. Really, I am."

"I'm proud of myself, too." Athena grinned. She took Monti's hand, which was still wrapped around hers, and settled it into her lap as she got more comfortable on the couch. "But that does still leave us to talk about."

Monti inwardly cringed. "There is no us, Athena."

Athena's shoulders tightened.

Monti hadn't said that well. She winced and tried to backtrack. "What I mean is that we haven't set any parameters on what we're doing. We haven't talked about any boundaries or goals—"

"That's what I want to do," Athena interrupted in a rushed tone. But then she settled again, as if now that the confession was out there, the biggest hurdle had been cleared.

Except Monti knew there was so much more to the conversation than that. But how were they supposed to do that without Monti truly confessing everything that was in her heart? And neither one of them were ready for that, were they?

Athena swooped in, pressing their mouths together in an unexpected kiss. Monti hummed, automatically raising her hand to cup Athena's cheek and pull her in. The kiss deepened, a tease of tongues and lips. Their chests pressed together tightly, and Monti felt every breath Athena took. Her heart raced.

"Athena," Monti murmured, trying to break the kiss. As nice as it was, they really did need to talk. "Athena, stop."

Athena pulled away, her eyes wide as she bit her lip. Monti moved in and pecked her lips in an attempt to reassure her that nothing was seriously wrong.

"I just want to talk for a minute."

"Okay," Athena whispered, staring down at their still-joined hands.

They were both bad at taking these risks. They both had the same hangups and tensions. Monti knew that. She was the one most aware of their similarities, which meant she was going to have to be the one to break first. She had to give up the idea that they could do this together. Someone had to take the risk.

"I don't want a traditional relationship," Monti started. As soon as the words started to fall from her lips, everything about this moment became easier. "But that doesn't mean that I don't want a relationship. I'm willing to step into whatever your current situation is, be it marriage or whatever."

Athena's entire face relaxed, the muscles easing in an instant. Were they both holding so much in that it was making it next to impossible to move in any direction? Monti tensed her fingers and then started a slow pattern with her free hand up and down Athena's forearm.

"I'm getting divorced," Athena said, sounding so confident in her decision. Perhaps that's all it was, the confidence for her to make the decisions she wanted. "And it has very little to do with you. You were a catalyst in a decision to change something I'd already been regretting for years."

"All right." Monti looked down at their fingers again, a little bit of the tension in her chest easing up. "So you're getting divorced. What does that mean for us?"

"Nothing really." Athena sighed. "I just wanted you to know."

"What do you want for us?" Monti's tension hinged on whatever Athena was going to say, whatever direction she was going to take them. She settled into allowing whatever emotions were going to come up to pass through her before she responded. Because if it was disappointment, she didn't want to respond with anger.

"I want to explore," Athena repeated what she'd said earlier. "I know that's not very defining, but I don't know what I want yet. I want to just experience and learn to live again. Whatever that means."

They still hadn't made any progress toward any type of definition. Athena was hedging. Monti wanted clarity. They were stuck in the same cycle they'd created from the start. Monti had to push for answers. The only difference was this time she had to push herself.

"I love you," Monti whispered, her voice so quiet. But the words that slipped from her allowed a warmth and a calm to settle over her in a way she'd never felt before. When she looked up, meeting Athena's gaze, she knew she was heard. She knew that Athena was right there with her in this moment. "But more than that, Athena, I want to be loved by you."

Monti's chest filled with that love, with the way Athena was looking at her, the softness in her gaze, the compassion and understanding. This momentous occasion wasn't lost on either of them. Monti wanted to move in and kiss her, be wrapped up in her. Instead of waiting, Monti did it.

She pulled Athena toward her, their mouths connecting. Monti's eyes fluttered shut. She poured every emotion she could into that kiss. Wrapping her arms around Athena's back, she held on tightly. She splayed her fingers in an attempt to move them even closer together. Monti breathed new life into her lungs with an ease she'd never anticipated.

This time, Athena pulled away, though only slightly. She started a line of kisses along Monti's jaw to her ear. She pulled Monti's earlobe into her mouth and sucked as she hummed. Monti's body was on fire in an instant. She knew they could do this, that they were comfortable with this. But what she wanted to know was if they could do more than just the physical. Could they continue this new cycle of sharing?

"Monti," Athena gasped her name. She pressed her face into Monti's neck and slowed her breathing. They sat together, wrapped in each other's arms, a small duo in the huge world around them.

Please, love me.

The thought slid through Monti's body like a dam breaking. She was back to being that little kid just searching for love in a world that seemed to turn against her. She was the preteen just trying to figure out who she liked—girls, boys, both, anyone. She was the freshman in college, wondering if anyone would ever want to be with her. She was the grad student knowing she couldn't let anyone in without hurting them. Monti blinked back tears as she clung desperately to that feeling and followed it along. To Tia. To Fallon. To the friends she'd made all over the world, and finally landing with Athena.

Athena kissed Monti's cheek, then her lips. "I love you."

The breath racked through Monti's chest as she inhaled. She nearly burst into tears from Athena's tender confession, from her approval and acceptance. They were both looking for the same thing—someone who could love them through all the pain they carried. Monti clenched her eyes shut, holding onto Athena. She felt as though she was floating, as if she was finding the lightness and peace she'd been struggling for.

Was this what making peace was?

The simple act of accepting someone else's love into her heart.

"I love you," Athena repeated with another kiss. "I don't know what that means for us exactly. I don't think you do either. But we're going to find out."

Monti melded their bodies together as best she could. She wanted to crawl up inside Athena and live there, in this moment, in this little perfect oasis of love and hope and peace.

"It'll be so peaceful," Monti whispered, accepting the truth of the moment. This was all she'd had to do to find peace. She had to allow it to happen.

Athena snorted, but when she spoke, her voice was so calm and truthful. "I don't think it'll always be peaceful."

Monti dug her fingers into the hair at the back of Athena's head. She pulled away slightly to look in her eyes, a grin on her lips, and a twinkle in her eyes. "Don't spoil my moment."

"Your moment?" Athena rested the full weight of herself on Monti's chest. "I thought this was *our* moment."

"Yeah, sure." Monti kissed her. Everything about this felt right in ways nothing had for a very long time. Monti would give Athena everything she asked for. "Our moment."

"Our peace?"

"Our lack of shame and expectations for sure." Monti kissed her again and again and again. "We're just here in this one single moment, bringing everything that we are."

"I didn't realize you'd be so sentimental in your confessions of love."

Laughing, Monti rolled her eyes and sat up a little. "Sentimental? What did you expect?"

"Oh, there's that word again." Athena ran her hand firmly over Monti's chest, over her breast, and down to her stomach. "I expected, for the record, that we wouldn't get to this point today. I expected we would drift apart after this trip."

"Why's that?"

Athena gave a wry smile. "Because you're a free spirit, Monti. And I don't want to force you to be anyone you're not."

"Oh, Athena." Monti pulled her in for another kiss. "Whenever you're in a relationship with someone–friendship, romantic, work, or whatever it is–you change. I'll change. We'll both become someone new. This is about us going forward together with open eyes and open arms."

Humming, Athena licked Monti's neck. "I think I know what I want in our immediate future."

Laughing, Monti slid her leg around Athena's side, effectively trapping Athena against her. This was right where she wanted Athena, and it was right where she wanted to be. "And what is that?"

"I want to fuck you into tomorrow."

thirty-six

"Seems we have a late night in store for us."

"Or an early morning," Athena countered. She bent down and kissed Monti deeply. She was so happy. She couldn't even begin to describe how elated she was, but it filled every nook and cranny of her body. She was willing to try anything tonight, because Monti would catch her when she fell.

And she would fall.

Athena had no doubts of that. They both would. But to know that someone was there to catch her? If she was there to catch Monti? They could limp through life together. Monti dragged Athena's shirt up and over her head, tossing it over the side of the couch and onto the floor. Her bra followed seconds later.

Monti cupped her breasts, palming them and teasing them. Athena whimpered and bent down to capture Monti's mouth in another bruising kiss. She wanted this. She'd wanted this so much and for so long. She just hadn't ever thought she'd find it. Before she knew it, her pants were halfway down her thighs and Monti was sliding her fingers up and down her legs and between them, always a slight tease at first.

"How do you want me?" Athena asked, not even sure what she was doing. But she wanted to render her heart to Monti in this moment. Monti had given her all the power in every sexual encounter they'd had so far, but for this one, Athena wanted to give the same.

"What?" Monti looked up at her, eyes wide with surprise.

"How do you want me?"

"Every way possible." Monti dashed her tongue across her lips, as if she was already imagining those ways.

"Right now."

"From behind."

Athena's lips parted, and her heart moved right into her throat, clogging it up. She almost told Monti no. She almost shook her head and asked for something else. To allow Monti to move behind her would be the ultimate submission.

"Yes," Athena answered finally. She moved back onto her butt and pushed her pants the rest of the way off.

Monti stayed where she was, watching Athena as she finished undressing. When Monti didn't move, Athena held her hand out as if to help her get up.

"I changed my mind," Monti said.

"What?" Athena furrowed her brow. A lick of fear lashed through her that Monti didn't want her anymore, but when she paused to think instead of feel, she knew that was ridiculous after the conversation they'd just had. "You don't want to do that anymore?"

"No, I want to. I want to do everything with you. But you..." Monti trailed off, her gaze tracing Athena's curves before flicking to her eyes. "I don't want to trigger you."

"I agreed to this."

"I know. I just..." Monti stopped and winced. "Are you sure?"

"Absolutely." If anything, this boosted her confidence that she had made the right decision. Athena pulled Monti until Monti was up on her knees and pressed their mouths together. She parted her lips, slowly deepening the kiss as she pulled Monti back into the moment. She wanted Monti to know without a doubt that this is what she wanted. "Take your clothes off."

"Yes, ma'am," Monti teased, but she was already moving to the edge of the couch so that she could stand up.

Athena blew out a breath as she gathered herself again. Allowing Monti to do this was a huge step, but she couldn't imagine what it would be like to truly have no control. Monti skimmed her hand up Athena's back and over her hip as she leaned in and kissed Athena's shoulder.

"Lean over the arm of the couch."

Athena moved in silence, preparing herself internally for what was about to happen. She dragged in a cold breath of air, held it in her lungs for the count of three, and then blew it out. Her knuckles were white as she gripped onto the edge of the couch. Turning her chin over her shoulder, she made eye contact with Monti. "Ready whenever you are."

"Are you sure?"

"More than ever." Athena smiled. She'd never felt more sure of anything in her life. She was completely in love, and Monti was right there for her no matter what. "Touch me already."

"Commanding as always." Monti winked. She got onto the couch on her knees and knelt right behind Athena. She pressed her hips into Athena's ass and rocked slightly.

Athena closed her eyes and focused, feeling the way that Monti dropped kisses all along her spine up to her shoulders and back down again. Athena pushed her butt back into Monti, needing to be touched even more. This surrender was more than she could have ever imagined, and she never would have allowed this with anyone else.

"Touch me," Athena whispered again, this time with a hitch in the words. "Monti."

"Hold on." Monti moved her hands all over Athena's skin.

Waves of goosebumps rose, following the trail that Monti

took. Athena swallowed hard, clenching her eyes closed. She focused as best as she could on everything that Monti was doing to her, losing herself in the caresses, in the sweet words, in the tender way that Monti took care of her.

"Monti," Athena whined, but she didn't know what she was going to say beyond that. She was tired of waiting.

"Patience," Monti said with a chuckle. "God, you're so demanding."

But Monti moved down her body, nipping and kissing and teasing Athena's skin. She rounded the curve of Athena's ass, and then she used the flat of her tongue along the backside of Athena's thigh. That sent every worry out of Athena's mind. She had never been touched so erotically before. She shuddered and wiggled, needing more of Monti against her immediately.

"I love it," Monti whispered with a kiss to each of Athena's butt cheeks. "Are you ready for this?"

"More than ever."

Monti slid her tongue against Athena. Athena hissed as she tried to hold back her groan, but it was impossible.

"Just what I like to hear." The tease in Monti's voice was perfect.

Athena grinned as she clenched the arm of the couch tightly. "Touch me, Monti."

"You know, you keep saying that." Monti's tongue was against her again.

Grunting, Athena rocked forward. This was intense. Monti's face was pressed against her ass, her tongue doing wild things that Athena couldn't even name. She couldn't even think. All she knew was that she wanted Monti to keep going, to deepen her reach, to never stop. Athena bit her lip and strained against the couch. She was so close.

Athena concentrated on the pleasure coursing through her. She pushed her hips back just as that last ripple of orgasm coiled around her before it sprang loose. Her voice was so loud in her ears as her orgasm ripped through her. Before she could even catch her breath, Monti was on her again. Her fingers were deep inside her as she thrust firmly.

"Fuck," Athena mumbled, barely able to keep up with what was happening.

Her ears rang, her chest was tight as she tried to take deep breaths, but it was next to impossible. Monti took the first orgasm and dragged it into the second. She reached forward, cupping Athena's breast with her free hand and teasing her nipple by rolling it between her fingers with a flick. Athena's mind was blank. There was nothing in it except Monti and her talented, talented fingers.

Athena slid onto her side before turning over, Monti straddling her legs as she moved. She grinned up, her legs jelly and her body so warm and pliant. "I'm not sure I want to know where you learned to do this."

"Practice," Monti winked, but her cheeks were red and wet. "But I'll only give you details if you want them."

Athena put her hands on Monti's thighs as she tried to catch her breath and figure out what they were going to do next. She wanted to keep the connection between them. She wanted Monti on top of her, covering her, pressing her into the couch. That would be the perfect way to begin tonight.

"What are you thinking?" Monti asked, leaning forward on her knees and ghosting her fingers along Athena's skin. The touches were so light, barely there. They left a tickle in their wake.

"That I don't want to lose this." Another confession. She had never found it so easy to talk to someone in her life. Athena grinned as that thought settled in.

"Are you scared of losing it?"

"Losing you?" Athena looked Monti directly in the eye. She was on a roll. Why stop now? "Yes."

"Why?" Monti frowned slightly, as if she was concentrating hard.

"Because I'm not good at keeping what's good."

Monti moved in and pressed their mouths together. "Like I said before, we'll figure this out together."

"If only it was easy to trust. Not trust you, that's actually easy." Athena ran her fingers over Monti's body, teasing and touching wherever she could. "Trusting myself is harder."

"I never said it would be easy." Monti bent down, their mouths pushing hard together. The kiss was raw.

Athena tilted her chin up, deepening the embrace. She sucked Monti's lower lip into her mouth and pulled Monti down on top of her. Athena wrapped her arms and her legs around Monti's body. This wasn't going to be easy. Nothing between them had been easy up until that point. That wasn't what scared her. It was the fact that this wasn't set in stone. That Athena had no idea what was going to happen next. That in a few days, when they flew back to Seattle, this could all still end.

She wanted to beg Monti to tell her what to do, to take the decision-making power out of her hands. Because it was over-whelming to have to decide. She started to shake, and Monti must have noticed, because her kisses eased up and her touches became far more soothing than inciting.

"Don't stop," Athena begged, not willing to slip into that worry and fear. "Please, don't stop."

"You're trembling," Monti answered.

"I know." Athena kissed her again, desperation in the touch. She clung to the familiarity, the hope that Monti gave her. The peace they'd made together. "I want this."

"But we don't have to go this fast."

"Monti." Athena stopped. She cupped Monti's cheeks and dragged her so they were staring at each other eye to eye. "I want this. I told you that I want to fuck you into tomorrow, and I plan to deliver on my promise."

Monti's lips parted, as if she was about to protest again.

"Don't." Athena dragged in a breath, and her trembling stopped. She wasn't going to let her trauma get in the way of something that was so good. "Don't make this about something that happened in the past. This is about us, right now, right here, in this moment."

"Okay," Monti murmured. "Okay."

"Let me touch you."

"How?"

"However you want." Athena trailed her nails, scraping along Monti's hips upward. She cupped Monti's full breasts. "Just tell me what you want."

"Together."

"What?"

"Let's do this together. I know it's sometimes an awkward position, but at the very least we can do it with each other. And isn't that what *this* is all about?" Monti kissed her swiftly before shifting.

Before Athena knew what was happening, Monti had flipped around and was straddling her. "You'll have to move lower on the couch to make the angle work."

Athena steadied herself as she slipped farther down on the couch. She spread her legs when Monti touched her thighs. This was so awkward, but Athena was here for it. She snaked her hand up between them and slid one finger knuckle-deep inside Monti.

"Perfect," Monti mumbled before her mouth was on Athena again.

Oh yes, that was a good idea. Moving her hand, Athena started with her mouth. Is this what Monti had felt like moments before? Face buried between Athena's legs, lost in all the sensations and reactions. Athena closed her eyes to concentrate. She kept her mouth on Monti's clit for a count of ten and then she slid her tongue through all the wetness that she found. She hummed as the flavors blossomed, as the heat from their skin intensified.

Athena focused only on what she was doing, trying to ignore Monti between her legs. When her third orgasm slipped through her, she was able to ignore it after a few steadying breaths and really concentrate on Monti. Athena clasped her hands around

Monti's thighs and pulled her down hard. This was her moment, when she could show Monti exactly what she'd meant earlier.

She had to stop being scared.

Fear was the enemy.

Nothing else.

Monti grunted before she whimpered. She kissed Athena's leg, licked her, scraped her teeth against her. But Athena didn't stop. She kept everything going, putting all her energy and effort into teasing Monti into oblivion. They were in this together. No matter what they did. And Athena wanted that with no one else.

Monti collapsed onto the couch, her hips twisted, which prevented Athena from doing anything else to her. Athena trailed her fingers up and down Monti's legs, where she could touch, and she held on, just letting the moment settle through them.

The silence was so comforting.

They didn't need to talk. They didn't need words for what was between them. It was just them, wholly and authentically.

Finally, Monti rustled around and moved. She flipped back and lay on top of Athena's prone form. They kissed, mouths pressed together, eyes closed. All Athena felt was comfort, sweet surrender, and more peace than she had ever dreamed possible. She wouldn't give this up for the world.

This right here was what she'd longed for.

And she hadn't even known it.

"I love you," she said again, ready to say it so many times that Monti would get sick and tired of hearing it.

"And I love you," Monti answered, with a kiss to Athena's cheek. "But this couch has got to go."

Athena laughed. "What do you suggest?"

"A bed. A really big, comfy bed with fluffy covers and heavenly pillows."

"Are you tired already?" Athena used her fingers to tickle Monti's sides.

Monti jerked sharply, a laugh bubbling up from her chest. "No! Not that you'd let me sleep anyway."

"Not yet. We still have a few hours before midnight."

"Oh Jesus."

"Oh yes." Athena found Monti's lips with hers. "Are you ready?"

"More than ever."

epilogue

Monti hooked her thumbs in her backpack as she straightened up and looked out over Kathmandu. The city below her was stunningly gorgeous. But it wasn't as gorgeous as the red-cheeked woman with ice blue eyes, huffing as she climbed up the rest of the mountain to join Monti. Athena had thrown her hair into a messy bun when they'd started the hike, and now she had loose strands around her ears from her exertion.

"You said this was an easy hike," Athena pouted as she reached the small area where Monti had stopped.

She was adorable. Monti would never deny that.

"I lied." Monti kissed Athena's cheek and dropped her backpack to the ground. It had been a relatively easy hike. Monti just forgot that Athena wasn't as used to these outdoor activities as she was. Without a beat, Monti pulled the hose from Athena's CamelBak and put it to her lips. "Drink before you faint. I definitely want you awake for this."

Giving a wry smile, Athena sucked down the water as commanded. When she was done, she dropped the backpack to the ground and slowed her breathing. Monti stood just over her shoulder, skimming her hands down Athena's arms and clasping their fingers together. She rested her chin on Monti's shoulder and hugged her from behind.

"Are you glad you came?" Monti asked, though she already knew the answer. They'd planned this trip on and off for the last year. A culmination of their relationship together. A next step they'd wanted to take.

"In more ways than one." Athena laughed lightly, sending Monti a teasing look before focusing back on the city. She reached up and snagged Monti's hands, pulling Monti more tightly against her. "But to answer your actual question, yes. I am."

"Good." Monti kissed her cheek, she dropped her lips to Athena's neck, sucking gently before she scraped her teeth. She had missed Athena's flirting, and she loved hearing it every time. "I'm so glad you agreed to come with me."

"Like I would have said no to this." Athena reached up, threading her hands in Monti's hair and pushing Monti against her.

"You had quite a few lawsuits going on lately." Monti continued to nuzzle her face into Athena's neck. A rightness settled into her chest. They had worked so hard to get to where they were, and the journey had been worth every step. Every day they'd woken up and chosen this. Monti couldn't have asked for anything else.

"Had. But it's done now. It's all done." Athena turned around in Monti's arms and wrapped her arms around Monti's back.

"And you won." Monti kissed her cheek, and Athena tilted her head to the side to give Monti more access. This was their celebration trip along with their commitment trip. The two couldn't have been better matched. "You got Gwen and Zoe some justice."

"Some, yes." Athena pressed their mouths together, sliding her tongue against Monti's lips. "It'll never be enough."

"It never is." Monti fell into the embrace. She'd waited a long time to bring Athena here, but every time Monti had mentioned it, Athena had held back. They'd traveled so many places in the last two years, but they'd never been here. And finally, they'd made plans and they were here. Finally, Athena's dream of coming back to Kathmandu was a reality.

But today they had special plans.

This wasn't just a trip for nothing. Or even a trip for an easy adventure.

Monti threaded her fingers into Athena's hair, keeping their mouths close and together. Monti had picked this place specifically, spending hours trying to find someplace that was secluded and beautiful, where they could do this, just the two of them.

"Are you ready?"

"No," Athena mumbled. "But I'm as ready as I'll ever be."

Monti kissed her again. "You're sure?"

"Yes." Athena laughed, putting her hands on Monti's shoulders. "Stop asking that already."

"You know me. I always have to make sure."

"It's only a small part of what I love about you." Athena slid her thumb over Monti's lips and then down her neck to her breast. Monti held back her moan, though barely. She loved how confident Athena had gotten in the last couple years. How willing Athena was to touch her. Kiss her. Love her.

"Hold that thought." Monti let go of Athena so that she could rummage through her pack. She had everything they needed.

She set it up on the higher part of the hill and then indicated to Athena to sit next to her. They faced each other. Monti had never been so elated in her life. There hadn't been peace every moment, but she'd found enough signs of it that she believed it was there. Perhaps more than that, she believed that she had experienced it.

"Now are you ready?"

"Yes." Athena fluttered her fingers over Monti's hand. "I've been looking forward to this."

"Have you?" For some reason that surprised Monti. She'd

figured that after agreeing, Athena would have avoided thinking about it in her best fashion.

"Absolutely."

As if on cue, Athena took hold of Monti's wrist, wrapping her fingers tightly in a squeeze. Monti turned her wrist and mirrored the grasp. Monti used her free hand to pull the ribbons closer. She'd spent hours weaving the fabric together into the rope it had become, choosing the material and the colors so that it would specifically represent them.

"This is for us, binding us together in a new way."

"We're already inextricably tied together," Athena responded.

Monti warmed at that thought. It was so true. In two years, she had learned more about Athena than she'd ever dreamed possible. They'd spent countless hours together, in each other's arms, talking, reading, sharing.

"I love you, Athena. You've shown me a world I never imagined existed."

Athena smiled brightly, her eyes lighting up. She leaned in and kissed Monti quickly. "I love how intuitive you are, how you take such good care of me when I don't even realize I need it, how you're always there."

"I love your strength and tenacity." Monti wrapped the rope she'd made around each of their hands carefully, following the pattern she'd learned and practiced. "I love how you've changed me."

"You've changed me in amazing ways. We've grown so much together." Athena caressed Monti's cheek, not dropping her gaze from Monti's face. "I love how you love me."

Monti couldn't wipe the grin off her face. Opening her heart to Athena had been the best decision she'd made in years. She finished the tying. When she looked down at their hands, she felt nothing but hope.

"We're in this together. Whatever this is. Wherever this is. Wherever this leads us." Monti started to pull her hand away and Athena released her grasp. They each snagged the end of the rope and pulled tightly, forming the knot perfectly. "This knot binds us together, our lives, our pasts, our futures."

"You and me," Athena answered, still holding onto the knot. "I'm never going to let go."

Monti sucked in a deep breath of fresh air. The grin lit her up, light filling her soul. Holding onto the knotted rope, she pulled Athena in for a deep kiss. Their tongues swept together in a tease of what was to come, but Monti knew they weren't done yet. She pulled out the small water bottle she'd packed, the one with the wine in it.

She twisted off the top and held it between them. "This is a sign of us coming together, of the work, the time, the effort that relationships take. And it's a sign of our commitment to each other to always come together when we're struggling, to give each other grace, to be joyful, to remember to take time to relax and take comfort in each other's arms."

Athena pulled the bottle from Monti's hand and took a sip. "This is a sign of our commitment to each other, from when we first met to when we part."

Monti took her sip, the red wine hitting her tongue, the flavors lingering in her mouth. She twisted the cap back on the bottle and set it down. This time, when she pulled Athena toward her, she wasn't going to stop kissing until she had to.

They stayed there for hours, laughing, talking, enjoying this peaceful moment for the two of them. No one knew. No one had to know. Monti dragged in a deep breath and blew it out when the sun started to go down.

"We should probably head back."

"Probably. I barely made it up here," Athena laughed lightly, resting her head on Monti's shoulder.

"It's a thirty-minute walk. I think we'll make it."

"So you say." Athena sighed, but she stood up and brushed the dirt off her pants.

Monti packed everything up and then held up Athena's CamelBak so she could put it on before sliding her arms through her own pack. They walked hand in hand for a bit until the path was too narrow for them to walk side-by-side. As much as nothing felt different, Monti knew it was.

"You know the best lesson I think you ever taught me?" Athena started as she waited for Monti to catch up.

"What's that?"

"It's better to live without shame."

Monti smiled, her cheeks flushing at the thought. "How's that coming along?"

"It's easier said than done." Athena chuckled. "I think you understand that."

"I do." Monti snagged Athena's hand and lifted it to her lips. "But I'm glad you understand that."

"I didn't realize how much shame I carried with me." Athena kissed her cheek. "The world is so different now that I'm aware of it."

Monti settled into the walk again. They talked amicably until they reached their hotel. Monti set everything down where it belonged. She hadn't planned anything beyond their day up on the hill, and they had a few more days to explore the city. She had no doubt that Athena had already taken to finding something for them to do.

As much as Monti loved Athena's love for planning, she also appreciated a simple walk through the city with nothing on their agenda.

"I wish there was a beach nearby," Athena called from the bathroom.

Monti frowned, not understanding. "Why?" They could have very easily done this anywhere, but Athena had wanted it to happen here. Something about wanting to explore her past again.

"Because I'd love to go skinny dipping with you." Athena stepped out of the bathroom and leaned against the doorframe. She raised her hand above her arm, naked as the day she was born.

Monti sucked in a sharp breath, her entire body ready to go. Her jaw dropped. This was Athena in all her glory and in all her confidence. The scars that marred her skin were nothing now. Her past only built her up instead of tearing her down. Monti had never seen anything as sexy as this.

"You are amazing," Monti breathed the words.

"Do you like what you see?"

"I've always loved what I've seen of you. Every single bit." Monti stepped in closer, their lips touching. She smiled as she kissed Athena again. "I love you."

"Fuck me already."

With a laugh, Monti answered, "Yes, ma'am."

about the author

Adrian J. Smith has been publishing since 2013 but has been writing nearly her entire life. With a focus on women loving women fiction, AJ jumps genres from action-packed police procedurals to the seedier life of vampires and witches to sweet romances with an age gap twist. She loves writing and reading about women in the midst of the ordinariness of life.

AJ currently lives in Cheyenne, WY, although she moves often and has lived all over the United States. She loves to travel to different countries and places. She currently plays the roles of author, wife, and mother to two rambunctious youngsters, occasional handy-woman. Connect with her on Facebook, Instagram, or Rcam.

facebook.com/adrianjsmithbooks

instagram.com/adrianjsmithbooks

goodreads.com/Adrian_J_Smith

bookbub.com/authors/adrian-j-smith

amazon.com/stores/Adrian-J.-Smith/author/B00B94LSPW

my boss's stalker: spoiler it's not me

An unrequited crush. A stalker on the loose. Will she be able to save her boss?

Zoe's boss is a force to be reckoned with. And Zoe has had a crush on Gwen Fudala for the last three years. In a twist of events, Zoe drunkenly ends up on the phone with Gwen while in a compromising position. But it sparks a wildfire that neither can put out.

Still, something isn't right.

Gwen is being stalked. Vowing to let nothing happen to her boss, Zoe winds up tangled in the stalker's game. Unable to see which way is out and loyal to a fault, Zoe sticks by Gwen's side through thick and thin.

Can they navigate a relationship under the watchful eye of a perpetrator?

Or does the stalker have a new target?

My Boss's Stalker is a steamy age gap sapphic romantic suspense. Follow these two as they navigate complicated relationships, fear, and unexpected serenity.

Read it today

<u>Romance</u>

Memoir in the Making

OBlique

Love Burns

About Time

Admissible Affair

Daring Truth

Indigo: Blues (Indigo B&B #1)

Indigo: Nights (Indigo B&B #2)

Indigo: Three (Indigo B&B #3)

Indigo: Storm (Indigo B&B #4)

Indigo: Law (Indigo B&B #5)

When the Past Finds You

Don't Quit Your Daydream

Love Me At My Worst

Inside These Halls

Maybe Someday

My Boss's Stalker: Spoiler It's Not Me

<u>Crime/Mystery/Thriller</u>

For by Grace (Spirit of Grace #1)

Fallen from Grace (Spirit of Grace #2)

Grace through Redemption (Spirit of Grace #3)

Lost & Forsaken (Missing Persons #1)

Broken & Weary (Missing Persons #2)

Young & Old (Missing Persons #3)

Alone & Lonely (Missing Persons #4)

Stone's Mistake (Agent Morgan Stone #1)

Stone's Homefront (Agent Morgan Stone #2)

Fantasy/Science Fiction

Forever Burn (James Matthews #1)

Dying Embers (James Matthews #2)

Ashes Fall (James Matthews #3)

Unbound (Quarter Life #1)

De-Termination (Quarter Life #2)

Release (Quarter Life #3)

Beware (Quarter Life #4)

Dead Women Don't Tell Tales (Tales of the Undead & Depraved #.5)

Thieving Women Always Lose (Tales of the Undead & Depraved #1)

Scheming Women Seek Revenge (Tales of the Undead & Depraved #2)

Broken Women Fight Back (Tales of the Undead & Depraved #3)

Deep Sounding Chaos (Love, Tails & Battle Wails #1)

www.ingramcontent.com/pod-product-compliance
Lightning Source LLC
Chambersburg PA
CBHW040853010826
48978CB00013BA/1000